SEND NO MORE ROSES

ERIC AMBLER was born in London in 1909. Between 1937 and 1940 he wrote six classic novels – including *The Mask of Dimitrios*, which many consider his masterpiece – then spent six years in the British Army, followed by several years writing and producing motion pictures.

Since 1951 he has written thirteen more highly-acclaimed books. Two (*Passage of Arms* and *The Levanter*) won the coveted Gold Dagger of the Crime Writers' Association. His most recent novel *Send No More Roses* (in America, *The Siege of Villa Lipp*) was published in 1977.

Mr Ambler now lives in Switzerland.

ERIC AMBLER

Send No More Roses

FONTANA/Collins

First published in 1977 by Weidenfeld and Nicolson
This continental edition first issued in Fontana Books 1978

© 1977 by Eric Ambler

Made and printed in Great Britain by
William Collins Sons & Co Ltd Glasgow

'Send no more roses to assuage your guilt, Mr Oberholzer,' I told him smilingly. 'Such flowers may, as you have already so painfully discovered, later explode while you are still in the blast area.'

Frits Bühler Krom
DER KOMPETENTE KRIMINELLE:
eine Fallstudie (Tr. D. Keel)

CHAPTER ONE

They stopped the car by the gateway in the wall on the lower coast road. Then, after a moment or two, the three of them climbed out stiffly, their shirts clinging to their backs. It had been a long, hot drive.

From the shade at the end of the terrace I could see them clearly through the binoculars.

Professor Krom, the older man, I already knew; there could be no doubt about him. The younger man and the woman, however, had to be identified from recent snapshots taken by private enquiry agencies on the subjects' respective campuses. Although I can never take photographic identification quite seriously – I have seen, and used, too many false passports for that – these two, I decided, looked sufficiently like the persons they were supposed to be for me to assume that they were indeed those persons.

The car was a rented Fiat 127 with Milan registration plates. Their baggage, except the hand stuff, was on a roof-rack. There was no unauthorized fourth person inside. They appeared, for the moment, to have adhered to the terms of the agreement I had worked out with Krom.

For several seconds they stood staring up at the Villa Lipp. Then, lips began to move and gestures were made. One did not have to be a skilled lip-reader to know what was being said.

'Are we expected to carry our bags up all those steps?' That was the woman, running sweaty fingers awkwardly through her hair as she spoke.

Krom, the leader of the expedition, gave her a fatherly pat on the shoulder. 'I doubt it, my dear. But why don't we go and find out?' He looked up again, showing me his teeth this time; he had realized that I had to be watching. 'I'm quite sure he's there.'

'And laughing his head off.' Dr Connell, the younger man, was eyeing the house with dislike and massaging his aching neck muscles. He had done all the driving. 'I'll bet there's an upper access road, too,' he went on. 'No one builds a villa like that without a driveway. This is pure one-upmanship. The son-of-a-bitch just wants us to arrive pooped.'

He was not entirely right. True, I had omitted the access road from the sketch-map I had sent Krom; but not simply in order to cause them discomfort. What I had wanted, too, was plenty of time in which to examine them and their belongings before they could examine too closely me and mine. Not that they would see many of my belongings in that expensively rented petit palais, but they would all see Yves and Melanie as well as me. There was no way of preventing their doing so – we had been rendered, to some extent, expendable – but the attendant risks could at least be minimized.

Evidence of the need for such precautions soon became visible.

Once they had decided that there was no point in their just standing there and that they had better start climbing, Connell took what at first looked like a portable radio from the car before he locked it. Then, when he turned, I saw that what he had in fact was a tape-recorder.

This flagrant violation of the agreed ground rules did not greatly surprise me. Dr Connell was, my sources had informed me, that sort of young man; the academic counterpart of the boardroom Wunderkind, always confident of being able to talk anyone misguided enough to disagree with him into seeing things his way.

Well, Yves would know how to deal with him. The one who had begun to interest me more, from a security point of view, was the woman, Dr Henson.

As they cleared the lower flight of stone steps and passed the fountain at the foot of the main stairway, she swung the embroidered satchel she had been carrying slung on her left shoulder over to her right one. The satchel looked ordinary enough, the sort of object that a slacks-and-shirt woman of her kind might normally carry. What bothered me was that, judging from the way she had to heft it across her body, the contents of the thing were much heavier than one would have expected them to be.

I spoke to Melanie as I went inside.

'Before you go out to meet them, tell Yves that the woman may have something in her bag that shouldn't be there. I'll be in my room when he's ready to report.'

While I waited, I went through the three dossiers again and reread my own notes on them.

The subjects, in order of both temporal and academic seniorities, were:

FRITS BÜHLER KROM, Professor of Sociology and Social Administration

Nationality: Dutch

Age: 62

Civil Status: Married, two sons, one daughter.

My own office had turned up that information after a few minutes with standard reference books. The only additional information that I had been able to get about his personal life, as opposed to his professional life at the German university where he worked and about which every piddling little detail seemed to be known, was that he had eight grandchildren with a ninth on the way.

GEORGE KINGHAM CONNELL, Assistant Professor, Department of Social Sciences

Nationality: USA

Age: 36

Civil Status: Married, one daughter (by first wife who divorced him), two sons (present marriage).

I had a note which said that he was currently in Europe to attend by invitation a seminar at the University of Freiburg im Breisgau, West Germany, and that his family was at a Maine lakeside summer resort.

The American agency commissioned by me to carry out the Connell investigation had complained about the deadline I had imposed on them. They had, however, managed to gather in the time available a surprisingly large amount of campus gossip. One item reported 'a widespread belief' that certain members of the university Board of Regents were objecting vigorously to any renewal of Dr Connell's contract which might result in his promotion to associate rank and securing of tenure. The objectors were all, it was said, lawyers.

GERALDINE HOPE HENSON, Research Fellow, Faculty of Social Sciences

Nationality: British

Age: 33

Civil Status: Divorced, no children.

At the end of a detailed account of her career and an estimate of her credit-worthiness, the British agency had added a cosy note. Henson had been her maiden name and after her divorce she had gone back to using it. To her many friends, however, she had always been known affectionately as 'Hennie'.

Krom, Connell, Henson.

Social scientists all, but with not much else in common, apparently. Then, one looks at the titles of some of their published books and papers and the picture changes. All three of these scholars are not only criminologists, but criminologists of a new and peculiar breed; they all have the same kind of bee in their bonnets.

Krom's *The Lombroso Fallacy in Contemporary Criminology* and *Frontiers of Criminal Investigation* may not be as conspicuously iconoclastic as Connell's *The Myth of Organized Crime* or Henson's *The Professional Criminal – Six Studies in Incompetence*, but his preface to the monumental *Criminal Statistics 1965–1975, an Analytical Appraisal* makes his position clear. Along with such authorities as John A. Mack of Glasgow and Hans-Jürgen Kerner of Tübingen, as well as younger scholars like Connell and Henson, he has joined the ranks of those criminological heretics who believe that most current ideas about criminal psychology, criminal biology and criminal psychiatry are either fallacious or irrelevant. They believe this because they hold that what criminologists have been studying so assiduously over the years is not the criminal as he or she may exist, but only those one or two species of the genus which are, and always have been, catchable.

They also believe, despite the angry merriment of old-school policemen, for whom the idea is naturally upsetting, in the existence of an entire criminal species or sub-genus about which little or nothing is as yet known: that of the Able Criminal.

Krom's description of the species is one of the more celebrated. It was part of a lecture delivered at a meeting of the International Police Association in Berne. Although he himself, writing in German, prefers to identify his quarry as *Der Kompetente Kriminelle*, on this occasion he was, in deference to the majority among his polyglot audience, speaking in English. Having uttered the phrase Able Criminal aloud on a lecture rostrum for the first time, he then went on:

'I am not, my friends, in any way alluding to the Master Criminal of blessed memory, that beguiling figment of nineteenth-century fictional imaginations who so often fell prey to amateur detectives, but to a present-day occupant of the real world.

'The Able Criminal, male or female, may be presumed to possess a high IQ, to be emotionally stable and "well adjusted", to exhibit none of the personality defects said to be characteristic of the accepted "criminal types" and to belong to none of the much-publicized crime syndicates so dear to the romantics in some of our law-enforcement agencies. He will, except in the protective cover role of worthy citizen, be unknown to such agencies and unsuspected by them. He (or she – gender has no relevance here) has no discernible and hence no classifiable *modus operandi*, and unless disease or advancing age causes deterioration of his faculties, he is virtually uncatchable.

'Of the kinds of crime he commits, fraud is naturally high on the list; yet fraud is not, for some of the species, the only, nor even a principal, source of revenue. Here in Berne it will be unnecessary to remind you that the laws on income tax evasion – not avoidance, evasion – vary widely between our different countries. In America and Britain evasion is a crime. In Switzerland it is not. In a great many other parts of the world, in places like Monaco, Grand Cayman, Bermuda and the New Hebrides, there are no income taxes to evade. Within the stratified complexities of international tax and corporation law the opportunities for the Able Criminal are boundless. On the evidence which has been available to me – unhappily not evidence of the quality upon which our democratic justice likes to depend – these opportunities include large-scale but non-prosecutable embezzlement and blackmail, plus undetectable forgery as well as property crime, chiefly connected with heavily-insured works of art, of the more traditional sort. I do not have to tell this audience that where there is crime for gain on that scale, however sophisticated it may be, there too will be found, sooner or later, its inevitable accompaniments, gangsterism and violence.'

Krom had gone on to list some of the technical difficulties to be overcome in researching the species, and had compared them with those which had confronted the physicists who first set out to investigate the behaviour of energized particles in a cyclotron.

'The investigators might *think* that they knew what was going on inside, but until they had devised an exact way of knowing what was going on, the validity of their suppositions could not be assessed.'

Connell, in his doctoral thesis, had commented sadly on the comparison. 'Professor Krom might have added that, while physicists have long since solved those and many other sets of even more complex problems, we, the new criminologists, are still grappling with the most basic among ours. We have not yet learned to recognize source material as such even when we are staring at it.'

Dr Henson, writing in *The New Sociologist*, had been more explicit about her difficulties.

'No matter how ingenious the investigative techniques employed, the likelihood of the student learning anything that our able criminal would prefer to keep secret is small. The writer, and she does not think herself uniquely handicapped, has had to depend largely for her data-gathering upon methods of enquiry which only the charitable could call serious. To put it bluntly, they involve unscientific fumblings with minor strokes of luck; for example, the accidental unearthing of a conventional criminal informer who talked unwittingly of matters the real significance of which he himself had not even begun to grasp.'

She had made her point. She might have been wiser to have left it at that. Instead, she had gone on to lambast some of her critics.

'Understandably, members of the older schools of criminology, recoiling from the difficulties, have chosen to deny the able criminal's existence. They have preferred either to continue cultivating the already over-cultivated study fields of juvenile delinquency and Mafia-style organized crime, or to dabble in forensic medicine.'

The critics had hit back fiercely. Among the politer was one who reminded her that phenomena which are so very difficult to observe without 'unscientific fumblings' frequently turn out to exist only in the minds' eyes of the committed few who claim to have observed them. The able criminal could well be compared in that context with such aberrations as the Unidentified Flying Object and the little green men from outer space. And were there not simple persons who still believed in ghosts?

Poor Dr Henson. With that truthful but unfortunate reference to fumbling she had handed her opponents the only weapon they could effectively use. Yet, her frankness did not go unrewarded, for the controversy it aroused brought her to the special attention of Professor Krom. He had known of her book, of course, but now he was reminded of her, and of the views she held, at a decisive moment.

Something remarkable had happened to him and he needed kindred spirits with whom to share the experience.

Connell has emphasized the difficulty for the new criminologists of recognizing a source when they see it. Henson has spoken of the remoteness of even that opportunity. Only Krom, with all his experience, having stumbled upon a major and reliable source, having recognized it as such and then decided patiently to wait and watch, may now know how lucky he has been.

I know of only two other similar cases of this magnitude. In both, the consequences for all concerned were most unpleasant. There were failures of nerve and regrettable lapses into primitive modes of behaviour, not quite as unexpected as those upon which I have to report but no less outrageous. In neither of those cases, however, were there any survivors.

So, whether he is prepared to admit it or not, Krom was lucky in a number of ways. The most important of them, undoubtedly, was the discovery of his windfall source in me.

By the failures of the world in which I move I have been accused in my time of possessing nearly all the anti-social qualities. It has been said that, both in my business and in my private lives, I have been consistently sly, treacherous, ruthless and rapacious, vindictive, devious, sadistic and generally vile. I could add to that list. But no one, *no* one, has ever yet suggested that I would even condone a resort to violence by others, much less promote or organize the use of it myself. Squeamishness? Timidity? Think what you please. I have seen enough of violence to convince me that even when it appears to succeed, as in some struggles for political power, the success usually proves in the end to have been more apparent than real.

I do not, of course, expect justice; that would be too much; but I believe that I am entitled to a fair trial before the only court I recognize, the only court whose judgements I now value; that is the court of public opinion.

Now that the real 'Mr X' has been identified by me and the full extent of his perfidy is no longer a secret, those who are prepared to consider the evidence with open and objective minds – evidence which proves beyond doubt and sans whitewash that far from being the villain of the piece I am his principal victim – should be allowed to do so.

If Krom is still reluctant to risk his precious reputation by disclosing in their proper perspective those facts which are known to him, but which he finds inconvenient, then I must do the job myself. Perhaps, too, Connell and Henson will be prompted by their integrity as scholars, to say nothing of common decency, to back me up. If they are not so prompted, well, for once, my own welfare and that of men of more conventional goodwill may be promoted together. For once, it is in nearly everyone's interests that a whole truth be generally known.

The house-phone buzzed.

'Paul?' It was Yves.

'We have complications,' he said. 'Dr Connell protested at my taking his tape-recorder from him. Said that he had had no intention of using it without permission, and insists that taping is his normal way of setting down case notes. Would be lost without it. Pointed out that he had carried it openly, and after obtaining Krom's reluctantly-given permission to do so.'

'What did you decide?'

'To let him have it, conditionally, because we might find it useful too, if you see what I mean.'

'I think so. What conditions?'

'I said that it would be placed in his room and must remain there. He could use it, but no voice tracks were to be made other than his own. I can easily wipe anything we find objectionable later on. Meanwhile, I'll check it out for added circuits.'

'Okay. Now, what about Dr Henson's shoulder bag?'

'Paul, that is far more serious. The heavy object you observed turned out to be one of those plastic cases which women use now when travelling to carry cosmetics in small quantities. They are fitted with leak-proof bottles and little jars to save weight.'

'Then why was it heavy?'

'Because of an arrangement of objects packed in the cavity below the main tray. They included a camera.'

'Oh, for God's sake! What kind?'

'Special job, but based, I think, on a body belonging to that small underwater Nikon. Among the accessories with it we have green and infra-red filters and two lenses, one a close-up. A very classy outfit. Must have cost a fortune.'

'What did Dr Henson have to say for herself?'

'What one would expect, I suppose. No intention of using it without permission. Indignant when reminded that you had made a point of disallowing cameras in the protocol she signed. Hit back. Tape-recorders were also verboten. Connell was carrying one. Were we going to made an equal fuss about that?'

'How did Krom and Connell react to all this?'

Yves sounded surprised. 'Oh, they weren't present. I saw each one separately.' He paused. 'But, Paul, she had more than just the camera stuff in that compartment.'

'Not a gun, I hope.'

'No, something perhaps a little more dangerous. A small aerosol spray. It had a printed label saying that it was a nail-varnish remover.'

'Which you didn't believe.'

'The nail-varnish remover that the women I know normally use comes in bottles, not aerosols. The label didn't look right either.'

'What did you say?'

'I asked her to show me how it worked on one of her finger-nails.'

'And?'

'Refused. Why should she spoil a perfectly good manicure for my amusement?'

'But you weren't impressed.'

'Paul, she doesn't *have* a perfectly good manicure. I think the aerosol's loaded with that Swedish chemical they are using these days for examining suspect documents like forged cheques, the stuff that reacts with amino acids to bring up latent fingerprints on paper so you can photograph them. They come up purple. Hence the green filter for the close-up lens.'

'Hence also the fact that she wouldn't spray it on her fingers. The stuff is called ninhydrin and it's highly poisonous, even in solution. Someone must have warned her.'

'Doesn't surprise me. The whole compartment, the whole kit, looks as if it had been thought out and packed in a lab by some police or other intelligence-gathering outfit, for use in the field.'

I sighed. 'How about Krom? Anything up his sleeves? Radio bleepers? Poisoned darts?'

'No, he was clean. I've got the key of their car. I'm going down now to drive it up.'

He would also search the baggage thoroughly after it had been taken up to their rooms.

'Where are they now?'

'Melanie's giving them soothing drinks.'

'Let me know when you've cleared the baggage. I'll go down then and introduce myself to our guests.'

'Okay, Paul. See you later.' He hung up.

With characteristic politeness he had refrained from commenting on the crass absurdity of the words I had just uttered.

There would be no need at all for me to introduce myself to Professor Krom.

Unfortunately, he and I had already met – and more than once.

That was the cause of the whole trouble.

I can still hear him pronouncing what could have been my death sentence, as well as his own.

'You were too kind, Mr Firman. In future, when one of your employees is called to meet his Maker, I strongly advise you to send no flowers.'

That is what he *actually* said, not what he now claims that he said. At the time there was none of that rubbish about exploding flowers and blast areas; and the word 'guilt' was certainly not used, 'smilingly' or in any other way.

What guilt, anyway? Only an idiot would attribute a sense of guilt in this case to me.

I am not the defendant.

I am the plaintiff.

CHAPTER TWO

Professor Krom's account of the events I am describing differs radically from mine; and it does so, I believe, chiefly because his was written while he was still too disturbed by his experiences at the Villa Lipp to think clearly. He is, after all, an elderly man unaccustomed to explosions. It is likely that, in all important respects, my account is the more balanced of the two.

That said, however, his initial achievement remains and should be recognized for what it is: a triumph of chance over all reasonable probabilities and, from his point of view at any rate, evidence that some of his theories may ultimately be capable of proof. His single-minded professional persistence aided by a photographic memory produced a moment at which two apparently dissimilar persons seen in totally different and unrelated contexts were suddenly identified as one and the same.

I was the person thus identified, and news of the identification had been given to me two months earlier during one of the tax-haven seminars organized by Symposia SA.

The place was Brussels.

That much admitted, the record may now be wiped clean of some of the mud with which it has been so freely bespattered. I wish to state categorically that neither the Symposia group of companies – specifically: Symposia AG, Symposia SA, Symposia NV and Symposia (Bermuda) Ltd – nor its connected consultative body, the Institute for International Investment and Trust Counselling, are in any country or in any way contravening or subverting established law. Not even our keenest competitors in the field of trust counselling have, however eager they may have been to take advantage of Krom's so-called 'revelations', dared to suggest otherwise. The idea is preposterous; and anyone who still doubts this has only to look at the long list of those bankers, trust officers, international lawyers and tax accountants who attended the April seminar, and at the names, all famous in the international business world, of the experts they came to hear. Men of that calibre understand and respect the law. The last thing they wish to do is to consort with criminals.

The subject of that particular seminar was of fairly general interest, a survey of the various pieces of anti-avoidance legislation currently being introduced by some ill-natured western governments, and the number of registrants was high. There were one hundred and twenty-three of them; and anyone foolish enough to suppose that organizing such affairs is in itself a road to riches may like to know that Symposia's net reward for that week's work was a mere twenty thousand dollars. Nobody can say that *that* part of the tax-avoidance business yields high profits. Without its fringe benefits the game would simply not be worth playing. Through organizing these affairs we get to know people and we get to know things.

Not that we ever spied on anyone; I don't mean that. If anything, as I now realize, we were too easy-going. Naturally, we always took an interest in the identities of those who attended our seminars, in their countries of origin, the passports they carried and the fields of their specializations; but those little dossiers we compiled were primarily for the benefit of our faculty lecturers. From the start it was always Symposia policy to admit to our seminars, however delicate the subject matter, all who were prepared to remit with their applications cheques for the registration fees. We expect the major government revenue services to be represented and they usually are, often adding – especially when the lecturer is himself a former revenue official – a certain liveliness to the discussion periods. The atmosphere, though, is essentially one of friendly rivalry and mutual respect. Both sides are simply doing their jobs as best they can and with pretty clear ideas about one another's strengths and weaknesses. Discretion is practised, of course, but almost never to the point of play-acting. I know of only two cases of persons registering under false names.

One was a journalist working for a French left-wing scandal sheet. The seminar he attended was devoted mainly to the subject of discretionary and exempt trust concepts. He pretended to be a lawyer. In the article he wrote following this masquerade, he managed not only to mount a totally irrelevant attack on multi-national corporations but also to reveal that he did not quite know what a trust was.

The other case was, as we shall see, different.

The journalist had been spotted immediately. Krom was not spotted at all; chiefly because the name under which he registered was not false enough. It had been borrowed, with its owner's knowledge and consent, so that the usual intelligence cross-check turned up nothing to alert us.

In my official capacity as Director of the Institute it was natural that I should take the chair and introduce the speakers at one or two sessions. The first of those I presided over was in the afternoon of the second day. It ended at five. An hour later Krom introduced himself to me.

His method of doing so had an unpleasant touch of the macabre in it and was for me, I freely admit, highly disturbing. No doubt he intended it to be.

The receptionist telephoned me in my room.

He was a man who knew me and my voice well. He still asked carefully if he was speaking to Mr Firman.

'Certainly you are. What is it?'

We usually spoke French. Now he began speaking in English. He was obviously reading what he had to say.

'I am asked to state, Mr Firman, that Mr Kramer and Mr Oberholzer of Zürich are waiting in the lobby here to see you.'

Since they were both dead men – Kramer being literally dead and Oberholzer figuratively so – the announcement gave me quite a jolt.

I said : 'I see. *Both* these gentlemen are there?'

'That is what I am instructed to say, Sir.' The tone of his voice was unnaturally formal. I thought it possible that he believed he was dealing with a police matter.

As we were in Brussels, I knew that possibility to be remote. We were on excellent terms with the authorities there. In fact, if I could have assumed that it was only a police matter, I would, at that moment, have been much relieved.

'I'll be down in a few minutes, Jules.'

'Thank you, Sir.' Still very formal, painfully so.

I didn't wait a few minutes. I went down straight away and by the emergency stairs. This enabled me to get a look at the vicinity of Jules's reception desk without crossing the lobby.

There were some new arrivals at the hotel checking in, or waiting to do so, and there was quite a crowd by the desk. None among them was known to me or looked in the least like a person who could have intimidated an experienced hotel receptionist.

Jules was pretending to study his reservation plot-board on the wall behind the counter, and I could see, even at that distance, that he was in a state of shock. I had another, more careful, look around, then went over quickly and elbowed my way through to him. The indignant looks his two assistants gave me were easy to ignore. I tapped him on the shoulder. It was as if he had been expecting arrest and was now resigned to it. He leaned wearily against the wall before he turned.

He was, I knew, in his sixties. Now, grey and sweating, he looked eighty and unlikely to last much longer. When he recognized me he fluttered his hands and started to protest weakly against my invasion of his territory. I cut him short.

'Stop yammering. Where are they?'

'There's only one, the man in three-two-six. But . . .'

'Name?'

'Dopff. He is over in the corner by the big flower arrangement, and he is watching us speak. I beg you, Mr Firman, please . . .'

I did not wait to hear what he was begging me to do, or not do, but turned and walked straight across to where the man was sitting.

My memory for names and faces is good, very good, but it has its limits. I could remember that a person named Dopff was registered for the seminar and that he was from Luxembourg, but I couldn't recall his profession. That meant only one thing: whatever he was – lawyer, accountant, banker, amateur tax-evader or government spy – he had been checked out as a potential client and, as such, found wanting.

As I approached, I recognized him; he was the elderly man who had been sitting in the middle of the third row an hour or so earlier, listening with rapt attention to my introduction of the main speaker. I had noticed him partly because he had actually seemed interested in my ritual listing of the speaker's qualifications – they were all there printed in the official programme he had in his hand – but mostly because he appeared to wear a permanent smile. The smile, I had noted later as we were all leaving the conference room, was an optical illusion which vanished when you came closer to him. It was produced by the combination of an upper lip shaped like a circumflex accent and a mouthful of large, very white teeth, the kind that look like cheap dentures even when they are not.

He was showing them to me now as I approached him; only this was no illusory smile; it was a blatantly triumphant grin. Had I not needed badly to know who he really was, what he wanted and what sort of threat he constituted, I would have walked straight on past him just for the pleasure of watching the result through the mirror on the adjacent wall. I took refuge instead in courtesy. The really heavy-handed, old-world stuff can make it possible for one to discharge an enormous amount of anger without the object of the anger becoming fully aware of it. He may suspect but he cannot be certain. With luck, one will cause him considerable unease without giving him any excuse to take offence.

Unfortunately, with a man as sure of himself as Krom, this form of attack can never be wholly effective.

The common language of our seminars has always been English, so it was in English that I addressed him.

'Mr Dopff, is it? I understand that you wish to see me.'

To the grin he added an insolent stare. 'No, Mr Firman, that is not at all what I wish. I have already seen you, clearly and unmistakably, before. That was in Zürich five years ago when you were calling yourself Oberholzer.'

'My name is Firman, Sir.'

He went on as if I had not spoken. 'So, I have seen you twice. What I intend to do from now on is to talk with you.' He patted the arm of the empty chair beside him. 'Why don't you sit down?'

I remained standing. 'I am sure that you will understand that I am a busy man, Mr Dopff. I simply came to tell you that the receptionist here gave me a strange message, from you he tells me, about two persons of whom I have never heard. It seemed proper and sensible to let you know that the message was either garbled or misdirected. That is all.'

He showed his teeth again. 'That garbled message brought you pretty quickly, Mr Oberholzer.'

'The name, I repeat, is Firman.'

'At the moment it is, yes. But it used to be Oberholzer, and I have no doubt that there have been, and still are, a great many other identities in your repertoire. How annoying it must be for you to realize that this time you can't just run for it.'

I gave him my little bow. 'Except to escape the acute boredom of this conversation, Mr Dopff, why on earth should I run anywhere?'

He was unruffled. 'You ran in Zürich. Here, as you have obviously realized, you must try to bluff your way out. No head-start possible, no suitable cut-outs available and no inconspicuous exits handy. Agreed? So why not sit down and join me in a little whisky? In spite of your impressive outer calm, I am sure that you would find it helpful.'

At that moment I had almost decided that he was some sort

of private detective, a retired fraud-squad type. Anyway, it was time to counter-attack.

I sighed and sat down in the chair beside his. 'Very well, Mr Dopff. You want to talk. May I suggest a subject?'

'Why not?' He snapped his fingers for the waiter. 'We can always change it.'

'Then, since the subject of identity seems to interest you so much, why don't we have a look at the one you're using?'

'By all means.'

The waiter came then and took the order for more whisky. It was given in what sounded to me like Flemish.

'For a start,' I said, 'I don't think you're a Luxembourger.'

'Absolutely right!' Beaming smile. He might have been playing a guessing game with a favourite grandchild.

'And your name is not Dopff.'

'Right again. My good friend Maurice Dopff, who lives and works in the Grand-Duchy, registered for this affair and then found himself unable to attend. He kindly allowed me to come in his stead.'

'Do you really expect me to believe that?'

'Of course I don't. He allowed himself to be used as cover.' He fished out a visiting card and handed it to me. 'Permit me to introduce myself formally. The name is Krom.'

I knew at once exactly who he was. In the tax-avoidance game our coverage of legal and financial publications of all sorts and nationalities is as comprehensive as we can make it. The Institute and Symposia between them employed a multi-lingual, and very expensive, full-time research staff of eight as well as numerous part-timers. With us, good intelligence is as essential for survival as discipline and foresight. Our coverage of specialized technical journals dealing with law enforcement at policy-making levels is extremely thorough. Krom's allusions to tax avoidance and evasion in the published version of his Berne lecture had been sufficient to ensure its being brought to my attention flagged with a red sticker. Even if he had not initiated our acquaintance by playing games with dead men's names, I would have known enough about Krom to be wary of him.

My first ploy, then, was to pretend that I knew nothing while working to find out more.

I gave the card a perplexed look. 'Well, Professor, this is all a bit surprising. As you may imagine, we gets lots of peculiar characters at these seminars of ours, all sorts of nosey-parkers, including, I have to say, some of our competitors in the tax-haven area. We don't object. If we can teach them something, well that is what we are here for, to teach. It *is* though a trifle irksome, I admit, when they make fools of themselves by wearing disguises.' I contrived a sudden look of anxiety. 'You really *are* Professor Krom, I hope? This –' I held up the card – 'is not, by any chance, a disguise within a disguise?'

He had been watching me intently and with a certain air of disbelief. Now he shook his head slowly. 'No, I am Krom. Why? Were you hoping that I wasn't?'

'On the contrary, I was hoping that you were. You see, this is the first time we have had the pleasure of entertaining a Professor of Sociology. This is an occasion. Still –' perplexity again – 'I'm afraid I don't yet see the connection between your field and ours. Unless, that is, you are seeking advice on how best a good Dutchman may avoid those onerous Netherlands taxes.'

He suddenly grinned again and clapped his hands softly. 'An excellent performance,' he said, 'really excellent. Just for a moment there you nearly made me forget. Forget Oberholzer and Kramer, I mean. You see, Mr Firman, my field is criminology.'

It was time to show *my* teeth. I said: 'You'll find no able criminals here, Professor Krom.'

He positively giggled. 'From defence to attack, eh? The pretence of ignorance is abruptly discarded in order to disconcert. Splendid impertinence!'

I went on as if he had not spoken. 'So I'm afraid your little fishing expedition will have to be written off as a waste of time. Sorry.'

Protesting hands. 'Oh, but it has got off to a most successful, a most promising, start!'

The drink arrived just then. I was glad of the diversion. The man was proving hard to handle, and I needed time to think. I could have done with more. It was necessary to find out from him what he considered success without actually asking, and I made a complete hash of it.

When the waiter had gone again I said: 'Then you must be easily satisfied.'

He read me instantly. 'I can well understand, Mr Firman, that you are curious.'

'I'm surprised, certainly.' No point in letting the adversary *see* your discomfiture even if he must have sensed it. I kept

'ou bait your hook with some mysterious substance
Oberholzer and Kramer, and catch an empty beer can.
ou think that's good fishing, naturally I'm surprised.'
The teeth flashed triumphantly. 'You've missed a trick,
Mr Firman!'

'I am sure that you intend to tell me which.'

'Of course I do. You fell into the trap of failing to ask yourself an obvious question.'

I smiled. 'How do *you* know what questions I ask myself,
Professor?'

'I know you haven't asked yourself this one because you
haven't asked me for the answer. Consider. You are told that
Oberholzer and Kramer are waiting to see you. Correct?'

'I am told that two persons of whom I have never heard
are waiting to see me.'

An upraised forefinger flicked the quibble aside contemptuously. 'Yet, in your anxiety to set eyes instantly upon the
person who uses these unknown names, you quite overlook
the oddity of the channel of communication he has chosen to
use.' He paused before going on. 'Do you usually in this hotel
receive messages about visitors from the receptionist? Doesn't
the concierge's, the hall-porter's, department function here?'

I managed, not without difficulty, a careless shrug. 'It
functions, yes, and quite efficiently. I presume you thought
that a busy receptionist was less likely to remember your face
than the concierge who gives you your room-key and who
might also be unsympathetic to practical jokers.'

He gave me a kindly look. 'Not bad for a spur-of-the-moment
invention, but it won't do, will it? Hindsight content far too
high. If you had never heard of Oberholzer and Kramer why
would the possibility of a practical joke occur to you? No,
you failed to ask yourself why I had gone to the receptionist
because the questions uppermost in your mind just then were –
who is this joker, what does he want and how dangerous is
he?'

I drank some whisky. I had begun to need it. As if to
humour him, I put the question: 'Well, why *did* you use the
receptionist to send me your message?'

He gave me a nod for good behaviour, but no immediate
answer to the question.

'In spite of his being one of the more active members of
your private espionage organization,' he said, 'I think I may
know more about that receptionist than you do. Naturally, all

your known associates have interested me for some time. Where possible I have built up dossiers on them. However, once I had decided that the birthplace of our collaboration would be here in Brussels, work on all your local contacts was intensified.' A peculiar twitching of his facial muscles began as he added: 'The possibility of an abortion occurring was, to this fond parent, a totally unacceptable risk.'

As his face went on twitching and he gazed at me expectantly, I realized that he thought he had said something funny and was waiting for a laugh.

When all he got was a blank stare, the twitching ceased and he said tolerantly: 'Perhaps you would find a military analogue more to your taste.'

'Perhaps.'

'Well then, this was the kind of operation in which success can only be won by immaculate preparation leading to the achievement of tactical surprise. A note delivered to your room, or left in your mail-box downstairs here, would not have worked. You would have had time to think, time to investigate and prepare defences, possibly time to make arrangements for my discomfiture. Or even,' he added coyly, 'not knowing of the precautions I had taken to safeguard myself, time to organize my removal from the scene.'

I looked suitably offended by the insinuation. 'For a criminologist you have a somewhat lurid imagination, Professor.'

'I was not, of course, being entirely serious, Mr Firman.' The teeth made a jovial showing, but the wariness in the pale-blue eyes told a different story. He believed not only that I was an able criminal but also a person capable of murder. I made a note of the fact. That sort of belief, senseless though it may be, can sometimes be quite useful.

'But,' he was saying, 'you are right about one thing.'

'Good.'

'The concierge might, as you say, have found the verbal message strange. There could have been several possible consequences of his doing so. You might, as we have seen, have been in some way forewarned and thus forearmed. Even more important, he might, without thinking, have talked, gossiped, and so compromised the entire operation. I had long perceived, you see, that if our collaboration was to be fruitful, absolute secrecy, in the early stages especially, was essential. *That* is why I chose the receptionist to deliver my message. He will not, I assure you, repeat a word of it, or of your subsequent questioning of him, to any third party. The poor fellow is far too frightened to disobey me.'

'I noticed that he had been frightened. What did you threaten him with?'

'Threaten him, Mr Firman? It wasn't necessary to threaten him.' He found the accusation quite astounding. 'As I told you, I have done, and had done for me, much intensive work on your people. This man spied for you, so it occurred to me to wonder if, perhaps, he spied, or had once spied, for someone else. I was simply looking in a routine fashion, you understand, for parallel associations. Well, I have friends in Bonn who are interested in my work, and they have access to the BND and its archive of Nazi SD files. And what do you think? During the Nazi occupation here our receptionist avoided forced labour recruitment by becoming an SD informer. Naturally, since he had never been exposed here – the victorious Allies couldn't be bothered with the non-German small fry and the Belgian Resistance never had free access to the files – he had come to believe that the past, or that little bit of his particular past, was buried for ever. Did you know about it?'

He was still trying to sell me the proposition that, no matter what game we ended up playing, he would hold a winning hand.

'No,' I said. 'I didn't know.'

'So it was unnecessary to use threats. All I had to do was speak to him using his old German code-name.'

'I see. And you didn't consider that a threat?'

He swallowed most of his drink – talking had made him thirsty – and savoured it with a genteel little smack of the lips before he answered.

'No,' he said finally, 'I didn't consider it a threat. Nor, by the same token, would I consider that the conflicting interests which will be the basis of our collaboration need be thought of as threats by either of us. We are both sensible men, are we not?'

'I am beginning to have doubts, Professor. That is the third time you have spoken of our collaborating. Collaborating in *what*, for heaven's sake?'

This time he showed me all the teeth and a stretch of molar bridgework as well.

'I intend,' he said, 'to make a complete, full-scale case-study of both you and your remarkable career, Mr Firman. For that, I shall require your close collaboration. Total anonymity will, of course, be guaranteed so that nothing need be left unsaid. You will be the great Mr X.' He gave a little snicker. 'In other words, I intend to make your craft and its associated skills as well understood by, and as recognizable in, the law-enforcement agencies of the world as common-or-garden burglary is now. Yes, Mr Firman, I intend to make you famous!'

Mat was in London, negotiating, on behalf of Chief Tebuke and the native population of Placid Island, the final settlement of their claim against the Anglo-Anzac Phosphate Company; or rather he was going through the motions of negotiating on their behalf. Everyone who counted knew that he was in fact negotiating more for his own ultimate benefit than anyone else's. They also thought that they knew what he wanted for himself out of the settlement. His connection with, then amounting to control of, the Symposia Group was at that time a very well-kept secret.

We maintained a fully-staffed office in Brussels. With its help, I was able to reach him by telephone soon after seven.

The emergency routine in use at the time involved sending a preliminary alert through a London cut-out via telex. That brought him to a safe phone to receive the call. Inevitably, though, there was some delay. I filled it by re-examining the file on Krom.

It had been his Berne lecture that had brought him to my attention, and it was to the lecture that I now returned.

One of the things that had most struck me about it at the time had been his casual use of the word 'criminal'. In my opinion and, I think, in that of most modern lexicographers, a criminal is one who commits a serious act generally considered injurious to the public welfare and usually punishable by law. Krom seemed to believe that anyone possessing the imagination and business planning skills needed to evolve a new way of investing time and money in order to make a profit, was automatically a criminal. The wretch need not have committed any illegal act to earn him the distinction. If he had been original and his originality had succeeded, that was enough. For Krom he stood condemned.

This is Krom on my old friend Carlo Lech's last fling:

'The classic coup by Able Criminals – we do not know exactly how many were involved, but it is believed that there were four partners in the venture – is, of course, the famous butter affair. For the benefit of those delegates here whose governments have seen fit to abstain from, or avoid, membership of the EEC, I should explain that between member states there is an elaborate system of import-export subsidies. What these clever rogues did was to buy a large consignment of butter, a trainload of the stuff, and send it on a European tour, claiming, each time it crossed a frontier, subsidies for its fictional transformation into some other butter-fat product. At the end of the tour they sold off the butter for what they had paid for it and pocketed between them ten million Deutschmarks in subsidies. Later operators in this field have not even troubled to buy the goods they manipulate in this way. Their transactions exist *only* on paper. Value-added tax rebates on non-existent but thoroughly-documented export transactions are currently in vogue. EEC regulations are constantly being changed, of course, to stop up the holes in them, but new holes continue to appear. Needless to say, even when such a criminal, or the corporate cover behind which he works, has supposedly been identified, there is no effective means of instituting a prosecution.'

Well of course there isn't. No criminal law has been broken, and nothing injurious to the public welfare has occurred; not, that is, unless you consider the spectacle of EEC bureaucrats going about with egg on their faces injurious to the public welfare. There are, in fact, large sections of the European public who find such sights highly beneficial, and worth every centime or pfennig of their cost.

And not even Krom, by the way, had been altogether unaware of the inconvenient questions which his theories invited. He had dealt with them, cutely, by asking them before his audience could do so.

'Why, I may be asked, should the word "Able" be used to categorize this well-adapted but minor sub-genus within the human race? Would not the term Successful Crook be at once more accurate and more suitable? My answer must be that it would not. The word "crook" is imprecise and the word "successful" would in this context be misleading, for it could be taken to mean "fortunate". The Able Criminal is, no doubt, fortunate in that he is successful; but he is successful not through some happy series of accidents or because the police authority concerned with him is incompetent; he is successful always and only because he *is* able.

'Why, then, is he a criminal at all? What, if he really exists, can possibly motivate him? The desire for wealth and the power that goes, or is said to go, with it? Hardly. Men capable of planning and executing the butter coup or having the fiscal wit to create illusory businesses which make real profits could surely become multi-millionaires quite – I was about to say "legitimately" – perhaps I should say instead "legally". As legally, anyway, as unit trust managers or currency speculators are said to conduct their respective operations.

'But our Mr X is not attracted by the blessings of legitimacy and legality, only by the extent to which the appearances of them may be put to use. He is a white-collar criminal in the sense that he is an educated one, yes; but his crimes are the products not of breaches of trust – the hand in the till, the falsified accounts – but of breaches of faith. And the faith he breaches is that of faith in established patterns of order. He is, in short, an anarchist.

'What kind of anarchist? Well, of one thing we can be certain. He will not be stupid. He will not have taken to his heart the works of the ineffable Marcuse, nor troubled himself with the ravings of those hapless social philosophers, those paladins of the lollipop set, Raoul Vaneigem and Guy Debord. He will believe neither in the Spectacular Society nor in Situationist Intervention. He will not be a carrier of bombs in plastic shopping-bags. But his tactical thinking will have much in common with that of some of the better-disciplined urban guerrilla groups – those who work by confounding bureaucratic controls and exploiting the resultant confusion for profit. Whether that profit be ideological or solely financial is a matter which need not concern us here. The first step is to recognize the nature of the difficulties facing us. In the jungles of international bureaucracy, including those of the multi-national corporations, there is always plenty of dense under-growth in which able men may conceal themselves and from which they may mount attacks. The task of those attempting to flush them out will never be easy.'

We had one room in the office suite which was regularly checked for bugs. I sat in there to take the call to Mat.

Our conversation lasted less than a minute. Most of it consisted of code-words suggesting that we were in the fertilizer business. They conveyed, however, first a top-priority blown-cover alert from me with a request for orders. From Mat came an instruction to go to London forthwith by the company plane, and be prepared to return to Brussels that same night. The journey was to be made unobtrusively. If possible it should not be known that I had left the hotel at all.

Finding the pilot took time because he was in bed with some girl; but he had obeyed standing orders, which ensured that he was always on call in an emergency, and, once found, he responded promptly. For the salaries we paid we expected efficiency. When I got to the airport he had already obtained a clearance to land at Southend and filed a flight plan. Customs clearances presented no problem. The only baggage I carried was my Brussels room-key with its heavy brass number-tag. By eleven-thirty I was in London.

Mat usually stayed at Claridge's, but this time he had chosen to hole up in a rather seedy Kensington hotel.

I had twitted him about it when I had seen him some weeks earlier. What, I had asked, had he been trying to prove? That he was just a simple island wog being victimized by the wicked monopoly capitalists who had stolen his forefathers' birthright? And whom did he hope to impress with this nonsense? The British Foreign and Commonwealth Office people he was dealing with, who knew to a man that he was a graduate of the London School of Economics and had attended Stanford Law School? Or Anglo-Anzac Phosphate who thought of him chiefly as the expert on Pacific tax-haven trust laws appointed by a Canadian bank to make sure that that mangy old Chief kept his nose clean and got his sums right?

There had been no answering smile. About some things one no longer made jokes.

'Paul, there is only one person I have to impress at the moment, Chief Tebuke. You ought to know why, without my having to spell it out for you. If we want real power in an independent Placid Island with a dollar-linked currency and beneficent corporation laws, the appearance of that power must be vested initially in the historically acceptable indigenous figure who can give it a glaze of respectability. The granting of independence must seem, especially in North America, to be a belated act of simple justice to which no honest man, whatever his race, creed or colour, could possibly object. For how long did the Australian Government tolerate the fiscal independence of Norfolk Island when they found that it was taking a slice out of their tax cake? Just as long as it took to pass the legislation cancelling Norfolk's right to take it. No effective right of appeal existed because there was no indisputably valid claim to sovereignty. Any rich fool can buy an island and proclaim it a sovereign state. On the mainland he need not even be so very rich. All he needs to do there is back an up-and-coming separatist movement, or a bunch of dissident army officers, and play it patiently by ear. But how or what he buys into is unimportant. It's getting the recognition that counts. Not just a tolerated measure of autonomy, but *de facto*, *de jure*, UN-approved, copper-bottomed sovereignty, the works.'

'I only asked why you weren't staying at Claridge's.'

'And I'm telling you. In this case the key to recognition lies in Chief Tebuke, our symbol of both legitimacy and self-determination. In order to control him I must retain his trust and affection. In the islands, trust and affection are based on the strict observance of certain social rules, which you might choose to call etiquette but which I prefer to call a code of manners. I am not the Chief, but an adviser. Therefore, I must live in a lesser place. He happens to be impressed by the Hilton. So, I must not live in Claridge's where heads of state are known to stay. I could live on a lower floor of the Hilton, of course, but the less I see of him the better. This is well out of his way. What's the matter with it anyhow? I've lived in worse hotels and so have you. You're getting soft, Paul.'

That one had been rather more long-winded than usual, probably because he had thought it necessary to mix some falsehood in with the truth; but, apart from that, you could call it a typically sanctimonious Mat reproof.

It has been said that the vision of the apocalyptic horsemen reveals only that St John must have had poor eyesight. Just *four* horsemen? For heaven's sake! Listen man, even *twenty-four* would have been too few.

The suggestion is, of course, that the consequences of war are of infinite variety and by no means always evil. Like many other platitudes, this one, too, has an element of truth in it.

Among the consequences of World War II in the Pacific, for example, the accident of Mathew Williamson's exposure to the world Boy Scout movement, and subsequently to the works and philosophy of Lord Baden-Powell of Gilwell, would probably be accounted by most right-thinking persons a good thing; and if there are those, more familiar perhaps with the ideological content of the works, who feel inclined to question that verdict, let them keep their thoughts to themselves. One thing is virtually certain: without the benefit of the Chief Scout's teachings, Mat – he was given a Christian name and baptized at the Methodist mission while he was in Fiji – would never have become the extraordinary businessman he is.

In view of the *kind* of businessman he is, that may seem odd; but I doubt if the author of *Life's Snags and How to Meet*

Them, Sport in War, Scouting for Boys and *Lessons from the Varsity of Life* could ever, even in one of his least humourless moments, have envisaged the effects that his homespun pragmatism might have upon the mind of a lad of Mat's peculiar antecedents, natural talents and disposition. His books were, in a sense, gospels, but they were not designed to withstand interpretation by a half-caste Melanesian sorcerer.

Mat's father was an Australian sea captain named Williamson, his mother the daughter of a village headman in one of the Gilbert Islands. There is no record of the pair ever having been married. She had lived on board Williamson's ship, a freighter owned by one of the phosphate companies, and Mat, whom she called Tuakana because it meant 'eldest', was born in the company dispensary on Placid Island. She had, though, no more children after him.

When he first told me about Placid we were sitting on the verandah of a hotel in the New Hebrides' capital, Port Vila, having breakfast. He was in his middle thirties then, an imposingly handsome, dark-skinned man with russet hair. I had assumed that the hair colour was a product of his mixed blood, but found later that in some of the islands it was quite common. However, eyes as blue as his were not. I found them disconcerting. They have had the same effect on others I could name.

I was not too disconcerted to ask questions, though. That after all, was what I was there for, to ask questions. So, I asked him where he came from and so received the first of many lectures.

'As we were taught at the mission school,' he began, 'the great Captain James Cook gave English names to many of the places he discovered or explored in the wide Pacific Ocean. So good of him, so kind.'

It was said in a high-pitched, nasal voice, startlingly unlike his own, and further distorted by a regional English accent that he later attributed to Birmingham. He has an excellent ear. I am sure that if I had ever met the missionary whose voice he was imitating that day I would have recognized the man instantly.

The voice was discarded as abruptly as it had been assumed when Mat went on, 'You know what I think, Mr Smythson? I think that by the time of his last voyage he was becoming bored with the problem of finding all those new names. I also think that he had a copy of Dr Johnson's dictionary with him and was just going through it page by page. You smile? I'm serious. Fiji had its own native name, of course, even then, but north-west of it what do we find? Ocean Island, Placid Island, Pleasant Island. You see? Successive discoveries all in alphabetical order, even though they're separated by a thousand miles. Placid and Pleasant are, anyway.'

'And very different, I imagine.'

'Oh, not at all different. In fact, very much the same.' He cut a slice of papaya. 'Neither of them was ever placid or in the least pleasant. Both, however, used to possess millions of tons of phosphate deposits. Most of these, naturally, have long been strip-mined and removed, leaving us with lunar landscapes of unlovely grey coral. We were both occupied briefly by Imperial Germany before becoming British colonies. In 'forty-two we were both occupied by the Japanese, who used us as communication centres, and later heavily bombed by the Americans. Both of us subsequently became UN trust territories administered jointly by Britain, Australia and New Zealand, who still wanted what was left of the phosphate. I was born on Placid.'

'I can understand your feeling bitter.'

'Bitter?' He grinned. 'Why on earth should I feel bitter? We were barbarians. You will note that I say "we". I include myself. What would we in our ignorance have done with so much old bird-crap, so much phosphate? Nothing. Our exploitation by the Powers was the best thing that ever happened to us. Even the American bombing was good. Simple people enjoy loud bangs. Unfortunately I was not there to hear them. When the Japanese attacked Pearl Harbour, my father was inconsiderate enough to leave me to be educated in Fiji while he took his ship off to fight for the British Empire.'

The Methodist missionaries who received him had been in for some surprising experiences.

At ten, Mat had had no education other than that provided by his parents and by his travels with them in the ship. From his father he had learned to read and write English and the mathematics of navigation; on his travels he had picked up smatterings of several island languages; from the ship's crew he had learned about the recreational facilities available in Australasian seaports; and, of most importance to him at the time, from his mother he had learned the pagan legends of her forebears. From her, too, he had learned about the power and practice of magic; above all, he had learned the secrets of death-spells and other rituals, defensive as well as offensive, through which personal safety or power over others might be achieved.

In the summer of 1942 news came that Mat's father had gone down with his ship, and a number of refugees from Singapore, off the coast of Java. Later that year his mother died of a kidney disease. It was at the time of his becoming an orphan that Mat was baptized.

The staff of the mission school, delighted to find that they had a gifted child to teach – in mathematics he was considered a prodigy – cannot, however, have deeply regretted the death of his mother. Having fought the good fight against pagan superstition with the weapons of Christian superstition for so long, they must have been disheartened to find that their gifted child could frighten the living daylights out of his wretched classmates with an ancient death-curse. He had shown no interest in the religion he was now being taught. His sudden enthusiasm for Scouting, strange though it may have seemed at the time, was undoubtedly accepted with considerable relief.

I once talked to a retired colonial officer who had served in Fiji for the last three of the seven years that Mat spent there. He had known about Mat chiefly because he had been concerned as an official with the arrangements for the boy's higher education; but that had not been the only reason. He had recalled with amusement that, even as Mat was winning a scholarship and applying, with the help of Government House, for the grants which would enable him to live as a student in London, his name was being submitted for the honour of King's Scout.

'I'll bet they didn't know *that* at the London School of Economics,' he said, then chuckled again. 'Do you know, there was a time when that boy was actually accused publicly by the parents of another, older boy of sorcery and weaving spells. It wasn't a proper court case because they were both minors and because there was no law dealing with junior witch doctors, but there had to be an investigation of the complaint and I was told off to handle it. Know what the cheeky young bugger did?'

'Mat Williamson you mean?'

'Yes. At the enquiry, he handed me, very respectfully, a list of the questions that he would have addressed to the other boy's parents had he been the defendant in an adult court of law. As, under the circumstances, he was not allowed to ask them, would I please do so? Well, it sounded such a reasonable request and he looked so solemn and upset that, like a bloody fool, I agreed. Should have looked more carefully at the questions first, of course. The parents' complaint was that, as a result of the spell, their boy had suffered agonizing stomach cramps for a week and that the spell had defeated all medical attempts to relieve the pain. That list of questions was like a medical cross-examination, only worse because it gradually became like a parody of a real one. Began all right or I wouldn't have started on it. What had been the diagnosis of the District Nurse? Colic. Had she prescribed medicine? Yes, but it hadn't worked, and so on. Then he really cut loose. What about bowel movements? What had the faeces looked like? Liquid or solid? Small or large? Round or sausage-shaped? Was there accompanying wind? What did it smell like? I wouldn't have gone on but for one thing. Every other question made evidential sense. Had the boy had such attacks before? How often? Real questions. But it was the others that counted. You know, those people have rather a broad sense of humour. They began to laugh and that was that. Nothing much I could do. It wasn't a court of law, but when-ever I hear of a case being laughed out of court, I think of that list of questions. If I could have found the little monster guilty of something, I'd have done so cheerfully.'

'But you didn't.'

'Of course not. I was too busy trying not to laugh myself. But afterwards I gave him a ticking-off. Not that he cared. Too clever by half, young Williamson. And I'm not saying that just because he made an ass of me and also won a scholarship. Lots of those very bright teacher's pets are emotionally immature. He wasn't. He had the sort of insights that a great many so-called adults never begin to acquire. He was also a bit cruel. He'd know exactly what was going through some other fellow's mind and use the knowledge to frighten him by dressing it up in that magical hocus-pocus of his. Cruel, as I say, but funny. As for the Boy Scout stuff, that was funny, too, if you looked at it from where he stood. Tribalism, that's what he saw, with lots of stern rituals and the chance to exercise a natural talent for leadership. A very spry lad, and a very deep one, that.'

'As a matter of fact he still quotes Baden-Powell.'

He sniffed. 'They say that the Devil still quotes the scrip-tures, I believe. I'd say that Mathew Williamson's idea of a good deed for the day now would be lending his best friend a pound and getting an IOU from him for two.'

In fact, Mat Tuakana, as he was calling himself then, made his first million not by using his own money but by arranging for other persons to spend theirs.

He was twenty-two when he graduated from the LSE. One of his student friends there was a native of what had formerly been the Dutch East Indies and was then emerging as the Republic of Indonesia. The friend's father had long been a Sukarno man, was close to the new President and had valuable patronage at his disposal. American aid to the new state was being given generously. In Djakarta educated men of ability who were neither Dutch nor Chinese were in short supply. When Mat and his friend arrived they had no trouble at all in making themselves useful. In a country where the average life expectancy was then no more than thirty years and the number of university graduates as a percentage of the population was approximately zero, their youth was no handicap. Within weeks they were in positions of authority and responsibility that in most other countries could only have been reached after years of determined in-fighting and conspicuous dedication. In Indonesia, too, positions of authority and responsibility were also, then, positions of considerable personal profit for those who held them. Mat's job in the Ministry of Trade and Industry was to act as a purchasing agent. The money he used was allocated from the millions of dollars of US aid which arrived in the form of American bank credits, and what he bought was what American advisers to the new regime appeared to believe the Indonesian people most needed: useful things like refrigerators, room air-conditioners, radio sets, modern plumbing and cars that would make the place more like home.

Of the millions of dollars Mat spent on buying such things, some, naturally, stuck to his own fingers. He got two commissions on each deal, one from the agent selling the merchandise for its US manufacturer and another from the merchant to whom he allocated the stuff when it arrived. He made his million in a little under two years and then, sensing that change was in the air and knowing that, while it is always a mistake to be greedy, in Djakarta at the time it was often a fatal mistake, he got out.

He had many American contacts now, so it was to America that he went. He was also given much advice on how best to multiply his million. This he ignored. The advice he took concerned his education. From Americans whose judgement he had come to respect he had learned that the great American law schools are not simply places where men and women are taught to practise law, but places where excellence in other kinds of social and political management is nurtured and developed. Believing his education to be in many such respects incomplete, he had applied to Stanford and, on the basis of his excellent showing at LSE, had been accepted. With the million sensibly invested, I am sure that he had no trouble at all in enjoying his spare time there.

Whether or not he enjoyed the rest of it I have never discovered. The only time I ever asked him he evaded the question. It may have been that those who assessed him there ultimately saw through him a little too clearly, and allowed him to know that they had done so.

The Kensington hotel was made up of two large, Victorian, terraced houses joined together and given a revolving-door entrance. The night porter was obviously a tippler, but still more or less sober when I arrived. Mat's name sobered him still further and, after telephoning up to announce me, he managed to operate a curious old lift. The hotel may have been sleazy, but Mat had made the best of it. Since I had last been there he had taken over most of the second floor with, according to the porter, four rooms en-suite.

The largest had been made into a sitting-room and Mat was waiting for me there. So was Frank Yamatoku, his boy-friend.

Frank is a Japanese-American whizz-kid from California who made a killing in the porn trade there before Mat found him. Frank's innovation had been in movie theatres. He had started in Los Angeles with the one house, a couples-only place in which there were water-beds instead of seats and triple-X films showing around the clock. When he had had six of these places going, he had sold out to a syndicate, thoughtfully giving the Vice Squad a list of the syndicate's members as soon as he had cleared their cheque and was in the overseas departure complex at the airport. Frank has a lot of imagination and is an absolutely brilliant accountant, but until Mat found him he often took risks and lived dangerously.

Mat had cured him of those tendencies, I thought, but I would still have found it difficult ever to like Frank. He knew it, too, and the feeling was mutual. Even though I knew that he was working on the fine print of the Placid Island settlement with the Anglo-Anzac accountant, I was not pleased to see him there with Mat.

'You made good time, Paul,' Mat said. 'No further problems?'

'No further problems, no. But the one I'm here about is quite enough, I assure you.' I looked at Frank and then back at Mat and waited.

After a moment Mat gave me his lazy smile. 'All right. Would you excuse us, Frank?'

Frank stood up. 'Surely. Good to see you, Paul.'

With a nod he left. I was quite sure that he would listen to what Mat and I had to say to one another, but even so it was better without him there.

'A drink, Paul?' Mat motioned towards the sideboard.

'A little later perhaps, Mat. We have that man Krom, the criminology professor, on our backs.'

He became very still. He knew who Krom was. All the stuff about the man and his views that had been passed by the researchers to me had been passed by me to Mat. He was now mentally reviewing it. After he had done so, he relaxed again.

'Tell me, Paul.'

I told him about the first stage of the Krom encounter and waited.

'A foolish man,' he commented, 'but you don't consider him stupid, I gather. If you did you wouldn't be here.'

'No, he's not stupid. He is, however, a little frightened by the step he has taken.'

'Frightened of you?'

'Of me, of us. He has friends in the Dutch Ministry of Justice sympathetic to his views on our business activities. He has friends of like mind in West German intelligence. The man under whose name he is attending the seminar is a rich Luxembourger with political connections. All were advised confidentially of Krom's reasons for attending and of his professional intentions before he came. He has also left affidavits concerning the Kramer affair with university colleagues.'

I paused and again waited for comment. After a moment he began to whistle softly. According to Baden-Powell, the good Scout smiles and whistles under all difficulties. Mat had given up smiling under difficulties, but the habit, acquired as a boy, of whistling under them he had never lost. The tune was always the same, that of a treacly Victorian ballad entitled 'Just a Song at Twilight'. He must have picked it up from some homesick Britishers. It sounded very odd coming from Mat's lips. He says that Baden-Powell himself admitted to having sometimes had trouble over his whistling. Frequent use in public of this antidote to difficulty during the Boer War had given him in some quarters a reputation for eccentricity and, on one occasion, had led to his being accused by a soldier of callous indifference to the feelings of others.

The whistling stopped. 'What leverage has he?'

'He has been working on Symposia, and me, for a long time. He has identified me in the Oberholzer role. He knows other things. If he can't know all and publish it himself *without* naming names, he threatens to leak what he does know to an American or German news magazine *with* names.'

'All he's got is hearsay. He's bluffing. You should have played polo with him, Paul.'

Another Baden-Powell prescription. To play polo with someone in this context is to out-manœuvre him by edging him away from the direction in which you want to go. The metaphor was first used by B-P, I believe, in his essay on the joys of pig-sticking.

'It didn't work, Mat.'

'You should have double-talked him.'

'I did. I asked him to define crime. I asked him if he didn't think that it was largely a fiction created by politicians posing as legislators and legislators pretending that their motives are free from political pollution. Didn't he agree that ninety-five per cent of so-called crime is committed by governments against, and at the expense of, those citizens in whose names they pretend to govern?'

'Yes, that's double-talk all right. What did he say?'

'That it was double-talk. You have to understand, Mat, that what he really wants now is to satisfy his professional vanity. You read his Berne paper. It amused us. Others, his professional peers, are not in the least amused when their lives' work is dismissed as irrelevant. In many quarters he's been attacked as a crank. He now wants us to help him demonstrate that, far from being a crank, he is the great innovator, a Darwin of criminology.'

'By publishing a casebook *without* naming names? Oh, I know that medical textbooks do it. Patient X and patient Y. The identities don't matter, not unless the doctor reporting the case is suspected of being a quack seeking to prove an untenable pet theory with invented evidence.'

'Exactly. In such a case, he either has to produce the patient or qualified witnesses to substantiate his evidence. That's what Krom proposes to do. He has his witnesses already picked, one

American, one English, both qualified persons. We meet in private for a four-day period during which I give them the story of my life. Place of meeting to be of my choosing. Strict security to be observed by all, especially witnesses who will be given only the sketchiest of preliminary briefings, enough to engage their interest and ensure their co-operation without giving anything substantial away. The text of this briefing will be agreed by Krom and me. All names, places and so on to be changed in order to protect the guilty. That's what he wants, and in my opinion that's what he means to get, no matter what it costs.'

He started whistling again, then abruptly stopped. 'I think you've allowed yourself to be conned, Paul. I think you should tell him go jump under a train and that if he makes slanderous or libellous statements about you, or the Institute, or the Symposia Group to anyone who dares publish them, we'll sue them *and* him till the pips squeak. Remind him that, in the circumstances, he will be a source no publisher can protect in the usual way. He'll have uttered his threats to the plaintiff in advance. He wouldn't have a hope.'

I shook my head. 'It's no good, Mat. I tried all that. I told you, he knows things. One of his juiciest suspicions is that Symposia is hooked into the Placid Island project. He only needs start a rumour to that effect to cause trouble. Do you still think I'm allowing myself to be conned?'

That did it, as I had known it would.

Mat's cynicism about the Placid Island deal is a pretence; it always has been, although he would never dream of admitting it. As a boy, he had heard of another phosphate island, once called Pleasant, which had re-discovered its aboriginal name of Nauru. As a man, he had seen that same Nauru, whose whole history was so like that of Placid, cast off her old trust-territory shackles, achieve independence from the British Commonwealth and become the Republic of Nauru, with prospects as a tax-haven.

Now it was Placid's turn. Placid had a better climate than Nauru and better port facilities than Nauru, which lacks a natural harbour. Placid was Mat's birthplace. With Mat to preside over its fortunes and its future – poor old Chief Tebuke could have a whole floor to himself in the Placid Hilton if he lived long enough – with Mat to provide the inspired leadership that his people so eagerly awaited, Placid was destined to become the most remarkable, the most prosperous sovereign state in the entire South Pacific.

Is Mat an able criminal as defined by Professor Krom? Possibly, but he is certainly no anarchist. What he wants is a kingdom, and if the national flag has not yet been designed – a pandurus leaf on a field of gold? – the banknotes almost certainly have. If sociologists like Krom must paste labels on men and women in order to classify them, I would say that Mat is, as I am, an adventurer; that is, in the old pejorative sense of the term, a healthy and intelligent person who could labour usefully in the vineyard, but who prefers instead to live by his wits.

There was no more whistling from Mat. He stared at me now with cold dislike.

'What does he know about Placid?'

'That I went there last November. He knows that Symposia turned down the offer of an interest in Nauru. He knows that Symposia has stopped steering its clients towards the New Hebrides and has something else cooking. He knows that a Placid settlement is imminent because word has got around that our competitors are trying to get a foot in there through Anglo-Anzac.'

'You said that he was frightened of *us*. Did you discuss me?'

I had, in fact, tried hinting at his existence. Why, I had asked Krom, should he assume that in which he called 'the Symposia conspiracy' *I* was the number one? How did he know that I wasn't just a figurehead, part of an elaborate cover-story designed to protect someone else? My intention had been to shake his confidence a little. All I had succeeded in doing was making him laugh. He *knew* that I was number one, so would I please stop trying to talk my way out of the situation.

I had no intention, however, of telling Mat all that.

'No, Mat. we didn't discuss you. Your name wasn't even mentioned. Obviously, he must know *of* you, the *éminence grise* of the Placid Island lobby. If he reads the financial papers I mean. That PR outfit Anglo-Anzac have working for them will have seen to that. But as for your personal connection with Symposia, he couldn't have a clue. If he had, he'd certainly have said so.'

There was a long silence, and then he quite visibly relaxed. 'So, Paul, you're the only one who's been blown so far. It's not *us* he's dealing with, but you. And all that he's looking for is dirt about operators like you and old Carlo Lech. Is that right?'

'You might have put it a little more delicately, but yes, I suppose that's about right.'

'Then you'd better go along with him, hadn't you? Throw him an old bone or two and hope that he keeps faith, eh?'

'Yes.'

'And that his witnesses keep faith. You're going to have to do rather a lot of trusting, aren't you, Paul?'

'That *had* occurred to me. I'm going to have to take out quite a lot of insurance too.'

'Well, we can afford it. You'll need team help too. Yves would be your best bet on the technical side, I think. And Melanie I know you like.'

I should have guessed then what was in his mind. Yves, we had both agreed in the past, was a first-rate man; but we had disagreed about Melanie. Although he is sexually double-gated, Mat's judgements about women are rarely sound. I considered, and still do consider, Melanie to be one of the best cover-builders and analysers there is. She learned her craft with the Gehlen organization and is brilliant. For some reason – perhaps because she is as brilliant at penetrating the most complex covers of others as she is at erecting full-proof lie-structures for her own side – Mat had never trusted her. He suspected her, he said, of being a security risk.

I should have asked him whether he had changed his mind about her, whether he had forgotten that he had told me of his suspicions or whether he was, in his tortuous way, giving me fair warning of what I could expect.

I did not guess, so I did not ask. He would not have answered anyway, but asked who I would like instead of Melanie. There would have been a reminder, too, that once he had delegated responsibility he never interfered. He might also have started quoting Baden-Powell on a Scout's honour.

Instead, we discussed which old bones could best be used to satisfy Professor Krom's appetite.

CHAPTER THREE

By the time Yves had cleared the visitors' baggage, the sun was down behind the tamarisks on the headland; and, for the first time since Brussels, I was feeling something like my normal self.

Yves's first report had made me too angry to think sensibly. It had not been until I had cooled off that I had perceived the obvious: that I had been presented with an opportunity of improving my position; not of escaping completely from the predicament I was in, but of improving my chances of surviving it without suffering permanent damage. I was certainly better off than I had been an hour earlier. How much better off would depend on how skilfully I could manipulate the modified situation.

Mat had spoken of tossing Krom some old bones as if all we had to do was to open some handy closet and dismantle one or two of the skeletons that had been hidden in it. I had gone along with the pretence, and he had let me do so; but we had both known that what Krom would expect and insist on getting was not a bag of old bones but his pound of raw, red flesh. It had also been tacitly understood that the only place from which the stuff could safely be extracted – safely, that is, from Mat's point of view – was my own personal deep-freeze. As he had so charmingly pointed out, I was the one who was blown, not he.

That Krom might himself somehow make things easier for me, even unintentionally, was a possibility I had not even considered before.

Among the ground rules I had agreed with him in Brussels had been one that gave me the final say on all matters concerned with the security arrangements at our subsequent 'conference', and another that laid it down, as a precondition of my giving him any information in the presence of witnesses, that the witnesses would be bound in all respects by the same security restrictions as those he himself had accepted.

I had not needed Mat to tell me that I would have to do an awful lot of trusting.

Well, I had trusted and at once I had been let down. Krom's witnesses had turned out to be about as trustworthy as that legendary Lebanese scorpion. So what about Krom himself? Was it likely, *really* likely, that he, when it came later to publishing my confidences, would prove to be any more reliable? Perhaps, in the end, I would be less seriously injured if I simply called his bluff and told him to do his worst without my willing co-operation.

I could not really do that, of course, out of loyalty to Mat; but Krom could not be sure that I wouldn't; he might well feel that he would be wise not to drive me too hard.

Anyway, I now had him in the wrong and would shortly rub his nose in the fact. If he wanted his pieces of raw flesh he was going to have to sit up and beg. That meant that he would get tired sooner and possibly be more easily and un-critically satisfied. If my luck held, I might not have to throw him any of the juicier bits at all.

At least I now had a bargaining position, or thought that I had.

They were in the cool of the drawing-room off the terrace and sitting in a stiff little semi-circle. Melanie, petrified by having to pretend for an hour to be the hostess, was doing her impersonation of a grande-dame. I had warned her when we had worked together before that it made her sound like a retired *poule-de-luxe* hankering after the good old days, especially in her rather peculiar English, but she had con-vinced herself in the end that I had only been joking. It is odd that someone who can build up with such marvellous ingenuity roles for other persons to play should perform so dismally when called upon to act a little herself.

She was in the middle of an anecdote about Coco Chanel which she had picked up from a women's magazine. Krom's eyes were glassy with boredom. Dr Connell was glowering at her. Dr Henson was holding an empty tumbler in cupped hands and staring into it as if it were a crystal ball.

In the doorway I paused and clicked my heels slightly.

Melanie stopped talking instantly and stood up.

Krom rose more deliberately and pointed at me. 'This,' he said to his witnesses, 'is Mr Paul Firman.'

I waited one more moment, until they were all on their feet, then I went forward with my most charming smile to greet them.

Connell made an instinctive movement as if to shake hands, but I ignored it and let one formal little bow serve them all. The sooner they were reminded that they were uninvited as well as unwelcome guests the better.

'Welcome,' I said. 'So glad you had a safe journey. This, as you have no doubt gathered, is my secretary, Miss Melanie Wicky-Frey, but – ' I broke off and threw a reproachful glance at Melanie – 'I see that your glasses are empty.'

Krom was first off the mark. 'Thank you, Mr Firman, but we are travel-weary. What I think we would all like at the moment, if you will be so kind, is to be permitted to go to our rooms.'

'That is,' said Connell tartly and in pretty fair French, 'if his Algerian truffle-hound has finished snuffling through our bags.' He went on quickly as I opened my mouth to reply. 'And if, Monsieur Firman, you could spare us the protestations of injured innocence, we'd appreciate it. We are, as the Professor says, tired.'

I gave him the thinnest of smiles. 'Oh, I wasn't going to protest, my dear sir, though Mr Yves Boularis might do so if he heard himself described as an Algerian. He is Tunisian. Of course your luggage has been searched, and most thoroughly. I must remind you that, even though you seem to speak French quite well, the language agreed upon for this conference was English. Am I not right, Professor?'

Krom cleared his throat. 'Yes, quite right, Mr Firman, though I think Dr Connell has a point. We all submitted with good grace to a body search, but is it really necessary that we should be treated with such deep suspicion, almost as if we were policemen in disguise?'

'Yes, Professor, I am afraid it *is* necessary.'

He gave an exasperated sigh as I went to the sideboard and poured myself a drink. Then Connell started again. My not shaking hands had rattled him.

'I suppose you're referring to that little tape machine of mine,' he began, and drew breath to continue.

I shut him up by turning to Dr Henson.

'What do *you* say?' I asked her. 'Am I being unreasonable, or are you forgetting that you signed a paper agreeing to abide by a set of rules while attending this conference?'

On closer inspection, she was an attractive woman with delicately structured facial bones, fine eyes and a mouth which suggested all sorts of possibilities. Not all of them would be agreeable, however; that brief marriage of hers must have been a harrowing affair. At that moment she was wondering how she might convincingly convert her embarrassment into anger and failing to find an answer. Finally, she just shrugged.

'You are not being unreasonable, Mr Firman. I haven't forgotten the paper I signed.'

'Thank you, Dr Henson. Now, do you mind telling me and your friends here whether it was your own idea to photograph and fingerprint the persons you were to meet in this house, or someone else's?'

Krom let out a kind of yelp.

Connell started a protest. 'Now wait a minute! Are you accusing Dr Henson of . . .'

But Dr Henson preferred to take care of herself. 'No,' she broke in crisply, 'he is not making an accusation. He is asking an awkward question about the special camera and other equipment found concealed in my handbag.' She surveyed us challengingly. 'The answer is that it was *not* my idea. The camera and other things were given to me, with instructions, by the head of my faculty, Professor Langridge.'

Krom yelped again. 'Langridge! You mean that you told *him* about this conference?'

'Of course. I was taking a leave of absence. Short, yes, but at a time when I was expected to be present. Ought I to have disappeared mysteriously and drawn public attention to myself?'

'You told Professor Langridge *where* you were going and on what errand? Couldn't you have accounted for your absence in some other way? Was it necessary to be so indiscreet?' Krom was becoming very angry indeed.

'I don't make a habit of lying to colleagues, Professor. Besides, I didn't *know* where I was going until lunchtime today.'

It was time for plainer speaking. 'You told Professor Langridge that you were going first to join these two gentlemen in Amsterdam?' I asked.

'Yes.'

'Did you know, when you told him, that he often does little jobs for British intelligence?'

She flushed. Connell muttered, 'Jesus!' She still had the empty glass in her hands and for a moment I thought she was going to throw it at him. Instead, she put it down carefully.

'I knew,' she replied, 'that he did some work for the government. But there's nothing remarkable about that. Scholars of most disciplines sometimes accept research commissions from ministries or sit on official departmental committees. I had always assumed that what he did for the Home Office, or whoever it was, had something to do with his long-term study of the European probation services. A reasonable enough assumption, I think.'

'When did you discover that it had been a false one?'

'About a week after I had told him that I was proposing to take this time off. One day he called me in and showed me the camera and other stuff.'

'You didn't object?' This was Krom again.

'Of *course* I objected!' Dr Henson was nearly as angry as he was by now. 'We had a flaming row about it, if you must know. An extremely unpleasant argument, anyway.'

'Which he evidently won,' said Krom bitterly. 'How?'

'He began by asking, yet again, what our exact intentions were. By "our", he meant those of us who have concerned ourselves with investigations of the able criminal. What was our object? Did we intend merely to establish his existence, in the way, say, that a microbiologist might, having established the existence of a dangerous viral mutation, simply record the fact? Or did we intend to make use of any knowledge or proofs we might acquire about such persons to assist others in eradicating them?'

Connell grunted sympathetically. 'Yes, I've had that one. What did you reply?'

'That I didn't know, that the question was in any case both premature and hypothetical as well as grotesquely unfair to microbiologists. He then said that his "masters" – he actually used the word "masters" like some pompous senior official – that his masters were already convinced of the existence of this new kind of offender and were determined to eradicate him.'

'Did he say what evidence they had?' Krom was almost boyishly eager now. The tidings of yet another band of converts to his private religion had quite dissolved his anger.

'Naturally, I asked, but I soon realized that he didn't really know much. He did, though, make two statements of interest. This wasn't a Home Office matter any longer because conventional police forces hampered by rules and restrictions were helpless in these areas. Not much in that. But he also said that for the less-inhibited forces acting on Treasury orders, *and* in concert with foreign counterpart services where collaborative relations existed, it would be a different story.' She paused. 'And then he threatened me.'

'Sounds a sweet guy,' Connell remarked.

'He said that if I refused to co-operate, that is endeavour to get photographs and prints and report fully and secretly on my return, his so-called masters would place me under surveillance of a kind which would frustrate the whole exercise.

It's not as stupid as it may sound. He knows, you see, how I feel about our work in this field.'

'I suppose he was talking about harassment, men in trench-coats breathing down your neck.'

'And your neck too, I imagine, Dr Connell.' She turned to me. 'What about it, Mr Firman? How far would we have got? Turin?'

'No farther, certainly,' I replied. 'Naturally, the possibility of one or all of you being under surveillance had to be considered, and not necessarily surveillance of the obvious kind with which Dr Henson was threatened in order to ensure her co-operation. Professor Langridge's masters had other options available to them. I had you very carefully watched all the way.'

Connell snorted disbelievingly. 'All the way, Mr Firman? Taking that amount of trouble to cover yourself costs money.'

'Yes, the overheads on an operation of this sort can be quite heavy.'

'Of this sort? I thought this operation was supposed to be one-off, unique.'

'It is.' I gave him the needed rap over the knuckles. 'But I was speaking in general of operations involving inexperienced persons, for whom, or from whom, one needs protection. Naturally it is expensive, but you don't have much choice. Either you accept the expense when the need for it arises or you resign yourself to the prospect of being very soon – what was Professor Langridge's word for it? – oh yes, eradicated.' I turned and looked Krom in the eyes. 'A serious question must now be asked,' I went on. 'We have breaches of security on your side and also gross breaches of good faith. How, under these circumstances, can we possibly continue our conference as planned?'

I did not really expect him to throw in his hand; he had too much at stake for that, but it was worth a try. The more defensive he was forced to become the better.

He responded shakily at first. 'I agree that you have cause for complaint, Mr Firman, but no damage has yet been done. Has it?'

'No damage? I don't understand. To me, the whole situation now seems completely compromised.'

He rallied. 'Why? Thanks to your own caution, security has been completely preserved. As for good faith, Dr Henson has admitted that she erred and satisfactorily explained the dilemma that led her to do so. You have the apparatus given her by Professor Langridge. What has been lost?'

'Trust, Professor.' In Brussels I had used Mat's phrase about trusting on Krom. I had also used it several times on myself. I used it again now. 'So far I have done an awful lot of trusting. In return I have been rewarded with deception and equivocation. As things stand at this moment, it seems to me that I have less to lose by telling you the deal is off and that you can do what you like with your researches to date, than by continuing to accept bland assurances that your side of the bargain will be kept because you are honest folk and that it is only I and my associates here who are villains.'

He showed his teeth. 'Oh no, you don't, Mr Firman. Who is deceiving or attempting to equivocate now? We on one side have been completely open and frank. Stop overstating your case.'

I laughed shortly. 'You're bluffing, Professor. Shall *I* ask Dr Henson or will you? When she took that apparatus and agreed to use it, what did she intend? With whom did she mean to keep faith when she brought it here? Professor Langridge and his masters or you and me?'

Connell said, 'Oops!'

Krom thought it through, then glowered at Henson.

From her came a shrug and an exasperated spreading of the hands. 'Several answers,' she said, 'all of them muddled. My first thought was simply to leave the camera and other stuff behind in England, but then I realized that leaving it would create complications.' Another spread of hands. 'Where was I to leave it? In my flat where it could be found by the friend with whom I share the place? She works for Langridge and adores him. Ought I to have tried explaining the whole situation to her? And how could I be certain that, even though I'd promised to co-operate with these people, they wouldn't send someone to watch me anyway? All things considered, it seemed sensible to go through the motions of co-operating by taking the box of tricks with me. Does anyone mind if I smoke?'

She started fumbling in her satchel, but Melanie was there so promptly with cigarette box and lighter that any respite Dr Henson may have been hoping for was brief. When she saw that we were all just waiting for the more crucial parts of her explanation and that no one felt disposed, at that stage, to assist her by making any sort of comment, she continued.

'In Amsterdam the only place I could have left it safely was in the airport consigne. But if I was being watched, and I still don't know whether I was or not, that would have given the game away completely. How could I have returned with my lie about having failed to use the camera through lack of opportunity, when they knew that I'd ditched it at Schipol Airport? So I put off doing anything about it and waited to see where we were going. It was after Turin when I first began to wonder if perhaps I had been making a mistake, if perhaps I'd allowed my personal dislike of Langridge and his Secret Service nonsense to cloud my judgement, or distort it sufficiently for me to reject any and every argument that he put up without even pausing to consider it. However, it turned out that, whether I liked it or not, one of his arguments, along with some of the phrases he used to advance it, *had* stuck in my mind.'

Connell said, 'Aha!' an exclamation she ignored.

'Professor Langridge said –' and she ran her fingers through her hair again in the way I had seen from the terrace – 'he said that this conference, as I had described it, seemed to have more to do with journalism than with scholarship. And not even investigative journalism of the socially useful kind. It sounded to him more like one of those exercises in sensationalism currently favoured by the popular press and the seamier television channels. A news or TV feature is manufactured out of interviewing at a secret rendezvous some notorious terrorist or other wanted criminal.'

She began now to stride about, slicing the air with the edges of her hands as she spoke. It was obvious that she had begun to reproduce Professor Langridge's physical mannerisms along with his rhetoric.

'And what is the object of these journalistic antics?' she demanded of the ceiling. 'I will tell you. For the new media which indulge in them the object is readier access to the eyes and ears of audiences of cretins. For the crooks and thugs who are the star performers the reward is a big jar of the most marvellous cosmetic ointment of all – free publicity. Smeared with that stuff even the most odious of men and the most detestable of causes can enlist a measure of popular sympathy and support. Many distinguished politicians as well as eminent divines have become involved in such tawdry enterprises, so why not an ageing Dutch professor of sociology?'

She avoided looking at Krom, who seemed to be more

amused than annoyed by what she was now saying, and continued to talk at, or to, me. 'The team-leader gathers the brainwashed and compliant subordinates before setting off into the wide, baby-blue yonder. What is different about this adventure? Two things. Journalists working for the established media are to some extent privileged. Unless the casework upon which *we* are engaged happens to confer on us quasi-medical standing, we most certainly are *not*. And neither are your collaborators. The only way you could refuse information about these criminal contacts you propose to make, should you be challenged on the subject by a lawful authority, would be by a pretence of ignorance.'

She paused, and then, with a grimace of disgust at the whole recollection, became herself again. 'His other point made more sense. Reporters on secret-interview assignments are invariably, and for their employers' as well as their own legal benefit and safety, accompanied by a cameraman, an assistant to fetch and carry and somebody to operate a tape-recorder. Even if the person to be interviewed elects to wear a hood or mask, a camera is still there to authenticate the fact that he has done so, and if he chooses to make a voice-track analysis difficult by speaking into a water glass, the tape-recorder will take note of that too. Why is this Mr X so shy? It is because, and *only* because, he wishes to preserve his total anonymity and all the cover identities with which it is ringed, or is the truth rather more drab? Could it be that Mr X is just another professional incompetent after all, and that, far from being unknown to police anywhere, he is very well known indeed to those forces with access to Interpol files? Only photographs and/or fingerprints of the subject could establish the truth.'

'We have a specimen like that who sits on our Board of Regents,' said Connell. 'He's known as The Syllogist.'

'The conclusion I came to,' Dr Henson continued firmly, 'was that I didn't yet know nearly enough to make even a preliminary judgement. When I had heard what Mr X had to say, and formed an opinion of him, then I would review the position. Meanwhile, I would attempt to conceal the camera and ninhydrin spray.'

It occurred to me that for a person who professed to dislike lying to colleagues this was a pretty cool admission. I was about to say so when Krom cleared his throat loudly. Thinking that he was about to deliver the admonition, I let him go ahead.

He didn't even slap her wrist.

'I think that answers the question in all its aspects,' he announced. 'Our agreement stands.'

'Of course it stands,' said Connell. 'Naturally, with a deal like this there are going to be little misunderstandings which need clearing up.'

Obviously, none of them had the smallest sense of right and wrong. I had one more try.

'They may be cleared up to your satisfaction, Dr Connell,' I said, 'but they are very far from being cleared up to *mine*.'

Krom grinned at me. 'But it's not *your* satisfaction that has to be considered, is it? If it were, the chairman of the Symposia Group and director of the Institute for International Investment and Trust Counselling called Paul Firman would long ago have disappeared in a puff of smoke, to emerge three or four days later with an entirely different identity in Sao Paulo or Mexico City. We wouldn't be standing here at all. But we *are* standing here, and we are doing so because Paul Firman can't afford just to disappear. Time and affluence have done their work. His cover is too well established now and his face too well known. He may even be involved in a pension plan. He is caught between two evils and he has sensibly chosen the lesser of them. Am I not right, Mr Firman?'

I almost gave up, but not quite. I managed, apparently unmoved, to meet his eyes. 'We'll see later who is right and who is wrong, Professor,' I said. 'Meanwhile, dinner will be in an hour. Melanie, perhaps you would be good enough to show our guests to their rooms.'

The listening post Yves had chosen was a storage loft over the garage. It had the advantage of being accessible from inside the house via an inner door to the garage, yet well away from the servants' rooms.

When I got there the receivers covering the guest rooms had already been switched on and I was in time to hear Melanie telling Connell that she hoped he would be comfortable and to ring if there was anything he needed.

Yves nodded to me gloomily.

'You handled them well down there, Patron,' he said, 'but I think it is hopeless. *Nous sommes foutus.*'

'Not yet, surely.'

'It's only a matter of time. That lot will never be able to keep their mouths shut about anything. They're supposed to be intellectuals, persons of probity. One feels tempted to treat them as common crooks.'

'It can do no harm if we *think* of them in that way. In fact it might be a good idea.'

He gave me a sidelong look. 'When we started here, I had a feeling that there was a lot I didn't know. Letting your arms be twisted by a party of amateurs, however clever they might be or think they were, didn't sound like you, Patron.' He paused. The fact that he was calling me Patron instead of Paul meant that he was really worried. He added a sigh for good measure. 'You handled them well, as I said, but you handled them carefully and gently. I'd have pushed their faces in and told them to walk home.'

'If it were as easy as that they'd never have arrived.' I had been listening to a bumping sound coming from one of the rooms. Now there was a loud scraping noise. I wanted to change the subject anyway, so I asked what it was.

Yves plugged in the earphone he was wearing. This action enabled him to concentrate on the sounds from one room without ceasing to cover the rest. 'It's Krom,' he reported after a moment or two, 'trying to locate our bug, I think. He's been dragging a chair from place to place, then standing on it, probably to peer at the cornices through that pocket monocular he had tucked away in his suitcase.'

'Any chance of his seeing the bug?'

'Well, if he knew what it looked like he just might spot one end of it, but I don't think he will. Anyway, he couldn't get at it. It's in the chandelier, and you know how high those ceilings are.'

'He could fall off the chair and break a leg trying to get at it.'

'He has nothing to try with. I went over the curtain rods and put extra fastenings on them. If he tried to get one of those down he'd make a noise as well as a mess.'

There, in a few words, are summed up several of Yves's virtues. His vices were not then in evidence.

His versatility was wholly practical and selective. He did not waste time learning how to make amateurish electronic monitoring gadgets; he made sure of picking the most reliable equipment by seeking out the little man near Lausanne who supplies the CIA.

When resourcefulness and imagination could be enlisted to solve unfamiliar problems economically, they were permitted to do so; the curtain rods, which might have been decked revealingly with alarm-bell circuits, were simply fastened more securely to their supporting brackets.

A voice came suddenly from Connell's room. He was speaking into his tape-recorder.

'Research project Alpha-Gamma, casette one, side two. As from Villa Lipp, near Cap d'Ail, France,' he said, 'July 13, 19.30 hours. Arrived, accompanied Krom and Henson, at 17.30 approx. having followed route and instructions already noted. Query. Is this room bugged? Casual inspection which says no as likely to be wrong as right. Lacking equipment necessary make proper check, no point in speculating.'

As Yves nodded his approval of that sensible decision, Connell went on.

'Our party was met by woman who described herself as Firman's secretary. Age, fifty plus. First impression that of a Madame de Stael pretending, with aid of faded, little-girl-type prettiness, to be bird-brained. Hair rinse: brunette with approximately one centimetre grey-auburn visible near scalp. Named by Firman as Melanie Wicky-Frey. Rhymes with tray, but I'm not sure of the spelling. Fluent English, but strong accent with mixed American-British usages. Must ask Krom, who has European ear, for his diagnosis of nationality.'

A longish silence. Then: 'On second thoughts, no. Don't ask Krom anything. You won't get a straight answer anyway. He's a jealous little god about this project. Continue. Secretary Melanie then hands us over to lean and hungry character named Yves Boularis. Expression, mournful yet threatening. Reminded me of that termite-clearance inspector who gave me such a hard time when we were selling house on Cheviot. Diagnosed this Yves as Algerian butler. Wrong on both counts. Not butler, but some sort of right-hand-man. Also doubles as security guard. According to Firman, not Algerian but Tunisian. My present disinclination to believe a word the man Firman says – have a suspicion that there's one who could enjoy lying for its own sake – leaves doubt in mind, however. Who trained Yves to search baggage and frisk? The French? Had big fight to keep this recorder, but sweet reason, or my open fury, prevailed. However, Henson got into serious trouble, and thereby hangs a tale.'

He proceeded to tell it to the recorder, while we listened in turn to Dr Henson taking a bath, and Krom, who had by then abandoned his search for electronic monitoring devices, breaking wind.

When we came back to Connell, he was comparing the British use of men like Langridge in amateur espionage roles with the deeper penetration of the American academic world by US government agencies such as the CIA.

He went on: 'Have left description of Firman character till last. Reason? Call it insufficient evidence. Just can't make up my mind. First impressions, all tenuous. Caucasian, yes. Country of origin? Take your pick. Anywhere from the Caspian to Gibraltar, including Cyprus and Malta. Can't I pin it down a bit? Sure. He has a one-hundred-and-ten per cent British accent. Only other guy I ever met with an accent like it is an Armenian with a Lebanese passport who works for UNESCO and was educated at the English High School in Istanbul before going on to the Sorbonne. He has brown eyes too. Very helpful. Be more specific. Age: mid-fifties, maybe younger. Difficult to judge. Height: two inches shorter than I am, say five-eleven. Looks like weight-watcher, sunlamp-user and wearer of steel-grey toupee. Could also look, with only a little help from the imagination, like ageing movie star who never really quite made it to the top, but who got out at the right time, with self-esteem and investments still intact, to make a killing in California real-estate. Hell, I don't know. Maybe what I am looking at is a retired con-artist who gets his kicks now out of sticking pins into the pretensions of academic clowns like us. Could be. He's already needled Krom, and Henson took quite a beating; though she did, after all, set *herself* up for that. Maybe, as old Krom started to say in Amsterdam before the sheer horror of the idea switched it off, he isn't Firman at all but a covering stand-in. Oh no, forget it. This guy's no stand-in; he reads the lines too well. Want to know something, Connell? As long as he was a deduced, theoretical phantom of the opera, a conceptual bundle of joy who stuck in the Establishment's craw, you believed in the existence of Mr X one hundred per cent. Now, confronted by a person who says he *is* Mr X, you cop out. You say: "Him? Can't be. He looks human!" What did you expect? Bela Lugosi? The Man in the Iron Mask? Or hadn't you given that side of the matter any thought? Ah, well, you're tired now. So how about a shower and a clean shirt? Then, just watch and wait. Okay? Okay. More anon.'

There was no more then from any of the receivers. After a few seconds, Yves switched both them and our own recording tapes to voice-actuated operation.

'An observant man,' he commented.

'Describing you or describing me?'

'Both, I thought. And the woman is even more dangerous. Patron, I think we are doing now what you have always said we should never do.'

'I've said that we shouldn't do many things.' His gloom was beginning to depress me.

'But, in particular, you have said that we should never step out into the street without looking up first to see if the woman on the floor above is about to empty a chamber pot.'

'I have never said anything so crude. I did once say that one should always look carefully where one is walking on certain streets.'

'Same thing, Patron. If you don't look, you're in the shit either way. I think that is where we may be now, and I would like to understand why.'

'Later, Yves,' I said. 'Later, perhaps.'

There was no point in confirming his fears before it became necessary to do so.

We dined on the terrace.

Personally, I dislike eating in the open air at any time, even when there are no insects to plague one; but it was a very warm night and, as Melanie had said, with six at table and the cook's sister-in-law in from the village to help the husband serve, a few moths fluttering around would be a preferable discomfort to that of the staff body-odour in a confined space.

All three of our guests, advised by Melanie that the most casual clothing would be *de rigueur*, had decided to take her at her word. The white-haired Krom in faded blue slacks with a pink linen sports shirt looked positively elegant.

I gave them a white Provençal wine before dinner. None of them refused it, and the large round table at which we could all sit comfortably made for general conversation. At least we looked relaxed though, of course, there had been no real lessening of tension. Their suspicion of me, only slightly modified by increasing curiosity, still hung over us; but their readiness to be physically comfortable declared at least a kind of armistice.

It did not last long. Refreshed by his shower and change of clothing, Connell had soon forgotten his decision to watch and wait. He was ready for action again.

It took the form of hitching his chair closer to mine and telling me in a confidential undertone that he had been trying to place my accent. 'I know it's British, of course,' he added quickly, 'but British from whereabouts? I know it's not Australian or South African. I suppose it could be . . .'

He got no farther. Krom was half out of his seat and leaning across the table with teeth bared.

'No, Dr Connell, no!' He swallowed a couple of times trying to get rid of some of his anger before it choked him. 'No, I shall not need that sort of assistance from you in questioning Mr Firman about his origins and background.'

He had begun in his vehemence to spray saliva, and Dr Henson hastily moved her wine glass out of the line of fire.

Connell was looking utterly astounded. It was a facial expression of which he made much use I was to find. 'Of course, Professor, of course, of *course*. I was simply making an idle enquiry.'

Krom was neither deceived nor appeased. 'It was agreed between us, let me remind you,' he grated on, 'that all enquiries of whatever kind will be made by me. Here, everything will be conducted throughout in the way that I decide and only in the way that I decide. That was positively agreed.'

'Sure, Professor, sure it was agreed.'

'But not,' I remarked distinctly, 'by me.'

They all stared at me except Yves, who poured himself some more wine. I continued: 'I will be the one who decides which questions are answered and which are not. I will also decide the areas of business activity concerning which information may be given. No, Professor, it's no good your huffing and puffing. Since our meeting in Brussels I have had plenty of time for reflection and decision. After Dr Henson's demonstration of her disregard for her agreement about confidentiality, to say nothing of Dr Connell's less covert breach of his, my conviction that none of you is to be trusted has been further strengthened.'

Krom made a gargling sound of disgust and sat back in his chair. 'No, Mr Firman, no. No more wriggling, please. Will you not even now accept the fact that you are hooked?'

'When you accept the fact that the fish on the end of the line is not after all the one you thought you had, yes.' I did not wait for him to answer but turned to Henson. 'Why did they give you ninhydrin to bring here, Doctor? Do you know?'

'Oh, not that again!' from Connell.

Krom did some more gargling.

She took no notice of either of them. 'Apparently,' she said, 'quite a lot of people still don't know that one can raise finger-prints from matt-surfaced papers if one knows how. They didn't think it would be prudent for me to try stealing some-thing else you'd handled and start dusting it in the old-fashioned way. Besides, the results wouldn't have been as good.'

'Supposing I hadn't handled any papers while you were here?'

'They said you would. As long as your hands were warm, a book, a newspaper or even a paper napkin would work. As a last resort I was to ask you to read the typescript of a book review I have just written and get your opinion on it as well as your prints.'

'I'll gladly read it, Doctor.'

'Unbelievable!' blared Krom.

'Rubbish!' I said irritably. 'What about you and your friends in West German intelligence, Professor? When they ask you confidentially for the precise details of your adventures in the quest of Mr X, are you going to remain, after all the kindness they have done you with their files, resolutely silent? Of course you aren't. None of you is going to keep his mouth shut. He won't be able to. So, what you are going to be given is not all the truth, if there is such an entity, but bits of it. And you, Professor, can take your choice. Leak what you know and you get nothing more. Play it my way and you get something.'

He thought about it, then glowered at me suspiciously. 'How much?'

'Some days in the life of Herr Oberholzer?'

'I have one already.'

'No, you haven't. You can't begin to know what happened that day. You don't even know what crimes you might accuse him of.'

'Extorting money by threats. Blackmail. There are more, but those will do to begin with.'

I laughed sufficiently to choke a little over my wine. 'Extor-tion, Professor,' I said when I had recovered, 'is, as you must surely know, the standard cry raised against those who collect, or try to collect, payment from delinquent debtors. Blackmail is often used to describe letters from creditors beginning with the word "unless". Oberholzer was no debt-collector in any case. If that's all you have . . .'

'I am not speaking about debts incurred for goods or services legally supplied. I am speaking of the exactions of criminals.'

'But the services which we supplied were always perfectly legal. Is it a crime to give good advice?'

'Some advice, yes. To advise a man who has himself committed a criminal act how he may, by giving you money, avoid the consequences is certainly criminal.'

'And, Professor, if you ask for information instead of money?'

Henson giggled and Connell smirked, but it took Krom a moment or two to grasp the implication. It did not please him. He straightened his back.

'Very well, if such hair-splitting amuses you, I have, in the interests of social science, become an extortionist. Maybe you will find it less amusing, Mr Firman, if I now ask you to start paying up?'

'Of course.' I looked at Melanie. 'Would you mind getting the copies of file number one for me, my dear?'

Krom stared at me suspiciously as she went. I sipped my wine and took no notice of him.

The moment had arrived, as I had known it would eventually, and I was prepared to serve Krom what I believed would look, smell and taste like the meat for which he had asked.

The work they are doing in the food laboratories nowadays to make protein artificially is really amazing. I believe that they have even been able to produce it from really unlikely substances such as oil. The only trouble with the artificial stuff, though, is that it doesn't really taste of anything much. You have to add a meat essence to give the concoction flavour.

If you are feeding social scientists, especially criminologists, you have also to add to the artificially produced material a little truth.

When I saw Melanie returning along the terrace I turned to Krom. 'In expectation of our meeting,' I said, 'I have prepared papers concerning Oberholzer, his employer and later senior partner, their business associates and their business activities over a period of three years. They are papers for discussion and, of course, I am prepared to be questioned by you on them. My answers may or may not satisfy you. We shall have to see.'

At that moment, the butler announced that, at the other table on the terrace, dinner was served.

Melanie had timed it perfectly.

Their eyes were on the files she held, their stomachs were thinking about dinner.

One can divide one's adversary without necessarily conquering him, of course, but any division is better than none. I had won at least something; not a battle, still less a campaign, but perhaps a minor skirmish on an outer flank.

The first course was a duck-liver paste. For the occasion I had called it Pâté Oberholzer.

I don't care for such things myself.

The others ate all of it.

CHAPTER FOUR

Krom said that he intended to write my life story and now has the audacity to claim that he has done so.

What rubbish the man talks! He does not even know where I was born. And why does he not know? Because *he* did not ask. Because *he*, with this fatuous obsession of his, this determined inability to distinguish between a criminal and a businessman, prefers to assume that I must wish to keep such facts about myself secret.

Utter nonsense!

If he had not intervened so energetically when Connell had asked me where I came from, I would almost certainly have answered. There was no reason why I should not have done so.

I was born in Argentina, and my family was, still is, one of the many there of British origin bearing commonplace British names. In our case, as with others like us, intermarriage with and absorption by the Spanish-descended majority has, chiefly for religious reasons, been a slow process. When I was born, even though we had been in the country for well over a century and thought of ourselves as more Argentine than British, our name was still free of Spanish collaterals and my birth was duly registered at a British consulate as well as with the local municipality. All very schizoid. With us, British nannies still supervised the upbringing of children, and we were still sent to England at the age of eight to endure the torments of its boarding schools. My father thought it proper in 1914 to join the Royal Navy. In 1939 I joined the British Army no less matter-of-factly. If I withhold the family name I do so for good reason. I have dual nationality, and the possibility that the protective cover which this could give me might, after all these years, become an asset is one that I cannot now ignore.

Allegations of the kind Krom has made, consisting of one part fact stirred into nine parts fantasy, are always the hardest to refute; and, in this instance, the task has been made still harder because the fragments of truth embedded in his slablike case-study were supplied by me in what he persists in calling my 'confidential papers'. He also makes much of their having been supplied in front of witnesses. What effect that could have on the value of the papers as evidence is beyond me. If I had handed him a forged ten-dollar bill, would the presence of Connell and Henson as witnesses have rendered it genuine?

The first paper – how much grander the word 'paper' sounds than the more appropriate 'hand-out' – dealt with some of the circumstances leading up to Krom's seeing Oberholzer in Zürich and some of the consequences of the whole incident.

And that was *all* it was, an incident. Krom's presentation of it as if he were Zola discovering for an amazed public the iniquities of the Dreyfus case is, no doubt, for anyone who knows the truth, pretty funny. Far from funny is his clear and instantly recognizable picture of me dressed up to look like the super-villain of his imaginings.

Melanie, who helped me concoct the texts of the 'papers' and who was responsible for some of the juiciest red-herrings in them, thinks that we overestimated him. She says that we relied too much on the scholarly scepticism allied to an ability to evaluate misinformation that ought to have been there, but which were not. In other words, we were too clever.

I say that we underestimated his capacity for self-deception. We gave him a kaleidoscope to play with and he used it as if it were a reading glass.

If there must be a picture, let it be a warts-and-all photograph, not a caricature; and if the world, or that small portion of it inhabited by criminologists and policemen, really wants to know about poor old Oberholzer, let it be one of his own many voices that is heard. My account will be full, reasonably accurate and free from Krom's distortions. It will not, of course, be free from *my* distortions. I happen to be one of those who believe that the ability to tell the whole truth about anything at all is so rare that anyone who claims it, especially if he does so with hand on heart, should be regarded with the deepest suspicion.

I can only attempt to be truthful.

I met Carlo Lech for the first time when I almost had to arrest him near Bari. That was in 1943 after our landings on the heel of Italy, when the Eighth Army had moved north to Foggia. I was in the British Field Security Police at the time, and I almost had to arrest him because a corporal in the detachment of which I was in command was an officious bloody idiot.

But what, it may be asked, was an English-Spanish bilingual doing in Field Security in Italy? Was this the British Army once more up to its ancient game of putting square pegs into round holes? No, it was not. During the year after I left school, I learned to speak very good Italian.

Where his children were concerned, my father was generous and, though far from being imaginative, always scrupulously fair. I was the youngest of his three sons, and when, in the summer of 1938, he was notified by my housemaster that my year in the sixth form had ended less disastrously than had been feared, I was offered the same choice of rewards as my brothers before me. I could go to a university before going into the family business; I could spend a year and two thousand dollars travelling in Europe before going into the family business; or I could have the sports car of my choice and go into the family business right away.

My brothers had both taken sports cars. I chose the year in Europe.

In three months I had spent the two thousand dollars — having had a very good time doing so, though — and was flat broke in Cannes. A cable would have brought me a steamer ticket home, a sermon on the value of money and, of course, immediate entry into the family business. I didn't send the cable because I didn't want to go home and didn't want to go into a boring family business which already had more junior executives than it needed anyway. As any good con-man will tell you, it takes most people a long time to spot the fact that a spender has turned into a sponger, and in places like Cannes it can take even longer for a credit-rating to slip. I gave myself a month to get out of the hole I was in before I ran screaming to Daddy or started doing silly things that could get me into trouble with the police. I made it in three weeks. I got a job as steward on a yacht.

The owner was an Italian banker and some of the reasons for my being hired were simple.

The Munich crisis had led in France to a partial mobilization, and the French steward had been one of those called up. It was not known when he would be released or, since he had insisted that local union rules entitled him to a full month's wages on leaving, whether, when released, he would be trouble to return. At that end of the season it would be hopeless to look for an experienced replacement. The rest of the crew, including the cook, were Italians, who did not care who poured the drinks and served the meals and made the beds. I had Argentine papers and, as the yacht was registered in Genoa, there would be no nonsense about labour permits and unions that the

63

owner could not deal with later should he decide to keep me on. Meanwhile, the job was strictly temporary.

Among the less simple reasons for my getting the job was the fact that the owner's wife had picked me up one morning at the Carlton beach. She had done so under the impression that I was a virgin youth seeking reassurance and instruction from the older-yet-still-amazingly-attractive woman she believed herself to be. Both my clothes and the hotel at which I was staying were of the expensive kind, and when I confessed to her that I could no longer afford to tip even the boy who put up the beach umbrellas much less pay my fare home, she had at once blamed the gambling tables for my predicament and easily understood, without my having to tell her of it, my fear of parental retribution. I never tried to disabuse her of any of those notions. She was friendly in bed, only sometimes demanding, and she always smelt nice.

With her husband my credentials were of a different order. The school to which I went has never been considered as better than reasonably good; but he happened to have heard of it, and the idea of having an English public-schoolboy – even one who was Argentine – as a servant seemed to appeal to what I assumed to be the Fascist sense of humour. I think that his original intention may have been to discipline his wife, and at the same time strike a blow for Il Duce and the corporate state, by firing me after a few days, or as soon as I had sufficiently demonstrated my incompetence. If so, I disappointed him. Being a steward on a yacht is not all that different from being a junior boy in the kind of school I had just left. I may also have misjudged the nature of their personal relationship. Possibly it did not include the friendliness with which she treated me. Perhaps, in that marriage, she was the one who had the disciplinary whip hand.

I very much hope so, because, although I have during my life encountered a great many unpleasant men and women, I still after all these years remember him as being one of the nastier.

When the weather broke on the Riviera we cruised south, first to Ischia and Capri, and then on down to Tripoli. There, east of the town, the owner had land, on which he played at citrus-growing, and a tarted-up farmhouse. His wife explained that he owned the place not because he wanted to or because it was profitable, but for some mysterious political reason.

We spent several days doing nothing much while he had meetings with the Governor and other local administrators.

Then we started off on a cruise that was supposed to take us to Benghazi. A north-west gale ended that, and within thirty-six hours we were back in Tripoli. There it was announced that the yacht would now be laid up for its annual refit, with just the captain retained to oversee the work. The rest of the crew would be off to their homes in Italy for the winter months. The owner and his wife moved into the house.

Nobody having told me where I stood, I counted my savings, wondered whether I could expect a tip from the lady, and eventually asked the captain if I was entitled to my fare back to Cannes. He mumbled something about my not having a labour permit, and then said he would enquire. Until the boat went into the yard to have its bottom cleaned, I could sleep on board. I was reminded of the end of one of those terms at school when there had been not enough holiday time in which to go home, and nothing much else to do but spend too much pocket-money.

To my surprise, the captain remembered to enquire about me without being reminded. Next day, I was sent for by the owner.

It was the first time I had been to the house. You took a bus to the nearby village and then walked along a dirt road between lemon groves.

His study was a hideous room with a tessellated floor and red, leather-covered walls. The writing table was a Second Empire monster with a matching chair of throne-like proportions. He had a mop of white hair and very black eyes. Sitting in that enormous chair, he looked like an illustration depicting the king greedy for gold in an art-nouveau edition of Grimm's fairy tales.

'I understand,' he said, 'that you wish to return to France. Why, young man? In order to gamble away all the wages I have been paying you these past weeks?'

His wife had told me of his stuffiness about gambling, but I had forgotten about it, along with the fiction that I was a gambler myself. So, instead of replying that what I did with the money I earned was my own affair, not his, I answered his silly question as if he had been entitled to ask it.

'No, Sir. I merely wish to regularize my position. As the captain pointed out, I still have no labour permit for Italy or Italian possessions.'

It could have been more happily put. He gave me a long, smouldering stare.

Then he said deliberately: 'For the work you are paid to do

in Italian possessions, the only necessary permission is mine.'

I was very innocent in those days. It took me a moment or two to grasp what he had said. When the penny dropped, though, several things seemed to happen at once. For the only time in my life I felt myself blushing. I had an almost overwhelming desire to hit him and, along with it, an equally compelling determination to get out of the room before I did anything stupid. Good sense won. I turned quickly and walked to the door.

'Come back here,' he snapped, 'I haven't finished with you.'

I didn't go back, but I stopped and faced him again. After all, I still had to know what the score was.

'You had better understand me,' he continued. 'I have considerable influence with the authorities both here and in Rome. I could have you in prison within the hour if I chose. I could also have you deported. In that case, you would certainly pay your own travel expenses. The only way that you can, as you put it, regularize your position is to do as you are told, not by that fool of a woman, but by *me*.'

He let that sink in, then a smile hovered. 'You may even find it less inhibiting to do as you are told here, rather than on the far side of a yacht bulkhead.'

When he was sure from my expression that I had thoroughly understood him, he sat back and seemed to relax. 'I leave for Rome tomorrow afternoon and shall be away for some weeks. You will place yourself at my wife's disposal for as long as she continues to find you useful. When she has finished with you, then you may go.' He paused, savouring the final insult before delivering it. 'One other word of warning. There *are* some possessions of value to me in this house. Don't try to steal any of them. My servants will know immediately if anything is missing. Now get out.'

I left without seeing her and walked to the bus stop in the village. When I got back to the yacht, however, there was a note from her waiting for me. It said that I must ignore her husband's bad manners. They were the result of too much association with politicians. She would expect me for lunch on Friday. From then on I would be *her* guest, not his. In case I had not yet been able to make arrangements for cashing cheques with a local bank, she was enclosing five thousand lire to cover taxi fares and any other incidental expenses I might wish to incur.

At that time five thousand lire would have gone some way towards *buying* a taxi, the kind of taxi they had in Tripoli anyway. Two days later I moved into the farmhouse; but one thing I had to ask her about before finally deciding to stay. Had she known from the first that he had listened to us?

The question seemed to perplex her. 'But he didn't listen to us from the first,' she said. 'How could he have listened to us in your hotel?'

'I mean on the boat.'

'Oh, walls on boats are always so thin.' She dismissed them with a shrug. 'But what does it matter? Who cares what is heard? It is what one *feels* that counts.'

It did not seem worthwhile trying to challenge that statement.

I stayed there over three months, and by then my Italian, although never altogether free of Spanish intonations, was fluent. By then, too, I had come to the conclusion that I wasn't going to be needing it for very much longer. Hitler had invaded what the French and British governments had left of Czechoslovakia. A few weeks later, and to show that he could be just as bold and bloody if he put his mind to it, Mussolini had ordered the invasion of Albania. From Rome, too, came word that the yacht would that summer be cruising only on the west coast of metropolitan Italy. Her husband added, as if as an afterthought, that an Italian steward had been hired and would report for duty when he himself joined the boat at Naples. The captain would be advising her of his sailing orders.

It was time for me to go. I left, by a ship bound for Marseilles, on my nineteenth birthday, though I didn't tell her of the coincidence. I don't think she was all that sorry to see me go – she was one of those who like change – but a birthday would have added unnecessarily to the emotional content of the parting. Perhaps, now I come to think again about it, she taught me quite a lot.

From Marseilles I went to Paris and lived, within my means this time, at a small hotel in the rue de l'Isly. In spite of the fact that my year of 'travelling in Europe' was almost over I was not unduly troubled by the thought that I might soon have to return home. That was probably because it was almost impossible to live that summer in Paris without knowing that there was going to be a major war; and because, as a result, I did not really believe that anything was going to turn out as planned for very much longer. Still, as a precautionary delaying tactic, I wrote to my father suggesting that it might not be a bad idea if I went home by freighter via New York, so that I could visit the World's Fair and see what our foreign business competitors were doing in the world market. I could, I assured him smugly, easily afford it.

I need not have bothered. Mail travelled slowly in those days and, by the time my letter reached him, the German–Soviet Non-Aggression Pact had already been signed. During the last week in August 1939, I cabled him saying that, subject to his blessing, I proposed going to England in order to join either the Royal Navy or, failing that, the RAF.

His blessing I duly received, but soon had to cable for supplementary assistance : more money and some introductions in the right quarters. Of course, at the beginning of the war, none of the British services was prepared to cope with floods of raw recruits, least of all the Navy and the RAF. The best he could do in the way of introductions not only landed me in the Army but also in one of the most boring parts of it – a searchlight battery stationed in East Anglia.

All I remember now about the winter that followed was how cold it was, and that in March we moved to a site farther south which seemed even colder. In May we were moved again, suddenly, to Wales; not because we were needed there, but in order to leave the hutted camp we had occupied free to receive troops evacuated from Dunkirk. In Wales we were told that the artillery regiment to which our battery belonged was to be converted from the searchlight role to that of mobile Ack-Ack with Bofors guns. Older officers and men were to be weeded out and transferred to static units. The qualifications of all personnel were re-examined and reassessed. The process happened to coincide with Italy's entry into the war and the issue of an Army Council Instruction requiring returns from all units listing the names of NCOs and men who could speak Italian. My name was one of three sent in, the other two being those of British-born Italian waiters. In due course, we were summoned to a barracks near Durham where we were interviewed and tested by an officer who spoke phrase-book Italian with a Scottish accent. He said, in the importantly secretive way which was then fashionable, that we were probably needed for guard duty at the new Italian internment camp on the Isle of Man.

I never knew what happened to the waiters, but two months later I was sent to an infantry battalion bound by troopship for Egypt and the Western Desert.

After we arrived, the battalion delivered me to the Intelligence Corps. Theoretically, I was there as an interpreter. In practice, I was used from the start to interrogate the Italian prisoners-of-war who were then pouring in by the thousands. An officer, with an NCO escort, was supposed to deal with each POW separately, but there were just too many of them for that sort of nonsense. So the work was split up. To give me a semblance of authority, I was made an acting-corporal and told to behave like a stage sergeant-major. It was all a great waste of time. During the months before Rommel's first big counter-attack, I interrogated many hundreds of POWs and wrote an equivalent number of reports on them. Never, during the entire time, did I learn anything of military value that I had not already learned from the intelligence briefings we were given. The only higher-ups who took any real interest in our findings were the political warfare people. Once or twice I was able to quote in my reports things said by a more-than-usually demoralized prisoner – generally one with wife trouble – or gripes, spotted in the letters from home some of them carried, that could be used in propaganda.

I was confirmed as corporal and there was talk of my being commissioned, but nothing came of it. Instead, I was transferred to Field Security Police and posted to Italian Somaliland as an acting-sergeant. After more than enough of that – why anyone should ever have wanted the place passes all understanding – I was posted to Eighth Army in time for the invasion of Sicily.

To see how it was that I came to arrest Carlo, you have to know what the Field Security Police in Italy were supposed to do. Some who were there at the time may need no reminding, but it may help others to recall that our opposite numbers in the American sectors of the front bore a rather more dashing title – Counter-Intelligence Corps.

The CIC and ourselves both had the same job and we did it in more or less the same way. While the ordinary military police were concerned briefly with military matters such as convoy traffic control, drunks, deserters, POW cages, stockades and so on, we dealt with the problems arising from the presence all around our forces – and, in the towns and villages, *among* them – of large numbers of civilians who, until recently, had been actively or passively on the side of our enemies. Some of them, a few but some, still were. Our main task was to see that, in the forward areas where such things mattered, those who were against us and in a position to do something about it were either removed or neutralized.

Or course, things were rarely as simple as that.

If a farmer stole a pair of army boots because his own had

gone to hell and he had to start ploughing his land again, was that petty theft or sabotage? Was an old whore wounding a soldier by hitting him in an eye with the heel of a shoe merely defending her democratic right to the rate for the job, or was she giving aid and comfort to the Waffen SS division dug in across the river north of us? And then there were the black marketeers who flogged bottles of a turpentine-like liquid they called peach brandy to the troops in exchange for cartons of army rations. How did you cope with that sort of traffic? By telling the troops that they were ruining their livers?

Well, no. What you did was try to catch the black marketeers, and you did this by checking as constantly as you could on the driver and occupants of every civilian vehicle moving in your area. The CIC used jeeps with two men in them. We used one-man motorcycle patrols.

It was one of my patrols who brought in Carlo.

I was operating from the cellar of a bombed house near divisional HQ. This enabled me to mess at HQ and also gave me reasonably easy access to a signals network without having to go through corps channels all the time.

The first thing I heard of Carlo was the sound of his car, a clapped-out Opel that made more noise than the patrol's motor-bike. When both engines had been switched off, I heard the corporal telling the owner of the car to stay exactly where he was. The corporal then came down to report.

'Highly suspicious, this one, Sir,' he said. He called me 'Sir' because I was by then a Warrant Officer 2nd Class, a sergeant-major. He also handed me a gasoline permit and laissez-passer issued in Naples by AMGOT.

I drew a deep breath and counted silently to ten.

AMGOT – Allied Military Government Occupied Territories – was one of the crosses the army had to bear at that stage of the campaign. AMGOT, it seemed to us, had been recruited by a committee of highly-placed saboteurs from the dregs of those ghastly pools, which both the American and British armies were obliged to maintain, of officers who had been commissioned in haste or ignorance and later rejected by unit after unit as unfit for any sort of responsible duty. Some were just stupid, some were alcoholics, a few were failed crooks and many were in need of psychiatric treatment. There were all sorts, including a number of former reservists. Among the more remarkable, and from our point of view the more dangerous of these, were those amiable, personally charming and often cultivated eccentrics who, having served honourably in peace-time regular armies had, over the years, quietly become gaga without anyone ever having noticed the change. They were more dangerous not only because they were often of quite senior rank, but because many of them tended to hold political views which even Gabriele d'Annunzio might have found reactionary. Their tendency to form warm personal friendships with the former Fascist bosses they had been sent to replace, and also to confirm them in office, caused much resentment in the Allied armies.

Naturally, some of the AMGOT scandals were successfully hushed up. The Town Major in Sicily who used his authority to buy up all the best buildings, including the hotel, at cut prices for his own post-war account, was quietly court-martialled and sent home to serve a short prison term. Only a few ever heard about that. The gasoline-permit racket and the shenanigans that went with it were less easily covered up.

They reached their full absurdity when a CIC patrol on the outskirts of Naples stopped an Italian civilian driver whose car looked unusually well cared for and asked for his permit. The driver responded sullenly. He slowly produced a wallet from his pocket and was about to extract the permit when the CIC man reached in impatiently and took the whole thing. Inside, he found not only the AMGOT permit and a considerable sum of money, but also a Gestapo permit to operate the car issued less than three months previously. The driver was later identified as a senior Fascist Party official who had denounced Badoglio as a traitor for arresting Mussolini, urged his countrymen to stay loyal to the Nazi alliance and, when possible or convenient, stab the invaders in the back. He was on the Allied wanted list. The CIC put him in jail. Twelve hours later he was out, released on the orders of a senior AMGOT official.

This was too much for the CIC, who promptly leaked the story to war correspondents. Questioned by them, the AMGOT spokesman began, not too badly, by admitting the facts and agreeing that the whole affair was absolutely deplorable. But, he continued, they were all men of the world who knew that, in occupied territories where states of emergency existed, occasional compromises, distasteful though some might consider them, had to be made. AMGOT had been given the responsibility of governing the country *pro tem*, but no one had explained how it was to be governed without the aid of experienced local administrators accustomed to giving orders and seeing that they were obeyed. Where, might he ask, were the democratic administrators willing and able to take over the duties of those he was being urged to discard? We had had serious outbreaks of typhus. Was he now being asked to permit outbreaks of typhoid and cholera because the senior city sanitary department engineer had once been a member of the Fascist Party?

The spokesman had chosen that moment to pause for breath. Unfortunately for him, there had been one correspondent there who particularly disliked rhetorical questions. He was on his feet instantly. But what, he asked, about this man who had been arrested and then released? Was *he* a senior sanitary engineer? 'Colonel, is he *any* kind of a sanitary engineer?'

That was when the spokesman had made his mistake. Instead of continuing to conceal his contempt for the newsmen, he had suddenly let it show.

He had smiled at the questioner. 'No, my dear sir,' he had replied sweetly, 'the gentleman is not a sanitary engineer, but – ' a slight pause – 'I happen to know that he plays an excellent game of bridge.'

Naturally, the whole story was at once censored, but the censors could not stop it spreading by word of mouth. It was at this time that some wag thought up the bitter little joke motto, *Amgot mit Uns*.

So, all that interested me about Carlo's gasoline permit and laissez-passer was the name of the officer who had signed it. As the name was unfamiliar, I was unable to tell how much weight the permit-holder might have behind him. Accordingly, I rang signals and asked if they could put me through to CIC Venafro. Signals said that they would try. Venafro was then on the right flank of Fifth Army on the other side of the mountains from us, but signals could sometimes patch me in through HQ Caserta.

I called the corporal to come back down. There was still a faint possibility that he hadn't made a complete fool of himself.

'Was he carrying anything in the car?' I asked.

'No, Sir, just himself. But he's way off his permitted route and out of his area as well.'

'Did you ask him why?'

'No need to, Sir. Standing orders. He shouldn't be here.'

Hopeless. You could never persuade that kind of idiot that, in some circumstances, he might get better results by using standing orders as threats rather than by blindly obeying them.

'I take it you've told him that he's going to be arrested?'

'Of course, Sir. He already *is* under arrest really. Clear case. Shall I bring him down now?'

'Not yet. I'll let you know. Has he said anything?'

'Not a word, Sir. Shall I question him?'

'No. *You* keep your mouth shut too.'

After a while signals came through to say that they had raised CIC Venafro. The man in charge there was an officer – trust the Americans to do things properly – but he never pulled rank on me and we had always managed to co-operate amicably. We had first met in Sicily.

'Hi, Paul,' he said. 'What can I do for you? Or do you want to do something for me?'

'I'm not quite sure, Sir, which it is. One of my lot has brought in a man named Carlo Lech.'

There was a small silence before he said: 'Paul, I think you may need help, but I don't think I have the right kind. Lech is a well-known bridge-player. You didn't, by chance, catch him with any of the actual goods on him?'

'No.'

'Then you'd better let him go before someone starts reaching for your balls with a pipe-wrench.'

'He's out of his permitted area.'

'You could ask him why and then let him go.'

'If I'm going to have to let him go, Sir, I'd like to ask him more than that. He's been picked up and my man has logged the fact. I've got to have a good reason for letting him go. He's got to buy his way out and not too cheaply. He's from your side of the mountains. If you were here what would you like to ask him?'

'Two nights ago twenty thousand cigarettes went missing off a truck between Caserta and here. There was an MP riding shotgun. His case is that the cigarettes were never loaded. I'd like to know what really happened because it's happened before and some of the loot has ended up right here. Makes it look as if you're a jerk who doesn't know what's going on in his own back yard. And if Mr Lech knows any good anti-Fascists, men of distinction whom we can persuade to come out of hiding so that we can give them posts as mayors, city councillors and police chiefs where their untainted records and democratic convictions can publicly demonstrate . . .'

'Yes, Sir, I've had that directive too. I'll see what I can find out about the cigarettes and call you back if I get anything. Funny name for an Italian, Lech. Sounds more like German.'

'It's Austrian. He's one of those Tyrolese Italians. Injured in a road accident when a teenager, which kept him out of any of the services. Party member though, and a smart lawyer. Watch yourself, kid.'

I cleared the line, then told the corporal to send the prisoner down but stay upstairs himself.

At that time Carlo was more than twice my age, a short, compact man with greying dark hair, grey-green eyes and one of the kindliest expressions I have ever seen. You felt instantly that he was longing for you to say or do something, anything, which would give him an excuse to let the smile that seemed always to be trembling on his lips blossom forth. Except for the leather overcoat he wore, which was too long and had obviously once belonged to someone else, he was neatly dressed. His slight limp, a legacy of the road accident, did not seem to bother him much. He walked down the broken stone stairs as if he were used to them, and he was taking off his greasy grey-felt hat as he did so.

At the foot of the stairs, he stopped, looked carefully at the crown on my battledress sleeve and then said in English: 'Good afternoon, Sergeant-Major.'

I replied in Italian. 'Good afternoon, Mr Lech. Please sit down.'

He inspected me again and then, after examining carefully the rickety wicker chair I had offered him, sat down opposite my blanket-covered trestle table.

I was curious. 'What were you looking for in the chair?' I asked.

'Lice, Sergeant-Major. I can't stand them and, as a civilian, have no access to the military's new ways of getting rid of them.'

Several years later, he told me that that had been the moment at which he had made up his mind about me. 'I saw you as a son, the kind of son I would have liked to have, one with whom, and at whose side, I could do business. I saw you, above all, as a potential associate, a friend and partner whom I could trust, under any circumstances, even when his private hubris was involved, not to behave stupidly.'

He may have been telling something of the truth. Carlo had a sentimental streak that few who ever did business with him can have suspected. He also had a son, a handsome, clever but rather vain boy, who later disappointed him profoundly by going into the Church.

Nevertheless, our first meeting was for me more like a family quarrel than the meeting of minds he chose later to recall.

74

The moment he was seated, I perched myself on a corner of the table from which I could look down upon him, and attacked.

'You are driving a vehicle in this area without a valid permit and have, I understand, admitted doing so knowing that it was an offence. Am I right?'

'Knowing that it was a minor, technical offence, yes, Sergeant-Major.'

'There are no minor, technical offences in this area, Mr Lech. An offence is an offence. Where were you hoping to go and why?'

'To Bari on business. I explained all this to your corporal.'

'What business?'

'Supplying the club for senior officers in Naples with brandy, Sergeant-Major.'

'*Peach* brandy?'

He looked shocked. 'Oh my God, no. The colonels and brigadier-generals would never commission me to supply them with that sort of rubbish.'

I noted that in spite of his shock at the idea of peach brandy entering a senior officers' club, he had tried to pull rank on me with his colonels and brigadiers and at the same time managed to flourish the word 'commission'. I had to mangle that line of defence before he could develop it.

'Are you claiming that you are in this area illegally but justifiably because you have been specifically ordered here by a senior British or American officer? If so, have you some written authority to substantiate your claim?'

'Oh no, Sergeant-Major, there is nothing like that. It is really quite simple. When persons of consequence ask the person of no consequence for his help, he endeavours, if he is wise, to oblige them. I am sure that if you would care to telephone General Anstruthers –' he had difficulty pronouncing the name but made a brave try – 'he would confirm that good brandy was requested. Of course,' he added thoughtfully, 'I doubt if the General will take kindly to being questioned formally by a warrant-officer on such a trivial matter.'

I tossed a packet of cigarettes into his lap. 'Any more,' I suggested, 'than the General will take kindly to the knowledge that his name is being used illegally as a black marketeer's laissez-passer.'

He handed back the cigarettes without taking one, so I went on. 'Whereabouts in Bari is the brandy?'

He threw up his hands in protest at the question. 'Sergeant-

Major, if I were certain that it even existed, I would not be committing this trivial breach of the regulations which you are now exploiting. I am told that the brandy is there, six cases of it, but I am not told where. For all I know it may by now have been – what is the word? – "liberated" by the British army. Or it may be that the original bottles have been refilled with wood alcohol. I have a contact, yes, but I do not know him personally and so cannot possibly buy sight unseen. But I explained all this to your corporal.'

'Who is your contact?'

'The man formerly in charge of what was the bonded warehouse.'

'If the brandy is there and up to standard, what do you propose to do about it?'

'If the price is not absurdly high, I shall buy it and then take it back to the General and his club wine committee.'

'In your car?'

'Certainly, in my car, and with a bill of sale to prove that the goods are my property.'

'What makes you think I'll let it through, Mr Lech?'

'Unless you are attempting to solicit a bribe, which I doubt, why should you even think of stopping it? Tell me, Sergeant-Major, how do you define this new term or phrase you use, this "black marketeer"?'

'One who has authorized dealings in goods that are rationed or otherwise in short supply.'

'Is dealing in pre-war French brandy unauthorized? I hope you are not one of those socialists, Sergeant-Major, who object to the law of supply and demand controlling prices merely because persons like me risk their capital in order to make a fair profit.'

'What is a fair profit?'

'If I succeed in buying this brandy, I shall add forty per cent to the price I have to pay. Bearing in mind the fact that, in addition to my normal overheads in a transaction of this kind, I must suffer the mental strain of trying to convince a suspicious British Field Security policeman that I am not a crook, is that excessive? I shall be glad to let you have a bottle for the same price as that which I shall charge the General. Is that what you call black-market dealing?'

I had, after all, been warned that he was a lawyer. 'All right, Mr Lech,' I said, 'let's try a different commodity. Two nights ago, twenty thousand cigarettes were stolen off an

American truck somewhere between Caserta and Venafro. How would you describe the act of selling them?'

'In civilized countries, Sergeant-Major, and in some uncivilized ones, dealing in stolen property has always been an offence.'

'But one which you would never commit yourself.'

'Certainly not. I have no need to commit it.'

'You wouldn't know, by any chance, who stole those cigarettes?'

'No, but I know *how* they were stolen.' He waited for me to ask him how.

'Well?'

'Would the knowledge be of use to you here in your area, Sergeant-Major, or are you thinking unselfishly more of your colleague in Venafro?'

He could not have made his meaning plainer. If I wanted to hear more, he expected a clear run to Bari and back, with no 'technical' obstacles in his path. It wasn't a bad deal, so I nodded.

'I'm thinking of both of us now, Mr Lech, so your information had better be good.'

On his private island, ten years later, we analysed that part of the conversation as if it had been a game, a form of exercise.

'I watched you very closely,' he said. 'You were throwing away an apparent advantage because you knew that it was essentially worthless. I could have had you in trouble with your own people within hours, and you must have known that too. Yet, you hung on by switching currencies. Sterling was out, but there was still the dollar. Your reply, reminding me of the more lasting penalties to be incurred by arousing American displeasure, could not have been bettered.'

The verdict of a bridge-player enjoying the benefits of hindsight. At the time he had protested vigorously.

'Of course my information is good, Sergeant-Major. Indeed, it is impeccable. Most petty professional crooks share the same weaknesses. One of them is that they can never refrain from boasting of their successes. In the matter of the cigarettes, it was arranged in advance with the military policeman on the truck that the driver, his accomplice, would stop on the way and leave the load unattended for five minutes in order to deal with a sudden call of nature. The place arranged for the stop was near the village of Galleno. There is no soft shoulder on the road just there, so it would be an easy place for a truck to pull off, and then get back on again, without getting stuck in the mud. I dare say that a very quick search might find some of the cigarettes still in the village.'

'Thank you, Mr Lech.'

I gave him back his AMGOT papers and then filled in one of the duplicated pro-formas we used for civilian vehicle movement control in the Bari area. While I was doing the filling-in I thought that I might as well see what his reaction would be to the question about anti-Fascists.

To my surprise, he did not laugh.

'Here in the south,' he said, 'you will find only three kinds of person who will claim seriously that they have long been anti-Fascist. First, there are the village priests, or most of them, as you must know well. Then, there are the very few real Communists, getting old by now. They are mostly still underground awaiting their moment. And finally there are the madmen.'

'Madmen?'

He stood up. 'Who, unless he was a priest or a Communist or in some other way mad, would have resisted Party pressure to conform for twenty years? And who but madmen could look around them now at the destruction of what little had been built up in this pitiful country and declare that it is better so or that the punishment was necessary?' He brushed the thought away as if it were a cobweb across his face. 'In the north, we shall no doubt find things very different. You will see. We will both see. There the Communists will be less old and better organized. I am at present cut off from my family in Milan, but even when I last heard from my wife, before the arrest of Mussolini, the situation had already begun to change radically. The partisans had begun to organize themselves instead of talking.'

He took the pro-forma from me, examined my signature and then spelled out my name. 'Is that right, Sergeant-Major? Good. I have no doubt that we shall be meeting again and I wanted to be sure. May I ask, I wonder, where you learned to speak Italian so well?'

'If we ever meet again, Mr Lech, I'll be glad to tell you.'

'Oh, we shall certainly meet again, Sergeant-Major.' The smile had finally broken through. 'Thank you. Thank you very much.'

With a stiff little bow he turned and went off up the stairs. By the time the racket of his car had died away and the corporal had been told why his prisoner had been sprung, signals had got me Venafro again.

My colleague was pleased with what I had to tell him and looked forward keenly to passing it on to the MPs commanding officer, whom he disliked. I did not trouble to tell him, though, about Carlo's views on anti-Fascists. He would not have liked them and might even have considered such talk subversive.

Two days later I returned from a session at Corps to find a package on my table. The orderly on duty said that it had been delivered by an Italian in a car holding a movement permit signed by me. Inside the package was a bottle of Martell V S O P and a bill for two thousand lire made out on paper with a printed heading in English, *CARLO LECH Doctor of Jurisprudence*, followed by a Naples address.

I wasn't going to pay two thousand lire for a bottle of brandy even though it was certainly worth more than that at the time, and it would have been most inadvisable to keep the bottle without paying at all. The prissy corporal who had arrested Carlo would be sure to hear of it and start telling everyone that I had accepted a bribe. On the other hand, the idea of sending the bottle back seemed offensively high-minded. So, I went to the senior Divisional HQ warrant-officer and asked his advice. He agreed that the price made it look like a bribe but also thought it too good a thing to miss. His suggestion was that the bottle be raffled in the HQ mess with tickets at fifty lire apiece, all monies in excess of two thousand lire to go to the Mess Comforts Fund. The bottle was won by an Ordnance Corps staff-sergeant. We had an air courier service to Naples which I used to send Carlo his two thousand lire, in AMGOT notes, together with a typed receipt for his signature.

The receipt was eventually returned. Under his signature Carlo had written: 'Many thanks. See you soon.'

CHAPTER FIVE

I have said that I gave Krom and the witnesses a white Provençal wine before dinner. That is quite true. What I failed to mention was that this was no ordinary Provençal white, I mean the kind that may be drunk with, say, a fiercely garlicked bouillabaisse and survive the ordeal.

What I gave them was the very light-bodied, dry white that comes from the immediate vicinity of the small port of Cassis near Marseilles. There is not a lot of it to be had, and it is very good in its unobtrusive way. It is, though, quite delicate – a bouillabaisse would kill it stone dead – and has to be treated gently.

Unfortunately, the cook's husband, who had the temerity to call himself a butler, was convinced that the only proper way to chill any white wine was to refrigerate it, or even, I suspect, to give it an hour in the deep-freeze.

I had already warned the fool against such brutality, but that night, possibly because it was so warm outside, he ignored my orders and served it far too cold. The result was that it tasted very much like water.

And that was how Krom proceeded to drink it. Yes, I know he had had a long, hot day, had sweated a great deal and was probably a bit dehydrated; but the bottle of Evian provided for him in his room should have taken care of that. What he seemed not to realize was that the liquid he was swigging down so thirstily – he consumed well over a bottle before dinner – had the normal alcoholic content of other white wines from the region of about eleven per cent. Or perhaps he did realize it. Perhaps he would have been happier if we had all had a boozy pre-prandial session of double dry martinis or schnapps.

I don't know. I can only say that before dinner he certainly drank too much, and that during dinner he continued to drink too much and ate, once the pâté had taken the edge off his appetite, practically nothing.

In a way, I can understand his not feeling hungry. That evening, as far as he was concerned, was the culmination of many years of dedicated labour. I happen to believe that the dedication has been misguided and that the labour will ultimately prove to be fruitless; but that is not how he sees things at present, nor how he saw them then. He believed that he was within reach of a goal, physically within reach of it. The files Melanie had brought in just as dinner was announced now lay on an adjacent coffee table. If he had stood up and reached out, he could have touched them, and he was having trouble keeping himself from doing so. His eyes flickered towards them constantly to make sure that they were still there. The burgundy that came with the veal went down almost as quickly as the Cassis.

'Nice wine, Mr Firman,' Dr Henson remarked.

'Thank you.' It *was* nice for a wine that had only been bought two weeks earlier from a local merchant, but I had not expected her to notice it. I had thought of her more as a claret drinker.

'But not nice enough to impair our judgement, eh?' Krom beamed glassily on his witnesses.

'One would hope,' said Connell pointedly, 'that while we are on an important field expedition nothing should be allowed to impair our judgement.'

'There you are wrong!' Krom stabbed a forefinger at Connell and then began wagging it like the arm of a metronome. 'I will tell you in advance something that you would later have had to discover for yourselves.' The metronome stopped and the forefinger began stabbing at me. 'Where this man is concerned, no unimpaired judgement can be made. Why not? Because he is like one of those creatures of the cephalopod family such as the octopus or squid, which, when attacked or threatened with attack, discharges an inky liquid to form a cloud in the water behind which it may retreat.'

Yves nodded appreciatively. 'Calmar,' he explained to Dr Henson. 'Good to eat, but only when cooked in the Italian way.'

Krom ignored the interruption. 'And what does this ink consist of? What is its composition when Mr Firman has brewed it? I will tell you.'

'We know,' said Connell. 'The answer's hog-wash.'

'Pardon?'

'You're forgetting, Professor. You gave us this lecture on the way down. Every time Mr Firman feels that he is in any way, even marginally, threatened, up goes the defence that, if anything not quite kosher has been done by anyone, ever, and he's been around at the time, it was never he who was basically responsible for what happened. He, it appears, has always been one of life's number-two men, always putty in the hands of some ruthless, clever, wicked number-one. Right?'

'Well . . .'

'I know I'm not putting it quite the way you did, Professor, but I think that's roughly the way your readings on him come out when they're processed. You call that sort of tactical fluid discharge octopus ink. I call it hog-wash. What do you call it, Mr Firman?'

'In this case, I think that I have to mix the metaphor a little and call it wishful thinking. Professor Krom clearly does not wish to believe that the cephalopod he caught was not the largest in the ocean. A natural reluctance on his part. But if he really believes that my version of the events which interest him is so little to be relied upon, I don't understand why any of you is here.'

Connell said: 'Olé. Nicely fielded.'

Krom rumbled back into action. 'Has it not yet come to your notice, Dr Connell, that when a structure of lies about a sequence of events in superimposed upon a schema composed of fixed points of known truth concerning those same events, more can be learned about the liar by comparative analysis than can be learned by listening to and endeavouring to make sense of so-called frank confessions?'

'I wonder, Professor,' Dr Henson asked blandly, 'if we could have a concrete example of that method of working in the case we are now discussing.'

'Certainly. Mr Firman maintains that, at the time I identified him, he was *not* in control of a considerable organization running a small, but staggeringly lucrative, extortion racket. He also denies that his operation was based on information gained by the suborning of bank employees and others holding positions of trust. He claims instead, absurdly you may think, that he was the helpless agent of an Italian criminal named Carlo Lech.'

This was too much, even from Krom. I stopped him. 'Just a minute, Professor. I have never said that I was anyone's helpless agent, and I have never said that my friend Carlo Lech was a criminal. I did say that we were for a time in partnership and that he was the older and senior partner. I also said that he was an extremely capable business man and that he had other partners besides me. At the time, you may remember, you told me that Carlo Lech did not exist, that he was a figment of my fertile imagination. Didn't you use those very words, Professor?'

'I did and I was right to do so. The Carlo Lech of whom you spoke and are speaking now, your "friend", *was* and *is* a figment of your imagination. Oh yes, there used to be a Carlo Lech in Milan. No doubt about that. He was a highly respectable and respected corporation lawyer. That doesn't mean that he was necessarily an honest man, of course, but after our talk in Brussels I made the most careful enquiries about him. Unfortunately, he died five years ago so we cannot ask him personally what he thought of you. He had, though, a son who is a priest. This son had never heard of you, or anyone like you. His second child, the daughter Maria, wasn't born until nineteen forty-six. Mrs Lech was, as you may or may not know, twenty years younger than her husband. The daughter married a young American orchestral musician, a 'cellist of talent whom she met in Milan, and now lives mostly in the United States. Shortly before Carlo Lech died, she gave birth to his first grandson, Mario. I wrote to her asking about you, but she knew nothing.'

'Even the most doting Italian father would be unlikely to discuss his business associates with a young child, particularly associates who used assumed names.'

'She wasn't a young child when I saw you in Zürich. Were you her trustee in Vaduz? Ha! That left the widow, who seems always to have been a semi-invalid and who has been for the past two years in a sanatorium. She now suffers from Simmonds' disease which is, I believe, something to do with the pituitary gland. She was not available for interview. Had she been available, though, I have little doubt that her reaction would have been the same as her son's. She would never have heard of you.'

He paused to let it all sink in,.and to empty his glass again, before he delivered the *coup de grâce*.

'The Carlo Lech you described to me,' he said, 'never existed.' And then, perhaps to convince himself as well as his witnesses, he repeated the word that mattered to him most and thumped the table with his fist as he did so.

'Never!'

In spite of the note I had received after our first meeting saying 'See you soon', it was, in fact, nearly two years before I saw Carlo again.

A lot had happened in the interval and, as far as I was concerned, not a moment of it had been pleasant. Crawling up the leg of Italy with an army which had gradually been stripped of its best British divisions so that they could be used in the battles for France would have been, for me, a lowering experience anyway. Specialist units like the one to which I belonged did not go with their divisions. We were part of the Italian front, for eternity it seemed. The succession of east-west defensive lines which it is so easy to build in that country, where the mountains and the rivers lay them out for all the world to see, let alone German generals, ensured that the attackers, no matter how brave they were, no matter how well and skilfully led, had to suffer repeatedly the despair and frustration of having to pay exorbitantly for every minor success. And the reward for a minor success was always the same: your first glimpse of the next obstacle to a major one. I have heard of no campaign in a modern war that was accounted enjoyable by any of those engaged in it, but the Italian must, in terms of futility as well as ordinary beastliness, have been among the nastier. In war's forward areas, the sights of the dead unburied and of the wounded before they have been cleaned up are not always the worst; and the battlefield depression that follows a hard-fought victory is often, no matter what the staged press pictures like to pretend, indistinguishable from that which follows a defeat.

It was just after we reached the Gothic line and I was quartered in yet another wrecked house, north of Ravenna this time, when Carlo came to see me again.

I almost failed to recognize him. Gone were the long leather coat and the greasy felt hat. He was dressed in what would now, I suppose, be described as a para-military uniform. He wore GI ankle boots, the kind that British officers were always trying to get hold of, those made of an inside-out leather that looked a bit like suède and had rubber soles; and on his head was a black beret. It was his topcoat that impressed me most, though. This was the short turned-sheepskin job that was issued to some of the units operating in the mountains above the snow-line. It was also worn by some of the more dress-conscious senior officers among those of the fourteen nationalities then serving on the Fifth and Eighth Army fronts. On the otherwise badgeless Carlo, the coat bestowed field rank at least.

'I've tracked you down, you see,' he said by way of greeting, and handed me a bottle wrapped in a copy of the *Stars and Stripes*. 'Whisky,' he added, 'but there's no bill this time.'

It was late afternoon and getting dark. I lit a pressure lamp, got two beer glasses out of the mortar-bomb box used for mess stores, and opened the bottle.

We raised our glasses to one another in silence and drank. Then he said: 'You are looking older, Sergeant-Major.'

'I am. A year and a half.'

'I was merely observing, not offering a shoulder to cry on that you neither want nor need.'

'What can I do for you this time, Mr Lech?'

His near-smile twitched a bit. 'For the present, thank you, nothing. I had meant to visit you again before this, but events and my work made it impossible.'

He went on to give me a rough idea of what had happened to him. He was now based in Rome and working for the reformed Military Government, mostly in his professional capacity as a lawyer.

When war travels slowly and devastatingly from one end of a country to the other, it is obvious that in its wake a multiplicity of legal problems, few simple and many highly complex, are going to have to be solved. Most, of course, will concern damaged property, often, except for the land it once stood on, totally destroyed. Who used to own it? What has happened to him or her, or, if the owner was a corporation, it? If the one-time owner is now defunct does a known successor exist?

He had seen and heard a lot on his travels about the country.

About his wife and family, he said only that he had been in indirect touch with his wife, and that she was well. I gathered from other things he said that he had been in some way assisting British and American liaison officers in co-ordinating partisan activity behind the Gothic line. Questioned about it, though, he at once changed the subject.

'Last time I saw you,' he said, 'I asked where you had learned to speak Italian. Later, I tried to find out about you from the British Adjutant-General's department at army head-quarters, but they preserved security most ingeniously by pretending not to understand their own filing system.'

'It was probably no pretence. But yes, I did say I'd tell you all if I saw you again. You mean you're still curious?'

'More than just curious. Interested.'

So, I gave him a reasonably full, though in parts censored, curriculum vitae.

I soon found that the censorship had been unnecessary. He was not in the least concerned with my moral character, about which, he told me later, he had already come to a firm conclusion. This was, that I could be counted upon never to do anything which it was not in my own best interests to do, and that my decisions as to where those interests lay at any specific moment would always be swiftly, as well as shrewdly, reached. Tripoli, except for the name of the banker on whose yacht I had served, was waved away as of no consequence. He did not want to hear about adventures. It was far more important to learn that I spoke Spanish. How about French?

'I get along. Schoolboy grammar, plus additions to my vocabulary picked up in Cannes and St-Germain-des-Prés.'

'But you learn languages easily, it seems.'

'Learning Italian when you already speak Spanish isn't difficult. I think there is a book that makes it easier both ways. Do you want to learn Spanish?'

'No, no, no. You speak English. You should have little trouble learning German.'

'Why should I learn German?'

'Because I think that it is soon going to be a very useful language to have.'

'Don't you mean Russian?'

'No, German.'

I must have looked blank. You have to remember that this was February 1945 and the Western Allies and Russia between them were tearing Germany apart. Anyway, Carlo saw that explanation was needed.

'As soon as this is over, Sergeant-Major, I intend to go into business. Oh, I shall re-establish my legal practice too. That is necessary to the business as well as important in other respects.' He looked into his half-empty glass. 'You see, I intend to go into the business of managing other people's money.'

This, in itself, did not seem to me to have much to do with German being a useful language for me to learn, so I said nothing. Then, suddenly, he leaned right back in his chair and, raising one hand to shade his eyes from the glare of the pressure lamp, stared intently at me for a long time, several seconds.

Finally, he said, 'Paul, what are *your* plans for when this is over?'

It was the first time he had called me anything but Sergeant-Major. I remember noting the fact and also being extremely puzzled. It seemed to me that I was about to be offered some sort of job; but what, in God's name, could an Italian lawyer contemplating going into the arcane business of managing other people's money want with a man of not quite twenty-five? The young man spoke three languages, true, but was he not totally inexperienced in any business other than that of acting as a security policeman during a war? Obviously, I had been mistaken. He was not about to offer me a job. Therefore, he must want something else from me. Play it straight, then; that is to say, cagily.

'Well,' I said. 'I suppose that I shall go home and see my family. There's a job there, if I want it.'

'But in the meantime, what?'

'I don't think there's going to be much meantime.'

'There, I fancy, you are wrong,' he said. 'For you, there may be more than you think. I expect that you have heard talk of demobilization plans.'

'Of course. There'll still be Japan to be finished off, but not for the old sweats. I hear they've already started sending the long-service men home from Burma. It's to be first in, first out, with a points bonus for every month of overseas service. On that basis, I should be home three months after it's over, even going by a slow boat.'

He shook his head. 'I intend no disrespect, but if you had been a fighting soldier, an infantryman, an engineer, a gunner, that might have been a reasonable expectation on your part; but you are not in those categories. I believe that, even after the Nazis are finished here, Allied troops will still be needed. There will be problems with the Yugoslavs about Trieste and other places, there will no doubt be problems with the French. Above all there will be immediate internal problems, social, economic and political, which will not be solved in weeks or months, and will not even begin to be solved without the presence for a time of occupation forces. With partisans in absolute control of vital areas in the north, we could not even administer a direct economic-aid programme without armed help. Your governments may choose to replace what you call the old sweats – I suppose you mean the experienced men – with younger conscripts or those who have seen less service, but specialists like you will have to stay on. You will be asked to volunteer.'

'Or else?'

'That's right. Or else stay on anyway, but forgo the rewards that would have been yours as volunteers.'

'Thanks for warning me. One of our people managed to get sent home and given a psychiatric discharge a month or two ago. I was surprised how easy it was, once he'd really decided.'

'Baby talk doesn't become you, Paul. I think that you would prefer to stay in Italy for a year or eighteen months and make your fortune.'

'In the army? That sounds as if we're back to black marketeering.'

He sighed irritably. 'It is absolutely essential that you rid yourself of this absurd idea that I am a criminal or that I have criminal instincts. I am a lawyer who respects the law. Illegality is for the immature and the foolish. The wise man has no need of it.'

'Sorry.' He seemed genuinely put out, so I poured him some more of his own whisky. 'But,' I went on, 'you must admit that when anyone speaks of making a fortune out of the army, the mind instantly turns to thoughts of . . .'

'No, no!' he protested. 'While *in* the army, not *from* or *out* of the army.' He made one of his brushing-away-a-cobweb gestures. 'The kind of cheating you are thinking of is already being done on a scale that you could not possibly emulate, even if you wanted to. And the scale is increasing. I told you, I have seen and heard a lot on my travels. There is an American quartermaster, for example, who is at present, according to my estimates, over thirty thousand dollars ahead in canned-food deals.'

'Then we *are* talking about the black market.'

'No, we are considering a problem that arises out of it. In a nutshell it is this. What does the quartermaster do with his money when the time comes for him to go home? Does he carry it in his musette bag? *Does* he?'

'I gather that you think that to do so would be unwise.'

'From his point of view, catastrophic. I can tell you that the Judge-Advocate's department is already preparing court-martial cases against two splendid old soldiers, regular army veterans, who were simple enough to do just that. Given the opportunity, any fool can steal money. It's accounting for the possession of it later that is difficult. Do you know that one of those fellows was stupid enough to claim that he had won it all in crap games? The trouble was that he couldn't remember any of the other players. I can tell you this. When the time comes for the rest of these lines-of-communication and base-area bandits to go home, or even be transferred to other theatres, they are going to find that there are obstacle courses for them to run that they never knew about and that they can neither beat nor avoid.'

'So what would you advise the quartermaster to do with his thirty thousand dollars?'

'Advise him to give them all to me, so that I can take care of them for him.'

He himself obviously found nothing strange about what he was saying. It called, consequently, for a careful reply.

'Carlo, you are, as I have reason to know, a trustworthy man. But, with respect, I don't see how you are going to persuade a man who has made thirty thousand dollars by cheating to believe that you, to say nothing of the rest of his fellow men, aren't just as crooked as he is. Isn't that the way the crook's mind works?'

'Certainly it is. For that precise reason he must be sold new ideas. First, if he is an American, he must be made aware of the various hostile moves that can be made against his thirty thousand by the United States Government and its Internal Revenue Service. For instance, that part of his nest egg which is in occupation money will be made worthless after a certain date unless it is declared beforehand. In order to declare large sums he must be able satisfactorily to explain them. That part of the whole which is in Italian currency cannot be converted outside this country except by payment through his own home bank. Once more he must explain. In the same way, if he remits dollars in amounts which exceed his accumulated base pay, he will also be required to explain. In other words, he must either lose all or he must trust, *and* pay, someone else to do what he cannot do for himself; that is, convert that portion of his equity which is not in dollars into currencies which will remain negotiable. Then, the whole of it must be kept safe until such time as he can reclaim it without ever having had to account to anyone for his possession of one cent. How will we perform these unique and quite invaluable services for him? My dear Paul, I will tell you.'

Thirty years were to go by before the Watergate investigation brought the word 'laundering' into metaphorical association with the word 'money'. In 1945 we did not use that particular figure of speech; but in fact 'laundering money', the process of giving large sums which have been criminally acquired the appearance of having been come by legally was what Carlo then began to describe.

Mr Q, the quartermaster, would hear, as if by accident, not only of the obstacle courses in preparation but also about an Italian lawyer of the highest repute who specialized in foreign tax law and was an expert on international currency dealings.

How did Mr Q imagine that all those rich Italian industrialists had managed to get the hell out and stay rich when all the rest of Italy was on the bread line? Obviously, they had switched all their loose cash to currencies and places in which it was safe, and it was this wonderful little lawyer who had made it possible for them to get away with it.

Once Mr Q's agile mind had grasped the fact that here might be a way of concealing his own ill-gotten gains until the heat was off, an introduction would be arranged and Carlo would go to work.

Of course, Mr Q, your problems can be very simply solved. No trouble at all. I will arrange to have your money converted into gold-backed bonds and deposited in my Lugano bank. As soon as you wish to reconvert and receive the money, you write from America and tell me so. In reply you will hear news of the sad death in Europe of a distant relative of yours. Your family emigrated originally from where, Mr Q? Denmark? Then the relative will die in Copenhagen and the money that this so-generous cousin bequeathed to you will be paid in Danish kroner. Any questions?

'Yes, Dottore Lech. How do I know that I can trust you?'

'A sound question, Mr Q. I like hard-headed clients who take nothing for granted. You trust me initially because I am trustworthy and of good reputation. You sit here in my office confident that nothing which is said here will go any farther. You entrust your money to me because I shall give you, first, a notarized receipt for it and, second, the name of the bank in Lugano where it will be held to your credit in an anonymous numbered account. Do you know about anonymous numbered accounts, Mr Q?'

Naturally, he didn't. In 1945 the numbered Swiss bank account was not the hocus-pocus cliché beloved of knowing crime-reporters that it was to become in later years. Refugees from the Nazis had used it, as the Swiss had intended it to be used, as a defence against Gestapo enquiries and Gestapo reprisals. Subsequently, top Nazis and Fascisti, having second thoughts and wanting to hedge their bets, had used it as a defence against the dark suspicions of diehard comrades and the awful penalties that awaited defeatists.

To Mr Q the concept was new and immensely reassuring. He hung upon the Dottore's words; and if he never quite got around to asking how it was possible for a numbered account to be opened for him in a Lugano bank without anyone *at all* in the bank knowing his identity, it was understandable. In

Italy and sitting on thirty thousand hot bucks it all sounded just great.

Now, of course, it all sounds so wide-eyed and artless that just recalling it makes me smile. Nevertheless, it worked. Parts of the set-up still work. When we started, it worked in all its parts because Carlo had thought everything through carefully and realistically down to the smallest detail. Not even Mat Williamson denies that Carlo was a superbly imaginative planner.

His choice of me as the contact man, the intermediary who knows how one can get in touch with the legendary Dottore Lech and what miracles the great man can perform, is an example.

'Why me?' I had asked.

'Because a man like Q would automatically suspect a fellow-American who dangled information like that before his eyes of being an agent-provocateur; and he could very well be right. You, a British non-com, one of those upper-crust limeys whose voices make them sound as if they're pederasts even when they're not, could never be suspect. And what more natural than that someone in your line of work should hear about someone like me? From our own point of view, you have freedom to move about and make new contacts. With the cessation of actual hostilities, that freedom will tend to increase, and so will your freedom to invent reasons for extending your liaison with the Americans.'

'What about the British Mr Q's?'

He raised his right hand as if he were about to swear an oath or deliver a blessing, and then said very sharply: 'No!' After a pause he went on slowly: 'Never, Paul, as long as we are associated, will you ever approach any of your own people, no matter what you may suspect or know about them. Remember this. Nothing we ever do will ever be illegal with our own, our respective, national authorities. In your case, talking about currency transactions to an American soldier, or a Polish or a French one, you would be taking negligible risks. Talking to a British soldier of the same things, you risk being charged with an infinite variety of military offences. If we trifle a little with the law, it must always be the law of others, never of our own. Besides, most of the marketable commodities are now supplied by the Americans, who also control the main storage and distribution facilities. I expect that state of affairs to continue. Oh yes, there will be, as there are now, British, French and Polish fingers in the black-market pie. I have no doubt of that. But most of the fingers will belong, apart from those of my own countrymen, to Americans. That is where the serious money will end up.'

'But what happens to the money, Carlo? I mean, if it's left with us for safe-keeping.'

He was surprised that I should find it necessary to ask. 'Naturally, it remains the property of the client. That we will have the use of it to finance our own market operations will be none of his business, any more than it is the business of the man who banks his money in the conventional way to oversee the bank's investment policies. In many ways we shall, indeed, operate exactly like a bank, but a bank unfettered by petty rules and restrictions.'

'At most ordinary banks the client can go and withdraw his money if he wants. Will he be able to do that with ours?'

'Certainly he will! He can have his money any time he wishes, plus a generous share of its earnings during the time we have managed it. Our own charges will seem modest when we are found to have doubled his money for him. The fact that we may have quadrupled it for our own account need not concern him. Of course,' he added thoughtfully, 'complications are bound to arise. They always do when laws are broken.'

I waited. Carlo was thinking how best to enlighten the innocent without seeming to condescend or over-simplify. He was a courteous man.

'Consider,' he said at last, 'the position of a client of ours once he is back in his home town, a civilian again with perhaps a job, and even a wife and family. How different it will all seem! And how unreal this faraway treasure of his will soon become!'

He contemplated that agreeable vision for a moment before sighing his way back into the real world. 'But let us assume a bolder spirit, or one who cannot bear the thought of money lying, as he thinks, idle in a Lugano bank. There are such men, Paul.'

'Yes, Carlo, there are, especially among those who have made killings as black marketeers.'

'Especially, you think? Among those who were always pilferers, thieves, even before they went into the army, stupidity is to be expected, I agree. But from those late-developing delinquents who will use our services we can count upon more sense, I believe. Take our prototypical Mr Q, for example. Longing for, or possibly needing, money, he decides to send for his nest-egg in the prescribed manner.'

'You mean he chooses to inherit? Yes? Well, we then have to find the equivalent of thirty thousand dollars in Danish kroner and remit from Copenhagen. Or do we just ignore him?'

The smile blossomed. 'Ignore him? That is the last thing we do. On the contrary, we at once arrange to have sent from Copenhagen direct to his local home town paper the magnificent news of this remarkable legacy and of the romantic story which lies behind it.' He looked at me expectantly.

'What romantic story?'

'What does it matter? You are being obtuse, Paul. Think of Mr Q and the strange position in which he would find himself. Think of the questions that would be put to him. Who is this mysterious relative? Why has nobody ever heard of him or her before? And it would not be only the local newspaper reporter who wanted answers. His friends and, above all, his family would want answers, too, and they would examine them somewhat more critically. Almost as critically as the Internal Revenue people. How quick they would be to note the source of Mr Q's surprising windfall and to request a copy of the probated Will when one became available! Do you know, Paul, I believe that Mr Q would very soon be countermanding his instructions to us and telling his local paper that the whole thing had been a case of mistaken identity. Same name, wrong man.'

'What about his notarized receipt? He could come here and collect.'

'He could, but would he? Have you thought of all the anxieties, the heartaches, that receipt must already have caused him? He will have realized, remember, almost as he saw me signing it, that to be found with that piece of paper in his possession could be as damning as to be found counting the money itself, perhaps more so. There could be no plea for leniency on the score of ignorance. Al Capone went to prison for income-tax evasion, not for the way he had made the income. No need to remind Mr Q of that. How he must, in the end, have hated that beautiful receipt! Where did he hide it when he left for home? In the lining of his tunic? In one of his shoes?'

'Supposing he went to Lugano?'

'They have never heard of him or his numbered account. He would have to come to us, where he would at once learn that, for security reasons, we had some months earlier transferred the money to a different bank. All is perfectly safe. What currency would he like it in? Or would he prefer to have it transferred to his domestic account? You see? He is back with his original dilemma, only now, from the tax-evasion standpoint, the offence is even more serious. He had an illicit hoard of dollars. Now, it has made a profit on which he ought to pay capital-gains tax if he were an upright, God-fearing citizen. But he is no longer that, and he knows it. Perhaps, if he has confided in his wife and she is a woman of courage, the pair of them will risk all and smuggle it back to the United States. Or try to do so. We would be failing in our duty, I think, if we did not warn them most seriously of the nature of the risks they would run. At the same time we might remind them that, if they leave the money with us to increase and multiply, there is nothing to prevent their using it later. They might eventually decide to buy a *résidence secondaire* in Italy, or somewhere on the Côte d'Azur, which they could rent when they weren't luxuriating in it them-selves. Then, no one ever need know anything.' He paused, closed his eyes and breathed in deeply as if he were already enjoying on Mr Q's behalf the cool evening breeze scented by pine trees. Then he opened his eyes again before narrowing them slightly. 'You see, Paul? There would never be, there *could* never be, a run on *our* bank.'

Does that sound like an anarchist speaking, Professor Krom? – a man against all settled order and systems of law?

I don't think it does. To me it sounds like a man who enjoyed making money not by breaking laws but by circum-venting them, not by destroying order but by utilizing it in unorthodox ways.

Yes, Carlo was vain; indeed he revelled in his own clever-ness; but the respect that he professed for the law was absolutely genuine. He was, too, something of a moralist and strongly disapproved of black marketeers.

He disapproved because he considered them parasites. He would have been affronted, though, by any suggestion that the same word could, with equal justice, have been applied to us. I only know of one person who had the temerity even to hint at the suggestion, and the consequences for that person were unpleasant. Carlo could, when angered, become quite vindictive.

In that respect he was different from Mat Williamson. Mat does not have to be in the least angry with a man before deciding that he must be destroyed.

The years immediately following VE Day were great ones for

parasites. Allied aid supplies, mostly American but some British, poured into Italy and West Germany at a prodigious rate.

However, since this is not a history of the post-World War II black markets – the writing of which I happily leave to a scholar of the Krom school of fantasists – I shall merely give some idea of the scale of them by reporting that, during our first eighteen months of operations, Carlo was 'entrusted' with nearly half a million dollars derived from the Italian markets *alone*.

I say '*alone*' because before long we were getting word of much larger sums needing our services in Germany.

The early reports from Carlo's man in Lugano told of a chaotic situation. Big money was being made, but those making it, mostly American senior NCOs and junior officers in transportation and supply units, seemed unaware of the difficulties into which they would soon be getting. This was not simply because they were new to the game, but because in West Germany the rules were complex and the conditions of play tended to promote over-confidence. For instance, there were three distinct occupation zones, in two of which – the French and the British – exchange control restrictions were maintained on their national currencies. In the British zone, these restrictions were enforced by a Special Investigation Branch squad of remarkable ferocity. So, the American wheeler-dealer, who already benefited from his access to the most sought-after market commodities, also enjoyed the advantage of being able to do business in the only freely convertible currency available, the dollar.

Soon, stories began to come in of American soldiers crossing into Switzerland for 'Rest and Recuperation'. On arrival, most of them made for the nearest bank. Perfectly natural, one would have said, if all that those fine boys were doing was exchanging a few of their dollars for francs to spend locally during their furloughs; but that, it seemed, was by no means all that some of them were doing; lots were opening bank accounts.

This, of course, was before the mere possession of a Swiss bank account by an American or British citizen rendered him, at least in the eyes of his native Revenue men, at best a jail-worthy tax-evader if not a Mafia narcotics-pedlar as well; but murmurings about refugee Nazi funds being protected by the Swiss bank secrecy laws were already getting louder, and a newspaper story about a black market in antibiotics involving occupation medical-corps personnel had caused a considerable fuss. As always when the nostrils of higher authority are assailed by smells of corruption other than their own, the cries of outrage and disgust are promptly followed by sounds of loophole-stoppings and stampings-out, of tightenings-up and clampings-down.

In the American sector, by the end of 1946, an efficient laundry service of the kind Carlo could provide had become essential. I do not claim that his was the only one in the field – we had our imitators by then – but it was unquestionably the safest and most reliable.

In November, having at last been told that the army no longer required my services, I asked for a travel warrant to London and was demobilized there. Acting on Carlo's instructions, I then obtained a British passport, as well as renewing my Argentine papers, before returning to Milan. From Milan I went to Lugano, where I spent a week or so learning a few more ropes. From Munich, I wrote to my family explaining that I had gone into the scrap-metal business.

The code-name given to me by Carlo for use when I needed to authenticate confidential messages was 'Oberholzer'.

In 1956, Carlo had an operation for the removal of his gall-bladder. The surgeon who performed it somehow bungled the job, and later in the year a second operation became necessary. He recovered all right, but it was a long, debilitating illness and it changed him. I don't mean that he aged prematurely, though I have noticed that serious illness can have that effect on persons in their sixties. With Carlo what happened was that, as his physical health returned, the pattern of his characteristic psychological responses seemed gradually to intensify. He became an exaggerated, larger-than-life version of himself. Things that would once have only made that smile of his blossom, now made him laugh aloud. Things that would once have been dismissed as annoyances now produced outbursts of rage. It was as if, in the struggle to regain his health, he had been obliged to shed the emotional weight of several old but crucial inhibitions. The result was in many ways a more engaging man, but also a more formidable and sometimes frightening one. I have said that Carlo could be vindictive. After his illness he could be cruelly so. The man who could dream up the butter-train coup was also capable of applying himself with relish to more disagreeable amusements.

His claim that ours was a bank on which there could never

be a run had proved to be justified. On that score we had no anxieties; and, after 1951, when the double-taxation conventions between Switzerland and the US and UK came into force, the possibility of a run ceased to exist altogether. Our 'customers', a cagey bunch of crooks with finely-tuned survival instincts, could never all go crazy at the same time.

That is not to say, however, that some of them did not over the years withdraw their deposits, having devised their own ways of accounting for them. Some of the ways worked. Few attempted, though, to use the legacy method of getting their money, and most who did chickened out, as Carlo had predicted they would, before the pay-off was finally made.

The typical American customer seeking to close his account with us was usually in Europe on a business or vacation trip. Mostly, they wrote, after leaving the United States and generally from London or Paris, to announce that they were on their way. Those who went unannounced direct to Lugano were referred to Milan, and Carlo was immediately given advance warning either by telephone or by one of our couriers. When such customers arrived they were usually, and quite naturally, a bit flustered. Doubt and greed, plus a little anger and a lot of fear, make a disturbing emotional mix; but most were easy enough to handle.

The one who so upset Carlo was exceptional in a number of respects. To begin with, he was not flustered, only bloody-minded. Furthermore, during the time that had elapsed since I had signed him up in Germany, he had returned to the United States and, under the GI Bill of Rights, qualified as an accountant. In addition, he had married a woman, also an accountant, whom he had met while they were both attending a post-graduate course in business administration. She had worked then for a firm of Wall Street investment bankers. After their marriage they had gone into business together, starting an employment agency specializing in trained data-processing staff.

This customer was so different from our prototypical Mr Q that I shall call him Vic – as in Victor and victim.

When I first met him, Vic had been dealing in the already overcrowded market for stolen PX goods, but later, thanks to a lucky posting and a promotion, he had been able to switch to army truck tyres and make real money. By the time his tour of duty in Germany ended we were holding over seventy thousand dollars for him, and he, although he had met Carlo only once, held nine of the notarized receipts. The courier service we operated made such transactions fairly routine, once confidence had been established at an initial meeting, as well as safer. The meeting usually took place near Zug, where Carlo's holding corporation was registered.

Vic gave no advance warning of his arrival in Milan, and none was received from Lugano because he had not bothered to go there. I had other projects to supervise by then, and was dividing my time between Milan and three other cities. It was by chance that I was there when Vic descended on us. A lucky chance, I think; not because the occasion was in the least enjoyable, but because it made me think more carefully than I had thought before about Carlo. Naturally, he called me in to greet his old client and my old friend.

At first, Vic showed no signs at all of bloody-mindedness. He was not exactly affable, but cool, polite and collected. He had a brand-new Gucci brief-case which he carefully placed on the floor between his legs. Then he told us what a wonderful little woman he had married and why he hadn't troubled to go to the bank in Lugano.

A month earlier they had been talking about expanding their business, of opening a second office in Chicago. They had spoken of the additional capital that would be needed and of the problems of borrowing it they would have to face. In the watches of the night Vic had revealed for the first time that while in the army he had not always been a simple soldier.

Mrs Vic had heard his confession with surprise but only token distress. They were both human, weren't they? Once her surprise had worn off, curiosity had taken over. Her Wall Street experience had given her some knowledge of Swiss banking customs. *What* sort of an account did he say he had? An *anonymous* one? Didn't he mean numbered? No, he meant one hundred per cent anonymous numbered. Well, honey, I have news for you. There are numbered accounts, but not one hundred per cent anonymous ones. Okay, your name's not on the account externally, but it's on it internally. The only anonymity lies in the fact that no more than five key bank personnel can match the name to the number. Exactly how did you open this account? What sort of application did you sign?

Now, Vic turned narrowed eyes in my direction. 'How many other suckers did you sign up, Paul baby?'

'You had an anonymous account.'

'There's no such thing.'

'There's no such thing *now*. The rules were changed when the double-taxation conventions were signed.'

'Bullshit!'

I gave him the weary look. 'If you yourself had not insisted that, for security reasons, contacts between us could only be made on *your* initiative, you would long ago have been formally notified of the situation. Why project your paranoia on us? If you had simply gone to the Lugano bank you would have been referred here automatically.'

'Well, now that I'm here *un*automatically, where's the money?'

I looked at Carlo. He already had his hand on the intercom to the outer office. He flipped the switch and said in English: 'Send in the current confidential fiscal account of Mr Vic.' To Vic he said: 'I am assuming that you can produce the original receipts that I notarized. You have them with you?'

'Sure.' He reached for the brief-case and took out an old-fashioned pouch file of the kind that is tied with a linen tape. He undid the tape, took out the receipts and spread them out elaborately in the shape of a fan. 'How many peanuts are they worth now?' he asked unpleasantly.

What interested me at once was their condition. I had seen a number of those receipts produced for inspection in Carlo's office, and always before they had looked unfit even for his elegant waste-basket. Either they had been dog-eared and greasy from years of furtive handling and re-examination, or so creased, folded and refolded to suit strange hiding-places that they were nearly falling apart. Vic's were all clean and smooth. As well as being astute and impertinent, he was also, it seemed, overwhelmingly sure of himself.

Carlo's senior secretary, the matriarch, came in with the statement of account and placed it reverently on the desk in front of him.

Normally, that is faced with a client who had minded his manners and was there merely to enquire about the state of his dream money, Carlo would have let the account lie there for a few minutes while he chatted away knowledgeably about some new sculptor whose work had caught his eye, or the follies of currency speculation, or anything else that had happened to come into his mind as he sat there. The truth was that the accounts, which were always updated twice a year, were his own particular pride and joy. He did them himself and they were masterpieces of obfuscation. One of his greatest pleasures was to see a client, on examining an account, purse his lips and then nod sagely as if it were all perfectly understandable. He believed that the preliminary chit-chat – what he called his abracadabra – helped the process along by bemusing the client.

With Vic, however, abracadabra was obviously not going to work. Besides, the fellow annoyed him. Almost before the secretary had left the room, Carlo leaned forward and tossed the account folder in Vic's direction.

Vic caught it neatly, opened it and spent about ten seconds glancing at each of the three pages inside. Then, he slapped it shut and skimmed it back so that it plopped on to the desk right under Carlo's nose.

'Mr Lech,' he said, 'I left you with seventy-three thousand dollars of mine. In eight years those dollars have become one hundred eighty-six thousand somethings. First question, what kind of somethings? Lire?'

Carlo put the account folder aside as if the sight of it now offended him. 'American dollars, of course,' he said. 'You have more than doubled your money.'

Vic did not look in the least pleased. He just said: 'How? How have I doubled it? Tell me, Mr Lech.'

Carlo touched the account folder without looking at it. 'It is all here, Sir. I thought you understood figures.'

Vic made a spitting sound. 'Sure I understand figures, when I know how they've been cooked. You, or rather your boy Paul here, now tells me that my money hasn't been in that bank after all. So where has it been?'

'Acting on your behalf, we held it in a deposit account.'

'Ah, now we're getting somewhere. Acting on my behalf, you said. Right? So what did you invest it in? German blue chips? Schering? Siemens? Daimler-Benz? Hoechst? What was the portfolio?'

Carlo had a small ebony-edged silver ruler which he used as a paperweight. With it, he suddenly rapped on his desk. 'That is enough, Sir,' he said sternly; 'I am a lawyer, not an investment banker. You found it convenient to utilize my services in order to hold your money in trust. I have held it in trust. It is more than intact. You can receive it back at any time you wish, less my proper fees but plus compound interest at bank rates as they have fluctuated over the relevant period. You have more than doubled your money. What is your complaint?'

Vic sat back, as if relaxing, then cocked an eye again at me. 'What kind of an account do you charmers say you put it in?'

'A deposit account.'

He made his spitting noise again. 'Now I *know* you're lying. If you had opened anything at all in my behalf, it would have been a discretionary investment account. No, let's cut the crap now, eh, Pauly? I've done my homework. I figure that, over the last eight years you've had them to play with, you and Mr Lech have made a cool million out of my seventy-three thousand. That would be par for the course. Now, you tell me you've doubled my money plus a few bucks, less your fees of course, and ask me what my complaint is. Are you serious?'

What did he think we were? Nice guys about to vote him a pension as sucker of the year? He had indeed done some homework, but not as much as he thought. In fact, thanks to the Lugano bank's post-war policy of investment in German industry, we had made over two million dollars out of his particular nest-egg. Now, it remained only to get rid of the man.

'How would you like your money, Mr Vic?' I asked. 'A draft on the Chase-Manhattan in Geneva? A telex transfer to your own bank in the United States? Cash?'

He examined us both carefully for a moment or two without answering. Carlo began tapping on the desk-top with his ruler.

Then, Vic broke his own silence with a short laugh. 'The shyster and his shill!' he said.

Carlo stopped tapping and I saw that he had gone quite pale. His colloquial English was not good, but it was good enough to understand the word 'shyster'. Rather than let him say something that he might regret, I got in first.

'Don't push your luck, Vic,' I said. 'We could always ship it back as truck tyres. It's cash, I take it. Dollars in century bills?'

'Fifties or centuries, but I want them right now.'

Carlo reached for the intercom and told the matriarch to get the bank on the phone. That was unnecessary because we kept a cash float of half a million dollars in a safe deposit box. He was playing for time; to think, presumably, though what there was to think about just then I did not immediately understand. When the bank was put through, he said first that I would shortly be requiring access to the safe deposit vault. Then he told the procurator at the other end to wait and, looking at Vic, asked him in Italian if, in view of the large sum of money he would be carrying, he would like a bank escort to his hotel.

I gathered, correctly, that this was a test question to see if Vic understood Italian. When it was evident that he did not, Carlo repeated the question in English.

No, Vic did not need an escort, thank you very much; he could take care of himself.

Carlo said goodbye to the procurator and then went on speaking in Italian to me.

'Paul, I want the receipt from him for the money to be witnessed by someone at the bank. Make a ceremony of it. And I particularly want those old notarized receipts of mine back. Then, I want to know as soon as possible which hotel he's in. Offer to share a taxi with him and drop him off. Then phone me the name of the hotel immediately. Unless it's within a couple of minutes of here don't wait until you get back.'

It was not the moment to ask him what he was up to, so I went ahead and did exactly as I had been told.

Vic made difficulties about signing for the money, but the actual sight of it and the solemnity of the bank officials quietened him down eventually. The old receipts he handed over without a murmur. Only about half the money was in hundreds and he had trouble stuffing it all into his nice new brief-case. He rejected my suggestion that we share a taxi – now that he had the money he seemed scared of me – but he let me flag one down for him and tell the driver where to go.

I called Carlo from the nearest café and reported.

'Good,' he said. 'You have all the receipts? Splendid. Now please bring them back here, Paul.'

When he had the originals spread out on the desk he looked at them as if they were old and much-loved friends.

'How could such an otherwise cautious man be so stupid?' he asked. 'If they had been mine, I would have set light to every single one myself before I handed you its ashes.'

'He was too worried about the receipt that *he* had to sign.'

'That is why I asked for it. Oh yes, it will be useful, but it will be the first ones which will count. Look at the dates! How interesting, and how devastatingly conclusive.'

'Conclusive of what?'

He did not answer straightaway. 'What is that name he called you, Paul?'

'Shill?'

'Yes. What does it mean?'

'Mostly it's the slang word for a professional gambler's accomplice who is there to make winning look easy, but con-men and other crooks also use shills. A shill is a person, man or woman, who persuades the victims to come and try their luck, to let themselves be swindled.'

He sighed. 'One would think we had *lost* this foolish man's money instead of doubling it. Well, he must pay for his insolence. As soon as you phoned me I arranged to have him tailed from his hotel.' He responded to my raised eyebrows. 'I wish to know what he does with the money.'

'If he has any sense he'll put it in a bank.'

'Yes, but which bank and where? It is too late today, but perhaps he will travel overnight. Where to? Lausanne? Basle?'

A wild thought occurred to me. 'You're not thinking of taking it back off him, Carlo?'

'It would serve him right, but we are not thieves. No, I simply wish to know which branch of which bank he chooses.'

'Then what?'

'The American Internal Revenue Service pays a ten per cent reward to informers who give them proof that a US citizen has failed to declare income.'

'You'd inform on Vic?'

'I? Great heavens, no! I have an associate in New York who will do that. I will just send him the evidence. Think of the wringing of hands when the IRS descends on our friend Mr Vic with their demands for back audits. What was the source of these large sums obtained while you were serving in the army and for which we hold receipts? Why did you not report them? You refuse to answer because to do so might incriminate you? Then answer this. We have evidence here of a capital gain by you of over eighty thousand dollars. Why was that not reported? Where is it? We'll tell you. It's in such-and-such a bank. And before you add perjury to the rest of the crimes you're going to be charged with, let us remind you of this. Swiss bank secrecy doesn't protect persons who can be shown to have committed criminal offences like stealing US army property. What a fine time they will have!'

I was beginning to feel sorry for Vic. 'You'd do that to him for a ten per cent pay-off?'

'Of that pathetic reward I shall not accept one cent,' he said contemptuously. 'My reward will be the satisfaction of *my* sense of the fitness of things. He insulted me. He insulted you. He will be punished, as a criminal, such as he, deserves to be punished, for his crimes against his country's laws.' He sat up very straight in his chair and gazed fixedly at the Moretto landscape on the wall behind me. Finally, he made the cobweb-brushing gesture he still used to punctuate thought processes. 'All this has taught me a lesson, Paul,' he added.

'You mean that, if we're going to blow him to the IRS, he's liable to blow us too?'

'Certainly not! What crimes have *we* committed? I was merely reflecting that it might be time for us to spread our wings again and to fly in a new direction.' He raised his elbows sideways, dropped his hands, then tensed his fingers into talons as if he were a bird of prey about to kill.

'Oh?'

'Yes. In future, Paul, we will have no more dealings with illegitimate money. It is contagious, it carries infection.' One of the talons brushed away yet another cobweb. 'By devoting ourselves diligently to the new arts of tax avoidance, I think that we may be able to create for our clients, and certain others, impenetrable and indestructible shields against the rapacity of governments.'

He went on to explain in detail what he had in mind.

I have admitted that, after he had recovered physically from his illness, I sometimes found Carlo a little frightening. The revenge he had taken on Vic, simply because the man had been foolish enough to speak his mind, worried me quite a bit; but the plan of action he then proceeded to lay out was wholly rational.

The idea derived from his belief – a widely-held belief, I know, but one that was in his case based on special knowledge – that the very rich are always also very stingy.

Thus, if you were able to show a rich man how he could avoid paying large amounts of money to the government which presumed to tax him and his corporate enterprises, he, in his turn, would be ready to pay a much, much smaller amount of money to you in the shape of a fee.

At least, he would be ready to do so for a time. That, sooner or later, he would become reluctant to pay you as he had previously been reluctant to pay the tax collector, was inevitable. Ultimately, he would probably try to cheat you as, once upon a time, he had tried to cheat the tax man. Therefore, you bore that possibility in mind from the start, armed yourself with appropriate sanctions and made sure that, if or when the attempts to cheat you were made, simple mechanisms to ensure their failure were triggered automatically. Ideally, Carlo thought, our relationship with our clients should be one of mutual, and permanent, trust.

Who but Krom could have had the breathtaking audacity to speak in this context of 'international parasitism' and make wild allegations about a 'multi-million-dollar extortion racket'?

CHAPTER SIX

I am not the only one who has found Krom hard to take.

Had our stay at the Villa Lipp not been cut short so suddenly, Connell and Henson would surely have ended by quarrelling with him. Obviously, they respected his earlier work and so were prepared to put up with a certain amount of his nonsense, including a lot of tipsy pontificating; otherwise, they would not have been there; but even on that first night, before we knew that things had gone seriously wrong and that we were in danger, there were signs of strain.

Krom had objected strongly to Connell's asking me questions; and I had made a bet with myself that, in due course, I would hear him insisting just as strongly that only he was entitled to receive my 'papers', and that only he would have the right thereafter to decide who saw how much of what was in them. I won the bet too.

When the coffee had been served, I told Melanie to pass round file number one to our guests. Krom stopped her instantly by clutching at one of her arms. He was as stricken as a child who has just been told that the bright new toy which was to have been his alone must, after all, be shared.

'I think, Mr Firman,' he said with a show of teeth, 'that, in your own interests as well as ours, the distribution of all documents ought to be strictly limited.'

'I quite agree, Professor.' I stared hard at Melanie's arm until he released it. 'There are only three copies of that document, one for you and one each for your witnesses. I shall insist that the last two be returned for me to destroy as soon as they have been read and compared with your text.'

He tried to think of an inoffensive way of saying that he did not want his witnesses having free access to material that was really his, and his alone, in case they stole bits of it from him. Naturally, he failed; there is no inoffensive way of saying such a thing. He tried stepping around the difficulty.

'Notes could be taken.'

'Of course. And I am sure that they *will* be taken,' I said cheerfully. 'Dr Connell has a tape-recorder and Dr Henson has a shorthand-writer's notebook in her suitcase. I dare say she also has an excellent memory.'

Henson suddenly laughed and received a glare from Krom.

She at once raised both hands in apology. 'Sorry, but I had an unworthy thought,' she explained. 'It crossed my mind, only for an instant but quite distinctly, that Mr Firman couldn't care less how many notes are taken because he has no intention of letting us see or hear anything that could in any way compromise him.'

Yves broke in angrily. 'There, Doctor, you are greatly mistaken. This meeting alone compromises him, and us.' His outstretched hand included Melanie.

'Don't worry, Mr Boularis.' Krom tried clumsily to pat him on the knee and seemed to resent Yves's instinctively flinching away. 'But don't deceive yourself either, or let him deceive you,' he went on with one of his saliva sprays. 'Your friend Firman was compromised years ago when I saw him in Zürich.'

Connell stifled what might have been the start of a low moan. 'Ah, yes,' he said, 'we're back at the celebrated Oberholzer-Firman identification. Are we now going to be allowed to hear exactly what was so compromising about it, or is that still "pas devant les enfants", Professor?'

He sounded as if he had become as tired of Krom as I had. Before the elder statesman had time to do more than glare and show teeth again, I had signalled to Melanie.

This time, she went the other way round the table so that the witnesses received their copies of the file first.

'Read all about it,' I said to Connell.

The witnesses' behaviour towards me since then has left much to be desired, inevitably perhaps; but I still regret that security considerations, now known to have been irrelevant, prevented my giving them more of the truth than I did. They might have learned something, not only to their own advantage, but, of more immediate consequence in this time of trial, to mine.

This is how it really came about that Krom saw me in Zürich.

The warning telegram did not reach me until late on Tuesday, over twenty-four hours after Kramer had been taken ill.

The text of it said only that he was in the emergency heart unit of the Kantonsspital in Zürich. The signature, however, was in a code form meaning that not only was there material urgently awaiting collection but also that the strictest security precautions should be taken. Use of the code signature showed that, ill or not, he had written or dictated the telegram himself and that his mind was still functioning.

I was in Lisbon at the time and the message had been re-transmitted from Milan by Carlo; and I mean by Carlo personally, not by some trusted underling to whom the job had been delegated. If that sounds an odd way to run a business making net profits in the five-million-dollar-plus region I shall have to agree. It was odd; but that was because the business was odd.

Carlo kept up his office with its appropriate staff in Milan mainly as a front. Otherwise the only persons we employed were our six couriers, four men and two women, who did exactly as they were told and never asked a question except when the answer was needed to clarify an instruction. All other operations in the ten cities we used as bases were handled through the neutral channels of 'business accommodation' services which provided mail-forwarding and phone-answering together with addresses to put on our various letter-heads. Our consultancy work was always done in hotel rooms. For the profits we made, our overheads were negligible.

The business I was doing in Lisbon had reached a delicate stage and it was impossible to respond to the warning message as promptly as I might have done. I don't think it would have made much difference though. When I received the message, the Kramer relationship was already unsalvageable. All that would have been different, possibly, would have been the nature of the trap set for me.

Anyway, it was Thursday before I could leave Lisbon. I reached Frankfurt later that day and rented a car. I was in Zürich at nine-thirty on Friday morning.

Why did I drive when I could more quickly have got there by air? Mainly because, if you are in western Europe and want to have a confidential business discussion on the other side of a frontier, it is more secure to travel by car. The days when an elaborate carnet recorded every frontier transit which the car and its passengers made are gone. All you need is an international certificate of insurance and they generally don't bother even with that, much less your passport; at most road frontier crossings they just wave you through. Airlines, on the other hand, keep copies of passenger flight manifests that can be checked by anyone with the right kind of muscle, and at lots of airports you may get your passport stamped. Train controls can be stickier than road, too, because the officials have more time. The only persons who should never use road frontiers are smugglers, because on some roads the Customs people like to play games. Instead of lining up beside the immigration squad, they move their checkpoint three or more kilometres back along the road on their side where a build-up of traffic doesn't matter. Then, they have plenty of time to nail the ones with the evidence on them, just as the poor slobs think they are free and clear.

I am not a smuggler and I use the roads. I did, though, go to the Zürich airport and park the car there before taking an airport bus into town. Anyone then becoming interested in my movements would have assumed that I had arrived by air. I got off the bus at the Haupt-Bahnhof.

From there I phoned the hospital and learned that Kramer had been dead for two days.

It was too early in the morning, I felt, to telephone a newly-created widow. To pass the time, I had a second breakfast while I decided how best to handle the phase-out-and-forget routine in this particular case. At that point, strange as it may seem now, the only grave difficulty of which I was aware was that of remembering the widow's first name without having Kramer's personal file there to check on.

I got it eventually – Frieda. After breakfast I went for a stroll and found a department store where I was able to buy a black tie.

By then it was ten-thirty, so I went back to the station and called the Kramer apartment.

The voice of the woman who answered was that of someone younger than Frieda; the married daughter, I found. She accepted my condolences politely enough on her mother's behalf, but when I asked if I could speak to the mother there was a marked change of tone.

'Is that, by any chance, Herr Oberholzer of Frankfurt?' she asked.

'Yes. I am an old friend of your father's.'

'So I have been given to understand.' Her tone was now distinctly cool. That could have put me on my guard, but didn't. Those nursing private griefs often resent attempts, real or imagined, by outsiders to share them.

'I am speaking for my mother,' she went on briskly. 'She has asked me to tell you that the funeral will be at eleven tomorrow morning. The crematorium is on the Käferholz-strasse. Flowers, if you wish to send any, should be delivered to the chapel of the hospital mortuary before nine-thirty.'

'Thank you. I am grateful for that information. However, I hope to pay my respects and offer my personal sympathies to your mother before then. I propose to call on her this morning, just before noon if that would be convenient.'

'No, Herr Oberholzer, I am afraid that that would not be convenient. Only family members are here today. But my mother has anticipated your anxiety and concern. She asks me to assure you that your papers are quite safe and that you may collect them at any time after the funeral tomorrow. There will be sandwiches and coffee here for those who can stomach them. Goodbye, Herr Oberholzer.'

She hung up.

Even then I wasn't really worried. Under the emotional stress of her husband's sudden death, Frieda had obviously been talking too freely about things she would have been wiser to forget; but, as her knowledge of them was necessarily limited to what Kramer would have told her in an unlikely fit of total indiscretion, it represented no serious threat to me, just a nuisance. Because she had disapproved of me and my relationship with her husband – though she could scarcely have disapproved of the money it had brought in – I was being made to stay in Zürich when it was neither necessary nor advisable for me to do so, and to attend a funeral.

Persuading wealthy tax and exchange-control evaders to pay you for advising them is not difficult; not, that is, when you have the right sanctions at your disposal; but, unless you are very careful, it can be dangerous.

It must be accepted that any rich man who chooses to *evade* his country's fiscal laws when, simply by taking a little trouble and obtaining good advice, he could *avoid* them, has to be, however superficially astute, basically stupid.

When, therefore, he has to pay up in order to conceal his folly he is unlikely to accept the loss philosophically. On the contrary, he will quite often go to extravagant lengths to avenge the 'outrage'. I know of one case in which the idiot actually went out, bought himself the most expensive rifle on the market, had it fitted with a telescopic sight and began practising to become a marksman.

The fact is that a lot of these very rich men can behave remarkably like old-fashioned psychopathic gangsters. Protecting your set-up from lunatic vindictiveness of that kind calls for more than ordinary care and attention. Where security is concerned, you have to be a trifle paranoid.

The moment Kramer's daughter hung up on me, I should have immediately gone back to my car and hit the road for home and a good dinner. I was married at the time to my second wife. She was really an excellent cook.

The wrong kind of greed, that was my trouble; greed, plus slow and very sloppy thinking. Kramer had said in his telegram that there was important material to be collected. So, there was I hanging about in the expectation of collecting; just as if nothing had happened; just as if Kramer had still been alive and well.

The weather was horrible, a bitter wind was blowing showers of wet snow. If I had been travelling on one of my real passports I might well have checked in at a first-rate hotel where I was known and would be cosseted. Luckily, I was travelling as Reinhardt Oberholzer. I say 'luckily', because if I had been using a real identity nothing I could have done would have saved the situation. There are some paper-trails that cannot be diverted or cleaned up because, before you can get busy with your little spiked walking-stick, the hounds will be there in the field waiting for you.

So, thank God for the Oberholzer passports.

Yes, that's right, Krom. Passports, plural. We used five. I had one. The four men couriers had one each, which they used when they were acting as cut-outs.

Carlo's unorthodox thinking would have sent any trained intelligence man crazy. For example, he had picked the cover-name Oberholzer originally because it was neither common nor uncommon but middle-ordinary in most German-speaking places. In an Anglo-Saxon community, Underwood or Overton would be in the same bracket. So far, quite orthodox. But what happened when the cover wore thin and began to unravel?

Orthodox opinion was that you promptly junked both it and its occupant. Carlo did not agree. By hastily junking a cover, to say nothing of the person who had been using it, you might well supply confirmation of what had until then been only a suspicion. You might even create suspicions where none had existed except in your own imagination. Was it not better surely, to present the opposition with a fresh set of doubts to resolve by putting a second man into play, one who in some respects strongly resembled his namesake, yet in others was confusingly different? If suspicions had existed before would they not now be allayed? Or, if not wholly allayed would not the reasons for them now have to be reassessed?

In view of the nature of the opposition we faced, an opposition which had always to rely upon reluctant or havering witnesses telling as little of the truth as they dared, such a reassessment could have only one result. 'Doubt demoralizes' was one of Carlo's favourite maxims. His tactical description of the Oberholzer-style multiplication manœuvre was 'dispersal' or, if he felt like being facetious, 'defence in width'.

I once played against a good three-card-trick man for over an hour. I knew exactly what he was doing and how he was doing it, and still he beat me three times out of five. That was how the Oberholzer game had worked. Only we had been winning five tricks out of five, until I lost one that made it necessary not only to change the name of the game but also some of the rules.

Zürich is a busy city and unless you have made reservations in advance or are a known and valued client in a particular establishment, central hotel rooms are not always easy to find. Since I could not go to a place where I was known, I went to the tourist bureau at the station, where they operated a hotel booking service.

Now I may have been careless that day, but I was not completely feckless. When you are using a cover, you always, and automatically, use it as little as possible simply in order to protect it from unnecessary wear and tear. So, when I gave my name to the girl at the tourist bureau I instinctively resorted to an old ploy.

In most countries, officialdom tends, when identifying you, to put your surname first and your given name or names after it. In many parts of Asia this name order is socially usual as well. On the European mainland and in South America, the social and administrative usages tend to overlap. Your insurance policies may describe you as OBERHOLZER, Reinhardt or Reinhardt Oberholzer. On a formal occasion among strangers you may click heels and introduce yourself as Oberholzer Reinhardt, while at a less starchy function you are dear old lovable Reinhardt Oberholzer. To the travel-bureau girl I gave my name as Oswald Reinhardt, slurring the Oswald slightly so that I could always claim, if necessary, that she had not been listening attentively.

By the time I had returned to the department store, bought an overnight bag and a change of linen and was back at the bureau, they had a room for me. It was in a second-category place up by the botanical gardens. The receptionist there had my name as O. Reinhardt from the bureau, and did not bother to look closely at the Oberholzer passport I fumbled with before filling out the police card.

The hotel was on a pleasant street with lots of trees which

probably gave it quite a rustic outlook during the summer. Unfortunately, it was also next door to a church with a clock tower. This had a full set of chimes which were, I soon found, in robust working order. The receptionist, showing me to my room, said with a false but practised smile that many guests enjoyed the sound of the clock striking. The prospect of going back to the tourist bureau and starting afresh was unattractive, so I asked the way to the nearest pharmacy.

It was several streets away in a little shopping district which appeared to serve a quarter which was mixed business and residential. In a miniature supermarket I bought half a bottle of whisky. In the pharmacy I bought, in addition to razor, soap, face-cloth and tooth-brush, some ear-plugs. Then, deciding to return to the hotel by a different route, one that I thought might be less exposed to the wind, I saw the flower shop.

Now, although I like flowers and normally find flower shops agreeable places, I am not one of those who cannot resist them. It was just that, in this particular shop, there was a remarkably handsome girl visible through the window. She was spraying the leaves of some philodendra, and the way she was raising her arms did something for her. As I slowed down to admire the view, the sight of her happened to coincide with an irresistible urge to get in out of the cold wind again plus the thought that a wreath from Oberholzer at the Kramer funeral might serve both to modify his women's hostility and to fortify their discretion.

So, I went in.

When the girl was not spraying plants placed high up on wrought-iron display stands, her posture was not so good, but she was cheerful and friendly. She wouldn't recommend a wreath, she said, because her partner, who was the real expert at making wreaths quickly, was away with 'flu. If I insisted, she would do her best to make a nice wreath in time, but as it would have to be at the hospital mortuary before nine-thirty the following morning, she really thought that flowers would be better. What about some of those hot-house roses over there? Of course, they wouldn't last beyond tomorrow, but in this weather neither would the flowers in a wreath. You couldn't just send greenstuff, could you? If I decided on the roses she would see that they were well wrapped and, as she was the one who would be doing the delivery, taken straight into the mortuary chapel when they got there. For a German like me they wouldn't be all that expensive, and if I took the lot – the red, yellow and pink would look lovely together – she would give me a discount. She was a good saleswomen with some miserable roses on her hands which weren't going to last the weekend anyway.

Once the bargain was struck, though, and I was seated at a little table writing conventional words of sympathy on a card to go with the flowers, and sealing it into one of the envelopes provided, she became curious. She knew from my accent that I was neither Swiss nor Austrian, but she couldn't decide whether I was a north or south German, nor could she figure out my relationship with the dead. When I had declined her offer of a receipt and she was ringing up the sale on the cash register, she remarked that they didn't have many foreign visitors buying flowers up there and asked me where I was staying. When I told her she looked genuinely concerned, but at once said bravely, but with even less conviction, what the receptionist had said, that lots of people liked the sound of the bells. She was no longer curious about which part of Germany I came from. She knew now that I would not be back, not in that quarter of Zürich certainly. When I left the shop, she was putting my condolences to the family Kramer into a little plastic bag that would protect them from the weather.

I lunched well, far away from the hotel, spent the afternoon in a cinema and had a good, early, dinner. The night, though, was dreadful.

The ear-plugs did little to help and the whisky less. Every time the clock struck, the windows rattled and you could feel vibrations through the bedsprings, or at least I fancied that I could; and, of course, after a bit you ceased to think of sleep and simply lay there waiting for the next assault.

At three in the morning I took a chair-cushion, the duvet and all the pillows and blankets I could find, and made up a sort of bed in the bathroom where, I had noticed, the sounds from the clock tower were slightly muted. There, I managed to doze through two lots of quarter-hour chimes before the bathroom floor made itself felt and four o'clock shattered the last hope of sleep. I sat up for the rest of the night in the one armchair, with the duvet over my head.

Excuses, it may be said. The man makes a fool of himself. Clearly, he has to blame someone or something, so he picks on a church clock and a sleepless night.

Not so. My mistakes on that occasion had all been made the day before. What is remarkable is that, having suffered the sort of sleepless night after which a man normally needs tranquil-

113

lizers if he is to function at all, I succeeded in behaving with such decision and efficiency.

I sat in the armchair until five-thirty. Then, I shaved, bathed, put on my new white shirt and black tie and waited for daylight. At six-thirty, while it was still dark, I went down and consulted the night-duty concierge about the possibility of getting a taxi. He said that it might take a while, but that he would phone for one. When he had done so, I asked about getting some coffee. The kitchen did not open until seven. Casting about in my mind for other ways of killing time, I thought of my bill and asked if I could pay it. Yes, I could. A surprise, until I caught the look of resignation on the concierge's face. I was evidently not the first guest in that place who had been in a hurry to get away. Nor would I be the last. Very early departures were normal.

So, I paid the bill and said that I would return later for my bag. That was my first piece of luck.

A taxi came eventually and I went to the Carlton-Elite Hotel. There, in the restaurant, I ate a large American breakfast and read the German-language papers. Later, in the lobby, I read the Italian papers and did the Paris *Herald-Tribune* crossword. By then it was nearly time to go to the funeral.

To the doorman I explained my wants; a taxi or a hire car with a driver who would take me to the crematorium, wait and then drive me to an apartment in the Hottingen district. That was where the Kramer apartment was. The doorman said that a hire car would cost no more for that sort of journey and would be more comfortable. He could have one there in five minutes.

It was a black four-door Taunus and the driver was an elderly man with beautiful iron-grey hair and a thin, sad face. He knew exactly where the crematorium was and obviously enjoyed funeral work, of which, he told me gently, he did a great deal.

'Was the departed a close relative of the gentleman?' he asked as he fought his way out of the central traffic.

'No. He wasn't a relation of any kind.'

'A close friend then of the gentleman perhaps?'

'A friend, a business friend.'

'Ah.' He cheered up at once and proceeded to give me some man-to-man advice. 'Then the gentleman will probably be wise to sit at the back of the chapel during the service. That way, one is able to avoid at the conclusion too much involvement with the close relatives if one does not wish it. A brief word of sympathy to the chief mourner in order to show that one has been present is all that is necessary then before leaving.'

'I expect you're right.'

I spoke distantly and he got the message. I heard no more about the theory and practice of funeral attendance. Unfortunately, he had made me think.

I had, in fact, been 'close' to Kramer and his wife for several years. But was I a friend? Even a business friend? A more accurate description, and one that Krom may smack his lips over if he wishes, would be 'co-conspirator'.

I recruited Kramer at an Interfiscal Society Congress in Monaco.

A director of one of the big-three Swiss banks had been there to give a lecture on his country's bank secrecy laws. It was a good lecture, neither as defensive nor as plaintive as such public-relations exercises usually are, and I said so to a man from the same bank who had accompanied the director to the Congress. That was Kramer and he was strictly middle management. He was there, I gathered, partly so that the director should be seen to have some sort of ADC in attendance, and partly to latch on to any worthwhile business that might be floating around among the delegates to the Congress.

The director was the man with the personality, the financial mastermind. Kramer had his dignity, too, but it was that of the good soldier. He would rise no higher in the bank hierarchy. He obviously knew this and was, for an otherwise sensible man, surprisingly bitter over what he saw as an injustice. He spoke over-respectfully of his superiors in the bank. The sardonic smile, of which he made much use, was the final give-away. He was, I decided, open to an approach.

I made it over a drink in the Hôtel de Paris.

'What I don't understand,' I said, 'is the nature of the penalties that your secrecy laws impose. They seem so light.'

'You think so, Mr Firman?'

'Well, supposing an officer of your bank, a man in the head office where you work, is approached by a stranger who is – oh, what shall we say? – an agent of the American Internal Revenue Service? Not impossible?'

He restrained his inner amusement. 'It has been known,' he said solemnly.

'Right. Now, supposing the agent offers this officer of yours three thousand dollars for the name of each and every American citizen on your books and the size of his account with you. What is to stop your man accepting?'

'Assuming that our man, as you call him, has management status in the bank sufficient to give him access to the information requested, what would be most likely to stop him, leaving aside the question of how law-abiding he might be, would be the risk he takes if he accepts.'

'A twenty-thousand-franc fine and six months in jail maximum? With a hundred thousand dollars, and most likely much more, in an entirely different bank, what's he got to lose?'

'I don't think our director made it quite clear, Mr Firman, that the penalty of fine and imprisonment you mention may be applied for every single offence proved against the accused and that the sentences would run consecutively. Ten offences against the secrecy law would mean five years in prison, twenty offences ten years.'

'But with zero risk the question hardly arises, does it? Do you mean to tell me that it doesn't happen all the time? I can tell you of a dozen cases. In one, the British Treasury got all they wanted on a dozen accounts for a measly two thousand dollars.'

He was drinking a silver-fizz, a long drink made of gin and egg-whites mostly. Some women like it and barmen usually provide a straw to drink it with to save the lipstick. He now removed the straw from his glass before he answered.

'There is no such thing as zero risk, Mr Firman.' He folded the straw in two and put it in an ash-tray. 'And what I mean is that, for the kind of information of which you speak, three thousand dollars per item is too little by half.'

It was so easy that Carlo became convinced that Kramer was a provocateur and had to be persuaded that there was no risk on our side. Above all, he said, I must not put myself in the dangerous position of pretending to be an IRS agent. I asked Kramer once whether he thought I was from the IRS, and it was the only time I ever heard him laugh. He said that I was not the IRS agent type. I was never able to decide whether he had intended that as a compliment or not. In time he must have arrived at a very clear understanding of the ways in which the information he supplied me with was used.

One thing I can state with confidence. During the years of our association, Kramer received from us, and in my opinion earned, considerably more than that notional one hundred thousand dollars we had discussed in the Hôtel de Paris.

When we reached the crematorium chapel where the service

for Kramer was to be held, the tail-end of a procession of mourners was just mounting the steps to go inside.

'Excellent timing,' said the driver.

In front of the chapel entrance, there was quite a large semi-circular forecourt with cars parked around the rim of it. A black Cadillac limousine with a driver waited by itself in front of the chapel steps. This was obviously the car that had brought the chief mourners and would presently take them away. There was, I noticed, a group of three men draped with cameras and camera equipment huddled by the entrance. I assumed that, since at least one senior bank official would be there to pay last respects to an employee, one photographer would be from the bank's PR agency, with the other two covering or hoping to cover for local papers.

As I got out, the driver showed me where he intended to park. I followed the last of the mourners inside and was allowed by an usher to take a back seat. There was taped organ music – Bach, of course – coming through loudspeakers, and on a stone catafalque at the far end of the chapel was Kramer's coffin. There was a single wreath of flowers on the coffin itself but the floor around the catafalque was covered with wreaths and flowers. I couldn't see my roses but assumed that they would be somewhere there. It is difficult to be certain about numbers, but I would say that the seating capacity of the chapel was a hundred, more or less, and that over half the seats were occupied, mostly by business-suited men. A good turn-out.

The service was conducted by a Protestant pastor and was brief. Then, sliding doors rolled slowly into place, hiding the catafalque, so that the removal of the expendable inner shell of the coffin, the part with the corpse in it, to the functional section of the crematorium could take place unobserved by the mourners. The piped music began again. It went on for about ten minutes. When it ceased, the pastor went to Frieda Kramer in the front row of seats and said something to her. After a moment she stood up and, on the arm of a man who was probably her son-in-law, began to walk slowly back along the chapel aisle. The funeral was over.

The others started to follow. After a bit I joined the procession. A man near me told his companion that one collected an urn with the ashes in it a couple of days later.

Outside, Frieda was standing by an open rear door of the Cadillac as, one after the other, the business-suited men and the women in peculiarly awful hats came to commiserate and express solidarity.

I joined the reception line not because I wanted to but because I saw that she had spotted me. Since there was something I wanted from her, there seemed no point in giving offence by going direct to her apartment without uttering a word of sympathy there in public with everyone else. So, hat in hand, I went forward.

As I did so, Frieda said a word out of the corner of her mouth to the daughter who immediately reached inside the car and picked up something from the back seat. The people still between me and the Cadillac made it impossible to see what it was. The payers-of-respects shuffled forward once more.

I heard a woman mumbling to Frieda something about the deep sense of loss that everyone who had known her dear Johann was experiencing and hastily composed a similar speech for myself.

Finally, the man immediately in front of me sidled out of the way and my turn had come.

Until then, Frieda had been standing there stiffly with her elbows at her sides and both hands clasping her handbag just below her breasts as if she were afraid that someone there was going to try to snatch it. She had looped back her black veil and had her double chins held high ready for the attack. I found myself wondering if she already knew how surprisingly rich she was. As she acknowledged the mourners, you could tell who were friends or family and who were acquaintances she scarcely recognized. With the former she would allow herself to be embraced, with the latter she would incline her head stiffly, ignoring the proffered hands and simply saying, 'Thank you, thank you.' But always, so far, she had kept her handbag pressed against her solar plexus.

It was I who broke the spell. There could have been no question of my embracing her, so I did what the other acquaintances had done and proffered a hand for rejection.

That is to say, I *started* to proffer a hand. It was already on its way to her and the preliminary 'My dear friend' was already on my lips, when her handbag shot outwards and upwards, grazing my knuckles.

She was not, in fact, trying to hit me. She was simply using her handbag to point with so that there should be no doubt in any of the spectators' minds about whom she was pointing at. She was pointing at me and, still pointing, when she spoke.

'This,' she said loudly and clearly to those present, 'is Reinhardt Oberholzer.'

At the same moment several other things happened.

A blunt instrument hit me quite hard on the right shoulder. It was the edge of a brief-case wielded by the daughter. The brief-case must have been the object she had taken from the back seat of their car.

'There are your papers, Herr Oberholzer,' she snarled, and let go of the brief-case.

As I caught it, I heard in the sudden silence that had fallen the clack of an SLR camera shutter. Almost at the same moment, a second photographer let fly with electronic flash. Both of them immediately moved in on me for more pictures.

Krom says that he was right behind the photographer with the flashgun, though I didn't see him. I don't say he wasn't there, just that I didn't see him; and the fact that I didn't see him doesn't surprise me in the least.

He says that I looked stunned. I *was* stunned. I have a mind that is capable of working quite quickly to solve reasonably simple equations and, as I caught the brief-case, my mind had informed me with breathtaking clarity that I was in some danger and – though I deplore the vulgarity there are times when one must be forthright – perilously close to finding myself up shit creek.

After the brief, horrified silence from everyone, except the cameramen who went on taking pictures, I decided that it was time to go. So I put the brief-case under my arm and then, with a little bow to Frieda, turned and walked over to my hired car.

The driver had neither heard nor understood what had happened but he had seen the photographers at work. That meant only one thing to him. He grinned as he opened the car door for me.

'I see that the gentleman is a person of importance,' he said.

'Yes.'

All *I* saw was a police car parked thirty metres away with a plain-clothes man leaning through the window to use the radio. His eyes were on the car I was in and he was obviously calling in its registration number. I have never been in a police identification line-up and been tapped by witnesses as the guilty party, but at that moment I learned exactly how it must feel to be in that predicament.

'Get moving,' I said.

'To Hottingen, Sir?'

'No. There is no need for that now. Just go, but go slowly for a moment.'

He was going slowly anyway down the long crematorium driveway, but I still had to have some time in which to think.

I had been set up by the Kramer women and publicly identified as Oberholzer. Photographs had been taken of me, but of no one else at the funeral. The police had been in on the deal. I had been given a brief-case. It was new and nasty, the kind of thing that could be bought for a few francs at a cheap stationers, and I did not think that there were papers or anything else in it. There had to have been a reason for their having given it to me, but any attempt at analysis of the *kind* of reason would raise questions that I couldn't possibly answer at that moment. I had too many questions to cope with already. The brief-case could wait. The overriding factor was the police involvement. What offence had I committed under the Swiss Criminal Code?

Well, I could be said to have induced a bank employee to breach the secrecy laws. That was an offence. But where was the witness to support a case against me? Kramer was dead. Frieda? She was co-operating with the police, it appeared, but why? And what would her evidence against me be worth in court? Nothing, because I would simply maintain that Kramer had approached me. What lies he may later have told his wife were no concern of mine. On the other hand, the Swiss police had a way of putting a foreign suspect in jail and leaving him there for a few months while the judicial authorities mulled over the possible charges that might be brought against him.

The first priority, then, was to get rid of the car with which I was associated, the one in which I was riding, the one with a driver who would both talk and invent. Next, I had to get out of the canton of Zürich and then out of Switzerland itself as quickly and as unobtrusively as possible.

'We'll go direct to the airport,' I said.

'At once, Sir.'

Only then did I open the brief-case.

I had been right about there being no papers in it, but it was not empty. Inside, were two of those transparent plastic slip-covers that many European businessmen use to keep loose papers or small amounts of correspondence tidily together without too many paper-clips. I knew that Kramer had used them because, on one of the rare occasions after our first meeting when we had met outside Switzerland, he had shown me how he kept the various sets of document copies that he thought I should see, after he had returned the originals to their proper places.

The volume of useful paper – statements of account, buy and sell orders in respect of investments, yearly audit sheets – had been small and those relating to the persons or corporations in which we were interested at any one time he had been able to keep in a single attaché-case. It had been fitted out with one of those concertina-like contraptions that turned it into a miniature filing-cabinet. Into each division went one of the plastic slip-covers. Along the outer edge of each was stuck an identifying strip of Dimo embossing tape with his own code-name for the account holder printed on it.

He had always, for 'sensitive accounts', used blue tape instead of the normal black. Sensitive accounts were those belonging to clients of the bank who had been judged 'unpredictable' – that is to say, marginally insane by ordinary standards – and who remained clients only by virtue of the size of their funds and the voting power of their shareholdings.

Both the empty slip-covers in the brief-case his daughter had given me still had their code-name tapes on them, and both were blue. One was KLEISTER and the other TORTEN. Kramer had had a love-hate thing about cakes and pastry – he had always been overweight – and his choice of blue names had invariably been used as a reminder that, for him, such things were bad. I knew Kleister and Torten all too well. The former was a Spanish land-owner, the latter the founder and board chairman of an American pet-food manufacturing outfit with European subsidiaries. They had in common two things: both were exceedingly rich and both suffered from that kind of obsessional madness which has been called, when it has affected whole families, vendetta or feuding, but which in their case may best be described as acute personalized revanchism. Or, to put things more simply, pure bloody hatred of one particular group of their creditors.

Those two had been the most persistently difficult of the clients monitored by Kramer, and in the end Carlo had felt obliged to discipline Torten. With the Spaniard, Kleister, the threat of discipline had been sufficient because he was more vulnerable. The mere possession of a foreign banking account of the kind he had was a serious offence under the Franco regime. Torten had chosen to do battle with the Internal Revenue Service, but Kleister had paid our fees. On the other hand, Kleister had also employed an expensive international private enquiry agent to identify his 'persecutors'. By one of those strokes of ill-luck against which not even a Carlo Lech can insure himself, the enquiry agent discovered – not because he was all that clever, but because Torten, when drunk, could be monumentally indiscreet – that the method of paying his fees that Torten had been instructed to employ was the same as the one his client Kleister had described. So, he brought the two men together.

Kleister went to America – the terms of Torten's bail pending his final appeal had involved surrendering his passport – and an alliance was concluded. A council of war followed at which it was decided that as soon as they had discovered who we really were and where we were to be found, they would have us killed.

The expensive enquiry agent had hastily washed his hands of those particular clients. Carlo's response, when word of the threat had filtered through to him, had been to demand a bonus payment from Kleister and to furnish the IRS with a supplementary dossier on Torten.

That had been over a year earlier. Kleister had paid the bonus and Torten was serving a prison sentence of three years for tax evasion, having already paid a heavy fine for the same offence. It was expected that he would be put on probation after serving a little over a third of his sentence. We had heard no more talk of our being sought out and killed. It had seemed likely that K and T were at last beginning to behave rationally.

The sight of those two names in that brief-case, though, gave me a peculiar feeling, chiefly one of anger. I had no doubt that they were there with the knowledge of the police. What was I supposed to do? Panic and throw myself under a bus? Tell them what the words really meant? Give them the missing recipes for Kleister and Torten à la Kramer? Beg for mercy? Confess to some unspecified crime? Drop dead?

I shoved the things back in the brief-case and very nearly wound down the window with the idea of throwing the whole lot out. Then I thought of how upsetting that would be to the driver, and calmed down. Anyway, we were nearing the airport.

When we got there I told him to go to the Departure area and murmured something about the urgent necessity of my getting a plane that would, if I changed at Frankfurt or Munich, get me to Hamburg that afternoon. Then I paid him liberally, saw him drive away and went through to Arrivals.

I had to assume that the police had put out some sort of alert on me, so I hadn't much time; but there were two things that had to be done before I started running.

In the Arrivals area among the rental car company desks was one belonging to the company I had used for the car from Frankfurt the previous day. So I told them where the car was on the park, gave them the ticket for it, turned in the keys and paid with my Oberholzer credit card. The police could make what they liked of that. I hoped it would tend to confirm what the driver would tell them, that I was on my way to Hamburg. It would take them ten more minutes or so to find out that there was no Oberholzer booked on any of the flights out to West German destinations.

The other thing I had to do was contact Carlo, or at least get an urgent message to him. I put the call through to Milan with the help of the restaurant telephonist, who didn't mind earning twenty francs for pressing a few buttons on her new PBX. It was just before noon and Carlo hadn't yet gone to lunch. I told him cryptically as much of the bad news as he needed to know at that moment and what I proposed to do about it. I then asked for immediate courier assistance and specified a rendezvous. Carlo did not argue or question, but said that I might have to wait a little. Then he hung up.

I went back outside to the bus stand. There was one just leaving. I rode, as I had done the day before, as far as the Haupt-Bahnhof; but this time I took a train from there, the one that left just after one o'clock for Geneva via Lausanne. There was a restaurant car but I stayed away from it. The man who clipped my ticket between stops along the way might remember me if asked, but there was no point in adding a waiter to the list of those who had seen the last of Reinhardt Oberholzer.

At Geneva the wind was even colder than that in Zürich, but there was no snow and the sun was shining. I walked to the rendezvous, an English tea-room in the rue des Alpes.

I had to wait an hour before the courier arrived. She was a small, stocky Frenchwoman in her mid-sixties, very lady-like but also quite formidable. A few months earlier two louts had attempted to snatch her handbag in the Paris Metro. Both had had to receive hospital attention for severe cuts and bruises before being charged by the police. The cuts appeared to have been inflicted with a razor blade.

She came into the tea-room, paused for a split second to locate me and then beckoned.

'You'd better come now,' she said, 'I'm double-parked.' With that she left.

I had the money to pay my bill ready on the table. All I had to do was get my coat from the rack by the door and follow.

She had a Renault with Paris registration, and the moment I was in the passenger seat beside her she was off. There was no conversation; she just drove, quickly and carefully, until she came to a main crossing where she turned on to the Avenue Henri-Dunant. Unless you drive north or north-east to Lausanne or the Jura, practically every main road out of Geneva will very soon take you out of Switzerland and into France. The Avenue Henri-Dunant joins the road to Annecy and I thought she was going to take that. Instead, she turned suddenly into a big filling-station with an automatic car-wash.

It was one of the men couriers who, when those things began to be introduced, first pointed out what an excellent security device they could be. For the space of about a minute and a half it was possible to cut yourself off completely from the world outside. There was no bug yet invented that could penetrate the defences of a car going through a tunnel of steel and concrete to the accompaniment of the sounds of huge brushes spinning against a car body and water being sprayed through dozens of high-pressure jets.

So, for a time, even though the chances of a courier's car having been bugged were small, all message exchanges of a confidential nature were delivered, whenever possible, inside cars travelling through car-washes. Silly really, because the message either had to be shouted above the din or written out and handed over. After one or two mistakes had occurred because of shouted messages having been misunderstood, the messages were always written and, since no bug was going to pick them up anyway, the use of car-washes for security purposes died out. One of the fringe benefits of the experiment, though, was that for the year or two it lasted, the trade-in value of couriers' cars showed a slight increase.

This courier had written the message out before we got to the car-wash.

Carlo had been brief: *Phase out entire Paris operation, repeat entire, then come and see me soonest.*

Before the car was under the blast of the hot-air dryer she had retrieved the message, put a match to it and mashed the remains in the ashtray.

We left Switzerland and entered France in the early-evening commuter traffic. Nobody on either side bothered with passports or anything else. Once over the frontier, the courier made a right turn and drove via Bourg to Chalon. From there I went by train to Paris.

When Carlo had told me to 'phase out' the Paris operation he had meant that he wanted every possible paper trail cleaned up; and when he had emphasized 'entire' he had been referring to something that not even the couriers knew about. This was that we rented a furnished two-room *garçonnière* in Paris. The object had been to enable me to come and go without registering in hotels. The place was rented on a year-to-year basis so that no question of residence arose. The *gérant* who handled the apartment concerned was a crook, naturally, and I dare say that if he could have found out who the mistress was for whom I kept the place, there would have been a little gentle blackmail. She didn't exist, though, except as a phantom presence represented by half-used make-up containers and scent bottles, some clothing, and a passion for the works of Simone de Beauvoir evidenced by a whole shelf of them, mostly falling to pieces from much re-reading. Melanie had done an excellent job in that case too.

The reason for Carlo's decision to close down the apartment as well as cutting off our accommodation service contacts was clearly based on the fact that all the clients monitored by Kramer had been dealt with through Paris, coupled with the conclusion arrived at by Carlo that everything even remotely to do with Kramer had become a threat to our security and must, therefore, instantly be discarded or neutralized. Why he should have come to that conclusion I did not then know, but it was not the sort of matter one could discuss at length over an open international telephone circuit.

The immediate difficulty was the weekend.

The accommodation service was relatively easy to cut off, because that was paid for quarterly in advance and all I had to do was write them an Oberholzer letter terminating the agreement on the last day of the year. Any communications received henceforth should be reported or forwarded to our Rome office – another accommodation service which relayed correspondence to Frankfurt.

Getting rid of the apartment was not so easy, because the *gérant* headed for the country on Friday morning and was not to be reached again until Monday afternoon. It was no use my just walking out, leaving everything and hoping for the best. A new tenant, or a policeman, or a forensic expert, must be able to walk into that place when I, and my true love, had vacated it and find no trace whatsoever there of any identifiable human beings. In addition, the *gérant* must be utterly convinced not only that he knew all, but also that he was going to have to forgo the kick-backs he had once received from the now grief-stricken Oberholzer and look around promptly for a replacement sucker.

During the weekend all I could do was enlist the sympathy of the concierge's wife, who had used to keep the apartment clean for me, and get her to pack up the belongings of the woman who had betrayed me by going back to her husband, as I could not bear to touch them. Quite an affecting moment it was when I took the suitcases down and put them in the taxi.

I got rid of them by going to the air terminal and buying a one-way ticket to Toulouse. I can't recall the name I used – something like Souchet, I think – but I remember that I had to pay excess when I checked the bags in because of the weight of Simone de Beauvoir; but with one lot of baggage on its way to Toulouse and limbo, all I had to do then was pack up the spare suit and other things I had kept there for my own use, and wait for Monday afternoon.

It was Tuesday before I reached Milan.

Carlo looked down as he listened to my report, and after I had finished he was silent for a while.

Finally, he stirred, heaved a sigh and said bleakly: 'I think we are in trouble, Paul.'

'We've been put to some inconvenience and expense, yes. We may also consider it necessary or advisable to abandon some profitable clients. The Oberholzer cover will have to go, of course. But we've had these spots of bother before, Carlo. No doubt we'll have others in the future. This is a nuisance, yes. Trouble? I don't think so.'

'We have been lucky,' he said contemptuously. Luck was something he had always despised. 'But you miss the point, Paul. I say that *we* are in trouble.'

'You mean our partnership?'

'As it exists now, yes.'

'Carlo, *I* didn't kill Kramer.'

'Did you take steps to enquire into the circumstances of his death?'

'No point. He was dead and his wife and daughter were making it clear that the less they saw of me the better.'

'I wasn't suggesting that you should have enquired from them. I myself enquired through Lugano.'

'And?'

'Kramer was taken ill in his office. He had a heart attack, as you heard. But, an hour earlier he had been questioned at length by men from the police section concerned with offences against the banking laws. The strain on him must have been considerable, don't you think?'

'Yes.'

'What would you have done if you had known what I have just told you?'

'I'd have got out.'

'Exactly. Lugano also reports that, after you had been identified and photographed at the funeral, police visited the hotel where you had stayed overnight. What had you done, Paul? Registered as Oberholzer?'

'Of course not. And there was never any chance of their finding me at the hotel. I paid the bill before I went to the funeral. All I lost by not going back there was some dirty laundry.'

'And the chance of meeting the men who had brought on Kramer's heart attack, surely. How did they know where to go? A few quick phone calls? Nonsense! Zürich is too big a city for that. How did they know?'

I thought back. 'The flowers,' I said slowly; 'it must have been the flowers.'

'What flowers?'

I told him the truth. Telling lies to one another was something we had never done.

'The police must have checked all the cards that came with the flowers,' he said morosely. 'When they found yours they checked the shop that had sent them. That must have narrowed their field of search considerably.'

I could have remarked that it had in fact pinpointed the hotel because I told the girl where I was staying when she had asked me; but enough was enough.

'So,' he went on, 'in addition to your photograph they now have a specimen of your handwriting and almost certainly your fingerprints as well. And you object when I use the word trouble? You amaze me. You have become soft through having so much money, Paul, and, I fear, something of a liability.'

'What do you want us to do? Split up?'

'Obviously you can see the difficulties in that course as well as I can. We both need time to think. Meanwhile, though, you must make yourself scarce. I think you should go to the island for a bit.'

The island he had bought was in the Bahamas. He and his wife loved it, my wife adored it, I loathed it.

'Anna will like that,' I said.

'Your wife will stay where she is,' he said curtly, 'where a wife should be, in the home looking after your child while you are away on business.'

'Very well.'

'I will come over next week perhaps. Then we can discuss the future, without emotion, like sensible men.'

'All right.'

It was a month before he turned up. I was being punished. And it *was* punishment, from the start. You went to New York or Miami and thence to Nassau. Then you took an island-hopping plane almost to the Caicos. Finally, you headed back north again in a stinking little tub that did a grocery round of ten or twelve of the 'Out Islands' delivering mail, gasoline, kerosene and bottled gas along with canned meat, powdered milk, bottled water and other necessities. At one of them, Carlo's cabin-cruiser picked you up and took you still farther off the map.

Anyone who holds the belief that a West Indies island all to yourself except for some servants is bliss, has to be crazy about sun-bathing, spear-fishing, underwater photography, or re-reading mite-infested paperbacks. If he does not enjoy any of those things, the boredom is deadly and complete. In November and December on that particular island it usually rains heavily, too.

Carlo's house was comfortable, I admit; but I had noticed on previous visits that it was still more comfortable when he was there to chivvy the cook and tell her exactly what he wanted done. Even on the day he arrived and was too tired from the journey to do much chivvying, the standard of cooking rose perceptibly. That evening the food was eatable.

Afterwards, he asked me whether I had given any thought to my future role in our partnership.

'My only thought has been that I seem no longer to have a role.'

'I don't agree. I have been observing the progress of the trends in tax-avoidance, not evasion mark you, avoidance. A few years ago, when you said that word, certain names came automatically into mind as tax havens. What were they?'

'Monaco, Liechtenstein, the Channel Islands, Bermuda, Curaçao perhaps, Panama, possibly Switzerland.'

'And now? What names would you add?'

'The Bahamas, British Virgin Islands, the Caymans, the New Hebrides, all sort of odd places. You need a geographical dictionary to find some of them.'

'Yes, and what are we doing about it? Nothing.'

'What would you like done, Carlo?'

'I would like a survey made by someone upon whose judgement I can rely. I cannot go myself because there is too much going on in Europe that I must attend to personally – ' he was at the time preparing the butter-train caper – 'but you will know what to look for and be able to assess the prospects. We should consider investing where it is necessary to safeguard our position against later competition.'

We discussed it for four days, then left the island; he to go back to Milan, I to scout the Caribbean before flying west to the Pacific.

I never saw Carlo again.

Krom was fidgeting with the file in his hand and I knew that he couldn't wait to get at it.

'I have a suggestion, Professor,' I said.

He looked at me suspiciously. Was I about to play some last-minute trick?

'Yes, Mr Firman?'

'I suggest that we now adjourn this gathering until tomorrow morning. Naturally, when you have read what I have written there, you will have questions to ask arising out of it. Would eight-thirty here be too early for a breakfast meeting?'

I looked at the other two to see how they felt about it, but Krom was not consulting them.

'I agree,' he said firmly. 'Eight-thirty.' He got to his feet a bit unsteadily, pulled himself together and remembered his manners. 'I must thank you for an excellent dinner. Good night, Mr Firman.'

Adroit use of the backs of the rest of the terrace chairs enabled him to steer a reasonably straight course into the house. Connell gave me a sly look.

'What was there about that white wine, Mr Firman?'

'Nothing, except that it was served too cold.' I stood up.

They took the hint and also said good night.

Yves and I finished our wine. Melanie said that she was going for a walk.

After ten minutes or so, Yves and I went up to the loft over the garage. There was silence from Krom and Henson; they were reading to themselves. Connell was making sure that his copy of the material was going to remain available for future use by reading it to his tape-recorder. Only an occasional grunt of surprise or doubt showed that this was the first time he had been through it. It was interesting to hear it all being read out – truth, rubbish, and half-truth – all as if it were some sort of Holy Writ.

I was listening, fascinated, when he was interrupted by a knock on his door. He switched off the recorder and went to answer the knock.

Dr Henson's voice said: 'Sorry to bother you, but I've just had this note from Krom shoved under my door. Have you had one?'

'Wanting a pre-breakfast meeting in his room at seven-thirty? Yes, I've had one.'

'Do we accept?'

'If our lord and master wants to make sure in advance that he asks all the questions and leads for the prosecution, why not? He'll take charge anyway.'

'I suppose so. I heard you talking. What were you doing? Recording it all on that thing?'

'Yes. Why?'

'Since you've been allowed to get away with it, how about giving me a copy of the transcript?'

There was a pause, then: 'Dr Henson, may I call you Geraldine?'

He made it sound like a joke and that was the way she treated it. 'Don't be a fool, Connell.'

'Gerry?'

'My friends call me Hennie, and I assure you that, as a nick-name, it's quite appropriate. Good night again.'

'Good night.' The door closed and he went back to his dictation.

It was at that moment that we heard stumbling footsteps on the bare, wooden stairs up to the loft.

It was Melanie and she was looking flustered. She was also out of breath.

I signalled to Yves to turn the sound down. 'What is it, Melanie?'

'I went for a walk you know, and I *think* – only think mind, Paul – that this place may be under surveillance. Cars stationary on both upper and lower roads. It's difficult to be certain at night, but I thought you'd better know.'

CHAPTER SEVEN

All three of us had a bad night, but at least Melanie and I got some sleep. Yves had none.

About an hour after Melanie's warning, he returned to the listening post over the garage to report his preliminary findings. Since he had spent most of the hour crawling between bushes and being bitten by insects, he looked a mess.

He borrowed my handkerchief and dabbed at some larger scratches on his hands and arms while he explained how he had got them. There had been parked cars on both roads, as Melanie had said. He had seen one on the lower road by the garden gate and two, one on each side of the main entrance, on the upper road. The latter were both at distances of about a hundred and fifty metres from the entrance. It had been in the oleander thickets along the upper boundary fence, where he had gone to take a closer look at the two cars outside, that he had run into trouble. At some time, the chain-link boundary fence had been damaged by a car or truck going off the road after taking the bend too fast. Concrete posts had been put up to prevent a repetition of that particular accident, but the gap in the fence had been temporarily blocked with a barbed-wire entanglement which no one had bothered to remove after the fence had been repaired.

Still, he had been able to get a look at both cars by waiting for the headlights of the occasional passing car to show them up. Each had two persons in it, though of what sex he had not been able to see, and each had a local Alpes Maritimes 06 registration. Each also had its front wheels on full left lock. In addition, both on the lower road and the upper, the places at which the cars were parked were where the roads widened slightly. If you wanted to park on those roads for any ordinary reason – you wanted a smoke and a chat, you wanted to neck or eat a sandwich – those were the places you would logically choose. Not as logically, perhaps, if you wanted to mount a simple surveillance operation against the Villa Lipp because your view of it would be so restricted; but if you wanted to prevent any of the occupants leaving the place without your knowing or, if you wanted to prevent their leaving by car altogether, you were in exactly the right position. You had the lower gateway under observation if they tried leaving on foot, and with your two cars on the upper road you could foil any attempt at a get-away by road simply by starting up, driving four metres and then standing on the brakes. If you kept your ears open for the sound of engines from below, you could have the road blocked on both sides of the entrance before the escaping cars could reach it.

And, of course, we, or rather Melanie, could be imagining things.

I would not have blamed Yves in the slightest if he had thought that possibility as being one at least worthy of discussion. In fact, he did not even hint at it. He appeared to respect Melanie's instincts as much as he respected his own.

'One parked car would be of no importance,' he said; 'two would be an interesting coincidence. Three parked cars at this time and in those places and postures I will not accept as explainable in terms other than those of surveillance until I hear that explanation. Then if I am able to snap my fingers and say, "Of course, how stupid of me," I will go to bed. Meanwhile, I must continue to ask obvious questions. Who are they? Who are they working for? What are their orders? Why are they behaving as they are?'

'There's one other explanation you might try on yourself,' I said. 'This is a rich neighbourhood. Oh, I know there may not be much in the way of valuables in the Villa Lipp, but one or two of the pictures ought to be marketable. The owner is known to be absent. They could be a gang casing the joint.'

'Then why aren't they doing so? Why are they just sitting there, all six of them, where they can see so very little but can so easily be seen? And why six? Looking a house over before deciding to rob it is a one-man job and he comes in the day-time with credentials from an insurance company. One is forced to conclude that these people mean to advertise their presence, that they mean to be seen.'

'Perhaps they're selling protection. There used to be a gang along this coast who'd strip your house of everything, including the carpets and the kitchen stove, if you didn't pay them.'

This was ignored. Yves had turned to Melanie again.

'I might not have gone for a walk,' she said doubtfully.

'But they did see you?' he asked.

'Oh yes.'

'Did they see that you had found them interesting or suspect?'

'I doubt it. I can't be sure.'

'Then I think,' he said, 'that we should see what happens when they know that they have been spotted.' He thought for a moment. 'Patron, either they are very close in because they intend to do something violent almost at once and will not allow anyone to escape, or they are applying psychological pressure to make us leave.'

'They might be out there to make us run, but I don't think they could be meaning to do anything violent unless they knew that, apart from your revolver, we aren't armed. There aren't enough of them. It really comes back to your first question. Who are they?'

'I could go and ask them,' Melanie said.

She does sometimes say stupid things. 'All you'd get would be a blank stare,' I said.

'I think,' said Yves, tactful as ever, 'that there may be a simpler way of letting them know that we are aware of them. We could just close the entrance gates. They can be seen from where the cars are parked.'

'Do they close? With all those shrubs growing through and around them, I would say that nobody ever closed them. They're probably rusted open.'

Yves tried not to look reproachful. 'When we moved in, Paul, oiling the hinges was one of the first things I did. The lower road gate also.'

'Sorry. Can they be locked? I know there are plenty of ways of getting into this place, but if one were going to be violent, charging in by car with a bunch of armed hoodlums would be the most intimidating.'

'There is a chain in the garage. I could arrange things so that undoing the chain from the closed gates would be a noisy operation.'

'Then do that, please. The lower road gate, too, if you can.'

'That has a lock and a key.'

He went off. Presently I heard the distant sound of the front gates closing and then a rattling of chain. Almost immediately afterwards, Melanie, who had been sitting by an open window in a room nearer the driveway, came to report that, on the gates being closed, both cars had at once started up and been driven away.

After Yves had dealt with the lower road gate, he returned to report that, on his opening and slamming it noisily before locking it, the third car had also left. He had one additional item to report. Just before he had done his opening and slamming act, he had heard someone's voice. It had been his impression that the voice had been coming through a small loud-speaker of the kind you would expect on a miniature walkie-talkie set, and that the set had been in the hands of the car passenger. He had glimpsed for a moment a short, chromium-plated whip-antenna, of the kind used on such sets, sticking at an angle through the passenger-side window space. The words he had heard the voice uttering had been: '. . . now. Okay. Out.'

The three words had been spoken in English, though by what nationality of English-speaker he firmly declined to guess at. All that seemed likely was that he had been hearing the end of a conversation between an occupant of one of the two cars which had been on the upper road and the passenger in the single car on the lower. The rest of the conversation had taken place while he had been moving from the main gate down to the one in the wall.

'So,' he concluded, 'as soon as we let them know that we are on to them they leave. What is the next move, Paul?'

'You could get some sleep. We all could.'

'Someone must keep watch in case there is an alarm to be sounded. You have our guests to deal with in the morning and so you must be rested. It had better be me who mounts guard. Melanie could relieve me for an hour, perhaps, so that I don't begin to see things that aren't there.'

'All right,' said Melanie. 'At two o'clock, say?'

'Okay, Paul?'

'Very well. Divide the watch between you as you like. I shall have to take a sleeping-pill now, I'm afraid, but I shall set my clock for six-thirty unless either of you wakes me before. I'll also monitor our guests' get-together at seven-thirty. If anything of interest happens outside, one of you will let me know, eh?'

In spite of the pill I had a poor night.

This wasn't because of the watchers outside the villa; at least, not directly because of them. Yves had brushed aside what I had said about protection racketeers, but that was the explanation I had settled for in my own mind; and I had done so because, at that point, I had believed it to be the most likely one.

There *are* such racketeers operating on the French Riviera, and, as their demands are not really exorbitant, it is, especially for foreigners, simpler to pay up than to take moralistic stands and suffer the consequences. The latter can be tiresome as well as costly. A German I know who has a house on Cap Ferrat, but who refused to pay a few thousand francs for protection, had the whole place emptied while he was away, the gang having brought in removal vans to do the job. The police received the owner's complaint sympathetically but without surprise. These things sometimes happened. After such forceful demonstrations the protection people obviously had much less trouble collecting dues, even from hard cases like my German friend. Though I could see that a man of Yves's temper might well find it unacceptable, my assumption that, with the cost of everything going up, it had become customary to put the bite on summer-season tenants as well as owners seemed reasonable enough. I quite expected to receive by mail the following morning, in addition to the good news that a protection service was available, a subscription form to fill in and return with my cheque.

So it wasn't worry that kept me awake, but my old trouble: the inability to wait before trying to solve a problem until all the available facts are in. Strange as it may seem, the problem that nagged, and went on nagging long after its solution had ceased to matter, was that of figuring out how best to use the presence of external enemies to get Krom and his witnesses out of my hair.

At seven, I went down to the kitchen, complained to the cook that indigestion from the dinner the night before had kept me awake, and appropriated the pot of coffee she had made for her husband and herself. Along with it, I had one of the petits-pains just delivered by the village bakery. The husband told me that during the night some unauthorized person had shut the outer gates. I said that it had been I who had shut them in order to keep out stray dogs. Obviously, and not surprisingly, he thought I was off my head.

I had one cup of coffee in my bedroom and took a second through to the garage loft.

Krom's seven-thirty meeting started more or less on time. Connell was the first arrival.

After they had exchanged greetings and told one another how tired they had been and how well they had slept, Krom said: 'I chose this room for our meeting because it is free of listening devices.'

'You know that for a fact, eh, Professor?'

'I have examined the whole room carefully myself.'

'And didn't find a thing. Ah, well . . .' Connell left his doubts at that. 'Do you think we could get a cup of coffee if we rang that bell there? Until I've had coffee in the morning, I don't feel altogether . . .'

He broke off as Dr Henson arrived. More good mornings. She, too, had slept well.

Krom said: 'Coffee would be desirable, but I think it is more important that we get down to business before we meet Firman. I take it that you have both read this paper? Yes? Then, I would like first to hear your general views on it.'

'On the whole true? On the whole false? Or on the whole half-and-half?' asked Henson.

'That for a start, yes.'

'I say half-and-half.'

Connell said: 'So do I, but I can't make up my mind which half is which. I'm hoping for help there from you, Professor. The part about the actual confrontation at the crematorium must be true because you were there and saw it. But how did you actually come to be there? It would help a bit if we could now be told, I think.'

'It would indeed.' Henson's voice.

Krom cleared his throat. 'This will all, of course, be in my book, but I think I can trust you two.'

He could have said right out that, if they dared repeat as much as a word, he would arrange slow and painful deaths for them, but his tone conveyed the message plainly enough.

Henson uttered a strange sound which was probably an involuntary giggle quickly masked by a cough.

'That's what we're here for, Professor,' said Connell. He managed suddenly to sound like the sheriff of Dodge City in a television western.

Krom hesitated, unsure how to take the performance. Then, deciding to ignore it, he went ahead. 'I had obtained the permission of the Federal judicial authorities in Berne to look into the background of a number of cases of blackmail or, to be more precise, extortion, involving persons and corporate entities who banked in Switzerland. These cases had been brought to my notice by an international private enquiry agent who has sometimes made use of tips I have been able to give him. This time, as well as giving *me* information he thought I should have, he sought advice. These cases of extortion in which he had been asked to act, sometimes in a defensive role, sometimes as a negotiator, covered a period of three years or so. The cases all had two elements in common. They involved tax evasion or breaches of exchange-control regulations under a variety of national jurisdictions, and they involved an organization calling itself a debt-collection agency with branches in most of the countries of Western Europe. Unfortunately, he had had little success to report to his various clients. Given a defensive role, there was nothing he could do except advise them to pay up. Told to negotiate, he encountered nothing but blank walls. He realized quite early on that he was dealing with a front, a façade, in this collection agency, but that those behind it were both well informed and impeccably disciplined. His clients, on the other hand, were mostly, as he put it, "at sixes-and-sevens" from the moment they became victims until they eventually decided to pay. None of them was ever able to deny the allegations of evasion or breach of regulations, at least not for long, and only one or two had the will or gall to fight anyway. There are always a few men and women who prefer fighting to surrendering, even in a cause they well know to be defective, even when they know that they cannot win or draw, that they have to lose. One can only marvel at such lunacy.'

It might have been Carlo speaking.

For a moment or two I found myself wondering what sort of a man Krom would have become without the burden of that overweight super-ego he carries around. What would have happened to all the 'anarchy' of which he is so afraid? Might he not have become one of our less scrupulous competitors?

An agreeable day-dream, but still a day-dream; he was on again about the troubles of his fat-headed friend, the private enquiry agent, who had unwittingly caused me so much inconvenience. I made myself pay attention.

'It was these diehards among his clients about whom he was specially concerned. And not simply because well-publicized losers were, if known to be his clients, bad for business. He feared too – as we shall see, rightly – that such unbalanced persons could easily decide to take the law into their own hands and commit criminal acts of violence. He wanted the whole matter properly investigated by some responsible police authority. *He* could do nothing more. The essential initiatives, he thought, could only be taken in Switzerland, though obviously not by him. With my academic connections there I might do better.'

'And you *did* do better.' Henson's longing for coffee was also now becoming audible.

'A little, yes.' Krom was savouring every moment. If his witnesses thought that they were going to hurry him along with polite proddings they were much mistaken. 'A little better,' he repeated, 'but *only* a little. Both the judicial authorities and the police had certain ideas on the subject of these extortion cases which I found it difficult to counter. They were aware, of course, that there were leakages of information from several of the so-called big banks and from some cantonal and private banks as well. These they were naturally determined to locate and stop, because Swiss law, *their* law, was being broken and the guilty must be found and punished. In so far as the information I brought them about specific leakages helped them to that end, they were interested. But when it came to talk of organized extortion, they lost interest.'

Henson let out a squeak of incredulity. 'The Swiss lost interest in an extortion racket?'

I was grateful to her. It was the question that had popped up instantly in my own mind.

'They didn't believe that it existed,' Krom explained. 'They thought, at that point, that I was merely trying to prove a pet theory. They said that, in order to do so, I was confusing two quite different anti-social activities. One wasn't even a crime. They were referring to the traffic in titbit information that was then being carried on with various US government agencies. For instance, there was the racket worked by those who sold luxury goods like furs and diamonds to rich Americans. In places such as London, Paris and Antwerp, the persons who did the actual selling often earned extra commissions by informing on their clients to the US Revenue as soon as the goods were sold. When a client was caught for smuggling, the informer received a percentage of the fine as a reward. Not nice, or kind, or good for business in the long run, but not illegal. Besides, it didn't happen in Switzerland. What they were interested in, as far as I was concerned, were the bank employees who allowed themselves to be suborned and the wicked men and women who did the suborning. Among those whom they were particularly keen to arrest and convict in the last group were, I am afraid, Dr Connell, agents of the United States Internal Revenue Service, which, with the blessing of the American Congress, had made no secret of its hostility to Swiss secrecy laws. Those agents, with their big money bribes, were then considered the prime villains. It had been thought at one time that Oberholzer might be an important IRS man, or possibly even CIA.'

Connell laughed. 'Oberholzer, an American government man? With *that* accent?'

'You have accepted a Secretary of State with a German accent,' said Henson crisply. 'I see nothing extraordinary about Oberholzer being thought of as a possible IRS or CIA agent.

Firman's accent – and I take it that we *are* talking about the same man – isn't contemporary British anyway. I'd call it expatriate mid-Atlantic. The same could be said of his vocabulary. If he had a Hungarian–American accent you wouldn't find the CIA notion in the least odd.'

'True.'

'And we are not talking about what, in retrospect, *we* may think, but what the Swiss knew and believed from time to time,' Krom reminded them. 'I said that not all the victims of the Oberholzer organization were prepared to submit. Among those who chose to fight were two clients of the enquiry agent – one Spanish, the other an American – whose cases had certain common denominators. Both had their accounts in the Zürich head office of the same bank. At least three other known victims also banked there. The other common denominator was the method used by the so-called debt-collection agency.'

'The one of whose methods Firman so much disapproves?'

'The one of whose methods he *says* he disapproves, yes, Dr Henson.'

'I didn't understand how that worked anyway,' Connell said. 'I made a note to ask him a question about it. How do you make a pay-off that can't either be watched or traced?'

'A good question,' Krom said; 'I will add it to my own list of clarifications required. Anything else?'

'The part played in the incident by Frau Kramer and the daughter bothers me,' said Henson. 'What were those two up to? Assisting or obliging the police? Getting back at Oberholzer for corrupting the good Kramer? Covering themselves against the charge that they had compounded a felony? That identity parade after the funeral doesn't sound like a good police idea. Why didn't they go through with the original plan and get Oberholzer out at the apartment? Then, he couldn't have run, not the way he did anyway. And what was the idea of giving him those plastic slip-covers with the code-names on them? That makes no sense at all.'

'Oh yes, it does, young woman.' Krom chuckled. 'And, as it happens, the sense that it makes ties in with your questions about Frau Kramer's place in the affair.'

I listened intently to the next bit because I was just as keen to know the answers as Dr Henson, more perhaps; the same questions had puzzled me at the time and, at intervals, ever since.

'Frau Kramer,' Krom went on, 'could not, I think, have ever

made her husband a very happy man. She was one of those women who, at the same moment as they complain that their men do not climb higher and faster on the ladder of success, hang on to their coat-tails to make the climb more difficult, perhaps impossible. They are moral saboteurs, you might say. To be specific, Kramer had reached, as do many men in big organizations, his natural level of maximum attainment without either understanding why he would go no higher or recognizing and accepting his own limitations. In this refusal to accept he was abetted by his wife. But when it came to Oberholzer's approach, things were undoubtedly different. Ambitious women of Frau Kramer's type often have broad streaks of self-righteousness in them. They desire the ends but reject the means. Or, rather, they do not wish to hear about the means.'

'As if Lady Macbeth were to say that she didn't want to know,' remarked Connell.

'Pardon?' There was a short silence while Krom grappled with the allusion. 'Well, yes, perhaps. But I am sure Frau Kramer *did* know of the Oberholzer arrangement. It was just never openly discussed, so that she could say, with her hand on her heart, that she had never been told.'

'Hence her and her daughter's dislike of Oberholzer,' commented Henson.

'The daughter's attitude was determined much more by the adverse effects on her own marriage and position of respectability that a criminal scandal would have had. After Kramer's second coronary attack in the hospital, and once she knew that he was unlikely to survive a third, Frau Kramer's chief concern was for the money her husband had accumulated. All she wanted to know was whether or not she would be allowed to inherit it. Naturally, the police were in no hurry to enlighten her. Equally, she was in no position to ask questions about her husband's private fortune without admitting that she had been a party to concealing the criminal acts that had made it. The daughter would probably have been prepared to abandon the money, or the prospect of it anyway. The mother could never have done that.'

'Didn't they have a lawyer to advise them?' Connell enquired.

'Of course. But what use is an honest lawyer when what you need is a dishonest one? No, she chose instead to give co-operation to the police. This, the police accepted gratefully, but remaining stiffly correct, without allowing their gratitude to show even for a moment.'

'Were you present at the original Kramer interviews?' asked Connell. 'I mean before he had the heart attack.'

'Oh no. That would have been quite improper. I was kept informed though. I was also there when the decision was made to allow Kramer's encoded telegram to be sent, in the hope that it would bring Oberholzer, his pay-master, to Zürich. As we know, it did.'

Dr Henson sniffed. 'Even such a stupid woman as Frau Kramer must have known that the police couldn't try and convict a dead man. If he *embezzled* that money from the bank and it could be proved that he'd embezzled it, even without his being there, things might have been different. As it was, the police had no case against either her or Oberholzer, and probably no claim to any money there might have been lying around.'

'You would be surprised,' said Krom, 'how great an appearance of power a senior Swiss policeman can convey just by looking absolutely serious. Except in one thing, Frau Kramer did exactly as she was told. The exception was in the matter of where the identification of Oberholzer before witnesses was to take place. She refused, practically at the last minute, to have Oberholzer in her apartment.'

'On what grounds? He must have been there before, she must have known him before, or how could she have identified him?'

'She said that until the police had told her that Oberholzer was a criminal she had not known.'

'*Had* the police told her?' Connell asked.

'Of course not. Challenged on the point, she maintained that the interest of the police in Oberholzer had been enough to tell her. It was obvious now that Oberholzer was a criminal. Her husband, who had known the man slightly, had been questioned about him, but had known nothing. Now, she was being questioned. She also knew nothing, but would assist the police in identifying the villain, anywhere but in the apartment sacred to her husband's memory and to her own memories of their happiness together.'

She hadn't *needed* a lawyer, I would have said.

'There is still the question of the code-names,' Dr Henson was reminding Krom.

'I am not forgetting it, young woman. My good relations

with the Swiss authorities obviously do not depend alone upon academic associations. When I am given information it is given on the understanding that the arrangement is reciprocal. I pick their brains, and they pick mine. In this case I helped them discover the real names of the two enquiry-agent clients, the Spaniard and the American, who had defied, or tried to defy, the Oberholzer organization.'

'Kleister and Torten, you mean? Oh, I see. You matched the code-names with the details found by the police in Kramer's private files.'

'Precisely.' Krom did not like Connell stealing his thunder like that, as he went on to make clear. 'But the question asked was not "how did the police get the names?" but "why did they give them to Oberholzer?". I will tell you. It began as a joke.'

'Huh?'

'Yes, I agree. A somewhat macabre joke but a joke nevertheless. My police friends had made enquiries about the then whereabouts of Kleister and Torten and found that Torten, the American, had, since his release from prison on probation, been enjoying his freedom in Florida. Kleister, his old ally, had recently joined him there. What was more, he had joined him not just for a brief holiday, it was understood, but on a permanent basis. Both men were widowers and, in spite of their costly troubles, both were still wealthy. It seemed likely that they might be preparing to resume operations against the Oberholzer extortionists. For two men of their ages with money to spend and a cause that they could think of as a crusade, what could be a more pleasurable way of passing the time than finding a man they both hated, and then arranging for his murder?'

'Yes,' said Connell, 'I can see that there'd be room there for loads of laughs.'

'I remember my police friends saying in their droll way that, if Oberholzer were going to be murdered, they would prefer that the crime be committed outside their jurisdiction because they would not have their hearts in the investigation. Someone suggested that they might give Oberholzer a warning of the danger by mentioning Kleister and Torten to him verbally. Later, when the confrontation was moved from the Kramer apartment to the crematorium, they put those marked folders with the code-names in the brief-case because they intended to stop and interrogate Oberholzer at the airport when he tried to leave. Their object, since they could not prosecute him, was, first, to intimidate him, second, to trip him if they could into some damaging admission about his relationship with Kramer and, lastly, to make it clear that he was considered an undesirable alien who would be well advised to stay out of Switzerland. They thought that the code-names in the brief-case might prove useful as an element in the interrogation. In fact, as we now know, he eluded them at the airport, though more by luck than by ingenuity. However, the warning of the code-names did not, it seems, go unheeded. He is still alive. I wonder about Kleister and Torten. Perhaps he knows. Perhaps I will ask him.'

'Well,' said Dr Henson, 'one thing's explained. I can see now why he objected so strongly to that field kit of Langridge's that I tried to smuggle in. With one set of fingerprints on record in Switzerland against an old identity, the last thing he'd want would be another set of prints, one attached to his current identity, circulating internationally. The two would almost certainly be matched. I must say, though, that he doesn't strike me as a man who has been labouring for years under a threat of death from a pair of half-witted tax-dodgers. If anyone's had the pleasurable time, I'd say it was he. Most regrettable no doubt, but my guess is that he doesn't know what a twinge of guilt feels like and that he has always thoroughly enjoyed himself.'

'He will not be enjoying himself for much longer, my dear. Of that I can assure you. As for us, I think it is time that we went down to breakfast.'

I was already seated at the table on the terrace waiting for them when they came down.

They all told me, in response to my polite enquiries, how comfortable they had been and how well they had slept, thank you, at the same time managing to make it clear that solicitude would get me nowhere and that, now they were rested, the sooner we got down to business the better. None of them asked how *I* had slept.

The coffee was not nearly as good as the earlier pot I had had, but they drank it appreciatively and ate their croissants. Krom did not wait to finish his, however, before going into action.

'We have all read with interest your first paper,' he said, spraying crumbs with the sibilants, 'and, while we find some of it useful, we all agree that it is far from satisfactory.'

'Full of holes,' Connell explained.

'And doth protest too much,' said Henson in her Langridge voice, 'against accusations that, as far as I know, haven't yet been made.'

'I'm sorry,' I said. 'Perhaps you should all try reading it again, and more carefully.'

Krom swallowed the rest of his coffee and reached for more. 'I myself have read it three times,' he said; 'and with each reading it has seemed less and less illuminating, except in one respect.'

'I am relieved to hear that my failure has not been total.'

'Sarcasm will not help you. What is illuminated so brilliantly is your determination to disclaim all responsibility for anything and everything concerned with this large-scale criminal activity except the humble part you played in it as a kind of superior, but none too competent, messenger boy.'

'Incompetent, yes. Humble? I sincerely hope not. The last thing I want to do is give false impressions.'

'Flippancy is even more tiresome than sarcasm, Mr Firman, so let us have no more of either. We at any rate are serious, and –' he whipped a folded sheet of notes from his shirt pocket – 'to begin with, I propose to ask you a series of questions.'

'As long as you understand that I may decline to answer those I don't like, go ahead.'

'You said that you had prepared a number of discussion papers and that you could be questioned on them. You did not say how many papers, only that they would cover your activities as Oberholzer for a period of three years. My first question is, what is the scope of the activities described? How is the material as a whole organized?'

'It's mostly anecdotal, I am afraid, like the first paper. So much is hearsay, of course. I can't help that.'

'No, not if you persist in trying to convince us of the existence of senior partners whose orders you meekly obeyed, of separate groups of evil men who did any dirty work that your leader might deem necessary. If you could abandon that pretence it would be helpful.'

'I said that I would try to answer your questions, Professor, not debate your assertions. You asked about the scope of the activities described in the other papers. I have tried to answer your question. Dr Connell complains that the first paper has holes in it. Do you agree with him?'

'I go farther. For me, it is in all respects unsatisfactory.'

'Not exciting enough do you mean, Professor? Not enough murder and mayhem?'

Connell tried to take over. 'He means that there's too much shadow and not enough substance. For example . . .'

Krom stopped him with a look.

'Dr Connell was about to raise a question which we all seem to have asked ourselves. Accepting for a moment the fiction that you were never a principal, only an agent, what about this debt-collection agency that you say was or is employed by your employers to extort their fees? Where is it based? How does it work? Please tell us all about this remarkable institution, Mr Firman.'

I smiled. 'That is the subject of one of the papers you were asking me about.'

'An entire paper?'

'It was a complex organization. And please note that it no longer exists. It was originally based in Luxembourg, with branches in Hanover, Rome, Paris and London. It went out of business years ago.'

'Soon after I saw you in Zürich, in fact.'

'The two events were not related, Professor. In any case I'm sure you would prefer to read what I've written on the subject rather than have it piecemeal.'

Dr Connell stuck his neck out again. 'Does what you've written about explain how you, that is they, got the money without the victims' knowing where it went?'

I waited expectantly for Krom to intervene, but this time he let the question through without protest. No doubt he was curious himself.

'I don't think I understand,' I said. 'By victims you mean debtors, I take it.'

'Call them what you like. I call them victims. Now, how did it function? I guess the process of collection would start with a letter saying that the Luxembourg Finance Corporation, or whatever you called it, had taken over the debt and so kindly pay up without further ado or get clobbered. Right?'

'*I* didn't call the agency anything, and the Lech-Firman partnership was very far from being its major client. Its name, by the way, was Agence Euro-Fiduciare.'

'Meaningless, but looks respectable I guess. Okay. Now, how about that first move?'

'It would be of the kind you described. It sometimes produced results.'

'But not often?'

'Not often, I would say, no.'

'So then you got tough. Yes, I know. *They* got tough.'

'When the agency purchased the debt from us they would naturally receive an account of the services we had rendered the client. This account would include a complete statement of the client's financial situation according to our records.'

'Everything *not* on the record back home, you mean?'

'A *complete* statement, as I said. This would include all assets, however held and where held, sometimes together with a summary of the last official tax return made by the client to his domestic revenue authority. Where exchange controls had been evaded, copies of the relevant documents would be provided instead. If, say, from some fringe of the sterling area, money had been transferred to finance a transaction in real-estate or gold, this would be documented as a reminder.'

'Oh boy!'

'At the same time new instructions about the way the debt was to be paid would be issued.'

'I'll bet they would. That was one of the holes I wanted to see filled in. How was it arranged so that Kleister, and others like him who strongly resented and resisted being screwed, didn't know, when they'd finally decided that they *had* to pay up, who'd been screwing them? Their first thought would have been you as the tax-consultant. Right?'

'The partnership always dealt at arm's length.'

'You mean through cut-outs, I take it. Okay, so when things got tough, they weren't able to find you. Right? But they *could* find Euro-Fiduciare, eh?'

'The agency had its own methods,' I said austerely. The pieces of real meat I had to give were not going to be tossed over in response to the first yaps.

Connell didn't like being told to wait. He tried jumping for it. 'So do kidnappers-for-ransom,' he said; 'have their own methods, I mean. So do blackmailers and extortionists. But there is a moment all of them have to face. That's the moment when they pick up the money. Okay, they tell the mark to leave it in the middle of a desert in used twenties and a transparent bag with "Don't Fence Me In" painted on it in red, but they still have to go there and pick it up. That's when things usually start going wrong. Their helicopter has engine trouble or the pilot turns out to be a gamma-minus navigator who puts down nowhere near the loot. The police have been brought in by the victim or his family after all. The bills have been chemically marked and are, used or not, traceable. Some cop or FBI man hidden behind a rock there watching the pick-up gets bitten by a rattlesnake and yells. A gun goes off accidentally. Anything and everything can happen. How did the agency make sure that, whoever else got hurt, they didn't?'

'In my paper on the subject I give examples to show how the whole thing worked.'

I stopped there and poured myself the last of the coffee. Henson was sitting motionless with an unlit cigarette in one hand and her lighter poised in the other. Krom and Connell were both leaning forward expectantly. All three were now, metaphorically speaking, and indeed almost literally, slavering.

'Tell us about it,' ordered Krom.

I shrugged submissively but with no thought of obeying. I knew that if they were allowed to gobble up all the food that had been prepared for them, just because the smell of it had reached their nostrils, there would be none left for tomorrow.

Yes, that's how I was still thinking. I still hadn't realized even then that, for me as host at the Villa Lipp, there wasn't going to be a tomorrow.

'It isn't really all that difficult, Professor,' I said. 'Look at it this way. The popular jargon now calls those services Carlo gave the old black marketeers, "laundering money". All the debt-collection people did was set up another sanitary process to suit their own special needs. In my paper on the whole subject, I call it, "waste-disposal". Laundered money is money cleansed of its associations with the pockets it has been in. Waste-disposal money just disappears into a sewage system, one with so many outfalls that no particular deposit can ever, once it has left the sink, be followed or traced to its ultimate destination.'

Krom looked sour. 'Your metaphor is appropriately anal, Mr Firman, but I didn't ask for metaphors. I want specifics, facts of the kind that a banker or a police accountant can get his teeth into.'

'And facts you shall have, I said. 'You'll find them all in my next paper. For now, though, you'll just have to be satisfied with paper number one and metaphors. Unless, that is, any of you would like to try solving the money-transfer problem that seems to worry Dr Connell. As a technical exercise, I mean. I don't mind giving friendly advice.'

Krom's lips tightened and he remained silent; but Connell wasn't so fussy about his dignity.

'What sort of friendly advice?' he asked.

'You know that banks all over the world transfer money to one another by means of what's called the "tested-cable" system? You do? Good. Then you'll also know that crooks have used tested-cables to swindle banks, often via their computers, out of millions of dollars which have proved to be untraceable. Well, if crooks can make untraceable transfers, think how much easier it must be when the payers are thought of as honest men and the payees are simply debt collectors.'

Henson made a cooing sound. 'What an absolutely *brilliant* idea!' she exclaimed.

'No, Dr Henson.'

'No what, Mr Firman?'

'No, I will not be flattered into accepting with only a token murmur of protest the suggestion that using tested-cables was my idea. It wasn't. The head of the collection agency thought it up.'

'Oh? And who was he?'

I wasn't falling for that one either. 'He? It may have been a woman. I don't know, Doctor.'

Krom gave his witnesses meaning looks. 'You see, Mr Firman is a slippery fellow. Do you know that, in Brussels, he actually had the impertinence to tell me that most crime is committed by government, and that delinquency is a function of the class struggle?'

'Oh dear!' Dr Henson choked slightly on the cigarette she had at last lighted. 'That sounds more like cut-price Trotskyism than anarchy.'

'It's double-talk,' said Krom, 'and I told him so. Quite unnecessarily, of course, because he is intelligent enough to know that himself.' He turned his attention to me again. 'We have heard the divided responsibility claim *ad nauseam*, Mr Firman. It is not accepted. You thought everything up. *You* were at the controls of the extortion machine you call a collection agency as well as those of the so-called tax-consultancy which kept it fed with information. Your version of the Oberholzer conspiracy is nothing but a pack of lies. What do you say to that?'

'That you are impolite, Professor, as well as mistaken.'

'Would you prefer me to call it the Firman conspiracy? What does the name matter? However you choose to masquerade now, you were the figure around which it all pivoted. Yours were the controlling hands, yours the organizing mind. That is the central, the essential, fact.'

'Central and essential to your case it may be, Professor. That does not make it a fact. To a man of your academic standing and repute I hesitate to use harsh language in a discussion of this kind, and at the breakfast table too, but I must tell you, and in front of your witnesses, that at the centre of your case is what used to be known as an *idée fixe*. Nowadays, it's called a hang-up.'

He said something loudly about my personal character. What he said was probably quite unpleasant and it may even have been true; but, as he said it in Dutch, I can't be sure. I was about to ask him to translate, when we were interrupted by Melanie.

She did not come out on to the terrace, but called to me from a drawing-room window. I turned and she beckoned. Obviously, what she had to say was not to be overheard. I excused myself and went to the window.

'What is it?'

'Yves wants to see you. He didn't want to show himself because he was rather dirty. He's up in his room.'

'Is it urgent?' I didn't want to leave just then in case they thought I was running away.

'Yes, Paul, I think it is urgent.'

'All right. You go over and tell them that I'll be back in a minute.'

I went up to Yves's room. He had been in the shower and was drying himself. He greeted me with the glum phrase that had begun to irritate. Only this time he varied it slightly for emphasis.

'*Nous sommes vraiment foutus,*' he said.

'Just tell me what's happened. I'll draw my own conclusions, Yves.'

He gave me the mournfully threatening look that had reminded Connell of a termite inspector he had known. 'I have not forgotten that I am under your orders, Patron.'

'Good. What's happened?'

He smiled disagreeably. 'What has happened is, Patron, that I am becoming more nervous every minute. Have you been all over this house?'

'Most of it. Why?'

'Then you will know that on the attic floor there are two windows from which, if one keeps moving from one to the other, one can in daylight see practically all the land surrounding this house.'

'Yes.'

'At sunrise I moved up there to keep watch with binoculars. At about six-thirty, I saw something I didn't like. It was on that piece of land beyond the lower road to the right of the bay.'

'You mean the headland with the tamarisks on it?'

'Those small trees? Yes. There are bushes too. There was a person there.'

'That land isn't on this property. It belongs to the commune, I think. What sort of person?'

'The first thing I saw was a flashing of light of the kind you get when sun reflects off lenses, but it was difficult to see because the flashing was coming from behind the bushes.'

'Someone keeping the same sort of watch on this place as you were keeping from the attic?'

'That's what I *thought*. I also thought that it must be an amateur, someone who didn't know enough to keep in the shadow of a tree to avoid sending reflections of the sun. So, when Melanie brought me coffee, I told her what I had seen and went down to take a closer look at the watcher. I thought too that perhaps I might frighten this amateur a little.'

'And?'

'It wasn't an amateur there and I didn't frighten anyone but myself.' He put on some clean undershorts and a pair of slacks as he continued. 'What I had seen flashing were the bottoms of two new, shiny cans of tomato-juice cocktail mixture. They had been taped together and hung by black thread from a tree branch so that they were just behind a bush. Attached to the tape was a cord going back through the other bushes for perhaps thirty metres. This served two purposes. It kept the cans pointing in this direction, and it enabled the person hidden at the other end to move the cans slightly as they would have moved if they had been hand-held binoculars.'

'So you followed the cord back and found that the person had gone.'

Yves sat on the edge of his bed and, reaching beneath it, picked up a shoe. 'That is not all I found.' He held up the shoe. 'Please look at that.'

It was a blue canvas espadrille of the kind which used to have plain rope soles but which now have soles of crepe rubber. What was odd about this one was that there were extensive burn marks on it, the sort of marks that you would expect to see if it had been worn to stamp out the embers of a brush fire.

'What happened?'

'I followed the cord to where it ended along a narrow path and then I trod on this.' He reached under the bed again and pulled out a square of charred plywood the size of a chess board, with a long bolt attached to the centre.

'What is it?'

'The pressure plate of a very small, insultingly innocuous, incendiary bomb.'

'What do you mean by innocuous? It burnt your espadrille.'

'If they had wanted to, they could have blown a foot off. This bolt broke a small tube of sulphuric acid when I trod on the board. All it ignited, judging from the smell, was a very small amount of chlorate of potash mixed with sugar. I was glad I was wearing socks though.' He took the shoe from me and poked a finger through a burn spot. 'They were just having fun, you see. But, Patron, I don't like practical jokes of this sort being played at my expense.'

'You didn't see *anybody*?'

'No one in particular. The motor cruiser arrived, the big one that anchors off the sand beach near the point.'

'At *that* time in the morning?'

'They like a swim before breakfast. I've watched them through the glasses. A crewman lowers the dinghy for them to go to the beach. One man, two women. They swim in the morning and early evening every day.'

'Did you see anything unusual apart from the booby-trap? Or *hear* anything, like a getaway car starting, for instance?'

'Patron, have you been across the road there?'

'No.'

'All you can see from where I ended up is part of the bay, the part with the little pier where we could bring in a launch for water-skiing, if we had a launch. All you can hear are the sounds of waves breaking on the rocks below and, very faintly because of the bushes, passing traffic on the road. And I will tell you this. After that little *pétard* had gone off I wasn't listening very carefully to anything. I have had time to think, however, and come to some conclusions if you would care to hear them.'

'Of course.'

'We were told last night that we are blown. We have now been told for a second time, and given one or two additional bits of bad news.'

'For instance?'

'That we are not just a little blown, but completely. They know, for instance, how we are organized, Patron.'

'Explain, please.'

'As I understand it, you are here to give information to this Krom and the others. No, I am not trying to pry. I don't want to know more. It's better the way it is. But you are the key figure, the one who is giving out the information to these educated half-wits. Those outside can only want to stop what is being done inside. At the moment, they *seem* to be trying to do this by scaring us into breaking up the meeting. Why? They can only wish to make us run so that they can more easily dispose of you.'

'By "dispose of", you mean kill, I take it. Aren't you imagining things?'

'You're the one with the information, Patron. How else are they going to stop you?'

'You said that they know how we are organized. What do you mean by that?'

'There are *at least* six of them and they are not amateurs. That we know for certain. Six pros cost money. You don't use them only to play practical jokes. Patron, they *knew* that I would see those reflections and go down to find the source of them. *I* and I alone.'

'What makes you so sure?'

'Because if they had thought that there was any chance of you're going down, they would have left something a little more important for you to tread on. They would have left something that would have killed you.'

I thought for a moment. He was wrong, and I could have told him why.

In Italy during the war I had seen a lot of booby-traps and the effects on those who hadn't made the right allowances for them. There was one trick the Germans had played that I have never forgotten. The hand-guns that their officers and senior NCOs carried had been much prized by Allied troops. The forward area people used to sell them for two or three hundred dollars a time to the chairborne warriors back in the lines-of-communications and base jobs. When the Germans found this out, they used to leave Lugers or Walthers behind when they moved out of a village and booby-trap them with grenades. The Allied engineer patrols got wise to that soon enough and used to carry lengths of cord with hooks on them. Then, when they saw a pistol left behind, they would put a hook on it and pay out the cord until they found a nearby foxhole to take cover in. Even if the pull of the cord set the grenade off, the pistol was usually undamaged. That game went on until the Germans found out, from some prisoner they took I suppose, what was happening. So then they used a bit more ingenuity. They'd still leave a pistol lying around, but it was no longer the pistol that they would booby-trap. Instead, it would be that convenient, nearby foxhole they'd fix; and not just with a grenade; they'd plant an S-mine in it that could cut a man in half. That's why Yves was wrong. If I'd seen a cord there leading invitingly into the bushes, I'd have been off, scared shitless, scrambling back to the house as fast as I could go. Once you become booby-trap conscious, or get land-mine jitters, you stay that way for life.

I decided to keep all that to myself though. My convenient protection-racket theory had, since I had left the terrace and Krom's indignation a few minutes earlier, ceased to make even a little sense. Yves was on edge, and now so was I. The immediate needs were calm and as much sense as we could bring to dealing with a difficulty we didn't yet understand.

'What would you advise?' I asked.

'That we should stop covering for certain persons who aren't here and start thinking of our own skins again.'

I didn't ask him who it was he thought we were covering for, because I preferred not to know that he had guessed correctly.

'By doing what, Yves?'

'That's a very conspicuous car we came in.'

He was quite right; a white Lincoln Continental with Liechtenstein plates is a conspicuous object; but he knew that the one in the garage was part of our cover story as tenants of the Villa Lipp and I didn't immediately read his thinking.

'What of it?'

'You asked for my advice. I say we forget our guests, take their small car, just the three of us, and make a quick break for it. Then we hole up in the safe-house and hire help to take care of the opposition.'

'How do you know that there *is* a safe-house?'

'With Melanie planning a set-up, there's always a safe-house.'

'I'll bear the suggestion in mind, but I don't like it at the moment. We know too little. Supposing the opposition turned out to be a government agency. You couldn't hire help to take care of that.'

'It isn't the French. They wouldn't play practical jokes. On their own ground, as we are, they'd have a complete frame-up ready – drug-smuggling or arms-dealing charges, something like that – and we'd be in police hands while they took us to pieces one at a time until they had what they thought they wanted. If it's a foreign government outfit operating with French permission, the last thing they'd want is the sort of trouble we could organize.'

'Maybe. I don't like the jokes any more than you do, but they bother me in a different way. I can't help feeling that whoever's out there must be waiting, hardly able to keep from laughing aloud, to see how soon we start walking like good boys into whatever stew-pot he's got waiting. We've let him know that we're not asleep. Before we do anything more positive than that, I want to know who's paying him or them and for what.'

'Perhaps Melanie was right after all. Perhaps we should try asking them.'

'The first persons we ask are the ones downstairs on the terrace. If any of them knows anything that we don't, it's time we found out. Besides, even if none of them knows anything new, they'll all have to be told what's going on. I don't fancy any more meals on the terrace. We make too easy a target. You'll probably be up again tonight, Yves. Why don't you just get some rest now?'

'Thank you, Paul. Later perhaps. At the moment I would prefer to hear the answers you get downstairs.'

'In that case you'd better bring your shoe and that other piece of evidence. Krom may be more inclined to believe you than me.'

Krom was not inclined to believe either of us.

At first all he did was cackle with laughter. That ended in a fit of coughing, then, the spluttering and hawking over, he went into a stern-father act broken by giggles whenever his own wit proved too much for him. Not until he had realized that his witnesses had ceased to be even mildly amused did he simmer down sufficiently to deliver a coherent verdict.

'No, Mr Firman,' he declared sonorously; 'yesterday we were tired, and so let you off lightly. Today, things are very different. Today, you will have to lie with much more skill if you expect to be taken seriously, much less believed. Diversionary tactics as elementary as these – sinister watchers lurking in the bushes armed with walkie-talkies, binoculars, booby-traps and bombs – will not help you for an instant. I beg you not to waste our time with them. Let us return to Oberholzer and the account you give of the ways in which the material he gave you was used.'

I glanced at Yves and Melanie to see how they were taking it. Melanie was wearing the expression of mindless impassivity that was her normal response to boredom or stress; and I had expected to see Yves sunk in his habitual gloom. To my surprise, and concern, his sallow complexion had gone a shade lighter and his lips were pinched in a peculiar way. It took me a moment or two to realize that he was in a towering rage.

As he caught my eye he stood up suddenly and looked down at me.

'Patron, I apologize. I came down, against your advice, because I expected to hear some questions answered or at least discussed. I now see that I underrated the difficulties.' He pointed at Krom. 'This old bag of piss and wind is too much in love with himself to be able to think, and these others only lick his feet. If you still think you can persuade any of them to listen to sense, that's your affair. I don't think it's worth the sweat. I think, with respect, Patron, that we should now take seriously the suggestion I made upstairs, and simply warn those you are covering for that from now on they'll have to take their own chances. These people here don't matter. We do. It's up to you, though, and I'm still at your orders. You told me to get some rest. That's what I should have done at once. So, that's what I will do now.'

He started to walk away. It was Henson who stopped him.

'Mr Boularis?' She spoke sharply but with a rising inflection, as if she were asking a visitor who was expected but who had not yet been introduced to identify himself.

He paused and half-turned his head.

'Mr Boularis,' she went on quickly, 'I'm sure that you're tired, but I would be grateful if you would repeat the explanation you gave us about this pressure-plate device.'

Yves turned round now to look at her suspiciously.

'I know,' she added, 'that the explanation you gave ought to have been sufficient, but for someone who doesn't know much about explosives it was a little puzzling.'

Yves answered her with his eyes on Krom. 'I'm surprised that with so much bleating going on you heard anything. What don't you understand?'

'Well, for instance, you described the thing as having been arranged so that the long bolt in the centre of the board acted as a sort of plunger going down into a small bottle holding the incendiary material. The end rested on a tube containing sulphuric acid which it broke when you trod on the board. Is that right?'

'That's how I reconstruct it from what was left.'

'Thank you. What I don't understand, though, is how hard it would be to make and set up such a thing.'

'Quite easy, if you have the stuff.'

'You mean if you know in advance that you're going to make it and roughly when you're going to use it?'

'Yes.'

'How long would it take to make and how long to install?'

Yves walked back slowly, deciding how to answer her. For a few delicious moments I was able to forget about Krom. One of our guests had suddenly started talking sense and the whole atmosphere had changed. Melanie, I saw, had felt the same. I wondered how long the improvement would last and concentrated on looking as if I hadn't noticed it.

'To fill a glass tube with sulphuric acid and seal it would be tricky,' Yves said. 'The best way would be to use a well-greased rubber cork with a hole in it for the bolt to slide through and break the bottom of the tube. You'd also have to see that the bolt was clear of the acid, or it would simply be eaten away. The whole thing would have to be carefully handled.'

'It wouldn't be something you might decide to do on the spur of the moment?'

'No. With those materials you would not wish to be hurried. An accident could be most painful.'

'So this device was made yesterday or before?'

'Certainly.'

Connell could no longer let Henson score all the points. 'How about siting the ambush? How about digging the hole for the device and doing the installation?' he asked. 'Would you do that at night?'

'Not unless you could use bright lights to see by.'

'So this harassment, or whatever you want to call it, must have been planned well in advance?'

Krom snorted. 'Of course it was planned well in advance. Mr Firman plans all his special effects well in advance. Think how carefully he planned to wave his magic wand and turn the unfortunate Carlo Lech into Beelzebub. Planning to conjure up, out of thin air, this band of goblins and evil spirits to frighten the children into being good, and obedient, and uncritical, would be easy by comparison.'

They all looked at me except Henson who was still watching Yves.

'What would *you* say to that, Mr Boularis?' she asked. 'Why should Professor Krom or Dr Connell or I, or anyone else who has read what Mr Firman is prepared to admit about himself, accept anything he now says at its face value? You see the difficulty?'

'What difficulty?' Yves asked. 'I am a skilled person who recognizes and respects managerial intelligence. What old piss-and-wind there is accusing him of is planning to play pointless, and therefore unintelligent, practical jokes on *me*!'

'And why shouldn't he?' demanded Krom. 'He is perfectly capable of hiring other skilled men to do just that.'

'Of course he is,' said Connell; 'but why should he? I mean, where's the mileage in it?'

'In your very own words, Dr Connell,' retorted Krom. '*That's* where the mileage is. You and Dr Henson are now arguing Firman's own case for him.'

'Professor, that's not quite true. You say he's trying to fool us. Okay. That's likely enough. All we're asking is, "why should he try fooling us *in this way*?" Where does it get him? To a point where he can say that he's sorry, folks, but he's being harassed by enemies so we'll just have to take rain-checks? He can't be as dumb as that. He's still over a barrel. You just take what papers he has now and re-convene at a later date. So there has to be another explanation. Either he's stalling for some reason that we haven't yet figured out, or there's an explanation that *he* hasn't yet figured out.'

They looked at me again.

'Quite right,' I said. 'I haven't yet figured it out. If Professor Krom can contain his disbelief for a moment or two, or at least keep it inaudible, I'd like to try again.' I glanced at Yves. 'Either sit down or go to bed, Yves. Don't just stand there, please.'

He sat down again.

Krom sighed heavily. 'Now comes the rabbit out of the hat.'

I ignored him. 'Nothing can be figured out,' I said, 'until we know who is playing these tricks. The *why* can be answered later. Yves, Melanie and I have the advantage of knowing for certain that I'm not the trickster. Perhaps you too will accept that as true for a moment. The only other things we can be certain of so far are, first, that all the elaborate security precautions we took have been penetrated and, second, that whoever did the penetrating wants us to know it beyond all doubt.

As I say, we'll have to leave the "whys" for later. Let's start with the "who?". Yves doesn't think that we're dealing with a French agency because of the methods being used. I agree with him. It could be, though, a foreign agency, German or British say, acting with consent on French territory.'

Dr Henson smiled slightly. 'Unless Dr Connell has some CIA connection that we don't know about, that leaves the Professor and me as those possibly responsible.'

'I'm afraid so.'

'Nonsense!' said Krom and wagged a finger at me. 'Either you have a bad memory, my friend, or you are hoping that I have. Yesterday, you told us that if any of us had been under surveillance we would have come no nearer to you than Turin. You had us carefully watched all the way. How could we possibly have led what you call a "foreign agency" to you, even if we had been prepared to act against our own interests as scholars as well as to breach our security pledges? If we did so unwittingly, then it can only have been because your vaunted supervision of our journey here failed. That is if it ever existed.' He grinned at Connell. 'You commented that it must have been expensive. If it had existed, I dare say it would have been – *very* expensive, *too* expensive. Composing a Firman fairy tale about it would be an easier operation and an infinitely cheaper one.'

The look Connell gave me was hostile. 'How about that, Firman?'

I motioned to Yves. 'Tell them.'

'About the cost?'

'About what was done.'

'Ah.' He cast his mind back. 'Well, there were several good, clean checkpoints. The first stage, you will remember, was air from Amsterdam to Milan and then, by rented car, to the Palace Hotel in Turin. Only Professor Krom knew even that much in advance. At the Turin hotel, you were still clear. The next appointment was waiting, addressed to the Professor. It was for lunch the following day at the Tre Citroni restaurant in Cuneo. There, the sketch-map was handed to you in a sealed envelope with the bill.'

'Aren't you forgetting?' asked Connell; 'we all knew the night before that we were going on to that restaurant in Cuneo for lunch the following day. Any one of us could have blown that.'

Yves nodded. 'You could have, yes. That was why you were given the opportunity. If any one of you had taken it there would have been no sketch-map at Cuneo. But none of you did take it. None of you made a telephone call either that night or in the morning except to order from room service. None of you left letters or notes behind you at the hotel to be picked up later. Overnight your car was examined carefully for beepers. The road to Cuneo is mostly through flat, open country of the kind which makes tailing difficult to conceal from alert observers. You were not followed then, nor when you took the road over the mountains beyond Cuneo. At the French frontier you were also clear. Nevertheless, as you began the final descent to Nice an extra precaution was taken. There was an accident on the road just behind you. Only a minor affair, but it blocked the road for nearly ten minutes. By then, you were either well lost in the late-afternoon Nice traffic jams or already out of Nice and heading along the lower road in this direction.'

They thought it all over for a moment or two. Connell was the one who broke the silence.

'Murphy's Law?' he asked.

I shrugged.

'What did you say?' Krom was suddenly on the edge of his chair. 'What law is this?'

Connell smiled kindly. 'Sorry, Professor. I was using an American folk-expression, a sort of joke proposition called Murphy's Law. It holds that, in all human affairs involving advance planning, anything than can unexpectedly go wrong will invariably do so.'

'What has that to do with Firman's precautions?'

'Well, it means that even if this security leak he's trying to trace was caused by one of our group, it could only have been caused by some outlandish mishap, like a tail, who hadn't for some reason been spotted earlier, accidentally picking us up again outside Nice. Personally, I think it more likely to have been the French police. A little thing like an accident blocking the road wouldn't have stopped them radioing ahead.'

Henson objected instantly. 'It simply doesn't work, you know. Suppose we'd been heading for a high-rise apartment in Monaco. Where were they going to put the booby-trap they'd been working on? If there really is anyone hostile out there, they couldn't have found this place by following us. They *must* have known in advance.'

'And since,' said Krom, 'we have no evidence that there is anything out there more hostile than the insects who bit Mr Boularis we may conclude that Mr Firman, after a lifetime of successful chicanery, has at last lost his grip. In his anxiety to get rid of me, he has accused us, his guests, of doing something to place him and his employees at risk, something that, *on his own showing* mark you, none of us could possibly have done. I find it very sad.'

Such leaden fatuities ought not to have angered me, but they did. My inner anxiety must have been telling on me. Worse, the invitation to reply in kind proved quite hard to refuse. I started to tell him to save his tears, but stopped myself only just before the words were out.

'No one so far is losing his grip,' I said instead, 'and no one has been accused. As your host, I am simply telling you that the arrangements for our safety and security here seem, in spite of all the care taken, to have broken down. It was my duty to warn you, so I have done so. There will be no more meals served at the round table by the balustrade over there. So far, these people have only annoyed us. However, they may have plans for more aggressive acts. Whether they have or not, I don't intend to present them with sitting targets.'

Krom gave the balustrade what was supposed to be a terrified look. 'I am amazed,' he said, 'that you don't call in the police.'

'If it becomes necessary to do so, Professor, I shall leave you to handle the reporters. As a sensational news story, the siege of the Villa Lipp should be just the thing for newspapers like *France Dimanche*. I dare say your colleague Professor Langridge would find it enjoyable, too. Meanwhile, if you want to take a walk and inspect the booby-trap site, by all means do so. With luck, the enemy can try playing a practical joke on you. That would make the walk more interesting and, when you get back, you'll be able to tell me how nearly you were killed. Meanwhile, I shall continue with my enquiries. You will be kept informed, of course, of my progress.'

The idea of sensational publicity had shaken Krom sufficiently to confine him to a sneer. None of them made any move to leave, however, and for several moments we all just sat there staring at one another.

Then Connell spoke. 'Going to be a bit difficult for you now, isn't it, Mr Firman?'

'Difficult? I don't think I understand.'

'I mean that looking for leaks now is going to be difficult. Now that we've been eliminated, you've sort of run out of suspects, I'd say.'

I smiled at him. 'Dr Connell, I said I was going to continue with my *enquiries*. I have no further need of suspects.' I paused to let him interrupt if he wanted to. He didn't. 'With you three disposed of, the mystery, or part of it anyway, is solved. I know now that the leak could have come from only one person.'

Melanie broke the silence that followed by emitting a little gurgling laugh.

They turned to look at her.

'Mr Firman means me,' she said.

CHAPTER EIGHT

Krom and Connell both looked startled. Henson was the only one amused by that odd laugh.

She offered Melanie a cigarette. 'Is Mr Firman denouncing you?' she asked.

'Oh, I don't think so.' Melanie declined the cigarette with a graceful hand movement. 'It's just that, having reminded himself that he and I are the only persons who were supposed to know in advance that this was to be the meeting place, he now finds it convenient to think aloud.'

'He doesn't pause to wonder if he himself could conceivably be the culprit? Two persons were supposed to know in advance, but only one of them could possibly have leaked the information – you. Can that be right?'

'Yes, of course.'

'Of course? You mean that you really accept that verdict or that you have no choice?'

'Oh, I accept.'

'The master is infallible?'

'Naturally.'

Melanie was displeased with me, and her innate bitchiness, usually well hidden beneath the surface appearance of bright-eyed stupidity, was beginning to show through. Had I not intervened then, she would soon have been talking nonsense of a less acceptable kind.

'You mustn't take Melanie too seriously,' I said. 'She has a weakness for ornate overstatement. I am always warning her against it, aren't I, my dear?'

Her instant, over-anxious nod aroused Krom's paternal instincts. 'Are you always warning her, too,' he demanded, 'that, as your secretary, she must expect to be used as a scapegoat?'

'No, Professor, I am not. No such warning would be necessary. As an acknowledged expert in the organization of undercover work, Melanie Wicky-Frey knows a great deal more about the selection and management of scapegoats than I do.'

Henson started to say something, but I shut her up by raising my voice as I went on: 'For your further information, she chose this place herself, composed all the cover stories we are using, and advised me on general security matters at all planning stages. What she is complaining of now is that I am not treating her as if *she* were infallible. I don't blame her. As you people should know very well, experts always tend to award themselves immunity from criticism.'

Krom looked expectantly at Melanie, ready to welcome and swallow whole any denials of my dastardly charges she cared to make. When all he drew from her was an empty stare, he sighed and returned heavily to me.

'So, when you introduced her as your secretary, that was a lie.'

'Don't be absurd, Professor. Why should I need a secretary here? I was surprised you didn't ask. The idea's so obviously preposterous. Actually, Melanie is a wholly special kind of PR expert.'

'A wholly special kind of liar, you must mean. It's hard to believe, though, that there could be anyone more special in that field than yourself.'

Yves cleared his throat. 'Patron, I thought that these people were going to take a walk. If they are not, I suggest that you and Melanie talk in the dining-room. You won't be overheard there.'

He meant that the dining-room wasn't bugged. 'Good idea,' I said and stood up, motioning as I did so to Melanie.

'Ah, no!' Krom was levering himself out of his chair. 'I refuse to be dismissed in this way.'

'No one's dismissing you,' I said; 'but it's clearly impossible to talk seriously here.'

When I started to move, he stood in front of me. As I made to go round him, he grabbed me by the arm.

Connell was on his feet instantly, bleating, 'No, no!' as if I had been about to hit the old fool.

I said to Melanie: 'Go ahead. I'll see you in the dining-room.' Then, I looked at the hand on my arm as I had looked at it the night before when it had been on Melanie. Like other compulsive arm-grabbers, Krom seemed not quite to realize that his habit could be objectionable. When I had to jerk my arm free, he looked cross, as if I had interrupted a chain of thought, and then wagged a reproving finger.

'Your statement,' he repeated, 'was a lie, and, as you now admit, a pointless one. You *have* admitted that, yes? Very well. We don't yet know what kind of man you are, but the evidence so far suggests that, although you may not be a criminal psychopath in any of the generally accepted senses of the word, you possess many of the characteristics often attributed to the so-called moral defective. Still, for the present we shall have to be content with an *ad hoc* classification, such as – oh, what shall we say? Variegated delinquent, perhaps?' His eyes sought the witnesses' approval. 'There is, in any case, one thing of which we can now be certain. Our delinquent is an inveterate as well as a resourceful liar.'

I was weary enough to lose patience with him.

'Where,' I asked, 'did you get this extraordinary idea that you have a prescriptive right to be told nothing but the truth? Does it come up through the seat of your academic chair? Or is there some tatty sociological saint who once taught that all who have to submit to your questioning are, by divine decree, automatically on oath? Of course, that must be it. And what happens when the poor souls perjure themselves? Obviously, burning at the stake would be too mild a punishment. Instead, we are slowly and brutally classified! Right, Professor?'

Connell chuckled, but Krom only nodded encouragingly. 'Slowly and brutally? Yes, I expect you're right, Mr Firman. And so?'

'And so, the only time you'll hear a truth from me is when it happens to suit me better than a lie or when none of the available lies is good enough to stand inspection. Truth games are dangerous, even for children. All I'm playing for is safety, safety for myself and my partners in what you choose to call crime.'

Krom beamed. 'This candour is *most* refreshing.' He switched the beam to Connell and Henson. 'Clearly, this tantrum of Firman's is a direct response to my diagnostic stimulations. We are making progress. If, as he says, defects in his cover arrangements have come to light, now might be the moment for us to probe his defences in depth.'

Although the witnesses could scarcely have failed to notice that Krom, with his third-person plurals, had suddenly conferred colleague-collaborator status on them, neither gave any sign of having done so. Knowing Krom as they did, they probably recognized that, from him, such courtesies could only be slips of the tongue.

'I agree,' said Connell; 'it's time we had a look at some of the nuts and bolts of this set-up. If he expects to persuade us that he's basically incompetent, he's going to have to produce something more convincing than a hunk of charred plywood.'

'Bearing in mind,' said Henson, 'that, according to Mr Firman, Wicky-Frey is the nuts-and-bolts expert, I would feel that we should concentrate first on her.' She flashed her appealing smile at Yves. 'Now, what do *you* think, Mr Boularis?'

She had succeeded with him before; but that had been half an hour ago and he had learned a lot since. He glanced at her casually and then returned to watching the small birds that were hopping about beneath the chairs and feeding on the crumbs from breakfast.

After a moment, he said: 'I *now* think, Madame, that you are *all* full of piss and wind.'

In the silence that followed this further diagnostic stimulation, I left to join Melanie in the dining-room.

I found her sitting, wreathed in tobacco smoke, at the head of the long table.

She rarely smoked except after dinner. The ashtray in front of her and the lighted cigarette in her hand were announcements of her need for relief from the intolerable pain of my displeasure. They also warned me that if I were not instantly apologetic and extremely kind to her, she might be driven to commit ritual suicide by inhaling.

As I had nothing to apologize for, and no intention of being kinder than I felt just then, I made no move to sit down. I have always found it easier to keep my temper and to remain civil when standing.

Besides, my assumption was that, having had ample time in which to review the entire cover operation step by step, Melanie now knew where the leak had occurred, how it had occurred, and who might have had the impertinence to exploit it. Once I knew those things, I expected to be able, having shrugged away surprise and exasperation, to start figuring out ways of capitalizing on my misfortunes. Krom's description of some of my tactical thinking as 'octopus ink' had not been all that fanciful; and, yes, even in the dining-room on the morning of that second day, I was still thinking in terms of using the jokers outside the gates to neutralize the jokers within.

Call it the last minute of innocence.

'Well?' I asked.

Melanie stubbed out her cigarette. 'I've drawn a blank, Paul. No, let me finish. I've been over it all as thoroughly as I know how, and several times, even while that horrible little lesbian was pretending to be nice to me. I've nothing to tell you that you don't already know. Nobody was told except you. *Nobody!* And only the two communications codes were issued.'

'Why two? What two?'

She sighed patiently. 'Brussels office has one in their safe for emergency use. Usual safeguards. The other was requested by Mr Yamatoku in London. That was properly authorized. Standard procedure was followed in both cases.'

That was it. I suddenly felt quite peculiar, as if someone had stuffed wool in my ears and started to inflate my head with a foot-pump. Because I knew, almost at once, that if I didn't sit down I would soon fall down, I gripped the back of the dining-chair nearest to me, eased it around slightly and sat.

Melanie says that I succeeded in making the move look as if I had simply become tired of standing, and that at the time she hadn't had any idea that I was nearly passing out. Most gratifying. In future, though, it may be advisable for me to carry one of those special medical ID cards with multi-lingual notices on them. I mean notices warning that the bearer has an implanted pace-maker or an allergy to penicillin, or is diabetic, things like that. In my case, the card should read, *Bearer May Refuse To Lie Down When Dead.*

'You say that the issue of this second communications code was properly authorized? What do you mean by that?' I asked her. 'Authorized by whom? *I* didn't authorize it.'

'It didn't have to be authorized by you, Paul. Surely you know that? The cypher requesting confirmation was telexed to London and the cypher confirmation was duly received.'

'You didn't think to ask me why London had a need to know our communications code for this operation?'

'Certainly not. Both the request and the response to Brussels' double-check conformed strictly to the rules. It was all standard procedure. Why should I have asked you or anyone else? What are such procedures for if not to be acted upon?'

I could see then exactly why Mat had thought her a security risk. He had spotted something that the Gehlen organization had missed. Once a security procedure had been established, she would cease for ever to question any particular use of it. She was insufficiently paranoid.

Our communications code system had been devised originally by Carlo as a means of controlling the courier network when normal routines were interrupted. If, say, a courier had to divert, or be diverted, from his standard movement schedule, the first thing he did when he ceased moving was to call in or cable, via one of the answering services, a sixteen-figure message dressed up to look like a price-range quotation. Decoded, the figures would give the courier's cover name, the area of the country in which he was located, and a telephone number at which he could be reached. After Carlo's death, of course, when the Symposia Group came into being and the old buccaneering ways had long been discarded, we had no need of courier networks or any other sort of covert-operations hanky-panky. If the decision had been left to me, I would have abolished the communications code system. A modern business ought not to need such toys. It had been Mat's idea that we should keep that particular one.

The reasons he had given for our doing so had looked shrewd as well as sound. The code drill was simple, it had worked well for years, it was cheap to run and, above all, it encouraged personal initiative in our field men. It told them, in effect: 'Don't call us – except to leave your number, or tell us that there's something too big for you to handle on your own – we'll call you.' His real reason for retaining the drill was that it enabled him to keep tabs on Brussels, and all those rich Symposia pies he had his fingers in, without anyone but me knowing of the connection. Even upper-echelon personnel like Melanie, who knew that Frank Yamatoku in London was a number-two man to someone, didn't know that the someone was Mat Williamson.

For Mat, with our communications code and Frank to make the long-distance calls for him, pin-pointing us at the Villa Lipp would have been no trouble at all. If he had been in a hurry and had had access to an Alpes-Maritimes area phone-book with Yellow Pages, the trace job could have been done in an hour.

I now knew, then, who had been responsible for the presence of those objectionable people outside the house. It only remained to find out who they were and what orders they had been given. It says something, I suppose, about the quality of my former relationship with Mat when I record that, faced with an urgent need for answers to what the pit of my stomach told me were life-or-death questions, my first thought was still to ask *him* for them; to ask, moreover, knowing with reasonable certainty that I would receive. The answers wouldn't be wholly untrue, of course, because Mat has always preferred to deal in ambiguities and half-truths rather than straightforward lies; but I knew that, if I listened carefully and ignored the literal meaning of the words, the kind of background music used to make them sound convincing would probably tell me a lot of what I needed to know.

Melanie, still the injured party awaiting a well-earned

apology, was studying her nail-polish. I sat back and clicked a thumb and third finger gently until she looked up.

'Go back outside,' I said. 'Tell them I have to make some phone calls. I'll let you know what's happening as soon as I know myself.'

She stood up. 'What about the second file?'

'We'll give it to them after lunch, perhaps. Not that it matters now, but the quieter they can be kept the better. I'll see. On the subject of lunch, we'd better have it in here.'

'There's the space beside the swimming pool. That isn't exposed.'

'All right.'

'We can dine there too. It's a long way from the kitchen but dinner tonight'll be cold anyway.'

'Why?'

'It's the Quatorze today. The servants want to get finished early and go to the local fête. They asked. I said they could.'

When we occupied it, the Villa Lipp was still on a telephone exchange that hadn't been fully integrated into the international direct-dialling system. This meant that, although we could be called direct by someone dialling from another country, we ourselves could initiate foreign calls only through an operator. You needed patience to keep dialling until one answered.

In that large house there were only three telephones: one in the entrance hall with an extension in the main bedroom, and, also in that bedroom, the one I was occupying, a phone on a second line with no extensions. I used this second one, having checked it for obvious bugs before doing so. There would have been no point in my calling Mat's London hotel. Even if he had been in and available, he wouldn't have taken an international call through the hotel switchboard. It took me twenty minutes to get through to the London cut-out.

The man on duty spoke very slowly and distinctly as if he distrusted the telephone and would have been happier with a short-wave radio. This was normal. Mat likes using radio hams as cut-outs, and does so in a number of countries; partly because hams are accustomed to staying awake at all hours and partly because some of them can be prevailed upon, in an emergency and for no longer than the few seconds needed to send a high-speed message track, to operate their transmitters illegally. Mostly, he chooses elderly men with pensions to supplement and a mild taste for conspiracy. If they are former Boy Scouts, so much the better.

I gave the number of the phone I was using along with my cover name and said that the matter was urgent. It would be thirty minutes, I was told, before I was called back.

I had fitted induction suckers to both phones, and it was just as well that I'd done so because the return call came through on the other line.

It wasn't Mat, though, but Frank Yamatoku.

'Hi, Paul,' he said; 'still in the same place after all. Is that right? When you gave the other number, we thought you might have moved without telling us.'

'And upset your planning?'

'Oh, we knew you hadn't done that.'

'You did?'

'Sure. We'd have had complaints if you hadn't been in the target area. What's that other number? A second line we didn't know about?'

I'd already had enough of him. 'It's been great hearing your voice, Frank, but it was my old friend I called and my old friend I want to talk to. Is he there?'

'Not right now, Paul. Later maybe. Meanwhile, I have messages. We've been expecting this call for hours, you see. Since last night. Why the delay? We were getting worried. What kept you?'

'Reaction times must be slowing down.'

He chuckled. 'Happens to us all, they say. But you're here now, so never mind. I'll get to the messages. He says you'll want various questions answered, and that the first will be, "Who". After that comes, "Why?". Finally, there's, "What shall we do to be saved?". That one must be religious, I think, from the way he said it. You still with me?'

'Listening carefully.'

'Then I'll get straight to the why of it. I don't have to tell you, Paul, that we've both been worried. Not about how you'd handle yourself, naturally, because we both of us know and respect you, but worried *for* and *with* you. So, we began wondering what we back home could do. We wanted you to feel that, when you were fighting that lonely battle of yours out there, you weren't alone. We wanted you to know that you had friends right behind you ready to give a helping hand when you needed it. You understand me, Paul?'

'Frank, it's those friends right behind me, and what they might do before I can turn around and stop them, that I called about.'

'Bear with me, Paul, and let me share our thinking with you.

Our first thought was that you were, we all were, in bigger trouble than you wanted to admit, and that you were going to need more than a paper towel to clean off all that shit you stepped in. I mean clean it off so there'd be no lingering odour. What you needed, we figured, was one of those deodorants that does more than just freshen up the air. You needed one that would destroy the opposition's sense of smell. Right?'

'You've lost me.'

'Look at it another way. What happens when one of these penny-ante Third-World governments has big trouble on the home front? You know what happens. It looks around for some foreign enemy who'll take the people's minds off all the troubles at home by standing up outside the gates and drawing fire. Xenophobia, right? Baddies from outside?'

'I see.'

'Of course you do. And you'll also see that, with the kind of non-belligerents you have there with you right inside the city walls, we couldn't take chances. You're not going to fool social scientists of that calibre with Hallowe'en masks and hi-fi scream tracks. They're serious investigators. You have to give them a taste of the real thing or they don't believe, do they?'

'Don't believe what?'

'That this investigation they're making is dangerous, physically dangerous. Dangerous for you, dangerous for your employees, and, thus, dangerous for *them*. In fact, so goddamned dangerous for everybody there, that the quicker they get their asses out the less likely they are to share the terrible fate planned for you. Death through proximity, that's what they have to fear, Paul.'

'They're not going to buy it.'

'You don't know yet what you'll be selling, friend. I'm trying to tell you. This is where we come to the "who" bit. Are you still with me? This is important.'

'Still with you.'

'Now, I'm not personally acquainted with the outfit that's been hired, but I've heard of it and I understand that it's talented enough to rate top money. Can't say more because I've been told to stay with hard fact. The word to you from our friend, though, is that the tab for the operation's been picked up by three guys acting in concert, three guys whose names he says you'll know. I have them written down. Let's see. Yes, here we are. The names are Kleister, Torten and Vic. Vic who, it doesn't say. Maybe you know.'

'Yes, I know.' The foot-pump connected to my head was being worked again.

'Good. Then you'll also know, Paul, that these three gentlemen are all, as far as you're concerned, somewhat prejudiced. That means that, although our friend made it very clear to them that harassment was authorized only insofar as it was needed to carry conviction, the possibility of these nuts overstepping the mark if provoked ought to be borne in mind. He asked me to mention that specially.'

'I appreciate his concern.'

'I hope you mean that, Paul, because it's something you *should* appreciate. He's still fond of you, in spite of everything, and he still wants to protect you if you'll let him. He says that before you went over the hill you played polo real good, and that if you found yourself in an emergency predicament you might still give these characters more trouble and make them real mad.'

'I might, yes.'

'The word is, don't. You'll only get hurt a lot instead of a little. That's only advice, mind. He still has too much respect for you as his old bossman, Paul, to presume to *tell* you. He's only asking you to accept a piece of friendly advice.'

'Is there anything else that I should accept?'

'He said to tell you that he'll be thinking of you all the time. He meant it too. *All* the time.'

'I'll be thinking of *him*.'

'Have a good day, Paul.'

He hung up.

I switched off and immediately pressed the rewind button. After I had played the whole tape through twice, I listened to the beginning of it a third time before writing a note to Yves and Melanie.

Yves, please meet me at CP now after passing this to Melanie, please distribute File No. 2 and then join us.

I found the cook's husband and gave him the note to deliver. Then, I took the recorder from my bedroom and went to our 'Command Post' in the garage loft.

When Yves joined me everything was set up and ready.

I pointed to the recorder. 'I've just taped a call from London on this. First, I want you to listen to the beginning and tell me if anything occurs to you, anything at all.'

He asked no questions, just nodded and sat down.

I started the play-back. After the first couple of sentences I stopped it and looked at him.

'Again, please,' he said, 'and this time as loudly as possible. The speech quality doesn't matter.'

I couldn't get it much louder because induction suckers aren't all that efficient and the recorder's amplifier hadn't much left to give, but I did my best. Oddly enough, Frank's voice quacking away through the tape-hiss was, though still intelligible, less offensive than it had been with the volume lower. I let it run on for a moment or two longer before switching off.

Yves pursed his lips. '*Anything* that occurs to me?'

'Yes, please.'

'You said that the call was from London. I don't think it was.'

'How can you be sure?'

'Calls from London to here are dialled. With long-distance direct-dialling, an electronic time-and-distance charge counter is activated as soon as the answering phone is picked up. It's connected to the computer that bills the customer. I don't know exactly how long it takes to start running – only a small fraction of a second I would think – but if you already have the phone to your ear when the circuit is completed you always hear it. It's like the sound of a stick being dragged for an instant along iron railings. Your recording here begins while the phone is still ringing. If the call had come from London, or Bonn or Amsterdam, we'd have heard the charge counter coming into action when you picked up the phone. The sound's not there. That call was made locally from no farther away than Nice or Menton. And it wasn't made from a pay-phone either. You'd have heard a charge counter start with that too. The sound would have been different from the long-distance counter, but you'd still have heard it.' He paused, then added: 'Is that what you wanted to hear?'

'Not what I wanted, but what I expected. I didn't notice until the second time I played the tape.'

'Most people don't hear it at all. The counter normally starts during the time it takes to pick up the phone and put it to your ear. You asked for anything that occurred to me. I also recognize the caller's voice. It's a man I know as Mr Yama-toku.'

He was watching me narrowly for a reaction. I nodded. 'I'm going to ask you to listen to the rest of the conversation, but let's wait a moment until Melanie gets here.'

We had to wait several minutes.

'Questions,' she explained peevishly. 'Paul, you should not

have so spoken about me in the ambience of such persons. They are incapable of maintaining the moderations of polite usage.'

The sudden deterioration of her English suggested that the questions had been inconveniently searching.

'Didn't the second file divert them at all?'

'Do you divert lions with carrion when there is fresh meat to be had? These people are most ill-mannered.'

'You're being too fussy,' I said; 'I'll be surprised if those other people with us, the ones we *weren't* expecting, have any manners at all.'

Yves shoved a bentwood chair against the back of her legs and she sat down abruptly.

'What do you know,' I asked, 'about a man named Mathew Tuakana? He sometimes calls himself Mat Williamson. Mean anything to you?'

I was looking at Yves as I spoke simply to notify Melanie that I had called the meeting to order and wanted no more of her nonsense. I hadn't really expected him to answer. In his line of work, he was unlikely to have become involved in any of the futile attempts already made to penetrate the dense covers concealing Mat's operations; but I had been mistaken. After a moment's thought, he nodded.

'Yes, I've heard of him. A Polynesian *métis*. Homosexual. A banker of some sort. Ultra rich. Is that the man?'

'Where did you hear that gossip?'

'I know someone who did some work for him. It's all wrong, I suppose.'

'It's right about his being a half-caste, but wrong about the non-white component. His mother was Melanesian, not Polynesian. Also, he's had women as lovers as well as men. Who was your informant?'

An impertinent question that ought not to have been asked. Yves didn't apologize for ignoring it.

'I was also told,' he said, 'that Williamson was one to stay away from if you were free to choose. Some of these ultra rich have a habit of ditching things when they've finished with them, even if the things have only been used once. I'm told Williamson does that with people. Was I wrong there too?'

I hesitated, so naturally he had to pounce.

'Is *he* the one you're covering for here?'

I didn't have a chance of deciding how fully or frankly I would reply. Before I could draw breath, Melanie was talking across me to answer Yves.

'Of *course*,' she told him, 'it must be Williamson. I should have thought of him before. He's the Placid Island man, the one negotiating on behalf of the natives over the compensation to be paid out by the phosphate interests. He's an economist with unorthodox ideas. You know? The kind of ideas that sound fascinating while they are being used to sell something, but that no one ever hears of again after the deal is set. He also acts for a Canadian bank. If that man had needed protection from Krom, I should have thought the bank would have provided it. Why trouble poor little Symposia?'

By bitching me with that snide reference to Symposia she was trying to recover the dignity lost minutes earlier when her buttocks had hit the seat of the chair.

'He doesn't control the Canadian bank,' I said, 'though his association with it is common knowledge. He *does* control Symposia, however, and he controls it through me. That is very far from being common knowledge and the thing that was to have been hidden at all costs from those with prying eyes and publishing voices, especially Krom. News that there existed a backstairs financial arrangement between Symposia, the trendy fast-buck artists' favourite tax-haven advisory service, and His Excellency Mat Tuakana, man of the people, King's Scout and patron saint of Placid Island, would kill for ever his chance of getting that international licence to print money he's always yearned for. And he'd never get another chance.'

I turned to Yves again. 'I'm the one whose cover was blown by Krom, so I'm the one who has to make good the loss, hold the fort, stick the finger in the dyke, fall on the exploding grenade or do whatever else is necessary to keep His Excellency's reputation safe, sound and spotless. Yes, he *does* like scrapping people when he's used them. Let's hope he hasn't succeeded with us.'

'*Us*, Paul?' Melanie again.

The look I gave her was as sour as her own. 'I think it's time I revealed, in case you didn't know, that *both* of you were hand-picked for this operation by Mat Williamson himself. And if you think that being chosen by the great man personally for this assignment isn't much of a distinction, you're mistaken. In your case certainly, Melanie, the choice was made with immense care. To prove it I'm going to play back a phone conversation I've just had with Frank Yamatoku. He's Williamson's left-hand man, Melanie. That's why I was a little upset when you told me that you'd given him our communications code.'

Yves whispered *'Merde'* as if it were a prayer.

She stared coldly at my chin. 'A capable operations director would have reviewed the standard security procedures before committing the team.'

I wasn't going to argue about that with her. 'When I called Williamson's London cut-out from here, I asked him to return my call personally. It was returned instead by Yamatoku, and it sounds as if he's calling from a local phone not far from here. Listen.'

They listened. They listened to the whole thing three times. Between play-backs I answered questions as truthfully as seemed prudent in the circumstances.

Who, for instance, were Kleister, Torten and Vic?

'No, they're *not*, much as they may sound like it, a slack-wire baggy-pants act out of a third-rate circus. There's nothing even marginally comical about those three. They're old business rivals still nursing their grudges against me for the defeats they once suffered in a couple of big deals. They said I tricked them. You know how it is with losers, *some* losers anyway. They think that winners only win through skulduggery, and that that makes it all right for losers to use skulduggery if it'll give them their revenge. We should try to feel sorry for the poor slobs.'

Of course, neither Yves nor Melanie believed a word of that soap-opera version of the facts; but they accepted its essential element. It was more than likely that I should have former victims gunning for me. But gunning for me with what?

How real was the threat implicit in Yamatoku's reference to the possibility of K, T and V's merry men 'overstepping the mark'? Was such sinister moustache-twirling to be taken seriously?

I told them that, when dealing with Mat Williamson, everything ought to be taken seriously, but nothing at its face value. However, for the purpose of our council of war, a few assumptions could safely be made.

Among those old acquaintances of mine with reasons for disliking me, K, T and V had been chosen not for their ability to exercise restraint where I was concerned – it was known that K and T had once threatened to kill me – but because, in spite of earlier misfortunes, they were wealthy enough as well as crazy enough to pay a team of professional hard men to carry out orders of which Mat approved. When implementing any policy of his involving even a modest cash outlay, Mat always arranged for someone else to foot the bill. He had known of K, T and V because their dossiers had figured in the inventory of Carlo's consultancy accounts which I had inherited; dossiers that I had later transferred to Mat as part of our overall deal.

Yes, Mr Yamatoku's hostility was plainly audible. Unfortunately, the idea, comforting though it might have been, that Frank had merely been indulging his personal dislike of me must be put aside. No doubt he had enjoyed giving me his bad news; but he hadn't invented it. He would certainly have taped our conversation, as I had, but *his* tape would have to be played back to Mat. With that hypercritical audience in mind, an audience prepared to evaluate every intonation, Frank Yamatoku wouldn't have dared to depart from the brief he had been given.

In my own mind the conviction was growing that Frank had had a well-prepared, all-eventuality script in front of him when he had been talking to me; but I wasn't quite ready then to start explaining, or trying to explain, Mat Williamson to anyone except myself.

There was something else I had to be sure of first.

Meanwhile, I thought, it might be advisable to get Melanie on my side again.

'You were right,' I told her; 'I ought to have reviewed the standard security procedures before committing them to your care. I apologize. But now, I think, it's time we started formulating decisions.'

'Decisions on whether or not you take his friendly advice, Patron?' Yves had hooked up the small tape-deck to the bugging amplifier and had been replaying my conversation with Frank through the earphones. He flipped a switch. 'What does this bit mean?'

Frank's voice came through the monitor speaker. '*He's still fond of you, in spite of everything, and he still wants to protect you if you'll let him.*'

Yves switched off. 'In spite of *everything*, Patron? What is this everything?'

'He means that he forgives me the inconvenience I have caused him by allowing myself to be seen years ago by a Dutch criminologist in a Swiss crematorium.'

'I am being serious, Patron.'

'I wasn't joking. That's simply Mat Williamson's way of informing me that I am what you call ditched.'

'And *this*?' He had wound the tape on. 'What does *this* mean?'

Frank's voice again. '*That's only advice, mind. He still has too much respect for you as his old bossman, Paul, to presume to tell you. He's only asking you to accept a piece of friendly advice.*'

'That was put in,' I said, 'with the idea of making it difficult for me to play the tape to Krom. Frank's idea, probably. I'd say Mat let it go through to humour him. He himself wouldn't have bothered. He knows I'll let Krom hear the tape.'

Melanie almost squealed her protest. 'And give him one more excuse to call you a liar? While you were upstairs with Yves, they were talking about you as if I had not been there. You have not convinced them of anything that we hoped and planned for them to believe. Do you know what Dr Connell calls you? "Mr Kingpin", that is what! Paul, you will never succeed now with Krom and these others. You have cut off your own nose with you denials of truth and spit in your own face. You have boasted of your amorality, that everything you say is a lie, and they are virtuously ready to believe that there, at least, you tell the truth. They have made up their minds, and nothing you can now do will change them.'

In an effort to keep my temper, I corrected her before answering. 'You cut off your own nose to *spite* your face, not spit in it, Melanie.' I paused to swallow a bit more anger. 'The situation's completely different now. Can't you see it? Hasn't the penny dropped?'

Yves gave her no chance to reply. He was having trouble with a different anxiety. 'You haven't yet answered the question I asked you, Paul. Do you or do you not take this friendly advice of Mr Williamson? Oh yes, the situation is a little different now, but there is still only one way out of it. Those bastards outside were not put there just to make you call London. We're being set up for a kill. I feel it.'

'You may be right.'

'Well then, Paul, let's do what I said. Let's forget about the guests. This was their idea anyway, and they don't matter now. We should think of ourselves. No consultation. No argument. We choose the right moment, we take the rental car, we head for the safe-house and then stay there until this place has been disinfected by paid bastards of your own.'

I tried to say what had to be said. 'It doesn't work, Yves. There's no right moment for us to choose. For one thing, it's too easy for them around here, too easy to stage an accident. You know? One of those accidents in which all the occupants of a small car are killed when it runs off a road on the corniche? It's happening every day for real. No one would even notice.'

He slapped his right elbow with the palm of his left hand, and then stabbed a forefinger at me. 'Paul, I give you a guarantee! If *I* am driving, anyone who tries to run us off the road – *anyone*, even if he is an Italian kidnap driver – will kill himself before he can scratch our paintwork. That little buzz-box is not heavy, but she steers well and on these roads that is good enough. Good enough, with me driving, to get us away from this fly-trap, free and clear to the safe-house. Paul, I *guarantee* it!'

I glanced at Melanie.

She shrugged sullenly.

My eyes went back to Yves. He thought I was still trying to make up my mind and out came the forefinger again, moving stiffly from side to side this time, to dispel lingering doubt.

'You think I can't do it, eh?'

I said: 'Our cut-out point was the hotel in Turin. Remember?'

'What of it?'

He hadn't even begun to understand. It was possible that his mind was still doing immaculate skid turns on the hairpin bends of the corniche while the opposition cartwheeled down the hillsides in flames. A good technician, Yves, but unreliably romantic. There was nothing left to do but speak plainly.

'Yves,' I said, 'I'm sorry, but this fly-trap *is* the safe-house.'

His look of anguish was of the predictable kind and I didn't waste time consoling him. I knew at that point where the score stood. I also knew, more or less, what I would have to do to change it.

'A remarkable man,' Krom said, 'remarkable by any standards.'

He knew, or thought he knew, all about Mat Williamson and had instructed his witnesses on the subject. He had never heard of Frank though. I spelled Yamatoku for him. They wrote it down, and then we all went into the dining-room.

I played the tape through twice. During the second play-back both Krom and the witnesses took notes. Finally, Krom sat back and looked questioningly at Henson.

'Any comments, my dear?'

She stubbed out a cigarette. 'Only obvious ones, I'm afraid. A shadowy figure named Vic has been added to the supporting cast headed by Kleister and Torten. I shan't be at all surprised if we find this Vic popping up again, wearing a devil suit and a smell of brimstone next time, in a later discussion paper.'

'A note of scepticism is sounded.' He nodded sympathetically and looked at Connell.

'I had that very same thought, Professor. And one or two others.' Connell consulted his notes. 'This Mr Yamatoku, for instance. His speech sounds American – could be from my own home state – and I'm sure we'll find when we check it out that the Placid Island banker, Williamson, has a Nisei accountant of that name on his staff. But that still leaves us with the question of provenance. In this Frank-and-Paul show we've been listening to, is the Frank character the real Yamatoku or is he some bit player hired by the old bossman here to read lines? I am assuming, by the way, that the lines contain hidden meanings that are going to be revealed to us later. To give one example, there is an allusion to the game of polo which at present makes no sense at all.'

'More scepticism, I fear, Mr Firman.'

No cackling now, no raucous sarcasms. Something had happened to Krom while we had been away. My guess was that the witnesses, impressed by Yves's outburst on the terrace earlier, had ganged up on their leader and persuaded him that he would get more out of us if he made less noise himself.

Henson was pretending coyly to have had a sudden inspiration. 'I wonder now! Wait a minute! If Mr Firman could telephone London and have his call returned promptly like that, surely we could do the same. Naturally, we couldn't be certain that the Mr Yamatoku we were talking to – have I got the name right? – was the genuine article, but we ought to be able to test the actor theory. Only a very good one could improvise in that turgid neo-revivalist manner.'

'I thought that one of you experts might have noticed that the call was a local one,' I said. 'Would you explain to them, Yves?'

Yves explained.

They listened quietly and attentively in a way that I didn't like. Krom's natural rudeness and the witnesses' sycophancy had been infuriating, and probably bad for my blood pressure, but they had had their psychological uses. They had enabled me, for one thing, to view the prospect of him and his witnesses dying violent deaths in the near future with only a token regret. So, I had been left reasonably free to concentrate on avoiding the same fate. The new politeness was not only disconcerting, and thus destructive, but also insidiously depressing. It would have to be countered. As Yves began going into detail, I cut him short.

'You're quite right, of course, Dr Henson,' I said; 'talking to Mr Yamatoku, even if you could, wouldn't help you all that much. Besides, my object in asking you to listen to that highly compromising conversation wasn't to prove anything to any of you. It was to save myself trouble. If you'll just accept for a moment that the man to whom I'm speaking on that tape is Yamatoku and that the "our friend" he's referring to is his employer Mat Williamson, I'll try to explain to you what's happened to change things here without wasting any more time. Agreed?'

Connell talked across me to Krom. 'You have to hand it to our host, Professor. He gives that Number-Two status claim of his everything he's got. He really *does* try harder. Secret watchers and bombs in the night didn't work, so now it's threatening calls from sinister Orientals and sudden cracks of hypothetical whips – all great stuff. But it does make you wonder, I find, about the kind of therapy he's been in, and the quality of it too. Some of these cruelty-is-kinder organismic groups we're seeing around nowadays can do the mind permanent damage.'

Krom squirmed with the agony of keeping a straight face, and then showed me his teeth as if they had all suddenly begun to hurt him. 'You must see our difficulty, Mr Firman. If we do not take you as seriously as you would wish, you have only yourself to blame.'

'That's quite all right,' I said evenly; 'I'm glad that you're in such high spirits. They may help to make the news I have to give you more palatable.'

'The whip-cracks I could forgive,' remarked Henson; 'it's the false bonhomie that *I* find tedious.'

Krom covered an involuntary snicker by clucking in mock-disapproval. 'With Mr Firman working so ingeniously to avoid keeping our agreement, we should be applauding him rather than poking fun. You must be good, my children, *please*!'

Yves stirred and I guessed that he was about to say something obscene enough to disgust even the 'children'. He had my sympathy, but I didn't need his support and snapped my fingers to let him know it. At the same moment, I stood up as if about to leave and then stopped where Krom would be forced to lean back awkwardly if he wanted to see my face.

'I spoke, when I asked you to listen to that tape, of re-negotiating our agreement,' I said. 'Clearly, I was being over-tactful. Perhaps it will help you to contain your amusement, Professor, if I tell you that we no longer *have* an agreement. The one made in Brussels is now completely null and void. What we can still discuss, if you wish, is what remains of your ability to blackmail me, and what is left of my ability to give you protection.'

'Protection from what?'

'The consequences of threatening Mathew Williamson. He's not as tolerant of common blackmailers as I am.'

'I've heard of your Mr Williamson, as I've already told you, but I'm not acquainted with him. Nor am I, as you perfectly well know, a common blackmailer.'

'Exactly what you are, Professor, and where, as a result, you now stand are matters that must be re-examined. Do you want to send your witnesses out, or don't you mind if they hear us talking about the messier details of our bargain?'

He showed a few more teeth. 'You're wasting your breath, Mr Firman. I refuse to be provoked. My young friends have experience of the problems of doing research in this field. Why shouldn't they hear the details?'

'Very well. The basic threat you made was that, unless I did and said the various things you wanted me to do and say, you would expose, I quote, the Symposia Conspiracy. That's what you called it. Right?'

'That's what I still call it.'

'Then you must still be, Professor, as big an intellectual and academic phony as you were when you dreamed up the phrase.'

I didn't wait for a reaction, but turned and went through into the drawing-room. It was well-bugged in there – and when an adversary is under pressure it's always better to have a tape, even when there seems to be no way of its ever being used. Besides, it was necessary to have him off balance. That's why I'd walked away after insulting him. A double goosing like that is really painful.

He certainly found it so. He came running. The others followed but he didn't wait for them before counter-attacking. He was too angry to wait.

'You won't get rid of your corruption by trying to hang it on me,' he snapped. 'Ask any policeman! Defence by projection is common among criminals.'

'It's common among all sections of the populace, Professor, including criminologists. I accused you of being a phony. With or without your permission, I intend to explain to your witnesses why I did so.'

I paused as if to dismiss his unspoken protest before going on. 'Symposia is an organization concerned with tax avoidance by strictly legal means. By coupling its name with the word "conspiracy", an imprecise but emotive term loaded with associations of illegality, you created an essentially meaningless but potentially lethal smear. You've wasted your talents, Professor. You should have been a politician.'

His martyred God-give-me-patience look brought in Henson for the defence. 'If it was meaningless, why should it have upset you so much?'

I gave her my best smile. 'How did your Professor Langridge put it? "More to do with journalism than with scholarship," was it? Something like that, I think. What would he have said, I wonder, if he'd actually heard his colleague, Krom, threatening to leak the whole smear package to the financial journals and news magazines if I didn't collaborate? "Collaborate" was the chosen euphemism. Moral blackmail and extortion were the realities.' I faced Krom again. 'Last night you allowed that you were an extortionist. Of course, as you have explained today, you were tired last night. But tired of *what*? *Only* of travelling, or of hypocrisy too?'

Connell rallied to the cause. 'You still haven't answered the question, Firman. If the charge was baseless, why are we here? Why didn't you tell him to drop dead?'

'I can't believe, Doctor, that you are simple enough to suppose that a smear can always be defeated by ignoring it. Only the invulnerable few, or those past caring what happens to their reputations, can afford to adopt that attitude. I would also remind you that institutions handling, or advising on the handling of, other people's money are among the most vulnerable to this kind of false charge, however baseless it may be.'

'But in your case the charge wasn't false or baseless.' Henson again, with Krom nodding his blessing. 'Your first paper admits as much, not just frankly, but brazenly. Oh yes, you're careful to point out that Oberholzer belonged to your pre-Symposia days, but surely that's mere nit-picking.'

I was finding it difficult to remain cool and had to make

a conscious effort. 'Let's be clear about this. What I have admitted is that I once committed offences against the Swiss bank secrecy laws by obtaining confidential information from a bank employee. That offence is, as you well know, one that has been committed time and time again over the years by agents and officials acting for non-Swiss governments. Among them have been the governments of most of the developed nations and a good many from the Third World as well. Within the international communities of income-tax gatherers, fraud-squad investigators and exchange-control enforcers outside Switzerland, the offence is regarded about as seriously as a parking violation. You seem also to need reminding that I have never been arrested in Switzerland or anywhere else, nor even detained for questioning, much less convicted in a court of law.'

Connell went into a world-weary, cut-the-cackle routine. 'Please, Mr Firman. We've seen the bleeding. Now, how about showing us the wound? All you've been given, you say, is a parking ticket. And yet, for the honour of dear old Symposia, you act as if you'd been busted for murder-one. Come *on*! The Symposia Conspiracy isn't about parking violations. It's about an extortion racket that relies for the fingering of likely victims on an intelligence set-up pretending to be a tax-haven consultancy service, and, for the raking in of its blood money, on a network of illegal debt-collection agencies making undercover use of international communications systems. That's what Professor Krom was proposing to shed light on, and that's what he still intends to shed light on. All he did to you was to offer the sort of deal that the law offers crooks all the time and all over the world. "Turn informer and we won't press charges. Tough it out, or try to, and we'll throw the book at you." You started by going along with the deal and now you're trying to renege. No need to apologize. We understand how it is. But don't bore us with crap about parking tickets. Okay?'

With almost no effort I was able to laugh. 'When you wrote your book about organized crime, Dr Connell, that was the sort of talk you put in the mouths of the stupider DAs and the more reactionary policemen. You disappoint me.'

'A nice try, Mr Firman,' said Henson; 'but we already knew that you could read.'

In spite of her confident tone, she was by then having several second thoughts and Krom had spotted the fact.

'He's only digging his own grave, my dear. Don't let us do the job for him.' He tried to sound as if he were at ease, but he was showing scarcely any teeth and his eyes had the wary look I had first seen in Brussels when he had been afraid of me. Now, he was afraid of me again; not afraid this time, though, of what I might be going to do, but of what he had sensed that I might be going to say.

He had had two months in which to forget the euphoria of his Brussels victory over me and to start wondering why that success had been so easy.

I found it meanly satisfying now to ignore him and give his witnesses the answers he so anxiously awaited. Besides, they were pleasanter to look at.

I said: 'You asked me why, if this threatened smear were baseless, I didn't tell friend Krom, the author of it, to publish and be damned. I've given you one answer. All smears that start no-smoke-without-fire talk can be expensive in one way or another. You pay off for the same reason that big corporations often settle nuisance actions against them out of court. It may be cheaper in the long run to pay rather than to argue rights and wrongs. I could have given you a second answer. If pushed, we could have called the Professor's bluff and then warned the publisher he went to that this was a source that couldn't be protected by the anonymity custom because this source had already tried to sell *us* the story. That way, ordinarily, we would have been on fairly safe ground. We didn't adopt that solution because to have done so would have been to take an unacceptable risk.'

'Aha!' said Krom.

I didn't bother to tell him that his relief was premature, but went on addressing the witnesses. 'In amongst all the hearsay, gossip, innuendo and straight falsehood that had been assembled to support the conspiracy nonsense, there were one or two sets of facts. Most were unimportant or irrelevant. One wasn't. I refer to the Placid Island material.'

'What's so remarkable about that?' demanded Connell. 'Placid's typical. It's been stripped of most of its natural assets. The only future it has is as a tax-haven outpost with a few high-rise office buildings. Its one extra asset seems to be this Williamson you mentioned – a banker, and an economist too, with a good academic background who also happens to be a native of the wretched place. Professor Krom noted that Symposia had made overtures to Placid and was trying to establish a monopoly position there. Was *that* what you didn't like?'

'That's what Mat Williamson didn't like. He didn't like it because Symposia wasn't just *trying* to establish a monopoly in advance, it already *had* it established. The Symposia Group is eighty per cent owned by Mat Williamson and always has been.'

'But I didn't *know* that!' Krom yelped. It wasn't that he was dim-witted, just that a bit of his mind was still refusing to listen to the disaster warning that had begun to paralyse the higher centres.

'Of course you didn't know,' I said. 'Practically nobody knew, or knows *now*. The Canadian bank for whom Mat acts as a consultant in such matters certainly doesn't know. Neither do the officials with whom Placid Island independence is being negotiated. Others in ignorance include Chief Tebuke and the lawyers for the phosphate company which is being squeezed by Mat for compensation. Dr Connell asked why we are here. Well, I'll tell you why I *thought* we were here, if that's still of interest to anyone but the birds. We were here, Professor, so that *you* wouldn't rock the boat, of which I'll admit to owning twenty per cent, by revealing the Williamson-Symposia relationship.'

'How could I have revealed it? As you have said, I didn't know about it.'

No doubt he was still in shock, but it was hard to remain civil. 'I can't believe, Professor, that you are as unworldly as all that. You must suffer from the delusion that only scholars are capable of doing research. You think that the corporate entities which make up the Symposia Group are an open book to you because you've looked at all the available records. They show me as a stockholder and also as a nominee for other voting stockholders. That's as far as you've gone because, thanks to the fact that you once saw me years ago in Zürich, you made an assumption about me that you weren't prepared to modify or even reconsider. From Mat's point of view, that was fine – while it lasted. But would it always last? The first thing any newspaperman worth his salt would do would be to question all your assumptions however pretty they looked. And, having questioned, he'd find ways of getting answers that satisfied *his* professional standards. They wouldn't be your ways, because he'd have to work a lot faster than you people. He'd dig patiently, yes, but he'd use those techniques that governments call espionage or intelligence-gathering, depending on whose side is doing what, and newspaper proprietors call investigative reporting. It doesn't matter what *we* call it. The point is that, if you'd been allowed to hand your Symposia rag-bag to the financial editor of a news magazine, the information connecting Mat Williamson with Symposia would have been found within days and the result wouldn't have been called a conspiracy. It would have been called a "caper", or worse. It would have been the Placid Island Rip-Off. *Now* do you understand?'

Silence. Krom looked like death.

'Well,' said Connell eventually, 'none of that's happened and no one's yet rocked the boat. So what's changed since you and the Professor made your deal? Our appraisal of the situation was faulty from the start, according to you. All right. So what?'

'Unfortunately, *my* appraisal of the situation has *become* faulty. That's what's changed. In London, the risk represented by the Professor's decision to use blackmail in his quest for information seems, after all, to have been judged uninsurable. That phone call was to tell us so, tell all of us.'

'I see. The best way of making sure that no one rocks a boat is to have no people in it. Then your revised appraisal is, I take it, that those friends of yours outside this place now intend to kill us all. Correct? Or is this to be a selective massacre? Just you? Just us? Some of each? What's the new ouija board starting to say?'

Melanie said brightly: 'It's nearly time for lunch.'

The cook's husband was at the door asking if he should bring the ice for the drinks in there or whether we would be moving out to the swimming-pool area.

I said that we would have the drinks inside. By the time we moved out to lunch by the swimming pool, a lot more had been said and the guests were thoughtful. Connell hadn't pressed me for an answer to his questions. He had probably decided that I had no answers.

CHAPTER NINE

For a few minutes they seemed to have stopped wondering how much truth there was in me, and to be asking themselves a question that their books had always said was irrelevant. Was there or wasn't there honour among thieves?

Could criminal relationships be like those·to be found in trade and industry? Were comparisons drawn from what was known of marriages or ménages appropriate. Or was the 'standard' criminal relationship one of convenience and collusion only, like a contract between politicians, cancellable without warning by either party the moment it became in any way embarrassing?

No one was very hungry. Henson soon gave up on the loup. I had already done so. It is an overrated fish.

'From what you now tell us, Mr Firman,' she said, 'one would almost believe that, once upon a time, you and Mr Williamson were really quite good friends.'

'We have had a long and profitable business association. Obviously, our relationship had a friendly element in it.'

'Friendly enough for you to compromise your own cover to protect his against the Professor's enquiries. That was very friendly, surely?'

'Back in May, it seemed to be in both our interests that I should cover for him. Remember, I have twenty per cent. Maybe that clouded my judgement.'

'Yet now, you don't seem to be very much surprised or upset by the fact that he's betraying you, and telling you so, moreover. He is betraying you, I suppose. That tape we heard wasn't by any chance a fake?'

Two stiff gins-and-tonic had almost restored Krom's self-esteem. 'You're learning, my dear. I've been wondering the same thing.' He cocked an eye at me. 'Is it a fake?'

'I wish it were.'

Connell's hostility towards me had returned to normal. 'You don't think much of our right to the truth,' he said. 'How do you feel about associates like Mr Williamson? I mean, after that call we heard, what's the word now about the usefulness of truth?'

'Carlo Lech and I always told one another the truth. To do

so was part of our mutual respect. With Mat Williamson, mutual respect is based on insights of a different order. When a question is asked there, you consider, first, not what the exactly truthful answer would be, but what the questioner wishes to hear from you. No, I'm not surprised by his betraying me, nor by his telling me, in that oblique way, that he's doing so. When you deal with Mat, there's always a chance that he may *try* to deceive or betray you. What you *should* do is make sure that he can't. I thought I *had* made sure. Upset? More annoyed, I think. Mat's a complex creature, difficult to explain.'

He and I had been in Singapore when I had heard of Carlo's death.

My reports on the Pacific tax-havens, existing and potential, had been written. I was waiting for Carlo's acknowledgement of the last one, and with it, the words pronouncing my absolution and telling me that my exile was at an end.

He died of heart failure following a virus infection, according to the Vaduz lawyer who acted for our various corporate set-ups there. The man's vagueness was understandable. There was legislation against Liechtenstein Anstalts pending in Italy as well as moves afoot to clamp down on citizens holding large amounts of their capital abroad. It would have been indiscreet of him even to have visited Carlo's Milan office, and highly dangerous to have communicated with the family. There would have been no business reason for him to do so anyway. Carlo's stashed-away fortune was, and still is, in trusts administered jointly by the Vaduz man, with his partners as successors, and me. Carlo's invalid wife, his son and his daughter all benefited, in accordance with Italian inheritance laws, under the formal will he had made there. The trusts benefit only the daughter, her musician husband and, above all, Carlo's grandson Mario. When he comes of age, that boy will be very rich.

However, according to the first letter from Vaduz, Carlo had, in addition, bequeathed me a piece of valuable real-estate.

This news had surprised me. My own holdings in our joint enterprises were already worth several millions and I had discussed the whole subject with Carlo long before. We both had plenty of money, earned by our joint efforts but apportioned in accordance with an agreement made when Carlo had been convalescing after his gall-bladder trouble. Aside from the agreement, neither of us owed the other anything except good faith and a single ' ty. When one of us died, the other would see, as best he could, that the dead man's family and other private obligations were taken care of in a proper fashion. For the sake of official appearances, the survivor would receive the fees and expenses normally payable to a trustee.

A second letter from Vaduz told me that the piece of valuable real-estate aforementioned was Carlo's island.

Surprise had then become confusion. In spite of my occasional white lies on the subject, Carlo had always known that the island bored me. That was why he had sent me to stew there after the Zürich fiasco. Bequeathing the place to me could have been the kind of stupid gesture that wealthy dotards have sometimes made in order to get the last word in some old and silly argument; but Carlo had not been stupid, far from it, nor had he been the kind of man who would give away a tropic island he had loved to a tropic-hater who would at once proceed to sell it.

The third letter explained all. Carlo's island was the property of a Netherland Antilles real-estate company, the shares in which would go to Mario when he was twenty-one. Meanwhile, I was asked to hold them in trust for him. To compensate me for the time and trouble of maintaining the place as it had been maintained during Carlo's lifetime – and as I had known it, complete with staff – I would, until Mario was old enough to take possession, have free and unfettered use of the island and its installations at all times, for my own personal enjoyment. Our man in Vaduz suggested thoughtfully that it might be a good idea if, on my way back to Europe, I called in at the island and took stock of the current situation there.

Carlo, an innovator to the last, had found a way of getting the last word in an old argument, and of making a ribald gesture from the grave, at the expense of no one but a cornered trustee. Vaduz would have thought it foolish of me as well as petty if I had refused the task. *Everyone* loved islands in the Caribbean, surely. They must do. Otherwise, why did all those tourists go there?

The only person near to me then who would have enjoyed the joke was Mat. Jokes about people stepping on metaphorical banana skins always made him laugh. Luckily, I never told him that one.

It was the order in which things were happening then, not caution, that stopped me. Mat had already known of Carlo and of my connection with him – I was never able to discover *how* he had known – before we had met in the New Hebrides. The only consolation for me had been that he had told me about the Lech–Oberholzer operation while still believing me to be a louche character named Perrivale (Perry) Smythson whose brains he was trying to pick about certain loopholes said to exist in the Anglo-French Condominium Law. I had begun by taking him for a local boy who had made good. When the matter of our identities had been straightened out, and sufficient time had been given to mutual inspection, exploratory talks about the possibility of joint ventures had taken us a little farther. I would report our talks to Carlo and get his reactions. A further meeting place convenient for both of us was chosen – Singapore. Of course, I never heard from Carlo on the subject; the virus must already have been at work; but his unexpected going stirred everything up and made it all move faster. I mourned Carlo and needed distractions. When next I met Mat our Symposia project had become a discussable deal. There had been neither time nor inclination then for banana-skin jokes.

In those early days of our relationship Mat treated me with the deference due to an elder statesman. Some of this, of course, was part of the process of buttering me up and at the same time making me feel old, but not all. I had knowledge that he might find useful. He would listen with more than token attention to what I had to say, even if it involved criticisms of his judgement. For instance, I hadn't approved of the pattern of business deals he'd been weaving around the Pacific, and I told told him so.

He went into a long spiel about the vacuums created by the abdication of old imperialisms. There was an urgent need of entrepreneurial skills to stimulate constructive business activity at provincial levels, to bring out the money hidden in mattresses so that it could work for all and to engage the non-Chinese in major enterprises.

'They're either just coming down from the trees,' he concluded, 'or emerging from extremely ancient feudalisms. *Someone's* got to get things moving for them.'

'That's what the invest-in-the-future type con-men usually say when they're finally caught.'

His ability to look mystified while deciding his next move used to impress me very much in those days. 'What have con-men to do with me, Paul?'

'Con-men like that are *also* very difficult to prosecute.'

'Also?'

'Those entrepreneurial skills of yours, Mat, are being used in a way that is well understood by any policeman. By the British, the offence of exploiting credit facilities on the here-today-gone-tomorrow principle is called "long-firm fraud". In Germany it's "Stossbetrug", in France "carambouillage", and in America most bunco-squads call it "scam", I believe. Authorities everywhere have difficulty in getting convictions mainly because they're always short of the kind of auditors who know *what* to look for, *where* to look for it *and*, above all, can work fast enough to grab the paper-work before it disappears. You, Mat, have something extra going for you because, as well as moving from corporate set-up to corporate set-up in an ingenious way, you're also moving backwards and forwards between national jurisdictions. You're almost impossible to catch, except in one area.'

The broad smile. 'I know nothing of sharp practices, Paul. Please enlighten me.'

'Two policemen of different nationalities could one day get together, maybe through reading an Interpol bulletin, and regret that there is nothing they can do jointly to bust you. *But*, one or other of them, or both, depending on the countries concerned, might decide to clobber you with a breach of some exchange control regulation. It would still be slow going for them, and they might never get a conviction on the fraud charge, but there's one thing a lot of these law maniacs can always get done quickly. They can have bank accounts frozen pending enquiries. For the victim, I'm told, it can be a nasty, lingering disease that prevents his enjoying life to the full.'

He tapped my arm gently. 'You're absolutely right, Paul. That's been my own view for a long time and I'm delighted to hear that you share it.' He made it sound as if he'd been testing me; and, for all I knew, he *had* been. 'In fact,' he went on, 'I took my name out of it months ago, and not just because I didn't like what some of those rascals I'd trusted were getting up to. It was the local Chinese who decided me in the end. That's one of the clubs that won't be licked and can't be joined. They're natural business leaders, the overseas Chinese. Some people compare them with the Jews – diaspora, ghetto life, preservation of cultural identity despite assimilation, that sort of stuff. I say that's superficial. I say that they're the one multi-national corporation that'll never be busted under any anti-trust law anywhere. Why? Complete local autonomy for every single unit of accounting is there for all to see, that's why. So where's the corporation? It's programmed into their genes. Tell you something else about the Chinese . . .'

He paused. He'd been talking more or less freely to a listener he'd classified as safe. Now, though, there was something that he considered important to be said; so he was reviewing it again before letting me hear it.

'Paul, the Chinese can't be frightened in the same way as the rest.'

By 'the rest', I later found, he meant the rest of mankind.

The nature of his peculiar ideas about intimidation and the techniques of frightening people into absolute obedience emerged from what he then told me about something that had happened to him in Java. He had, of course, been making his first million at the time, so his recollection of the incident was pleasantly light-hearted.

'Just getting about the place was terribly difficult,' he said. 'There were bandits calling themselves religious patriots raiding the villages, and bits of the civil war still going on everywhere outside the large towns. It wasn't safe to travel by road, even from Djakarta to Bandung, without a military escort, and not all that safe with one. So, all the sizeable towns were jammed with people. A top priority got you a bed, but not much else. A room to yourself? Rare, very rare. The Russians were among the greatest friends of the revolution, but the Soviet Embassy had to function for months from a bungalow in the Hotel des Indes compound. It gradually got a bit better in the western areas, though in East Java, and especially in places like Surabaja, Jogjakarta and Semarang, it stayed difficult. That was because the hard-cores on both sides were still using the interior as a battle-field. God, how I hate hard-cores! Give me the pragmatists every time.'

'I hadn't realized, Mat, that you'd ever found it necessary to give that choice any thought.'

'You've never worked for a revolutionary government, that's for sure. Well, I had a top priority then, *and*, let me tell you, whenever I had to take trips East I used that priority as if I were Genghis Khan. I'd found that the best way of getting through your business in comfort in those parts was to commandeer a foreign consulate. There were several available. No foreign consuls in them just then, of course, on account of the troubles, but the compounds and houses were still there, and in most cases the old native servants had stayed on. In theory they were there protecting property belonging to friendly foreign governments entitled to diplomatic status and immunities.'

'How did you get around that?'

He gave me his boyish smile. 'Servants protecting foreign property on behalf of the central government were responsible to the central government. When one of that government's officials decided to inspect the property to see if the protectors were doing their duty, they'd better co-operate. Otherwise, they'd find themselves out on their ears or, more likely, in jail.'

'So they co-operated.'

'Yes. But they also resented and hated and wondered how to handle the interloper, this man who was suddenly giving them orders, making them work instead of resting up, sitting at the consul's dinner table, sleeping in the consul's bedroom. What would you have done in their places, Paul?'

'Pretended you were the consul and tried to kill you with kindness, I expect.'

'They could do that and they often did. But sometimes the effort seemed to cost them too much and then they'd try to redress the balance in their favour. That happened once when I was staying in a French consulate. I'd been to dinner with the official in charge of the port installations because I'd had business to do with him. He lived in a compound two minutes away, so, after an early dinner and a brief chat, I walked back to the consul's house. You know how those places are arranged? Square lot of half a hectare maybe, high wall all around with barbed-wire on top as optional extra, house in the centre, separate servants' quarters in back of compound, gap in the wall for gate, driveway from gate to house?'

'I know.'

'Well, when I got to the gate I found it unlocked. In that place and at that time, that alone would have given me pause. I also heard and saw movements inside. There was a moon, so I waited by the gate till my eyes had adjusted to the light and I could see what was going on. Have you met many French consuls, Paul?'

'Not many, no.'

'Those I've met haven't, on the whole, been great hobbyists. There was one who was a bit of an ornithologist and made a hobby of his bird-photography, but I haven't come across any who cultivated their gardens much, except career-wise and metaphorically. I think this particular consul may have had an English wife.'

'You'll have to tell me what you're talking about, Mat. I won't try to guess.'

'That place had a rose garden in front of the house!'

'It's not a flower I care for much.'

'But an English rose garden in Java, Paul. It was crazy. They were a crummy lot as you'd expect. Still, there they were, planted right after the Japs had pulled out in 'forty-five, no doubt, and tended with care by Madame Consul until the new war came and the servants had had to take over. Now what I saw, as I stood in the darkness by the gate, was a couple of those servants, the two men, digging up the rose garden and burying something in it. Paul, what would you have thought they were burying at dead of night, eh?'

'With you, a self-proclaimed government snooper, on the property? Small-arms I would say, or possibly the last of the old consular hoard of vacuum-packed Gauloises Bleues.'

'Or ammunition, or stolen car-parts? Sure. As I stood there just outside the gate, watching and waiting for them to finish the job, I went through all those possibilities and more. I also realized that this had to be a one-off, amateur-night deal or they'd have had a boy out on watch in case I came back early. When at last they did finish and the rose bushes were all replanted, I had to move away a bit because then they remembered that they'd left the gate open and came over to lock up. I heard them giggling over something, but couldn't hear what. Then they went off to their own quarters. As soon as they were out of the way, I let myself in and went to the house.'

'Not stopping to look at the roses by moonlight?'

'I wasn't interested in the bloody roses, and neither would you have been. The trouble was that they'd taken the shovels they'd been using away with them. There was no electricity on at that time of night, so, with just my flashlight, all I could find in the house to use as a digging tool was a silver card-tray kept by the front door. In darkest Java with tray and flashlight! Are you with me?'

'Out there in the rose garden digging up the consul's cash-float box? Could be. I hope the silver tray stood up to it.'

'That tray wasn't solid silver,' he said quickly; 'it was plate.' I hadn't known it then, but Mat's scout training instilled in him a respect for the property of others, apart from their money I mean, that has never left him. 'Besides,' he went on, 'the soil was all loose where they'd been digging. I washed the tray carefully afterwards. There wasn't a scratch on it.'

'How about the consul's cash box?'

He took a deep breath in order to regain lost calm before he answered.

'What they'd buried there, Paul,' he said solemnly, 'was the entrails of a pig.'

Now I may not have known much, at that early stage, about his concern for the preservation of borrowed objects, or about any other by-products of his unusual education, but I *had* already learned that, if you let him adopt his preternaturally solemn tone with you without instantly taking counter-measures, he could become insufferably condescending. He had expected to surprise me, so I was very careful to look un-surprised.

'How did you know they were a *pig's* entrails?' I demanded suspiciously. 'They could have been a sheep's or a cow's.'

'In Java?'

'All right, an ox's entrails maybe.'

'They were a pig's entrails. I know about such things, Paul. Take my word for it.'

'Okay, I take your word. So what? Dried blood and bone meal are supposed to be good fertilizers. Why not pigs' entrails? You said that the roses looked crummy. The poor men were simply anticipating your criticisms by feeding the things while they thought you were safely out of the way.'

'And giggling while they did so?'

'A cultural curiosity. Golden Bough stuff. The peasants of Java consider entrails highly amusing.'

I had been baiting him of course. He had now realized that, and didn't like it. He gave me a long, bleak look before he spoke again.

'They were there,' he said slowly, 'to cast a spell, to render me helpless in their filthy hands.'

'Oh.'

Once he had started on spells, there was no point in trying to comment, or interrupt. He knew what he was talking about and he liked playing teacher. If he sounded on those occasions as if he were explaining the facts of life for the last time to a strangely backward adolescent, that was probably another hangover from his Fijian scouting days.

Those servants knew that the rose garden was of the greatest importance to the owner. That I wasn't the real owner made no difference. As the person in command of the place, even temporarily, I had taken on the attributes of the owner, his strengths and, above all, his weaknesses. I was dangerous to them because I could put in spiteful reports about the number of illegals they kept hidden in that compound paying squeeze for a patch of roof and a place of refuge from authority. I was a nuisance to them because I made work for them to which they had become unaccustomed. I messed things up, I wanted food, my bed made, my clothes dhobied. They wanted me out of there, but couldn't tell me to go. So what was there left for them to do? Only one thing. Reduce my capacity for mischief to a mimimum. How? Let the spirits of the dead render me impotent. By what means? Let them emasculate me through my rose garden. Let the embodiment of the most aggrieved and jealous spirits be placed in that earth where I was vulnerable. Got it?'

'Mm.'

'So what do you do when hostile spirits have been put in to subvert and suborn you? You turn them around, make double agents of them, that's what you do. Hah! Those offal-buriers didn't know the man they'd challenged. They soon learned. Next morning at breakfast, just to start with. The head man can't wait to run tests, of course, to see if the spell has started to work. So, he changes what they serve me for breakfast. I'd ordered papaya. He brings me bananas. Moment of truth! If I don't notice because I don't remember what I ordered, or if, having noticed and complained, I still accept the substitution, then the spell's beginning to work. I'm spooked and they're getting the upper hand. If, though, I *do* notice and do complain and tell him to take the goddam bananas away and bring me papaya, then maybe they'll have to wait. Until the next meal, that is, to test again with my food or to see what happens when they starch a shirt so hard that I can't do up the buttons. Maybe the day is adverse. Maybe these entrails need to get a bit riper before the spirits feel comfortable in them. Got to give it time, eh?'

'I suppose so.'

'No time, nothing! You throw a scare into the head man right then and there. You don't accept the bananas. Instead, you ask him what you ordered. You ask him slowly, and as you speak you rap the table in time with the words. He will be a little afraid and say that, although you ordered papaya, the fruit available were not good. Then you address him in the manner of a death spell – a spirit-of-eating-alive type intonation maybe – and tell him that it was mango you ordered, not papaya. Now he's in bad trouble. He doesn't know what to think except that the spirits are not on his side. And that's just the beginning. After that, you see that nothing he does is right. You order meat for dinner and he tries bringing you fish. You give him hell, but tell him you distinctly ordered vegetables. What's he trying to do, poison you? You order meat again. Worried, he tries to back off by bringing you meat. You give him hell again, and this time you threaten to put the lot of them in jail for stealing meat when the country is starving. Now they're really on the skids, I mean panic-scared and shaking. The spirits in the entrails have turned against them. Only one thing left for them to do, isn't there?'

'Dig up the entrails and get rid of them, I suppose.'

'Oh yes, they'll have to put back the clock, but appeasing the spirits won't be so easy. They'll have to work at it. Work hard. Do as they're told without trying to outsmart you. Be good citizens. Do what comes naturally.'

'What's that?'

'For them? Being obedient.'

I smiled.

He remembered at once that the good Scout is at all times chivalrous, a parfit knight who never kicks a defeated enemy when the slob's down. 'Of course,' he added, 'as soon as they'd decided to behave themselves I was as nice as pie. That's the way spells work, like a storm. One moment it's all thunder and lightning and cleansing fear. Then, when the gods and the sorcerer are appeased, out comes the sun again.'

That was only one of his analogies on the subject of spells and sorcery. Many of them I came to know quite well. For me, though, the thing he was describing – often quite poetic-ally – was merely a primitive, and only slightly more deadly, version of what western man nowadays calls gamesmanship. A death-spell can kill in two ways: by frightening the victim to death or, since few men are totally susceptible to fear, by frightening him into doing something foolish – like taking too many sleeping pills or stepping in front of a bus.

It was Mat's belief that Lord Baden-Powell was a natural sorcerer of great potency, and that, but for the accident of his having been born an Englishman, his world leadership would have extended far beyond the confines of the Boy Scout move-ment. He would have had the will to use his superb skills and cunning politically.

Mat had made a close study of the Chief Scout's defence of Mafeking during the Boer War. The famous siege, which began in October 1899 and lasted for over eight months, was, accord-ing to B-P who commanded the town's defenders, a 'minor operation', and his successful defence against overwhelming odds, 'largely a piece of bluff'.

Mat says that he put a spell on the enemy. An official

historian said that he made imaginative tactical use of the modest resources at his disposal. Either or both could be right. By constantly moving his one acetylene searchlight around, B-P made the enemy believe that no night attack could possibly succeed. He disturbed their sleep by using a megaphone to give orders to imaginary trench-raiding parties. He harassed them with snipers who only fired during the late afternoon when the sun was behind them and in the enemy's eyes. His men lobbed bombs at the enemy with fishing rods as if they were casting from a beach for flounders. When he had pushed his line of forts and his trench system far enough out from the town, he even began sniping with field-guns. And all the time he kept up a cheerful correspondence with the enemy who was trying to starve him out or wear him down – the Scout smiles and whistles under all difficulties. In a presumptuous attempt to cast spells – or wage psychological warfare? – in the B-P manner, the Boer Commandant at one point proposed a cricket match between the two sides. B-P's reply could not have been bettered, in Mat's opinion. 'You must bowl us out first before your side can come in.'

With Mat, I have never really been sure where cleverness stops and low cunning begins. Inside that second-rate mind, there could be a third-rate one struggling to get out.

Among things said by Mat that I repeated to Krom and the witnesses was this:

'A man once called me a shark. You know what imbeciles some so-called businessmen are. *He* loses money, so he calls *me* a shark. He thought he was being offensive. I took it as a compliment. Know something? In the islands, my mother's people worship sharks. That's because sharks are the greatest of all the spirits of the dead. Super-saints, you might say, godlike beings. So, when he called me a shark I only laughed. What's wrong with being told you're a god? As a matter of fact, I rather enjoyed it.'

'That was *very* nice,' said Dr Henson.

She and Connell were in her room. After an interval the bed creaked again.

I was alone with the bugging gear in the loft over the garage. Yves had been sent, at his own request, on a tour of the perimeter fences. Melanie was on watch at the attic windows. Krom was in his room studying File No. 2, *and* licking his wounds no doubt. He would also be casting about feverishly for some way of retrieving his position. He couldn't wholly succeed now, but he still had a negotiating position of sorts; and, in spite of the wounds I had inflicted on him, he would make the most of it. More hard bargaining lay ahead.

That is, it lay ahead as long as the two parties at present under attack remained in reasonably good condition.

Connell and Henson had begun to talk again.

'It's the old man's own fault,' he was saying; 'if he'd levelled with us in Amsterdam and we'd talked it through with him, even a little, we'd at least have had *some* chance. We wouldn't have had to stand there like dummies while Firman threw curve balls that the old man couldn't even *see*.'

'One sympathizes though.'

'Oh, sure. That Oberholzer identification was his big break-through, so everything that came after had to flow from it, whether it should really have done so or not. He was wearing blinkers and we weren't allowed to comment or even notice.'

'Hindsight, friend.'

'Admitted. Even so . . .'

'Even so, what could we have changed? We might have had private doubts, but can you see either of us trying to tell the old man that he'd got the wrong end of the stick? Another thing. Firman's right. If *we'd* been doing the research, we'd have taken months to track down Symposia's tie-up with this Australasian witch-doctor Boy Scout. You know we would. By the way, I think my right leg's going to sleep. Do you mind easing over just a fraction of a . . . ?'

'Sorry.'

'No, that's fine. Don't go away. Were you ever a Scout?'

'Never. Nobody ever asked me to join. Don't tell me you were a Girl Guide.'

'I was wondering about the total ethos of a movement that could accommodate Mr Williamson and his peculiarities with such ease. My brother joined the Scouts when he was a boy, but he's eight years older than me so we didn't discuss the experience while it was happening. All I heard was grown-ups discussing it. He dropped out. I'm not sure why. I do remember one thing he quoted from the Baden-Powell book on scouting. It was the twelfth edition my brother had, an enlarged and revised one. I know that because when he quoted from it, my father pricked up his ears. Thought it might be the Edwardian first edition and therefore valuable.'

'Because the thing quoted was an Edwardian value judgement?'

'Not exactly. The book said that a tenderfoot was sometimes

timid about handling dead or injured men or seeing blood.'

'Here's one tenderfoot who still is.'

'Well, Baden-Powell said that if you were to visit a slaughter-house you'd soon get used to it. It didn't say how often you had to go. Until you *were* used to it, I suppose.'

'Used to seeing dead men in a slaughter-house?'

'Used to the sight of blood. That's a problem Mr Williamson's never experienced, I imagine. Did you like the shark-worship thing? We have an anthropologist who did her doctoral thesis on one of those island groups. I've never completely trusted her or her Pacific-island colleagues. I mean the khaki-shorts-and-beard brigade. You know? Out there, with all those animistic tribes for them to batten on, they can't go wrong. You fancy a sub-culture that's taken to keeping the souls of the departed in used Coca-Cola bottle-caps? All you have to do is seek, find, and then get lots of sixteen-millimetre colour footage before anyone else can. Your reputation's made. If shark-worship hadn't existed, Mr Williamson would have had no trouble at all inventing it.'

'The way I heard it, Williamson has no trouble at all doing anything, ever. That bit about his enjoying being told he's a god had a certain ring. And there were other bits I thought un-Firmanlike too. Our host may be a son-of-a-bitch, but he wouldn't get his kicks out of brain-washing domestic help who couldn't talk back, and I doubt if he'd be capable of dreaming up the entrails story. Hell, I'm beginning to buy his Number-Two pitch.'

'I bought that after hearing Yamatoku. Those whom the gods wish to destroy they first call up with the advance warning of the holocaust.'

'It isn't only the gods who like to do things in that order.'

'Sorry, my fault. I wasn't thinking just about sour marriages though.'

There was a pause. I waited patiently while they made themselves more comfortable. Then she went on.

'Mafeking was what made me think. Or, rather, the mirror-image of it that was held up so thoughtfully to demonstrate the nature of our predicament. It's got everything, *nearly* everything anyway, that we've got here, hasn't it?'

'*Almost* nearly everything, yes.'

'A garrison besieged, but somewhat short of field-guns to snipe with? That sort of almost-nearly do you mean?'

'I was thinking more along the lines that, in this mirror version of the siege, the good old Chief Scout's on the outside doing his whistling and weaving of spells, instead of standing firm on the inside, and either socking it to the enemy with bombs on fishing lines or writing sardonic notes about cricket.'

'There's that, I agree.' But she sounded doubtful. She was nearly there. 'What bothers me isn't in the mirror.'

'Nothing to do with Mafeking?'

'Oh, very much to do with Mafeking. The reason why the siege of Mafeking is remembered and why it added to the language a new word for crowd euphoria, you'll recall, isn't that it made Baden-Powell a popular hero, but that its long-awaited relief caused such wild rejoicing. The *relief* of Mafeking, *that's* what's remembered, not the siege. So, what bothers me is not that Baden-Powell is shown on the wrong side, but that there's no relief column on the way.'

'I see what you mean. No distant trumpeter, no cut-away of the cavalry galloping through murderous enemy fire to the rescue.'

'The police here have motor bikes. But yes, that's part of what I mean.'

'The old man's already rejected the police once. Okay, the situation seems to have changed. But what do we, or they, complain of to the local commissaire. The burns in Mr Boularis's shoe? Mr Yamatoku's used-car-lot courtliness?'

'Don't you think, friend, that we may still be missing the point? That phone call was a threat, but only if one knew enough to understand why. When we began to see that our leader had made a number of quite bad mistakes, you asked Firman a question. What kind of danger were we in and what was the extent of it?'

'A question he didn't answer.'

'A question that he didn't answer *immediately*. Supposing he'd told us, there and then, that his boss and partner, Williamson, had decided to terminate that uninsurable risk we all represented by killing us. What would your reaction have been? The same as mine, I expect. We'd have tittered merrily then moved on to the next question. "What must we do to be saved?"'

'Still tittering merrily?'

'Merrily enough, I think, to make it certain that any answer we received would be either facetious or evasive. Boularis is no longer even nominally polite to us. Firman's still doing his best, but our academic conceits must bore him stiff.'

'I'm afraid you may be right.'

'So, I think that Firman *has* answered your question.'

'With all this stuff about spell-casting and Mafeking studies?'
He was having doubts again.

'Authentic anecdote, I call it. What other currency has the
wretched man left? What currency, I mean, that we'd accept
from him without saying that it was unquestionably forged?'

'All right. We have our answer. "Yes, you're all for the
chopping-block. Sorry." Now, how do we tackle the matter of
survival? I think we'd both be grateful if his answer to that
was a little less Delphian and didn't have to be interpreted.
Always assuming, naturally, that there is an answer and that
he has it.'

'Perhaps we should try asking him about that first. I have
another suggestion.'

'Shoot.'

'That we don't ask Firman anything more in front of
Professor Krom.'

A pause, then he sighed. 'Difficult.'

'Why? Krom, if he ever gets back to civilization, will undoubtedly write all this up as if everything turned out exactly
as he had planned it. It'll be back to the dream world for him.
We decline to comment on anything except the authenticity
of those papers we've seen. End of obligation. What's difficult
about that? Do you mind passing me my cigarettes?'

Two reliable allies would be sufficient for what I had in mind.
I switched off and went downstairs to the garage.

When I'd found the things I'd been looking for I hid them
under the stairs.

Back in the loft, I went through the carton with the tapes
in it. The boxes containing the ones Yves had used were
numbered. I removed the tapes, adding the one I had just
recorded to the pile, but left the numbered boxes in the carton.

In my bedroom I put the tapes away in a safe place before
going up to the attic.

Melanie had Yves's binoculars on her lap with her hands
folded over them. She looked up as I came in but had obviously
been dozing.

I told her to go to her room and have a nap and that I
would keep watch for a while.

When she had gone, I used the binoculars to see where Yves
had got to on his tour of the perimeter. I spotted him down
near the coast-road gate, well away from the house.

I returned to the garage. The job I had to do there should
have taken no more than half an hour, but it took me much

longer than that. I have never been much of a handyman. Persons like Yves who can work so quickly and surely with their hands have always made me envious.

But at least I did the job properly; did it without being disturbed or attracting attention and got back upstairs without being seen on the way.

This time, when I searched with the binoculars, I couldn't locate Yves. An hour earlier, that would have worried me.

Now, it didn't. I went down to my bedroom, cleaned myself up and then, after pushing a note under Melanie's door, descended to the drawing-room. The note told her not to bother returning to the attic as I had revised our security arrangements.

Now, there was no point in having a sentry up there.

Now, all I had to do was to continue to think clearly and to give Connell and Henson, already heading towards me from the terrace, the prescription for our collective survival.

Oh yes, and I had to decide, too, how to reply to Mat.

He would call, I knew; not just to make sure that his spell was working – he would have few doubts on that score – but to make sure that I remained faithful unto death, and that, if the process of my dying should happen to take longer than planned, I wouldn't spend the extra time drawing unpleasant conclusions and making wild statements to ambulance attendants.

That was one chore he wouldn't leave to Frank Yamatoku.

Moulding the minds and hearts of men was work for gods.

CHAPTER TEN

The fireworks began soon after dinner.

When the first rockets went up from a boat along the coast off Monte Carlo, they seemed to act on Krom as a signal.

We had eaten simply, as Melanie had arranged, so that the servants could get off early to their local Quatorze juillet fête. While they were clearing the table we had moved to the terrace, though keeping close to the house in what even a sulkily nervous Yves had had to agree was an unexposed area. A drink tray had already been set out for us. I had opened a bottle of brandy.

As the popping sounds of the distant red-white-and-blue bursts arrived, Krom leaned forward and raised his glass. For a moment I thought absurdly that he must be about to propose a Bastille Day toast, but no; he had seen an insect drown itself in his brandy.

'I am glad to tell you, Mr Firman,' he said as he fished out the corpse with the tip of a napkin, 'that I am now prepared to discuss your Paper Number Two and to receive your Paper Number Three as per our agreement.'

'What agreement is that, Professor?'

I had avoided him after my talk with Connell and Henson. They might be allies now, but only allies of a sort. I couldn't expect them, when it came to fresh haggling with Krom over the threats and promises made in Brussels, to ignore his just claims on their moral support. It had been important, therefore, that they had time to get used to the idea of helping me with what mattered without having to oppose me again over something that by then scarcely mattered at all. The solution had been to stay in my room, leaving Melanie to ply Krom with pre-dinner drinks. Mat wouldn't, I knew, call unannounced. First, there would be a figurative rolling of drums or a clap or two of stage thunder calculated to strike fear into the hearts of us simple men. One could only wait for such a great moment. I had used the time to get all the tapes properly wrapped and hidden in the small bag I intended to take with me on the escape run, and to check out the local radio-taxi services. The bottle of frozen champagne brought to me by the cook's husband had thawed out sufficiently for me to be able to drink two glasses and the burgundy with dinner had been good enough. The strain had been there all right, but it had been under control. When we had moved to the terrace I had been ready to be kind to Krom.

Now, he was showing me his teeth again, and not just in normal quantities.

'I speak of our original agreement,' he said, 'and it is no use rolling your eyes, Mr Firman. I intend to enforce the original terms in all respects.'

'Using what sanctions to enforce them, Professor?'

He gave me the wide-angle view of his bridgework. 'Twenty per cent of what I could have used before, my friend. Twenty per cent of Symposia instead of one hundred per cent, *plus* the knowledge that, even if it were one per cent and we were dealing with a figurehead criminal, the Director of the Institute for International Investment and Trust Counselling still has to maintain the fiction that he is a man of probity.'

'Any attempt on your part to contend that I'm not, Professor, will land you with actions for libel, slander and defamation of character, depending on how you make your allegations and where. Meanwhile, take my advice. You're going to need all your strength before long, so don't push yourself too hard. I have more files prepared for you and you shall have them in due course. Melanie has the copies ready and waiting. At the moment, however, she's listening for the phone call I'm expecting, the one from Mat Williamson. You can hear it if you like. In fact, I think you *should* hear it, all of you.' I had turned, as I spoke, to Yves. 'That could be arranged, couldn't it, with some of the equipment you have?'

Yves squirmed visibly, then tried to pull himself together. Sulkiness was succeeded by pomposity. 'With respect, Patron, I think that with such a conversation, if it takes place, it would be wiser if you used your own recorder.'

'Yves is sensitive about his special skills,' I explained. 'It was just an idea. I thought you might all like to hear it as it's happening.'

'I'm for that,' Connell said. 'More authentic, I'd say. Don't you agree, Professor?'

'If Mr Firman wishes us to hear a telephone conversation, the question of its authenticity doesn't arise. It may be presumed false.'

I shrugged. 'Well, it's up to you. I thought I'd mention it.'

That was when Yves cracked. He suddenly stood up.

'Patron, why trouble to wait? Why wait for bad news?

Because it is polite to do so? I will have no part in it and I have told Melanie so. I think that she now feels the same.'

'About what, Mr Boularis?' Dr Henson was smiling up at him. 'What would *you* like us to do?'

'You?' He looked down at her as if in surprise and then made a sweeping gesture of contempt. 'You can do what you like, Mrs Doctor. You belong with your friends. You can die with your friends. Why should I . . . ?'

He broke off. Something beyond the terrace had caught his eye. He stared, then turned again, bewildered, to me. He had given up trying now to retain his dignity.

I got up, too, to see what it was that he hadn't been expecting at that moment.

The big motor cruiser which, until then, had arrived only at breakfast time was gliding past the headland into the bay. She was carrying a lot of lights. Beneath the awning over the after deck, there was a dinner table set and awaiting a party of four. Around another table, with bottles and an ice bucket on it, were gathered two couples. The women wore denim jackets with their slacks and one of the men had put on a sweater. It was probably cool out there on the water. There was much animation. I had no binoculars handy, but I didn't think I had seen any of them before.

'I thought there were only three passengers,' I said; 'the one man and the two women who swim from the outer beach.'

'The one in the pullover must be a guest or the other husband.' He gave a strangled sort of laugh. 'They all look drunk to me.'

And indeed they did, in a way; the falling-about, arm-waving way of film extras pretending to be drunk in the orgy sequence of a biblical silent. Sounds of the revelry came faintly across the water. Much louder was the sound of diesels suddenly going astern and the squawk of the chain as an anchor was let go.

To celebrate their arrival, the man in the sweater rose unsteadily to his feet from the cushion on which he had been sitting cross-legged and flung a hand in the air as if to call for three cheers. The next moment he had swooped on a long cardboard box lying on the deck by the table and was staggering forward with it to the bows. The crewman there securing the anchor took no notice at all when the man with the box dumped it beside him and began tearing at gummed-paper fastenings on the lid.

'What the hell's he got there?' Connell demanded. 'Bunting? Fairy lights?'

The guests were standing now too. After Yves's outburst, I suppose, any diversion had been welcome. I saw the crewman walk quickly away. Henson's eyes were the sharpest. Her exclamation was one of outrage.

'Oh no!'

Then, I saw. For a swaying-about, fumbling drunk, the man in the bows was suddenly displaying remarkable dexterity. In the space of a few seconds he had lighted from a single match no less than three strings of Chinese jumping crackers and had them bursting simultaneously all over the deck around him. What's more, he wasn't even bothering to watch them. He was already rummaging in the box for fresh delights.

I could sympathize with Henson's cry of protest. I remember thinking to myself as he lighted the first string that the motor cruiser had to be a chartered one with a bad crew easily bribed. No one who owned or had any other normal concern for such a boat would have allowed a good deck to be scarred in that way. Decks are sacred, and expensive, surfaces. The Italian banker had kept sets of overshoes for guests ignorant or oafish enough to come on board wearing leather soles, and smokers on deck had always been required to carry ash-trays.

'Paul!' It was Melanie.

'Telephone,' she said. 'An old friend. And I think it's long distance.'

'On which line?'

'The listed number.'

To Krom I said: 'If you want to hear this conversation with Mat Williamson, there's an extension in the entrance hall. Melanie will show you where.'

I didn't wait to see if he accepted the offer. As I turned away, though, a sudden glow from the sea made me look back.

The vandal on the boat had lighted a Roman candle. As he held it aloft, balls of red fire were spurting up and falling to the deck all around him. His friends began to applaud.

I went up the stairs slowly. Mat would wait and I didn't want to seem even a little breathless when I took his call. After starting the recorder I waited an extra moment or two before picking up the phone, and then began to speak immediately as if I had just snatched it up.

'Mat? What a pleasant surprise!'

I tried to make my surprise, if not my pleasure, sound genuine, but of course he wasn't fooled.

'Sorry to take you away from the fireworks, Paul, but this is by way of being an emergency. Besides, I'm returning your call to me this morning.'

I had to think very quickly then. He was using the high-pitched, nasal voice of one of the English missionaries who had taught at the school in Fiji. I had heard it first when he had told me about Placid Island. It was his anti-imperialist voice, and also the one he sometimes used to make the saying of a highly unpleasant thing seem as if it were funny. He was probably using it now, partly anyway, as a disguise, but it startled me and I knew that I would have to watch myself. I ought not to have been startled by an English Birmingham accent. With the recorder going, though, it couldn't be allowed to pass without comment.

'What a strange voice you have, Grandma!'

It was a mistake. He came back promptly, sketching in, for the record, a portrait of the faithful henchman driven at last by mockery into a small loss of temper. 'I said I was sorry to spoil your fireworks, Paul, and I'm sorry to disturb you when you have so much on your plate already, but this isn't a bed-time story.'

'That's twice you've mentioned fireworks, Mat. Where are you? Along the road somewhere? Watching the fireworks too?'

'You know where I am, Paul. There are always fireworks along the coast there on the Fourteenth of July. If I'm a bit upset, that's because I've been speaking to Frank, so bear with me. I've also listened to your conversation with him earlier, and . . . Paul? Are you still there?'

'I'm here.'

'Paul, what Frank said to you this morning was one long lie.'

'You mean one continuous lie or a lot of separate lies strung together?'

'I am *not* joking, Paul. From understandable motives, possibly, but with absolutely no authority from me, Frank has made a dangerous bloody fool of himself. In trying to be helpful by running interference for you, he's done a number of things he ought not to have done. He's tried to be clever and only succeeded in being horribly stupid. As he's my responsibility, the first thing I want to do is apologize.'

'Apology accepted.' I tried then to throw him. So far, every word he'd uttered had been that of a loyal lieutenant addressing a capricious martinet. I tried to throw him by suddenly becoming a martinet, and by speaking to him in a way that he hadn't been spoken to, I was sure, for a long time, if ever. 'But,' I snarled, 'you said that apologizing was the *first* thing you wanted to do. How about the *second* and *third*? Or have you been sitting around on your black butt waiting for somebody else to do your thinking for you?'

He seemed not to have heard what I'd said. All he did was move calmly into his second-stage position. 'Paul, do you remember that time some years ago when we – you, that is – were thinking of buying into that Malay-Chinese rubber syndicate? We went to stay with those people up near Kedah.'

'No, I don't remember that at all and I've never been to Kedah.'

'*Near* Kedah, I said. You'll remember when I tell you. It was just after that American went for a walk in the jungle and disappeared. The American who'd built up that silk business in Thailand and was taking a vacation in Malaysia? Staying as a house-guest with friends? Remember now, Paul?'

'How about getting to the point?'

'But that *is* the point, that he disappeared and was certainly killed. The local theory was that after he told his friends that he was going for a walk he was accidentally killed, not because he wasn't used to jungles – in fact he was very much at home in them – but because he fell into a tiger trap the village people had dug there on the path he took. It wasn't the villagers' fault, of course, but they were scared because *he* was an American and it was *they* who'd dug the trap and planted the bamboo spikes. So they buried the body and didn't report it. That's why *our* friends didn't want us to go for any walks outside the compound while we were their guests. Our disappearance would have meant police enquiries, trouble. Besides, I think they liked us. I think they wanted our money, but I don't think they wanted us killing ourselves on their doorsteps.'

'Any more than you want me impaling myself on the bamboo stakes that Frank's been so busily sharpening? That's nice, Mat. I'm glad to know. Where's Frank staying down here?'

'It's not nice for anyone, Paul. And I'm including your guests. I don't know why. If anything should accidentally go wrong in spite of all you've done to protect them, they have to be the guilty parties. I hear through the grapevine, by the way, that two of them at least have intelligence links. I've asked friends about the Brit and they confirm. There's nothing nice about any of it. Oh, I agree with you, that doesn't excuse

Frank. He's made a prize idiot of himself. These people he used your private files to learn about and contact, these old acquaintances of yours, were never the simple-minded hay-seeds he wanted them to be. He knows that now and he's not staying in any one place. He's buzzing about like crazy, because he also knows now that trying to win medals by relieving you of an unwanted presence was never a good idea anyway. Not without consultation. I've told him. He'll be lucky if he doesn't get the chop. But let's be realistic, Paul. The fact that he knows all this, and that he's doing his damnedest to put things right, doesn't help with the immediate problem. Calling off the kind of people he's had out digging traps for you isn't as easy as setting them on.'

'I don't suppose it is, Mat. Frank's advice, as you'll know, was non-resistance. Yours appears to be a little different and slightly more reassuring – no walks in the jungle. Have I got that right?'

No plain answer, of course. I hadn't really expected one. It was time for that final, all-important move to the third stage of the ritual. The preliminary declaration that a moral authority was properly vested in him, along with its appro-priate powers, had formally been made. In other, cruder words, the softening-up process was over. Now, it was time for the decisive incantation. I know of no simple way of describing that process accurately. The carnivorous plant treating insect prey with enzymes before eating them is a clumsy comparison. Mat doesn't want to eat his victims; he only wants them to oblige him.

He spoke slowly, and was probably tapping a table or desk in time with the words as he said them.

'Paul, there's something I'm going to remind you of now that I'm quite sure you haven't forgotten. You won't have forgotten this because it was something you once told me. You told me, too, in a moment of personal loss and sadness when you were trying to recall worse things you'd gone through. It was about when you were in the army in Italy, before you got to know Carlo up in the north. You recalled seeing another soldier, one of the men under your own personal command, go to obey an order you'd given. And then, a split second later, he'd stepped on a land mine – an S-mine you called it – and been cut clean in two.'

A three-tap pause.

'How far away was he from you? Only a few yards, wasn't it? Close enough for you to be deaf for a few days, I know,

210

and close enough for you to see what his guts looked like while his own eyes were still wondering what had happened. Less than a minute to die, though, with all those arteries severed. But the awful thing for you, aside from your having told the man to do something that killed him, came afterwards, didn't it? I mean after the first physical shock, when you realized that, although *you* were still alive, there was death all around you. When you stood there with all that singing in your ears and knew that you'd strayed into a minefield, and that if you moved so much as a fraction of an inch in any direction, or maybe even leaned over a little and changed the weight distribution under one of your feet, *your* guts could be slopping about on the ground there too. So, you did what others have sometimes done when they've found they were in a minefield and seen what a mine can do to the soft human body. No disgrace, not when you're in shock and looking at the results of making the wrong move. Some men would have turned and run blindly. Not you. You froze. And you *stayed* there frozen until, eventually, someone from an engineer patrol came. Remember? He was a sergeant. He took you by the arm and persuaded you, and finally *made* you walk. It was a step at a time, much slower than a funeral march you said, left-and-right and left-and-right, until you both reached a piece of ground where tanks had been. The mark of their tracks were new, so from there you had places to put your feet where there couldn't be unexploded S-mines. You walked back in the tank tracks. You listening, Paul?'

'Yes.'

'You asked for my advice. You don't need it. You already know what to do. You're in a minefield. Freeze. Right where you are. And stay frozen until I can get things straightened out and made safe, safe for you to walk away. Will you do that for me, Paul?'

'Yes, Mat.'

It would have called for a serious effort on my part to have said anything else.

Besides, it would have been foolish to have said anything else. Better if he believed that the spell was cast; or, to use the jargon he probably now prefers, that I was correctly programmed.

'I'll be there to take your arm,' he said.

The line went dead.

Green, orange and red lights glowed and flickered in the sky.

From my bedroom there was a good view of the bay, and I had brought Yves's binoculars down with me from the attic floor. I took a closer look at the motor cruiser.

Most of the deck lights had been switched off now, as if to make the fireworks show up better; but there were several Roman candles burning at once and some of the orange balls from them stayed alight longer than the others on the way down to the water. I could see quite a lot of her.

The stern gave her name as *Chanteuse*, and her home port as Monrovia. She had Liberian registration. By the autumn she would be among the dozens of other boats just like her tied up along the yachting moles of Cannes and available for charter next year. It must have been expensive, I thought, to get hold of her at such short notice. Although there were always a few charterers who had their coronaries in June or early July, and so were obliged to forfeit their deposits, you had to be right in there with bundles of dollars or D-marks in both hands to buy your way on to the yacht-brokers' sucker lists of last-minute clients.

Mat must have hated that; but Frank wouldn't have minded.

That Frank was on board the boat, I now had no doubt at all. I knew where he was, too. The people with the drinks on the after deck were merely set-dressing. There were lights on below. The only place in complete darkness was the bridge. It was a big all-glass affair like a greenhouse, with sloping sides that reflected the glare of the fireworks. He'd be there in the darkness with a walkie-talkie, where he could see and control but not be seen.

The man in charge of the fireworks was using a flashlight to set up a Catherine wheel on a plank lashed to the bow rails. As he stood back and felt for his matches again, the beam shone straight down on the rest of the entertainment, the fun-things still to come.

There was nothing more to see. I checked both phones. Then, I rewound the tape and took the recorder downstairs so that the others could hear what had been said.

Krom tried to stop me. He had been listening on the extension and was very agitated.

'We must call the police,' he said.

'We can't. And time's running out. Keep still and listen.'

They listened. Krom seemed not to hear, though. A tic had started under his left eye. I watched the others, Yves especially. He kept catching my eyes on him and then looking past me over my shoulder. The cassette switched off.

Henson had a question. 'Did that minefield thing really happen to you as he describes it?'

'Not quite as he describes it. That's a Camp Fire Yarn version for Scouts. Mat's a prude, you see, and he has blind spots. He thinks that people are unalterable, for instance. It would never occur to him that the mere fact of my being able to tell him about that paralysing experience meant that the memory of it had become tolerable. After over thirty years, it can't paralyse me any more, only make me curl my toes.' I stood up. 'It's cooler outside and we can watch the fireworks.'

'We must call the police,' Krom said.

Connell had questions. 'What's Williamson think he's doing? Sniping with field-guns?'

'And disturbing the enemies' sleep, too, I imagine. The accent he was using, by the way, came from Birmingham in England a long time ago. It came via Fiji and used to belong to an inoffensive missionary.'

'We must . . .' Krom began, and then paused. He put out his hands and gripped his knees tightly. 'They're there and he can't stop them,' he went on. 'He won't get here in time.'

'No,' I said, 'he won't, I'm afraid.'

There was no considerate way of explaining the position, either to him or to the others.

The Catherine wheel on the boat suddenly went haywire and flew off into the sea.

'Mat's telling me to freeze because his sorcerer's calculations tell him that, after the softening up I've had and Frank Yama-toku's warning, I'm going to behave irrationally. By talking about tiger-traps and minefields, he thinks he's compelling me to run, head for the hills with most of you following. Herd instinct. He wants us to run the way we came, in two parties.'

'Why us?' asked Connell. 'You're the one who knows him. You're the danger. And why in two parties?'

'I've blown him to you. He knows that, just as he knows that Dr Henson came bearing gifts from a British intelligence branch. The same person will have told him. I'm sorry, but you asked me. It's a special occasion. You get the truth. He just wants to do the killings quietly, with a minimum of fuss and expense. Two small parties are cheaper to kill than one big one. In this case particularly, because separate explanations would be cheaper.'

'Cheaper?' Henson was indignant. 'And what have explanations to do with . . . ?'

'Killing can be very expensive these days, or it can be cheap.

213

It all depends on what's left behind and how difficult the mess is to explain. On the roads or just off them, they're the easiest dumping grounds. All you need leave behind on them is either another ugly monument to our vulgar autoroute society or, if there are bullets to be found in any of the bodies, another tragic by-product of gangster-ridden monopoly capitalism. That's as long as you don't complicate things for the traffic police by mixing criminologists with tax-consultants.'

Or by letting a victim talk before he dies. How thoughtfully I had been programmed! Should my final moments be unduly prolonged, I could spend them reminding myself sadly that dear old Mat had been right after all. He'd told me to stand still, and like a fool I hadn't listened.

'Are you saying the Professor's right?' demanded Melanie; 'that we should freeze?'

'No, dear, I'm not. Mat will be doing everything he can to make us run because that would give him what he wants for the lowest price. But he's not too proud to have had a contingency plan prepared and ready. By using the agent in place he has here, he should be able to mount a quick two-birds-with-one-stone operation with no trouble at all. It can't be as tidy or as cheap, though. That's the difference. Cars with bodies in them aren't news. A bunch of psychos rampaging through an expensive villa, and killing five foreign-visitor occupants, would make headlines. And think of the cost! With all that easy money going on the tycoon kidnap circuit, the reliable people want danger money and fringe benefits if there's the remotest chance of their being caught, or even identified.'

No, better by far if I acted as programmed. Better for me. Better for our friendship. That was what he'd been telling me with the sob in his throat at the end.

Connell said: 'The agent in place you're talking about must be Yamatoku. Right?'

Wrong, and the look that Henson gave me said that she knew it was wrong, but Krom was suddenly emphatic.

'We must stay,' he insisted, 'stay here . . .'

That beautiful spell, woven to impose the sorcerer's will upon me, had failed with me because its beauties had been too knowingly and lovingly displayed for my taste. However, with Krom, not a man to be put off by schmaltz if he found the tune familiar, it had succeeded remarkably; though not in producing the effect Mat had intended.

He hadn't been telling Krom anything in particular, except possibly that this wasn't the *real* Mat Williamson speaking;

but Krom had listened and what he had heard had made the most exquisite sense to him. Mat had said freeze, so that was what Krom had found he wanted to do, *all* he wanted to do – stay absolutely still where he was, until some kind stranger came to take his arm and lead him to safety.

It wasn't, I think, that he was over-susceptible to the brand of hypnotic suggestion that Mat favours and can use with such effect when dealing with the unwary, or even – since, as far as I know, Krom was never in his youth caught in a mine-field – that the evocation of an intense fear experienced in the past triggered an irrational response to events occurring years later. What threw the man so completely was that set of facts which Mat had used to construct his Mafeking-sur-Mer fantasies happened to be not only familiar to Krom but also essential to his own fantasies, those about that arch-liar and able criminal, Oberholzer-Firman. He had known for years that there was nothing imaginary about the two men code-named Kleister and Torten. His original Swiss police contacts had confirmed the men's existence and their strange, psychotic retirement hobby. With those and other vengeful bogeymen like them crouching out there in the darkness, nursing pent-up hatreds and waiting, fingers on triggers, to kill anyone who broke cover, what else was there to do but stay put and keep your head down until help came?

'Stay here and telephone for the police,' he repeated.

Connell glanced from Krom to me. 'I can see, Mr Firman, why you might think it inadvisable to try busting out of here. I can also see why you'd consider this garrison a bit short on the arms and know-how needed to beat off an attack by trained assault troops. Unless you have guns as well as brandy to hand out I mean. I don't see what's wrong, though, with calling the police. If the Professor thinks it's a good idea and we can figure out a way of requesting protection that they'll take seriously – suspected prowlers, maybe – I say let's do it. And in view of the other prospects and possibilities you've been outlining, I say let's do it right now. Let's call in the relief column, dammit!'

'Yves will tell you why we can't,' I said. 'Tell them, Yves.'

He stared out fixedly at the boat.

'Yves has a gun,' I went on; 'he's the only one amongst us who has, and he's being very careful to sit where none of us can get behind him. He's worried because he's badly afraid of the consequence of failure at the moment. He couldn't shoot more than two of us before the others jumped him, so he's playing it cool, or trying to, and waiting for his friend Frank to tell him what to do next. We can't use the phone because he cut both lines right after Mat's call. I know because I checked. He's not going to let us try finding the place and repairing the lines, I'm sure. The gun's inside his shirt under his left arm. I think we'd like it to stay there.'

Krom nodded. '*Status quo*,' he said, and reached for the brandy bottle.

Henson sighed. 'Oh dear.'

'Oh dear, indeed. Our forthright, no-nonsense Mr Boularis has been very busy here. Busy making booby-traps, busy reporting progress at the lower-road gate, thoughtfully recommending instant flight as the way out of all difficulties, even offering to drive Melanie and me to our own private holocaust in *your* car. Mr Williamson and Mr Yamatoku wanted us to leave in a particular way, so naturally Yves did his level best to see that we did. My goodness, how hard he's been working! Not his fault that I'm nervous of drivers who tell you how good they are. Didn't you wonder too, Dr Henson, how Mat had found out about your connection with British intelligence?'

'Yes, I did. Especially as the only connection that exists is the one I told you about. Mr Boularis wasn't present when I told you about it though.'

'He must have been listening at the door.'

'Or else . . .' Connell hesitated, wondering if what he had suddenly thought of saying might be tactless. About some things he could be very quick on the uptake. It had been he, I recalled, who had voiced aloud his doubts of modern man's ability to spot a room-bug just by looking for it.

Melanie dealt with him firmly. 'Well, it no longer matters. Look! His friends on the boat are sending him signals.'

A couple of cardboard volcanoes had begun to spout red lava and golden rain.

'Signals to say what?' Connell's mind was still with the room-bug hypothesis, but he looked at Yves.

Yves didn't answer. His face was shiny with sweat.

I answered for him. 'Signals to say that the fun's over, I would think. Now, he's waiting for the bangs he's been warned to expect. Mat Williamson is a great believer in the loud bang as an argument. Simple people respect it. Not-so-simple people can often be fooled by it. As a means of inducing sensible people to behave stupidly or irrationally there's nothing to equal it.'

I was talking by then to keep my own courage up. I had seen

the launching rack on the deck out there from the bedroom window. It looked like an office-furniture designer's idea for an umbrella stand made out of a bundle of drain pipes. The fire-work man had been using the glare from the volcanoes to see by. He wanted no mistakes with that lot.

'Coming back, if you don't mind, to the subject of relief columns,' said Henson; 'you did say something about a need for concerted action when the right moment came and you gave the word. Aren't you leaving it a bit late?'

'No.'

I didn't try to elaborate. It would have been silly to tell her that there wasn't, after all, going to be any word. Allies are notoriously unable to understand why, when the time comes, they are quite often no longer needed.

Besides, at that moment the rockets were fired.

Visually, they had nothing to offer: no graceful arcs of coloured fire, no pretty second-stage bursts to surprise delighted onlookers, no candelabrum flares on parachutes, none of the ooh-aah stuff that was dished out in Monte Carlo. As the first salvo went up, all we saw were the jets of orange flame that lifted the things out of the umbrella stand.

Then, with apologetic plopping sounds, they seemed to give up and disappear.

The explosions on and near the terrace were not big, but they were far from apologetic. I doubt if there were more than a few ounces of HE in any of the charges. That's about what there would be in a modern hand-grenade; just enough to create a really jolting anti-personnel blast-wave with a radius of three or four yards. The shallow hole gouged out of a patch of Bermuda grass could have been made by a dog burying a bone. The stonework of the terrace suffered no more than pock-marks. There were several broken windows though.

No one was hurt, but the effect on Krom was remarkable. With him, the noises seemed to act like the traditional snap of the fingers employed by a stage hypnotist to bring his subject out of a trance.

I must say, too, that for a man of his age with half a bottle of brandy in the bloodstream, his reflexts were amazing. When the first salvo exploded, he did a racing dive on to the flagstones. He had found cover behind the pedestal of a marble-topped table before I had even started to move. By the time the second lot arrived, he was already wriggling and rolling his way over the broken glass by the drawing-room windows towards the comparative safety of the room itself.

'You see? You see?' he was saying as he went.

We did see; at least, we saw that it was necessary to get off the terrace. The third salvo, which broke another pane of glass and left one of the outside chair-cushions smouldering, was followed by a brief silence. Melanie broke it.

'Those people must be insane!'

'Of *course* they are insane.' Krom was lying curled up on the floor, busy searching the front of his shirt for slivers of glass. 'They have been insane for years. They were *driven* insane by our host.'

He may have been snapped out of a trance, but all spells were still in full working order.

'Are you suggesting,' Connell demanded in the most disrespectful tone I had yet heard him use to Krom, 'that the middle-aged jerks playing with explosives on that boat are Kleister and Torten?'

'Who else would fire mortar shells to maim or kill their tormentor?'

'Those beer-bellied cretins out there are in their forties.'

'And they are not firing mortar shells,' said Melanie; 'anyone who has ever been near a mortar bombardment would tell you that. Those were signal maroons, defective ones.'

'Not defective,' said Yves; 'only modified for aiming. They have death there. That was a rehearsal. Do you want to wait for the real thing? Take no notice of what Firman says. Get up and go, while you still can!'

Yves was a tryer; no doubt of that. He had much to lose.

I had begun to move and was almost at the door when Henson noticed the fact. As it was important just then that I shouldn't have further attention drawn to me, I gave her a meaning nod. I hoped that she would interpret it as the promised 'word' and as a sign that the time had come for a diversion.

She did not disappoint me.

'How do we *know* that the telephone lines are cut?' she asked Connell accusingly. 'Have *you* tried them? Has anyone tried them? Because if they haven't, I don't feel like taking the man Firman's unsupported word for it. There may be *one* line still working. If so, I think that Professor Krom should immediately call the police on all our behalfs.'

A good effort. Melanie moved in at once to cover the sound of my opening the door.

'If anyone is to telephone the police it must be me, Professor, because I am the official tenant here in this villa. It is I also who must telephone the *gérant* acting for the owners so that the damage can be reported and assessed. Please remember, too, if there is a telephone working, which I doubt, that the name of the tenant and present occupier here is not Firman or Wicky-Frey. It is Oberholzer.'

'Aha!' said Krom happily. 'Be sure I shall remember. Oberholzer! How could I forget?'

The jerrican was of metal and a real World War II veteran, not one of the plastic imitations they make nowadays. It had probably been sitting there in the corner of that garage for years; since one of those times when it had been thought prudent to keep a little gasoline put by for emergencies in case the local pumps ran dry. After which Middle East war had it last been filled? The '73? The '67? The Suez fiasco of '56?

I hoped that it hadn't been the Suez, because a top-sergeant who used to flog the stuff had once told me that gasoline stored for years gradually loses its potency. I also hoped that the man had merely been rationalizing his misconduct. Neither of the two cars had much left in its tank, and I wanted an event not an incident; it had to be a huge blaze, one that would quickly be seen and reported but not easily put out.

I was worried, too, about the roof problem. Before I had known that Mat was going to oblige me with fireworks, I had rigged the thing to look like a short-circuit following insulation failure in antique wiring. It wouldn't have deceived an arson investigator, but I had been prepared to face that difficulty later in return for the presence, when needed, of some fire trucks and their crews along with a back-up force of police cars and gawking spectators. The fireworks had given me a cover story potentially better than the one about antique wiring; but would it in fact be better if there were no hole in the roof to show where the firework had smashed through? Wouldn't that look fishier than a short-circuit? Even fishier than the remains of The Device?

I thought for a few moments of taking a hammer up to the loft and breaking one or two roof tiles. I didn't in the end; partly because I couldn't find a hammer, but mainly because I was, I have to admit it, beginning to panic.

The rocket-firing could well have been accompanied by a signal to the waiting clean-up team. 'That's zero, kids. Start counting. Give them ten minutes to get themselves together. If the bastards haven't begun to come out by then, you go right in and start earning your money.'

Or words to that effect. Besides, I didn't even know if The Device I'd cobbled together would work. I might have to waste valuable time finding out. Someone – Yves, for instance – might come looking for me while I was doing so. If, through having sweaty hands and being in too much of a hurry, I botched the job, I might end up by having to go in there and try blowing myself to bits with lighted matches.

The passage that led to the garage ended at the inner door of what had obviously once been a cubby-hole, with lavatory adjoining, for chauffeurs. Now, it was cluttered with such things as water-skis, old schnorkel masks, a wickerwork chair with a broken seat and a set of golf clubs with hickory shafts. On the wall by the far door were two switches, one controlling the passage lights, the other the lights in the garage. That second switch was necessary because there were no windows or skylights in the garage. When the big outer doors were closed it was pitch-black inside. I made sure that the second switch was in the 'off' position.

To arm The Device, I had to enter the garage without the lights on and feel my way around the cars to a work-bench against the opposite wall. On the bench was a trickle charger with spring-clip connectors on long leads for attaching the thing to a run-down battery without removing the battery from the car. The Device was made out of the two spring-clips, three adhesive bandages and one of the cigar-lighters belonging to the Lincoln. It was fastened with a piece of string, just inside the unlatched lid of the jerrican – in the place where the most vapour would be.

Arming it meant connecting the mains lead of the charger to the light-bulb socket above the bench. That was its regular source of power. There was no wall outlet. Switching on the light would then do one of two things: either blow a fuse somewhere in the house or, more likely, cause the cigar-lighter filament to heat up and ignite the gasoline vapour.

I could smell the vapour as soon as I opened the door. If the stuff had deteriorated in storage, it still smelled like gasoline, almost overpoweringly so. But could one tell by the smell of it? On the way around the cars I was tempted to take the caps off the tanks or loosen them. I didn't do either of those things though. A tank with no cap on it, or no signs of having burst under pressure, would be the sort of thing an arson man would spot instantly. Forget it.

Even if I'd had a flashlight, I doubt if I'd have used it. The night was very warm and the sun had been on the loft roof directly above for most of the day. The place fairly reeked of gas. I'd have been afraid of even the tiny little spark there might be inside the flashlight's outer case. The faint light from the door into the house, although most of it was blocked off by the cars, gave some help. Memory and the touch of sweaty fingers had to do the rest.

Finding the light-bulb socket over the bench was the most difficult thing. Standing there with one hand above my head, groping for the damned thing, I began to feel disoriented. Twice, I had to stop and find the edge of the bench again to make sure that I was still facing the right way. Once, when I had found the light socket, I dropped the charger lead and had to start all over again. But it was done at last. Only halfway through my sigh of relief did I remember that, now, if Yves or Melanie came along the passage looking for me, and switched on the light by the door before I could stop them, The Device would . . .

I scrambled out of there so fast that I bruised myself quite badly against the rear end of the Lincoln. I also gashed a shin in falling over the foot of the loft stairs. Panic. Bloody stupid panic.

Back outside the door again, with only a residual smell of gas still clinging to me and the pains in my left arm and right leg beginning to make themselves felt, I was suddenly quite sure that none of it was going to work, that I'd forgotten something of crucial importance.

Wearily, I leaned against the door and pressed the switch.

The passage light went out but nothing else happened. I had pressed the wrong switch.

I wiped the sweat out of my eyes and pressed the right one.

The *whoof* of the ignition felt like someone putting a shoulder to the door, not to try to force it open, just to see if it were latched.

Very gently, I unlatched it. It tried, equally gently, to close itself again. I used the handle of a ping-pong bat to keep it from closing completely, and then opened the lavatory window to make sure that there would be no shortage of oxygen inside.

I shut the inner door behind me as I left.

There were raised voices coming from the hall, but I had no way of getting up the stairs without being seen.

'It is for Mr Firman and no one else,' Melanie was saying, 'to decide what shall be done and when it shall be done. He is your host, and you, while you are his guests, must respect his wishes.'

Her defiant whine suggested that she was losing the argument. It was no surprise to find that she was losing it to Krom.

'As we are in danger,' he said acidly, 'such niceties of etiquette hardly seem relevant.'

'Quite right,' I said.

They stared at me with understandable curiosity. As well as having torn slacks, I must also have looked filthy and my shirt was black with sweat.

The curiosity changed to suspicion.

'What have you been trying to do?' asked Connell. 'Make it through the enemy lines?'

'No. Looking for the cavalry.'

Melanie was holding my tape-recorder. I had left it in the dining-room earlier. I took it from her, then turned to Krom.

'I have to tell you,' I said, 'that it will shortly become necessary for us to leave here. All of us. Any further meetings, if there should be any, will have to be held in another place.'

Krom started to open his mouth. I talked him down by raising my voice.

'No arguments. You have time, I think, to collect your passports, money, notebooks and other valuables from your rooms, but no time to pack anything. I must ask you to assemble here in no more than ten minutes.'

When Krom again opened his mouth, I let him speak.

'May guests be permitted to know what fresh disaster *now* postpones our detailed examination of your criminal past?'

'Certainly. The house is on fire.'

For a moment I thought that his tic had returned. Then, a most curious muscular spasm flattened the circumflex of his upper lip and covered the teeth behind it.

He was trying to stop himself giving me a smile of resignation.

The departments of Var and Alpes-Maritimes in southern France have suffered much from forest fires involving buildings and lives. As a result, the regional fire services are well equipped and well trained. On the Fourteenth of July an exceptionally high state of readiness is always maintained.

Our fire was first spotted by a man in a villa up on the corniche to the east of us. He reported it promptly, no doubt, because there was a slight breeze blowing from us to him, and because we might have been out for the evening. Fire travels quickly in those parts.

The braying of the approaching fire trucks and police cars began as I was stepping out of the shower.

Yes, I showered. I put on clean clothes too. Anyone who believes that the best way of convincing the police that you're not an arsonist is to look as if you've been in there fighting the flames with a wet towel and a garden hose, has to be mistaken.

By the time the leading truck turned into the driveway, I was ready to greet it. All I had had to do first was park my small bag with the tapes and other oddments I would be needing later in a safe place on the terrace. There was no point in lugging the recorder along too, so I opened it to remove the last cassette. Someone had already taken it.

Yves? That wasn't the moment to ask. I went downstairs. When the first police car arrived, I was out there with Melanie, wringing my hands, getting in the firemen's way and generally behaving just as any other right-minded person would have behaved in those circumstances.

My story was simple. Madmen on boat. Dud rockets. Old stabling converted for use as garage probably tinder dry. Hadn't seen fire start at back because dealing with burning cushions on terrace. Phones by then out of order. Witnesses, including distinguished Professor, would confirm. Thank God you're here.

I named the boat and told them to look for burn marks on her deck. No, they wouldn't be the kinds of burns you could wash off with soap and water. Power tools and much time would be needed to get rid of those scars. When they caught the villains, as they surely must, I would dearly like to be on hand with a shot-gun. Yes, I understood that one mustn't take the law into one's own hands and that I was over-wrought, but no doubt they understood my feelings.

I needn't have worried about there being no hole in the roof to show where the spent rocket had smashed through. When the firemen got there most of the roof had already fallen in. They concentrated on trying to contain the blaze and on confining it to the older, unremodelled part of the building. The senior firemen thought they would succeed, but it would be a long job, and some of his men would have to stay with it to watch for flare-ups. No, he certainly wouldn't advise any-one to sleep in the house. The fire had already got to the main electricity cable, and, when the pipes began to melt, the water would have to be turned off. Better start thinking about a hotel.

Since I didn't intend to be available when the insurance investigators started wondering how best to avoid paying out on the owner's claim, that left the cut phone lines as the likeliest source of trouble with local officialdom. If they could be seen to have been cut, there would be unpleasant questions asked and suspicion aroused prematurely. I consulted Yves.

'It's all right,' he said; 'the lines came in by the garage and that's where I cut them. The fire won't have left anything for anyone to see.'

'Good. Now I'll take that cassette.'

'What cassette?'

'The one that was in my recorder. The call from Mat.'

'Krom took that. He thinks nobody saw him. It's in his shirt pocket. You could try snatching it. I'll bet he won't give it to you.' His eyes narrowed maliciously. 'Did you know, Paul, that all that beautiful equipment of mine was charged to Symposia? You've lost that lot of tapes too. Bad luck.'

I tried to look as if he'd driven yet another nail into my coffin.

A gendarmerie radio van had arrived to handle communica-tions with the various authorities along the coast who would be concerned with tracking down the *Chanteuse* and bringing in her passengers and crew for questioning.

The cook and her husband returned on their motor scooter, having heard in the village about the fire. The extension to the house that contained their apartment, though badly scorched on the outside, was otherwise undamaged. After preliminary lamentations, they set about making a list of the valuable personal possessions they had left in the kitchen, the laundry, the wine-cellar, the pantry and one or two other rooms adjacent to the garage which had also suffered. A colour TV set, that they claimed to have bought themselves and installed in the pantry next to the freezer, was high on their list. The insurance investigator who diagnosed arson would have a choice of suspects.

The upper road had been closed by the police to non-essential traffic as soon as the alarm had been given. The coast road, however, became jammed with sightseers who had stopped their cars to watch the fun. Motor-cycle police had to be sent to move them on.

A television crew, who had seen the fire while covering a 'folkorique' happening up at La Turbie, were allowed in to get pictures for the regional news. Yves slipped away immediately, and so did I. Fortunately, the TV men didn't stay long. The blaze was already under control. I avoided the cameras by taking refuge in my bedroom, and used the time, with the aid of a candle from one of the sconces in the hall, to pack the rest of my things. I also smudged those surfaces likely to yield clear fingerprints to anyone looking for such things. The cook's husband and the daily woman would get around to cleaning up when we had gone; but, since the whole place wasn't going to burn down after all, the less there was of me there to find the better.

Melanie had no problem with the cameras, She was closeted with the police. As the owner of a burned-out car, she had to file a separate report on that incident as well as making her statement as tenant about the house fire. Connell too, the one who had signed the rental contract for the Fiat it appeared, would have to file a separate report to complete the paper work.

By then, it was eleven o'clock.

I could be certain of at least one thing. When the *Chanteuse* was picked up, Frank would not be among those found on board. It was also likely that, with all the police activity in and around the Villa Lipp, his squads of hired helpers on land had been withdrawn from the vicinity. Now, they would be waiting at assembly points farther out – waiting to see what my next move would be.

It was time I made it.

I found Krom sitting with Henson and Yves in the drawing-room, and set the ashtray I had been using as a candlestick down on the table nearest to them.

Krom was obviously very tired. However, my hope that fatigue would make him easier to deal with was a vain one.

'We have no electricity,' I began cheerfully; 'and the fire-man tells me that someone will shortly arrive to turn off the main water supply. There is still the swimming pool, of course, if you don't mind the taste of chlorine and care to use buckets, but most of it has already been pumped on to the flames by one of the fire trucks.'

He flicked me away contemptuously. 'Spare us. You meant

to disperse our gathering. You still mean to disperse it. The enemies outside having been disposed of, you are now ready to dispose of the enemies within. Dr Henson agrees with me.'

Her eyes were unfriendly. 'The relief of the beleaguered city having been completed,' she said, 'the garrison is ready to march out with colours flying. The cavalry are left in possession after their ride to the rescue.'

I knew then what the trouble with *her* was. The quip about cavalry riding to the rescue had been made by Connell while he was in her bed. By inadvertently throwing the word 'cavalry' back at him when he had accused me, facetiously, of trying to escape, I had let them both know that I had invaded their privacy. I could expect no more co-operation from them in dealing with Krom.

'The garrison may march out,' I said, 'but I wouldn't advise flying colours. You don't think Mat Williamson's going to give up just because of a little set-back here, do you?'

Krom's teeth were back in service. 'I, too, think it unlikely that the person who made that telephone call to you will give up. Was he the "Vic" we heard mentioned earlier? I think he must have been. So, he won't give up any more than Kleister and Torten will give up. They want their revenge, and they have waited a long time. Now that someone has shown them how to find you, they can follow you to the ends of the earth if necessary. We are more fortunate.'

'I wouldn't be too sure about that.'

'Oh, but I *am* sure, and my witnesses agree with me. The truth about you will be our protection. All we have to do is publish it. It's you that they want dead, not us. Mr Boularis has made that clear.'

I glanced at Yves. He smiled slightly. His closed session with them had been highly profitable. It was time for me to cut my losses.

I moved over and sat down by Krom. 'I think you have something of mine, Professor.' I pointed to the cassette in his shirt pocket, and then extended a hand as if to grab it. 'That!'

He drew back, clutching it to his breast fiercely. 'Ah, no! No, Mr Firman. If you want *this* back, you'll have to buy it. And I'll tell you what the price is. Don't you want to hear?'

His protective embrace had been passionate enough to smudge beyond recognition any of my fingerprints that might have been left on the thing, but to please him I nodded.

'How much?'

'I want two things: I want the rest of the papers you had prepared for me, the ones I would have had if we hadn't been interrupted, and I want a resumption of our meetings by this time next week at the latest. And they will be in Brussels, if you please. We have met discreetly there before, and in a public place. Why not again? I'm sure you know how to protect yourself there from fireworks, and your victims are used to waiting for satisfaction. Besides, they are obviously careful men. They are not likely to attack you in the lobby of the Brussels Westbury. So, in not more than a week's time, we can continue, eh? I shall be expecting you. What do you say?'

I stood up. 'I think it's time we thought about leaving, and I at any rate intend to be very careful *how* I leave. With luck, I may be able to persuade the gendarmerie to assist.' I looked at Henson. 'Melanie's still with the local police. The Professor's tired. I'd be glad of some help, but it's up to you.'

She followed me out to the gendarmerie van, and stood by while I explained to the sergeant in charge what the fireman had said about going to an hotel.

He pulled a face. 'At this time of year? You won't find anything near here. Monte Carlo might have something of the kind you're used to, but if you just want a place to sleep, Nice is your best chance. One of the commercial places near the central station.'

'Would it be in any way possible, Sergeant, for you to use your radio to call us a taxi?'

Henson gave him a most appealing look. 'Or even two taxis, Sergeant? There are six of us, as you see, and we have baggage.'

He said that taxis might be in short supply on the night of the Quatorze, but that he would use his influence with the radio dispatchers, those who were sober, and see what could be arranged.

The taxis came from Beaulieu, and were there within half an hour.

Melanie left the house keys with the cook's husband before joining me in the back of the second taxi. Henson said that they would take the sergeant's advice and head for Nice. No goodbyes were said. The whip had been cracked. Obviously, I was going to be sensible and safeguard what was left of my reputation by reporting for duty in Brussels the following week. They owed me no courtesies. Why should they pretend that they did?

As they were about to leave, I noticed that Yves wasn't with them. At the same moment he slid into the front seat beside our driver. He had no bag with him, nothing.

I said, 'Hallo.'

He didn't turn his head. 'Where are we going?' he asked.

I had already told the driver that we wanted to take a night train to Paris from Monte Carlo. There probably wasn't one, but modern taxi drivers only know about planes. I had no intention of going anywhere by train in any case, only of losing that taxi in a convenient place.

'Monte Carlo,' I said. 'The railway station.'

No more was said until we were up the hill by the Hotel de Paris. Then, Yves suddenly told the driver to stop.

'Leaving us?' I asked.

'I have a bad migraine,' he said as he got out, 'and there's an all-night pharmacy just over there. Won't be a moment.'

I waited until he was out of sight inside the place, and then told the driver to go ahead.

Melanie looked surprised.

'He isn't coming back,' I said, 'just hoping to delay us a few extra minutes. He's telephoning Frank, trying to re-establish credit. His rating must be pretty low at present. They may even believe that he *knew* I was setting the fire. A report that we're on our way out by train may help him for a few hours. If it had been true, if we were going to be there at the station waiting to be picked off like sitting ducks, they could have ended up forgiving him.'

'All this violence, I detest it! When did you suspect him?'

'When he said that he knew people who had worked for Mat Williamson, and that Mat was one to stay away from because he had a habit of ditching them.'

'You mean it's not true?'

'It's true in a way, but "ditching" is Frank's word, part of the formula he always uses when he's briefing someone who mustn't suspect that Mat's the boss. You can see why. Who would ever believe that the man hiring you would talk against his own head man like that? So, I knew that Yves had been briefed by Frank. Incidentally, Mat never speaks of ditching people, even when they have caused him deep distress, only of losing them.'

'Then what do you mean by "true in a way"? What way?'

'When Mat loses someone, it's because the person is being discarded or ditched. That's true enough. But nobody ever talks about it, as a rule, because nobody ever knows it's happened, the losing I mean.'

'Not even the lost one?'

'Least of all the lost one. He's dead.'

'Detestable!'

As we neared the station, I told the driver that we had changed our minds and now wanted to go to the Hotel Mirabeau.

I was quite sure that the Mirabeau wouldn't have rooms for anyone arriving without reservations at that stage of the season, and at that time of night. The driver was of the same opinion. I silenced him by declaring in a lordly way that I would demand a suite, and paid him off the instant he had our bags out. Because he was now in Monaco, and so not allowed to pick up another fare, he was on his way back to Beaulieu even before the Mirabeau's night man was out there to tell us we hadn't a hope.

A hundred francs got us another taxi and we didn't have long to wait. The Monagasque driver had a charming manner, and his price for taking us to Menton, ten minutes away, was only mildly exorbitant.

We stayed in a no-restaurant hotel in a back street near the Sacré Coeur; and we didn't go out more than was necessary.

The only time we went near a main road was to buy a couple of cheap radios. We bought newspapers at a kiosk on the nearby *quai*. There was a café-restaurant at the corner of the street. We had our meals there, and used their pay-phone to make our calls rather than go through the hotel switchboard.

Yves had an apartment in Paris and, since he was a keen skier as well as a highly-paid technician, a chalet near Megève. We took it in turns to call both his phone numbers, and we called three times each day. There was no reply from either until the evening of the fourth day.

It had been Melanie's turn to make the calls, and her blank look as she returned to our table told me that there'd been an answer.

'Paris,' she said as she sat down. 'A man's voice. I asked twice for Yves. He asked who wanted him, and then offered to have Yves call me back. Pressed most flatteringly for my name and number. I hung up.'

'A police voice?'

'An over-friendly, coaxing voice. I thought police. Why don't you try him?'

'I'll take your word for it. They say dialled calls are hard to trace, but that was last year. Who knows how hard or easy it may be now?'

We ate our food because we had ordered it and because it would have looked odd if we'd suddenly paid the bill and left. We couldn't risk drawing attention to ourselves just then.

In our rooms back at the hotel, we stayed glued to the radios. I switched between the hourly France-Inter news from the local transmitter and an Italian FM station. Melanie stayed with Radio Monte Carlo. The first announcement came through on France-Inter, at the end of the ten o'clock local news and before the sports round-up.

Earlier in the evening reports had been received of a bomb incident in the vicinity of Cagnes. They had since been confirmed, though detailed information was still awaited.

The incident involved a car found standing on the scrubland beside a drainage ditch a few metres from the west-bound access road to the autoroute. The driver, a man in the late thirties, appeared to have been '*plastiqué*' inside the car.

A curious feature of the incident was that the car itself had scarcely been damaged at all, according to Jean-Pierre Something-or-other, the man who had found it. He was a night watchman employed by the contractors working on an adjacent building site. He had seen nothing of the car's arrival. He had been led to it by his dog while making his hourly tour of the area he was there to guard.

The car was the property of an international rental service. It had been signed for earlier that day by a man with a credit card in the name of Yves Boularis and an address in Paris. Other papers found on the victim, along with the credit card in question, identified the dead man as Boularis. There was a description of the car and a request to anyone who had happened to notice it, either in the Cagnes district that evening or earlier in Nice, to contact the police.

At eleven, there was a repetition of the same story, but with additional details.

Boularis was a Tunisian who was listed in the central file of foreign residents as an import-export dealer in electronic equipment. The possibility of his having also been involved in the narcotics traffic had not been overlooked. Friends of the dead man and business associates were being sought for questioning.

There was a cryptic tail-piece.

A police spokesman had said that a disquieting feature of the case was the bizarre method that seemed to have been employed by the killer or killers. The dead man had been sitting with his seat belt fastened. The *plastique* had not been detonated by an ignition-key contact or by any of the other methods commonly used in these cases. A possible suicide? Certainly not. Out of the question.

The newspapers the following morning were a good deal more explicit, and one of them sickeningly so.

There was no doubt that Yves had been driven to the place of execution. He had been unconscious or semi-conscious at the time. There was evidence to suggest that force had been used to make him submit to an injection. The nature of the drug would doubtless be determined later. He had then been placed in the driving seat of his rented car. The charge of *plastique* that had killed him had been attached to the diagonal portion of the seat-belt where it crossed his stomach. Both his wrists had been lashed with bailing-wire to the steering wheel. A time fuse had been used to explode the charge. It may have been intended that he should regain consciousness and know what was being done to him before he died. A murder of revenge was indicated. It seemed likely that more than one assassin, and certainly a second car, had been needed to commit the crime. The body, which had been eviscerated – indeed, almost cut in half – by the explosive charge, was undergoing the most thorough forensic examination. The autopsy findings, together with scientific investigation of the car's interior, were expected to supply much-needed leads to the identity of those responsible.

'Bestial!' said Melanie. 'They are vile gangsters.'

'I dare say those who did it are. But what do we call those nice people, Mat and Frank say, who specified exactly what was to be done, *and* paid for the doing of it? What do we call them?'

'Ask Professor Krom. He always has a word for things. Ask him, Paul, and send me a postcard with the answer.'

'You won't be going to Brussels with me?'

'Thank you. I prefer to keep my stomach.' She gave me a sidelong look. 'Will you go?'

I managed a thin smile. 'Mr Williamson seems to have made his position very clear. Until the Placid Island negotiations are safely concluded, I am advised not to show my nose in any of the usual places. I must remain completely unavailable, physically unavailable, for questioning by any inquisitive journalist who may have heard rumours put about by Krom's witnesses or listened to the great man's schnapps-induced ramblings. The same applies to you. My work at Symposia will have to be delegated for a while.'

'To whom? Frank Yamatoku?'

I actually chuckled. 'We'll have to see. Meanwhile, I too would like to keep my stomach. We must both vanish. Of *course* I'm not going to Brussels.'

'Krom won't be pleased.'

'Then I must learn to live with his displeasure.'

Why have I failed?

Possibly because the form taken by Krom's displeasure hasn't greatly encouraged me to try living with it.

Some things are too difficult for a man of my sort ever to learn. Among them is the art of living with the displeasure of a fool.

His anger at my failure to commit suicide – by joining him and his witnesses in Brussels – was promptly expressed.

Two months later, a whole Special Issue of *The New Sociologist* was devoted to a piece by Krom. Its title was: *The Able Criminal*, Notes for a Case-study.

I made no complaint about it at the time.

That wasn't simply because, in order to oblige Mat Williamson, and discourage him from having me murdered, I was making myself scarce. I may have been incommunicado, but I wasn't out of touch. I could have instructed lawyers if I'd wished to, or I could have told my people at Symposia to instruct lawyers. There were, indeed, some of them who urged me to do so. I didn't because I thought it best to ignore the thing. Most international corporation lawyers and accountants are too busy trying to keep abreast of new tax legislation affecting their clients to bother their heads with publications like *The New Sociologist*.

I am not the first libelled person to have made that sort of mistake, and I won't be the last. However, it wasn't until German publication of Krom's book, *Der kompetente Kriminelle*, produced a whole crop of articles on the subject in the international news magazines and business journals, that I knew I had made a mistake.

So, it is against Krom's irresponsible book, not his irresponsible article, that my formal complaint is made.

Not that there's much to choose between them. The book,

ow being translated into four other languages, is essentially
revamped version of the article, padded to size with long-
winded footnotes, appendices, a bibliography and an index.
here is little new material. The journalistic crossheads used
o break the article up into digestible sections – phrases such
s *The Anarchy of Extortion* and *The Criminal as Moral
Philosopher* – have become chapter headings.

Not many changes otherwise. The inaccuracy, falsity and
otal dishonesty of the original remain unqualified.

Frits Bühler Krom is a phony.

He came to see me in Brussels with his head full of pre-
conceived notions. Nothing has been permitted to modify
them. He knew what he had to say in order to prove his case.
He has now said it.

Why, then, did he risk his skin on the battlefield of Cap
Ail? Though he couldn't have known the kind of danger
he would be running into, he was clearly prepared for trouble
of some sort. The precautions he took in Brussels against the
possibility of my being the kind of man who might like to
have him killed tells us that. Why then?

So that he can now apply the respectable label of 'case-study'
o the drivel he has written, of course. Why else? Now, he
an pretend that, having journeyed bravely into the unknown
nd observed its wonders, he is simply reporting what he alone
as seen for the enlightenment of scholars.

As poor Yves might have said, he is 'all piss and wind'.

For what does this criminological Münchhausen have to tell
s about his travels?

Well, once upon a time when he was in Zürich, he identified
his man Oberholzer. Years later, he saw him again. Ober-
olzer, now, as then, the sole and supreme overlord of a vast
nternational extortion conspiracy, agreed to talk and even
make written statements about techniques used by able
riminals in exchange for immunity from certain pressures
rom was in a position to apply. There were two victims of
berholzer's extortion racket who happened to be known to
rom. Their code-names were Kleister and Torten, and . . .

And so on, and so. Until we get to the shrewd analysis
f my 'papers'.

Sample questions. Why, if the tax-avoidance consultancy
ervice wasn't a mere front, was it necessary to employ
nformers like the unfortunate Kramer? A genuine tax-
onsultant would naturally be given access to his clients'
anking accounts by the clients themselves. Isn't it obvious

that men like Kleister and Torten were never clients, onl
victims?

It doesn't occur to him that men like K and T – men who
even he is prepared to describe in another part of the boo
as 'moneyed psychopaths' – lie to the consultants they emplo
as readily as they lie to the revenue authorities they hope t
cheat. When such clients tell you they have three accounts, yo
naturally assume that they have six. For your own sake, if no
for theirs, you'd better know for sure just where things stan

His is a monochrome world of good-and-evil, innocence-an
guilt, truth-and-falsehood. If such a world exists, and perhap
it does exist in the privacy of some minds, then he is welcom
to it. What he may not, *must* not, do is people it with real-li
human beings such as Paul Oops-nearly-said-it Oberholzer, rea
life business enterprises such as S...a Inc., and real-life pro
fessional bodies such as the Institute of No-I-shouldn't-mentio
the-name.

There are some things he's very good at not mentionin
They're the things about which you're not supposed to hea

There's no mention of Mat Williamson.

No mention of Placid Island.

No mention of Frank Yamatoku.

No mention of the murder of Yves Boularis.

No mention of the gift to us by his colleague, Professor Lan
ridge, of an aerosol spray of ninhydrin and a camera.

There's no mention of a lot of other things.

But there *is* the smear, and I'm the subject of it.

No one who has read Krom's book, certainly no one wh
matters in the trust management field, has any doubt abou
the identity of the man and the Group he is indicting.

And it's no good his retorting: 'If the cap fits, wear it.' As
told him at the Villa Lipp, no one concerned with the manag
ment of other people's money can afford to ignore a smea
We're too vulnerable.

I have the scars and mutilations to prove it.

What figure do I put on the damage?

Well, none of the cases against Professor Krom and h
various publishers is yet *sub judice* so there can be no har
in my making a rough estimate. There's still plenty of tim
for some of them to decide not to publish at all and for othe
to settle out of court after withdrawing the book.

To begin with, during a single month following the public
tion of *Der kompetente Kriminelle*, attendance at the tw
scheduled Symposia seminars was sixty per cent down.

mporary set-back? Far from it. During the month following, egistrations for our big one of the year, the annual Paris get-together, were down seventy per cent. We also received polite otes of regret from all but one of our star speakers.

So, I decided to cancel.

Note that, please. *I* decided.

I have spoken of 'my people' in Brussels. I was referring, of ourse, to my senior staff – the head of research, the internal ecurity man, those I had hand-picked myself – to whom I had lways delegated a certain amount of authority. The Mat Villiamson 'ultimatum' had made it necessary for me to elegate more, but I had managed.

I had managed by going back to using the methods Carlo nd I had used before I'd been fool enough to send those upid roses to Kramer's funeral.

I used an office accommodation service in a city where I asn't known. It was a good service, properly equipped with elephones, telex and trained operators, and efficiently run. hat was how I kept in touch. That was how I went on aking the important decisions. Some wouldn't have called delegating at all.

That, it seemed, was not what Mat had intended.

I used to go to the accommodation service office every day t noon and look at any telexes that had come in for me uring the morning. Then, if I thought it necessary, I would all Brussels and talk to one or two of my people there.

Three months after the publication of Krom's book we had uite a lot to talk about. The virtual boycotting of our seminars ad been only the beginning of our troubles. An old and valued ssociate, a tax lawyer with whom we'd done a lot of busi-ess, had described the nature of our ultimate predicament in ncompromising terms.

'No, I daren't do business with Paul Firman any more, nor ith anyone connected with him. The banks won't have him. obody'll have him. I don't wonder. I've read the Krom book oo.'

That's when I decided to take action; after hearing what an atelligent man who knew me was prepared to accept from rom, a man who didn't know me at all.

It was Wednesday. I was impatient to hear what Symposia's erman lawyer had had to say at the meeting that morning. called Brussels just before noon.

Neither of my people was there.

I waited twenty minutes and then called again. The operator

knew my voice of course, but hers sounded odd. I soon under
stood why. The person she put me through to was Frank.

'Hi, Paul.'

There was a tightening of muscles, but I managed to keep
my voice level. 'There seems to be something wrong with thi
line. I'm calling Brussels.'

'Nothing wrong with the line, Paul, just with your thinking
I'm sitting in what used to be your office.'

'I see.'

'Well now, that's what seems to be at the heart of th
problem. You *don't* see.'

'So you're going to explain. Is that it?'

'No, Paul, it isn't. Nobody's giving you any more explana
tions. You don't listen to them. Nobody's giving you any mor
advice. You don't take it. So I have the job of telling yo
what you *are* going to get from now on.'

'I can hear a squeaking noise, Frank. It isn't just your voice
You must be rocking backwards and forwards in that chair o
mine. I wouldn't do that. I keep the spring adjustment on th
tight side. If you lean too far back the whole thing's liable t
flip right over. You could hurt yourself.'

I tried to make my concern sound genuine. It sounde
genuine enough to make him lose his temper.

'Don't get cute with me, Dad. Just shut up and try to listen
You were warned to keep a low profile. You didn't. You blew
it. If Krom had taken you seriously a lot of damage could hav
been done. Luckily, you didn't impress him. But now you'v
had it. You were warned extra plainly last time. For a while
we thought we'd finally gotten through to you. But no. You'r
like all the rest of the old farts. You're told, you act lik
you've heard and then you forget what was said to you.'

'What did I forget, Frank? To fasten my seat belt?'

'Don't joke about serious matters, Paul. You've had you
chances and you've been lucky. The Krom situation was co
tained, no thanks to you. *Now* what happens? You want t
start suing that big prick and open the whole can of worm
again.'

'You're mixing metaphors on an open line, Frank.'

'You don't have anything left to hide, old-timer. It's a
hanging out for everyone to see, including the shareholder
and nobody likes the look of it. So, as of noon today, you'r
out. No need for you to worry about the chair I'm sitting i
It's been fixed, and if you think it can still be unfixed, forge
it. You're out on your arse.'

That I could believe. Keeping in touch is never the same as being on the job and Frank has always been an ingenious accountant. He has other skills I'm told. When signatures are needed from persons not immediately available, or willing, to give them, he is able to produce excellent forgeries.

'You're not forgetting that I'm a major shareholder myself, are you?'

'Twenty per cent is what you have, and I'll tell you what the deal is there. It's been okayed from on high, so you can believe me. Right? Want to hear?'

'I'm listening.'

'Call off the dogs on Krom, buy that nice retirement home you've always dreamed of owning in dear old Senior City, and you get a golden handshake. We'll buy that twenty per cent of yours at book valuation, *your* book valuation. So what do you say?'

'Drop dead.'

There was a pause. Then: 'Paul, that offer's quite genuine. We mean it. Just lay off Krom.' The effort he was having to make to remain civil was nearly audible.

'Drop dead.'

'Paul, I'd like you to reconsider that answer.'

'Okay, I've reconsidered. The answer's no.'

'Because if anyone's going to drop dead, it's not going to be anyone here.'

'Frank,' I said, 'you wasted money on Yves. Why did you have to hire people to kill him? You should have just tied him down and kept talking to him. The way you're talking to me. It wouldn't have been a pleasant death, any more than the *plastique* was, but it would have been a whole lot cheaper for Mat. And it would have left no traces. Well, scarcely any. Just the sort of rictus a man gets on his face when he's been hit by a poisoned arrow or dies yawning.'

There was another pause. My chair at the other end had stopped squeaking.

'Paul,' he said then, 'I'm going to read out some numbers to you. You know about communications codes. Well, this is yours, your current one. It places you and your Kraut helper about four hours from here by road, and about three from the guys with the know-how that you tell me is so inefficient and over-priced. So, better take a deep breath. If you're going to run again, this time, you'll have a long way to go. Ready? Okay. This is your code. Prefix reads . . .'

I listened to the first seven figures, just to make sure that my old security man hadn't thought he owed it to me to make a slight error.

He hadn't. The Brussels old-pals act had been repealed. It was time I got moving.

I hung up and called Melanie.

She always knows best how to make travel arrangements.

CHAPTER ELEVEN

Carlo's house smells like a handkerchief out of an old drawer. Even when it was newly built one had been aware of a certain mustiness. Carlo had attributed it then to the brackish water used in mixing the concrete and said that it would gradually go away. It never has gone away; instead, it has ripened. That verbena-scented anti-mildew spray which Melanie gets at the general store on the Out Island only makes it worse.

She does the trip on our boat, with Jake to navigate and nurse the engine, every week; and, every week, she returns with our mail and our groceries and our drinks and a denunciation of the Out Island hairdresser. Every week, too, she says that that is the last time and that next week, no matter what the risk, she is leaving for Nassau or Miami and the joys of Elizabeth Arden. She adds that bad food can kill you just as surely as *plastique*.

She has my sympathy. Tonight, though, when I've thought everything through again and treble-checked it, it is possible that I may at last have an escape plan to submit to her.

Yesterday, the mail she brought back with her consisted of two letters.

One was from a real-estate agent in Kingston, and it was to tell me that my asking price for the island was a bit too high. We get lots of letters like that. I mention it only to explain how we've been operating. Just in case somebody working for Mat and Frank somehow, somewhere, accidentally got on to the fact that I had access, as one of Carlo's trustees, to a Caribbean island, we have an early-warning system. There are hundreds of small island properties around here; and, since the real-estate people know more than the government records office about who really owns what, they're the ones who always know first if anyone starts making enquiries. Who but a prospective buyer would make enquiries? So, although I haven't the slightest right to be, I am a prospective seller. In that way, I get the benefit of the real-estate agents' intelligence network. Thus far, only one prospective buyer has actually reached our dreamy lagoon. After a special lunch prepared by Carlo's cook – getting a little old now but still resolutely awful – he left and we heard no more.

We have been reasonably secure against everything except excruciating boredom, malnutrition and the possibility of those conditions becoming permanent features of what's left of our lives.

That's why that second letter was so important.

It was from the man who has helped me prepare this account of the 'siege of the Villa Lipp' for publication.

I had sought him out because I had liked something he had written and deduced from it that he was a person who would be unlikely to strike high-minded or other tedious attitudes. My approach was made by sending him a copy of Krom's book and a commentary I had written on the original *New Sociologist* piece. At the same time I had him vetted as a security risk.

At our first meeting on the Out Island we reached an understanding. Neither of us, I am happy to say, has since had reason to remind the other of the terms of it. Our relationship has developed remarkably. From being my amanuensis, he has become my literary mentor, then a business intermediary dealing on my behalf with publishers and, finally, my trusted legal adviser.

He anticipated that final role on several occasions during the writing of the book by sending me warnings – 'You can't say things like that,' or 'Nobody's going to stand for this' – that I had simply ignored. Then, when the first English-language text was submitted to our publisher, the blow fell. The publisher made his acceptance conditional on legal waivers being obtained from those persons whom his lawyers said were libelled in the book as it stood; namely, Connell, Henson, Langridge, Williamson, Yamatoku, Symposia SA and, of course, Krom.

For me, that could have finished it. I was tired and unusually depressed. Indeed, at a gloomy last meeting on the Out Island with my adviser, I told him to have all those expensive typescripts – expensive because they had been done on that special paper that goes black if anyone tries to photograph or photocopy it – retrieved and destroyed.

He persuaded me not to be hasty. Let the publisher, who was willing to persevere with the book, try to get the waivers. If massive deletions or other vital changes were required, we could decide then whether or not they were acceptable. Possibly some name changes would be sufficient. There was nothing to be lost by finding out.

I told him to go ahead and see what happened. He gets a

percentage of any royalties that the book may earn, so I could see his point of view. Mine was that, providing the book wasn't totally emasculated, he and the publisher had better be left to do the best they could for what they have been polite enough to refer to as my Cause.

The first reaction we had was encouraging though somewhat surprising. It was from Connell and said simply: 'Publish and be damned.'

An accompanying letter from my adviser explained that Dr Connell was now teaching in a different university and also being divorced by his second wife. However, the lawyers seemed to think that his brief note constituted a waiver.

Dr Henson's reply puzzled me.

'Publish by all means,' she wrote; 'recent school-leavers and college drop-outs should find some passages in the book heartening as well as instructive. Funnier than Smiles's *Self-help* and likely to be preferred by modern teenage readers. Probation officers everywhere will love it.'

I wondered if she had been sent the wrong book, but was assured that she hadn't. It was thought that her reply may have been designed to cause annoyance to the head of her department.

He objected strongly to the use of his name and the attribution to him of certain statements. His name was changed to 'Langridge' and some deletions of references to British security service personnel were made.

The response from Mat was most strange. I was sent a photocopy.

The letter came, beautifully typed, on paper with the heading, GOVERNMENT HOUSE, PLACID ISLAND, in discreet capitals. It was signed by a Personal Assistant.

'I am directed by His Excellency Mathew Tuakana to present his compliments. He has read the manuscript of the book described as the edited recollections of Mr Paul Firman. It may, he agrees, be of some sociological interest to specialists, particularly in the field of psychiatric social work. It is not a field with which His Excellency has had occasion to become familiar. On Placid Island psychiatric illness, even in its milder forms, is virtually unknown. Mr Firman's account of a western criminal sub-culture seems, possibly for that reason, as far-fetched as the one he would like to give of Placid and its people. It is to be hoped that his recollections of the former are as unreliably based on hearsay as his speculations about the latter.

241

'Since His Excellency could not conceivably be the Mr Williamson described in this book, he feels unable to comment at greater length. I am instructed to add for your information, that there are no less than twenty families named Williamson with Placid Island nationality. If the author, or Mr Firman himself, cares to communicate direct with our Office of Information, it may be possible to clear up any confusion existing in Mr Firman's mind, at least on that point.

'I am further instructed to say that the only Mr Yamatoku who could be described as being in His Excellency's employ, is financial counsellor to the Placid Island mission at the United Nations. Counsellor Yamatoku is presently stationed in New York.'

My adviser thought the letter quaint: but said that my credibility had suffered a set-back. *Twenty* Williamson families on Placid? Hadn't I known that?

I explained the joke Mat had once explained to me. On Placid, changing family names was a popular sport, far more popular than the European political sport of street-name changing. In 1946 there had had to be a bye-law passed declaring a moratorium on name changing for two years. That was because every family name on Placid was suddenly MacArthur. All those Williamsons simply meant that Mat was becoming a potent cult figure.

And I don't consider that communication in the least quaint. I think it plainly serves notice on me that, book or no book, I'm still on the run; and that if at any time I should feel disposed to think otherwise, I can put my belief to the test by writing direct to Mat's Office of Information.

Well, I may now decide to do that.

The only reply from Symposia SA was a form letter from an official in a tribunal of commerce. It stated that Symposia was in voluntary liquidation and that any claim against it must be made by such-and-such a date. Very sad; but, as my adviser pointed out with unfeeling satisfaction, you can't in Anglo-Saxon law libel the dead.

That left Professor Krom.

He was in no hurry to reply; and, after some weeks of silence, it was feared that he did not intend to do so. Enquiries established, however, that he had been in the United States, attending another of his international police conferences, and also absent on vacation.

His reply has now been received. A copy of it was attached to the letter that arrived yesterday.

What I had expected, at best, was a tongue-lashing and a stern demand for the deletion of all references to himself and his work that he considered disrespectful. What I have received instead is – well, I haven't yet quite made up my mind.

The waiver he gives is a conditional one, and my adviser seems to find it in some way entertaining. The conditions the Professor lays down are that, along with my account, there must be published in the same volume and as a postscript or appendix, his own brief Commentary on it. The Commentary must be published exactly as written, in full and as an uninterrupted whole. Furthermore, I may not change or modify anything in the text already submitted to him, my text that is, as a result of anything he has had to say about it or for any other reason. 'All those false hopes, doomed expectations, demonstrable lies and unintentional errors must remain in their original state, unspoilt and undisguised by the scratchings-over of hindsight.' If these conditions are accepted, he will waive any objections he might have had to the submitted text.

There is a supplementary condition. While Professor Krom has the greatest respect for the publishers concerned, of whose reputation for integrity he is well aware, he must still insist upon receiving a final corrected proof of the book before it goes to press. He will wish to see for himself that the nominal price he has asked for his blessing has been fully and properly paid.

The publishers tell me, with evident satisfaction, that the Professor's conditions are entirely acceptable to them.

They assume that his conditions will also be acceptable to me.

Well, of course they are acceptable. They must be. If I want my voice to be heard at all, I obviously have no choice in the matter.

The Professor's Commentary is translated from the original Dutch.

I have read the edited version of Paul Firman's book [he writes] with the keenest pleasure, the liveliest professional interest and, yes, a good deal of wry amusement too.

It has in it so much of what I always felt was there but failed completely to bring out myself. The reasons for my failure are plain. When the investigator-subject relationship is clouded by a basic personality conflict, the best that can be hoped for is that the investigator will ultimately succeed in functioning as a catalyst. To that modest extent, at least, I may claim success. My colleagues, Henson and Connell, both thought this subject exceptionally difficult, the latter going as far as to say that, with defences arrayed in such depth, one had to ask oneself not simply what was behind them, but whether there could be room enough for a recognizable fellow creature. The simile he offered, that of a battle tank with armour so thick that it could accommodate a crew consisting only of trained mice, did not seem fanciful.

Well, Mr Firman has now set our minds at rest. The defences are formidable, yes, but there is a human being inside them. What kind of human being still remains, I think, to be seen; but we have available now a much clearer view of him. A self-serving effusion such as this, written by a delinquent of Mr Firman's rare calibre, will always reveal more about its author's internal world than the attempt at self-appraisal of an equally complex but less irresponsible mind. The scatological excesses of a Genet tell us more than the managed insights of a Gide.

Let us take a closer look at the material of Firman's outer defences. At the Villa Lipp, I compared his clouds of verbiage with octopus ink, a comparison which the octopus himself faithfully reports. It is surprising, however, to find the comparison holding good for his written word. Any spoken one – its meaning so easily changed by the voice and body-language of its speaker of the moment – lends itself naturally to deception. Comedians, evangelists, fortune-tellers, demagogues, all who traffic in the human personality, know and depend upon the fact. The written word is usually less obliging. It can be examined more than once. It can be analysed and parsed. Doubters suspecting soft spots may prod and poke at it. Only those accustomed to appealing to the semi-literate, or those as full of bile and adverbs as Mr Firman, can make the mistake of believing that, if a statement is made with sufficient vehemence and a neat turn of phrase, the conviction it seems to carry will always be unquestioned.

At one point in his book, Mr Firman has much to say about the technique of the 'smear'. By no means all of it was said, as he claims, at the Villa Lipp, but no matter. To anything Mr Firman has to say about ways of smearing an adversary, I am prepared to listen. He is an expert on the subject.

Consider, for a moment, his descriptions of me and the way that I behave, socially as well as professionally.

Few men are without their vanities, idiosyncrasies and petty weaknesses. Many, I among them, possess visible physical peculiarities as well, although I am in no way abnormally handicapped. About his appearance, a sensible man of my age will have only vestigial illusions; and, if he has been much photographed at conferences and heard his platform voice coming back at him through television and radio, he will probably have dispensed with even those vestiges.

I have a prognathous upper jaw and what are commonly called 'buck' teeth. Because they are so prominent I try always to keep them very clean. I express disgust or disbelief by making a hawking sound in the throat. When we were young, my wife tried unsuccessfully to cure me of the habit which she thought unbecoming, and at times offensive. I also suffer from an arthritic condition of the spine that my doctor calls 'parrot's beak' and is properly known as spondylitis. It afflicts many other persons of my age, causing discomfort or inconvenience in varying amounts. Long, hot journeys made in small, nervous cars on mountain roads are bad for parrot's beak. In my case, such a journey will result in muscle spasm and lower back pain; and, until I can take recuperative rest, my gait will be affected.

What does Mr Firman make of all this?

A monster, naturally; a staring blue-eyed monster with gleaming white fangs and circumflected lip, a monster who slobbers down all that lovely wine as if it were water, sprays his flinching companions cheerfully with gobbets of saliva, insults the food and then reels away, supporting himself with practised ease on the furniture as he goes, to sleep it off. The monster does not speak, he only yelps, yaps and blares. The monster does not take a bath, as Dr Henson does for the benefit of the eavesdropping microphones, he only breaks wind.

As the monster's creator himself would say, 'And so on.' Mr Firman must be taken with many grains of salt.

Where then, I may be asked, is the human being we were promised? Is there no truth at all here? Is this merely dreamstuff, clinical casebook material that will only become useful when it has been processed and interpreted?

By no means. As Mr Firman admits, indeed claims, many of the conversations he reports are transcribed from the tapes he took with him from the villa. I have consulted my colleagues, Henson and Connell, on the point and both agree with me. As long as one disregards Firman's interpolated comments, though some of them have evidential merit of their own, his accounts of what was said are in the main accurate.

When he is reporting from memory, however, we have to be very much more careful.

The recollections of his adolescence have yet to be checked. The passages concerning his war experiences have been read by a German scholar, a friend of mine who served as an infantry soldier in the Italian theatre from 1943 to 1945. He reports one error. The only German army pistols he can remember as having been issued were the Walther and the Sauer. However, while a prisoner of the Americans, he had heard German pistols referred to as 'Lugers' as if the word were a generic term for every type of German automatic hand-gun. Firman's reference to 'Lugers or Walthers' may be dismissed then as a mistake belonging to another time and place. It is not his memory that is at fault.

The same cannot be said of his mistakes over certain vital dates. All of a sudden he is grossly unreliable. He cannot even place correctly the year of my identification of him in Zürich!

Was the blunder intentional? I really don't think it can have been. Firstly, because I had already published the correct date in my Notes for a Case-study, and I can't see him passing up an opportunity to pour scorn on any factual statement of mine with which he disagreed. Secondly, because Mr Firman is far too astute to make mistakes that look as if they could have been intentional, unless he wished for some reason to draw special attention to them. But why should he? The Zürich date, for one, is among the 'neutral' facts that nobody disputes. A secretarial error then? No, because the rest of his typescript is singularly free of error. The editorial assistant must have accepted those wrong dates too, so presumably they were given him by Mr Firman.

I shall return to this problem. It touches one of Mr Firman's basic contentions concerning the guilt of the man he calls 'Williamson'. Among the charges levelled against me – other than those involving my teeth, my drunkenness, my timidity under fire or my stubborn refusals to concede that black is white – is a list of some of my sins of omission.

In one case, his complaint is certainly justified.

Unfortunately, I did not hear about the murder of Yves Boularis until several months after the event. It was not, I understand, reported outside France. Dr Henson came across a reference to it in a French medico-legal journal that I normally read only in précis. She wrote to me drawing attention both to the oddity of the method employed and to the timing of the murder.

Was it possible after all that the Villa Lipp had really been besieged? And could there really be a wicked Mr Williamson? The political leader who, having gained power and been proclaimed his people's saviour, wishes to obliterate all traces of his corrupt or criminal past is a familiar figure in the history of nations.

The possibility of my having done Mr Firman even a minor injustice was troubling. The true identity of the speaker whom he addresses as 'Mat' in the cassette of the telephone conversation that I took with me from the villa that night proved impossible to establish. Nevertheless, although Mr Firman may not believe me, I made every effort I could.

Through friends in London, I was able to obtain a copy of a BBC sound archive recording of Mathew Tuakana's voice. It was part of an address of homage and welcome to Chief Tebuke on the occasion of the Chief's inauguration as head of state at the Placid Island independence ceremony. It was in the Placid Island language.

A colleague who specializes in the techniques of 'voice-print' comparison reported to me on the two voices. He identified the man speaking with Firman on the cassette as being British from the English Midlands. Dr Henson had thought Coventry or Birmingham. The Tuakana recording, however, presented difficulties. This wasn't because he couldn't understand the language, but because it couldn't be used for the purposes of comparison. It is the *sounds* of the voice specimens that are analysed and compared. These two lots of sounds were of two completely different orders: one for the most part labial and nasal, the other wholly glottal. One cannot compare a fingerprint with a palmprint, even when they have been made by the same hand. There was no available and authenticated recording of Mr Tuakana speaking English or any other phonetically comparable language.

The doubt nagged at me, however, and, after the San Francisco conference two months ago, my wife agreed to my suggestion that we might spend the vacation due to me in seeing something of the South Pacific. We obtained a visa for Placid in Fiji, and went there, along with some cargo, on one of the bi-weekly island-hopping planes.

A hotel is nearly completed, but not yet in business. The old rest-house is primitive, but our reception there was warm.

As an outspoken critic of what Mr Firman calls the 'tax-haven business', I am fairly well known by name among those who earn their livings in it. It did not at all surprise me that

247

the Canadian lawyer, who acts as Placid vice-consul in Suva, and who issued our visas, had sent advance warning of our visit. Letters from Mr Tuakana and from a daughter of Chief Tebuke awaited us on arrival. Both were invitations to lunch the following day. My wife's hostess would be the Principal of the Island's new high school for girls. Mr Tuakana looked forward to meeting me for an informal discussion of matters of mutual interest to us. He hoped to prevail upon me and Vrouw Krom to attend a reception by Chief Tebuke later in the week. Meanwhile, lunch at Government House would be *à deux*. A car and driver would be at my disposal during our stay.

Government House consists of one two-storey house and four bungalows, the accommodation used by the British Resident Commissioner and his senior officials in colonial days. Mr Tuakana, as Chief Minister, occupies the largest bungalow and has his offices in it as well as his private quarters. His domestic staff, I noted, seem to be exceptionally well-trained.

In studying Mr Firman's book, I have tried from the start to remain objective, and to remind myself at regular intervals that all statements in it must be presumed false until there is evidence to the contrary. When I say, then, that the Firman description of Mat Williamson fits Mathew Tuakana like a glove, I mean that the description is not only visually correct – there may be two names but there is only one man – but that it also gives an impression I found recognizable, that of a man somewhat too well aware of his ability to deal with subordinates.

The way in which he introduced himself, however, had little of the charm Firman's account had led me to expect.

'I am the Tuakana whose baptismal name is Mathew Williamson,' he said. 'I am not the Williamson in this man Firman's book, any more than you, I imagine, consider yourself to be the Professor Krom he caricatures. As long as that is clearly understood, I see no reason why we shouldn't talk fairly freely and frankly.' He rang a small glass bell standing on the table beside him. 'What would you like to drink? Schnapps?'

'No, thank you, Minister.'

When the servant appeared he ordered iced water. I should record that his voice was quite unlike that on the cassette. I can usually tell the difference between American and British spoken English. His *sounded* more American, but I really don't now. Firman's assertion that the man is a clever mimic was obviously uncheckable.

After ascertaining that the rest-house had made us comfortable, he went on: 'Professor, tell me something. You and your wife went for a drive this morning. You saw mainly the port and the old phosphate-company workings. What did you think of the little you were able to see of us?'

'Somewhere in our friend's book this place is described as like a lunar landscape. That seemed a fair description of the mining area. Though I also saw what looked like efforts being made to improve things. Are they yours?'

His fleeting smile of satisfaction suggested that what I had seen had been a show put on for my benefit and that our driver had been briefed. 'Not mine alone, Professor. As helpers I have a number of those persons of whom you so steadfastly disapprove.' He poured me a glass of water from the jug that had been brought. 'I mean the ones you call tax-dodgers.'

I was wilfully dense. 'The men operating the earth-moving equipment looked like Islanders to me.'

'They were. But do you know the procedures for registering a corporation or creating a trust on Placid?'

'I could recite the exempt company and trust laws of half a dozen of your competitors in the field, Minister. I would be surprised if yours were much different.'

'Not much different, no, but a little. Part of our corporation and trust registration fees must be paid in kind.'

'A nice gimmick. Plant and machinery?'

'Topsoil. Most of Placid's was stripped away and lost by the mining company. A delivery of five thousand metric tons of good, black topsoil ensures the best of everything here for a newly arrived corporation. In subsequent years we'll take a thousand tons annually as long as the quality remains good. I'll take no sub-soil fill. The only clock we mean to put back here is the ecological one. And I think we have just enough time in which to do it.'

'You have a deadline, Minister?'

I received a cool look. 'People who think as you do are our deadline, Professor. There is writing on the wall. Tax authorities everywhere, especially in the high-tax jurisdictions, are getting tougher every day. And the writing is not only on walls. In the European Common Market Official Journal, the sin we are committing, the crime you so deplore, has been given a name of its own – Incitement to Anti-Social Tax-Avoidance!

Doesn't that sound wicked? Ten years from now we'll ha
been legislated out of our economic existence if a career
crime is the only one we're trained to follow. We have
illusions, I can assure you. If the western powers prefer
have us as neo-colonial Third World pensioners rather th
as self-respecting exporters of fiscal services, we must lo
elsewhere for salvation. But where? Yes, we could sell o
port facilities to the highest bidder and become somebody
nuclear naval base. Or we could lease ourselves as sites f
missile-tracking or microwave stations. Fates worse than dea
I'm afraid. No! With sufficient topsoil and a well-research
development programme, surely we can use our sinful ta
avoidance years to purchase a better future. What do y
think, Professor?'

'There's a lot in what you say, Minister.'

The arrogance of his answering smile was insufferable.
made a decision. If he could test Firman's verdict on me
making impertinent offerings of schnapps, I could test Firma
gossip about him by asking impertinent questions.

'How active is the Boy Scout movement here on Plac
Minister?'

Not an eyelid flickered. 'There is no Boy Scout moveme
here as yet. The Legislative Assembly has been asked
authorize the establishment of the movement here. The ne
Protestant chaplain is interested, I'm told, but we have mo
important things to do with our time at present.'

Over lunch – canned ham, salad, instant coffee – he told
about the public-works programmes he had scheduled and t
problems of getting low-interest loans.

I asked if Mr Yamatoku advised him at all on such matte

He looked mystified. 'Mr Yamatoku is with our mission
the UN in New York.'

'Minister, I shall be returning home via New York. Would
be possible for me to meet Mr Yamatoku?'

'If you were to call his secretary, I dare say he would t
to make time to see you. He is a busy man of course.'

My patience ran out there. I made detailed notes of t
conversation that follows as soon as I returned to the re
house.

'But not as busy as you, Minister, I'm sure. Where and wh
did you first meet Mr Firman?'

He stared over my right shoulder for a moment in a w
that nearly had me turning to see who might be there. Su
well-worn interviewing tricks sit oddly on so pretentious a ma

When he saw that I wasn't going to respond, he played at folding his napkin carefully as he answered.

'The place of meeting was the one he gives,' he said. 'Port Vila in the New Hebrides. He was calling himself Perry Smythson. Almost everything else he says is, either wholly or in part, a pack of lies. If it were not we wouldn't be talking. I'm quite sure you don't believe that we are sitting here privately like this because I am eager to hear your views on the methodology of international tax planning.'

'No, Minister, but you might be curious about my intentions where Firman's book is concerned. I am naturally curious about yours. I'm hoping that they may help me to make up my mind. For a man in your position, public controversy of the kind that libel actions can generate is a thing to be avoided imagine.'

'Avoided like the plague, Professor. The same goes for book-banning by injunction, or censorship through legal blackmail. My intention is to do nothing, and I will tell you why. After reading the Firman script, I sent off at once both for your book and the *New Sociologist* essay. The German of the book was a little beyond my understanding, but the essay fascinated me. Yes, fascinated! It confirmed something that I had long suspected.'

'Essays that do that are always fascinating.'

I earned only a fleeting smile. 'Tell me something, Professor. Firman quotes a definition of the able criminal which he says is yours. Is it?'

'It's the simplified, lecture-platform definition I normally give.'

'Then I'm afraid it can't be applied to Smythson-Oberholzer.'

'Shall we just call him Firman, Minister?'

'By all means. He's had too many aliases, I agree. But, whatever name you use, you can't call him the well-adjusted, emotionally stable man of your definition. That, Firman certainly is not. It was one of the first things I came to understand about him.'

'Could you be specific?'

'Certainly. The death of Carlo Lech was a great blow to him. I know, because I was with him when he heard the news.' He held up a defensive hand as if I had started to interrupt him. 'Bear with me, please. Lech was never the father-figure whom Firman portrays. There, I'm completely with you. *But,* Firman always chose to *believe* that he was. The child blames a suitable *alter ego* for its own misdeeds. That is natural. The neurotic adult, the boy who will never grow up, continues to project, but he does so on a different scale and uses different mechanisms. One such mechanism is called role-reversal, I believe.'

'Please go on, Minister.' The amateur psychiatrist is rarely as dangerous as he is often made out to be. As long as he has no patients, the injuries he inflicts are usually more painful than serious, like blows on the elbow. The kind of rubbish he talks, however, can tell you a lot about him.

'The Lech you dismiss, rightly, as a figment of the imagination was desperately real to Firman. Is *that* your emotionally stable, well-adjusted man, Professor?'

'It doesn't sound like him, no. Have you any other examples of this instability?'

'There are other examples staring at us from the pages of his book. He quotes you as saying that Lech had died five years previously. Wrong. He himself says that you saw him at the Zürich funeral five years previously. Wrong again. But why?'

'Those dating mistakes puzzled me too, Minister. Lech had died seven years previously, not five. I identified Firman in Zürich eight months before Lech's death. Those facts have never been in dispute. What was so special about the number five? Why the mistake?'

'Shall we call them Freudian slips, Professor?'

'Unintentional mistakes can be made by a copy typist who needs new glasses or an editorial adviser who can't be bothered with details.'

'But not these mistakes, Professor.' He was glad of my stuffiness; it made me a better audience. 'I know for a fact that the five-years-ago we are talking about now was of deep psychological significance to him. I'm no coffee-house analyst, Professor, and I only know what I've read about abnormal behaviour. But no one could have made a mistake about Mr Paul Firman then. It's not the sort of thing you forget. He went nowhere near Zürich or anywhere else in Europe. He spent the year shuttling between Singapore, Sydney and Hong Kong. That was the year his own mysterious Mat Williamson, the man on the telephone speaking with a Birmingham accent, seems to be talking about. He refers to a moment of personal loss and sadness, or sadness and loss. I made a note somewhere. It's on page . . .'

'Thank you, Minister. I know the place you mean. How did you come to see so much of him that year? Was that when your partnership began?'

'Partnership?' He didn't like the word. It occurred to me suddenly that Mr Tuakana was in a position to have me arrested, jailed and charged with insulting his government if he felt like it. 'That's what he calls it now. I was working for him as what he called a talent-spotter. I had no money worth talking about, and lobbying a company like Anglo-Anzac into facing the inevitable, even in a place like this, takes plenty. Firman paid me well, but I had to work for it. He had a short list of companies, corporations, that interested him. Usually they were in trouble. I investigated them for him. He was what some people call an operator. Quickly in, quickly out. Sometimes there were assets to be stripped. Sometimes there was a loss position to be parlayed. Sometimes there were other things. Partnership? I never saw it in that light. I was his hot-shot auditor. We never got around to discussing any of my long-term plans. That was the year of his crack-up.'

'A physical crack-up or a mental one, Minister?'

He placed his smoothed and folded napkin neatly beside his plate.

The hand that had held it twitched for a moment and then was still. He may have decided against rapping the table in time with the words.

'Professor, surely we can see now. Isn't it plain enough how those date mistakes came to be made? Five was the evil-magic number because five years before had been the evil-magic time. That was the year of the most terrible death and of the catastrophic disaster. As a result, it ends up as the year of *all* death and *all* disaster – Lech's death, the Kramer folly, the encounter with you, the exile from Europe, *everything*. The year of ultimate misfortune! And, by the way, that was the year he got himself into trouble with the New South Wales police. In Sydney, at one point, there was serious talk of starting extradition proceedings to winkle him out of Hong Kong.'

'Do you know what for, Minister?'

'Indeed I do. You asked for other examples of his instability. I can give you a perfect one. It's another of his role-switching ploys. Do you remember the long lecture he says he gave to that mythical Mr Williamson? Remember, Professor? The one about the perils of international fraud and the terrible fate that awaited those who didn't obey the laws?'

'I remember.'

'Professor, that was a lecture I gave *him*.'

He paused, shrugged slightly and then gazed into my eyes

253

with that peculiar look of engaging frankness that I have learned to associate with guilt sure of its defences and completely at its ease.

'My job,' he went on, 'was investigation and I could see the overall picture. Some corners of it were pretty murky, believe me. What provoked the lecture was a kind of multi-national thimble-rigging scheme he had going. This was a chain of twenty different corporations, all having what looked like serious assets – mining properties, real estate, palm-nut plantations – and all making paper profits. That chain was just the debris left from his asset-stripping deals. So he's given the mess a coat of paint. Why? Well, it seems he's acquired this little ex-British insurance company registered in ex-British Singapore and still operating under the old British free-for-all rules. That means minimal regulation by American standards. Most of its business is done in Malaysia and the Islands and it has a cosy Chinese name that means "faithful tiger". So guess who ends up owning all those paper corporations. Yes the faithful tiger, only now he's called Fidelity Lion and does his investing through nominees. The only mistake Firman made there was to let that mangy lion write annuity business in Australia. He'll never go back there again. They don't like insurance grifters, especially when they can't pin anything on them.'

'No country likes them. But you spoke of a terrible death and a catastrophic disaster, Minister. Was that what you meant? The collapse of a fraudulent insurance scheme?'

'Oh no. His Chinese directors nearly had him in trouble, but he moved fast enough to get out from under that. It was the business of his son that hit him so hard.'

'He mentioned a child by his second marriage.'

'That was a daughter. The son was by his first wife. Brilliant boy, handsome, great charmer. Snapped up by one of the Ivy League colleges. Firman doted. Terribly proud of him. Actually used to carry a photograph of the lad in his wallet.'

'What happened?'

'He died suddenly. All very unfortunate it was.'

'Drugs? Alcohol? A car crash?'

'Nothing as simple. The boy committed suicide, hanged himself. It destroyed Firman completely for a while. I've never seen a crack-up like it. Almost total withdrawal. He'd just sit.'

'Was there any explanation?'

'Of the suicide? The college had one. Overwork, examination pressures, unjustified fears of not meeting the high expectations

254

of others. Most of these places must have a form letter they send out. But Firman thought that he'd been the only one at fault. When he spoke at all then it was always to say the same thing. "I seem to have made a habit of failing the people who love me." No arguing with him. I for one would never be surprised if Firman decided to kill himself. There's a suicidal streak somewhere there.'

He stood up. It was time for me to leave. I asked if I could have copies of some of his speeches. A Personal Assistant was instructed to take me to the Office of Information.

I asked for tapes.

Later that day two envelopes were delivered to the rest house. In one there was a number of Mr Tuakana's speeches translated into English. A covering note from the Information Officer explained that there were no taped recordings of the speeches available in a language I would understand.

The second envelope contained the promised invitation to a reception by Chief Tebuke later in the week.

I had nothing more to do on Placid. There was a plane leaving the following day. With my wife's agreement, I answered the invitation with an apologetic letter explaining that we were expected back in Suva and much regretted our inability to attend the reception.

Firman's Mr Williamson cannot, in my opinion, be described as able.

He is not even a good liar.

Melanie finished reading the Commentary in a state of high excitement.

'If you still have those company accounts,' she said, 'this is a wonderful gift that Krom has sent you.'

Bedtime on the Island had usually been nine-thirty; but that night, with Melanie smoking to keep the insects at bay, we sat up later.

'It's not only a gift,' I said; 'it's a gift horse with a mouth I'm looking into. Oh yes, I have those company accounts all right. I had them all microfilmed in Hong Kong at the time. Mat's accounts were very good, but not to anyone who'd been trained to read figures by Carlo. The only thing I could never discover was the name of the suckers using his nominees. Now, we have the name – Fidelity Lion. No wonder the Australians were treading on Mat's tail.'

Doubts assailed her. 'It's several years ago now. What about statutes of limitations?'

'With our knowledge we could get him in trouble any time we wanted, and he'll know it.'

'The uncrowned king of Placid?'

'*Especially* the uncrowned king of Placid. He's totally vulnerable. There'd be no more topsoil for a man suspected of fraud. No more anything else. All we do is what Professor Krom did in Brussels. We leave copies of all the evidence in sealed envelopes to be opened in case of either of our sudden deaths, particularly if my sudden death looked like a suicide. Then, we just tell Mat. Perfect!'

'If it's perfect, why aren't you happier?'

'Because, along with the gift, there comes a disturbing message. Krom has finally confirmed beyond doubt the truth of something that I have resolutely denied. He is telling me again that I have been Number One all the time. The Number One anarchist!'

'Why should that disturb you?'

'It's a lie.'

'You've had too much to drink, Paul.'

'Very likely. They say there's no taste in vodka. There is in *this* vodka. There's a taste of scorched paint.'

She filled her own glass again. 'Did you really say it?'

'What?'

'That thing about always failing the people who loved you.'

'I may have said something to that effect. I was wallowing in self-pity at the time. Even so, Mat's version sounds a bit mawkish for me.'

When Melanie thinks hard, her lower jaw drops a little, giving her a hangdog look. She had it now.

'Failing people who loved me is something I have never done,' she said after a while.

'Good for you.'

'Not good at all.' Her mouth resumed its normal shape. '*I* have always been the one who loved.'

'Oh.'

She disposed of the subject firmly. 'Food, that's the important thing.' She emptied her glass again and banged it down on the table. 'I must tell you, Paul, that I shall think a lot tonight about food. About the good food I'm going to have away from here.'

'Yes. Yes, so shall I.'

I did.

I thought of good food, cold days and decent glasses of wine.